YA

THE
IVORY
KEY

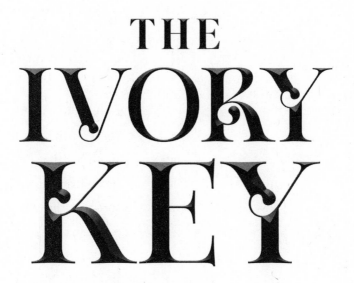

THE
IVORY
KEY

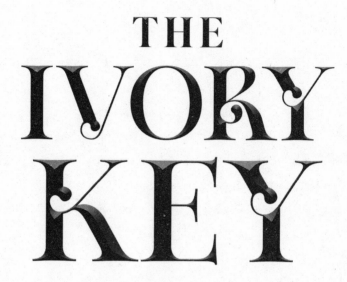

AKSHAYA RAMAN

CLARION BOOKS
An Imprint of HarperCollins*Publishers*
Boston   New York

Clarion Books is an imprint of HarperCollins Publishers.

The Ivory Key

clarionbooks.com

Library of Congress Cataloging-in-Publication Data has been applied for.
ISBN: 978-0-358-46833-2 hardcover
ISBN: 978-0-358-61331-2 signed edition
ISBN: 978-0-358-72301-1 special markets edition

The text was set in Minion Pro.
Map illustration by Jared Blando
Cover and interior design by Dana Li

Manufactured in the United States of America

1 2021
4500841798

First Edition

CV 10.04.2021 0624

For my first storytellers: Sugandham Paati, Kothai Paati, and Srinivasa Raghavan Thatha

Koranos

Ritsar

Simha Fort

Syena Fort

Trisore Fort

EXCURSI

Fron

C
K

New Border

Hima Mahal

Banagha
Stepwell Ruins

Ithana Fort
Ruins

Visala?

Lyria

Maravat

Ish

Gadhor
Fort Ruins

Gauri Mahal

Jhaner Fort

Chan

Vrin

Possible Location
of Visala?
See Letter from S#21

Great Library
of Elendha

Jhaner
Lake

Kasturi

Ravas

"Sacred Scrolls
Madhvi's Lament"??

Gates
of Savitri

Madhkot
Fort

Handhar
Ruins

Swapna

Moon
Temple Ruins

Dvar

Great Arch
of Dvar

Dvar Fort

Dwaramatha

Forest

Lighthouse
of Dvar

Maghgiri

Daks
Fort

Nayan
Fort

Excursion #6

Nayan
Island

Southern Sea

BLANDO

Mountains

Varaya Fort

1K Map Piece?

Yodh River

Note ... head
EXCURSION #13

Fire Temple
of Paliya

Port
of Harya

n a a r

O n a a r

h

lap

Fort

River

a r y a

Rayu
River

Tasgarh
Fort

Maghya
Ruins

Vengiri
Fort

A d h u r a

Excursion #2

Isles
of
Kaanch

Elarai
Monastary

ntains

Eastern Sea

N

The LANDS of

ASHOKA

Notes from Papa's Journal

CHAPTER ONE

— VIRA —

THE DEAD BOY'S face was as gray as a cloudy sky moments before a storm. His short black beard sculpted and whittled his cheeks down to a point. Thin lips glittered in the watery moonlight that managed to penetrate the canopy, brighter than the famed rubies of his home province.

But Vira knew it was blood that made them shine so enticingly.

She lifted the flameless lantern higher. The ball of yellow light within crackled with magic as it washed over his embroidered sleeve, illuminating the row of silver fish encircling his wrist. A wave of nausea hit her. The crest of Onaar.

The scouts hadn't been wrong. This was her betrothed — Lord Harish, son of the Viceroy of Onaar — now dead in the city of Dvar.

Vira's legs wobbled as she rose from her crouch. But she steadied herself. A maharani didn't show weakness. She took a deep breath, squaring her shoulders before turning to face the warriors who had found the body.

Three girls stood in a row, dressed in matching red kurtas and loose black pants, whispering to one another. One leaned against a neem tree, propped up by a shoulder, using the edge of a knife to file her fingernails. She straightened and nudged the others when she realized they'd garnered Vira's attention.

"Where's his horse?" Vira's voice rang out sharper than she intended.

The girl with the knife, who looked barely older than Vira herself, toyed with the end of her braid. "There wasn't one around here, Maharani."

"And his convoy?"

"He didn't appear to be traveling with one."

Vira bit back a snarl. These warriors — ones her Council had claimed were the best in the country — were obviously missing something critical: common sense. "Lord Harish did not journey here on foot with no mount and no supplies. *Find them.*"

For a moment Vira thought the warriors would refuse. But then they bowed in unison, palms pressed together in front of their chests, before scattering into the woods without another glance behind them.

Wind raked through the Swapna Forest, and leaves from the mango and neem trees cascaded down, enveloping Vira in a cocoon of green and brown. Now that she was alone, an uncomfortable lurch tugged at her stomach.

She looked down at Harish again. His kurta was light enough in color to reveal the three pools of blood that had killed him. An arrow pierced the center of each red stain, black feather fletchings quivering in the late-summer breeze.

He was to have arrived at the palace days earlier, but there had been no letter, no news of a delay. And when he hadn't shown up, she'd assumed that he was a reluctant noble plotting an escape from a marriage he wanted even less than she did. She hadn't expected this.

This wasn't the plan. It wasn't how any of this was meant to happen. She couldn't face the Viceroy of Onaar. She couldn't face her Council. She couldn't —

Breathe.

Reason broke through her haze of panic as her mother's voice sounded in her head.

A maharani never runs away from a problem. She faces it head-on.

She could picture her mother's severe face as if she were standing right there, hissing the same lessons in Vira's ear a thousand times, not expecting Vira to retain any of them.

Face it head-on.

Find out who killed Harish — quickly. Guards had already been dispatched through the forest and the surrounding neighborhoods of Dvar, searching for witnesses, for any clues that might lead them to a suspect. But it had been more than an hour since the scouts had reported the body. If the guards hadn't yet found the killer, Vira had a sinking feeling that they never would.

Find a way to appease the viceroy. It would be only a matter of days before he learned of his son's fate — a precious few days in which Vira had to strike a new deal with him or find some other way to protect the country from Lyria, their northwestern neighbor. Lyria hadn't made a move in months, but the threat of the war she'd inherited had been a constant shadow lingering over Vira's rule from the moment she'd become the maharani eight months earlier.

How do I do this, Amma?

But her mother had never offered comfort even when she was alive.

Vira's hand drifted down to the iron hilt of the talwar strapped to her waist, as if it would give her strength. It had been pried from her dead mother's stiff hands and thrust into hers. It was polished and sharp, the curved silver blade gleaming, as if it had never been covered in the blood of her ancestors. It hummed against her hand with latent magic, a demanding buzz that Vira was still unaccustomed to.

In truth, everything about the talwar was unfamiliar — the weight, the balance, even the elaborate designs carved into the hilt. *This is a maharani's weapon* was the only response she'd received when she fought to keep the one she'd trained with for years. That weapon was simple, elegant, comfortable. But because it hadn't been forged with magic, it now hung on the wall opposite her bed, mounted there as a reminder of the life she'd left behind.

At the sound of rustling, Vira turned to the shadows, her talwar drawn. Its magic grated against her palm, harsh and unforgiving, as her hand trembled. The blade glowed white, crackling with sparks of lightning as she braced herself for the return of Harish's killer.

But it was Amrit who stepped out of the trees. Vira's grip relaxed, the magic waned, and blood rushed back into her fingers. She shoved the talwar into its sheath, trying to ignore the weight of her mother's ever-present judgment.

A maharani's talwar is an extension of her rule.

She couldn't even hold a talwar. How could she expect to hold on to her country?

"You should have waited for me." Leaves crunched under Amrit's feet as he crossed the length of the clearing, walking toward her. A dull shard of moonlight illuminated his angular face. He hadn't changed out of his formal guard attire, and a thick silver bangle wrapped around the silk sleeve of his upper left arm. She couldn't see it from where she stood, but she knew there was a medallion in the center that was stamped with a swan — a sign of his rank and service to the royal family.

"Contrary to what the Council believes, I can protect myself against a few wild deer," she said.

Vira kept her voice light, but her mouth burned with the bitter aftertaste of the lie. She hadn't been able to wield a blade with a steady hand since the battle at Ritsar eight months before. Not since she'd failed to command Ashoka's armies to victory. Not since she'd lost Ashokan land for the first time in four hundred years.

Not since she'd erred so badly, the viceroys of two provinces had walked out of her Council, taking with them countless troops and resources she desperately needed.

Amrit looked at her, and for the span of a heartbeat she was certain he could see right through her. She hadn't told him — told anyone — about the nightmares, about the way her hand shook each time she had to draw her weapon. But Amrit sometimes seemed to know her better than she knew herself.

"I should certainly hope so," he said. "I did train you, after all."

And what a great student she had turned out to be, freezing in battle, letting innocent citizens die in her stead.

"You were busy. And I wasn't recognized." Vira gestured to herself. With her plain red kurta and simple braid, she could have been twin to any one of those careless warriors. She'd even taken off all her jewelry except for the thin gold chain she always wore around her neck, the small pendant hidden beneath her collar.

Amrit gave her an exasperated look. "That's precisely what concerns me. You don't have to do this alone, Vira."

Vira. Yet another thing her mother would have disapproved of. Amrit was the captain of her guard now, but he'd been her friend first. And she hadn't been able to bear the thought of him calling her Maharani and bowing to her with deference. No, this one small thing was a reminder that not everything was different. That there were still some parts of her the title of maharani couldn't strip away.

Amrit crouched before the body. "This is bad."

"The Council won't be happy." That was an understatement. It would be a miracle if the Council was anything short of furious.

"They're your elders, Vira. They don't want to take orders from an eighteen-year-old. You have to charm them."

"Pretty words woo councilors, not angry demands," Vira recited. Another saying her mother had drilled into her head. But frustration laced her voice. She wasn't her mother. She didn't have the gift of pretty words.

Even the alliance with the Viceroy of Onaar had been difficult to negotiate. The engagement to Harish had been a last-ditch strategy to convince the viceroy to return to serve on the Council, to lend his province's troops and considerable wealth to secure the western border. But it had always been shortsighted, a temporary solution meant to delay the mounting problems. Because it wasn't armies that Ashoka needed. It was magic.

Vira reached up to grip her pendant, her thumb tracing the familiar, comforting grooves of the image carved into the gold coin: twin blades crossed over a lotus. Magic was how Ashoka had maintained its independence over the last five hundred years. Magic that was mined from the quarry beneath the palace — a source of raw power, inherently useless until the mayaka, those who worked with magic, processed and used it to forge items of immense power.

Magic was woven into the very fabric of Ashokan society. It was threaded into the currency — into the skinny seyrs and square tolahs and gold jhaus, ensuring that they couldn't be forged. It was laced into every brick that made up the border walls, shielding and protecting the country from intruders. It powered their carriages, their lamps, their messages. It was even Ashoka's biggest export, traded to Lyria and other countries for painted pottery and plush rugs, for medicines and crops not found in Ashoka.

Or it had been. Trade had stalled months ago, the bustling ports and endless caravans already a fading memory. The Emperor of Lyria was convinced that Ashoka was hoarding all the magic they had. But that wasn't why Vira hadn't renegotiated the trade agreements.

It was because there was no magic left to trade.

It was her biggest secret: the horrible truth of just how little was left in the quarry. Magic waned with use, and without regular replenishment,

Ashoka's magical borders were already wavering. And if Vira couldn't protect Ashoka against invaders, there would be no Ashoka for her to defend.

"Look," Amrit said, tilting Harish's chin. Purple veins spidered down the dead man's neck and chest, disappearing into his kurta. "Poison, likely."

Amrit yanked out the arrow embedded in Harish's stomach, turning it over in his hand before holding it out for Vira to see. The arrowhead wasn't flat and notched, like the ones she'd used in her brief and catastrophic attempts at wielding a bow. This one was conical, the metal twisting in half a spiral. It was beautifully elegant, and unlike anything she'd ever seen. But judging from the look on Amrit's face, he had.

"You know who killed him," Vira said.

Amrit hesitated and then nodded once. "I can guess."

"Who?"

He said nothing for a long moment. In the distance, a mynah bird trilled. Another one answered its song. "Later," he promised. "We should move the body before —"

"Amrit —"

A twig snapped.

"What was that?" Vira's hand slid to her talwar as she turned. And froze.

Three figures stood several feet away, arrows nocked and aimed. They had dupattas wrapped around their faces, covering their mouths and noses, masking their identities.

Amrit stepped in front of her, talwar drawn.

The boy in the middle spoke. "Put down your weapons, intruders. We have you surrounded."

As proof, an arrow whistled from behind, traveling over Vira's head to lodge in a tree trunk in front of her. She whirled around, her heart racing as she scanned the dark tree line for invisible figures.

7

"Who are you?" Amrit demanded, not lowering his weapon.

"Who are *we?*" the boy mocked. "I'm surprised you don't recognize us. We recognize you. *Guard.*" The word was spat out like a curse.

There was only one group of people who were arrogant enough to expect their reputation to precede them, who would dare speak the word *guard* with such hatred.

"Ravens," Vira breathed. The boy's eyes snapped to her. She stepped out from behind Amrit. "You're thieves, not killers."

Stories of bandits who lived within the Swapna Forest and robbed merchants and travelers and anyone associated with the crown had been circulating for years. The Ravens, as they called themselves, had pledged to fight against the maharani long before Vira had ever taken the throne. Another war she'd inherited from her mother.

The boy pointedly glanced at Harish's crumpled body. "Clearly, the same cannot be said for you."

"We didn't kill him." Vira let go of her hold on the talwar, raising both her hands to showcase her empty palms.

The boy was unmoved. "That may very well be. But your fate is a matter for our leader."

Desperation drove her forward. "You don't und —"

The figures drew their bowstrings back. Vira stopped.

"Make no mistake —" The boy's voice was sharper than a blade. "We don't *like* to kill, but if you run, we will hunt you." This wasn't a warning. It was a guarantee.

Vira blinked, licking her lips once. Twice. They were outnumbered. She glanced at Amrit, and she could see him coming to the same conclusion. He lowered his weapon.

Her breaths came out in small, shallow pants as thick gray smoke suddenly swirled around them — curling around her knees, snaking around her waist and chest.

Amrit coughed. "Vi —" He coughed harder as the fog enveloped him.

Vira's eyes watered. "Amrit?"

The smoke burned down her throat, her lungs, her stomach. She gasped for breath. She coughed, too, reaching for Amrit. But there was only air. She couldn't see anything. Or hear. Or . . . think.

She had . . . she had to find . . . Amrit.

Vira fell to her knees. Dirt coated her hands, lodging under her fingernails. Her arms could no longer hold her up. The faintest scent of neem clung to the air.

And then there was only darkness.

CHAPTER TWO

— RIYA —

THERE WAS SOMETHING sacrilegious about breaking into a temple.

Riya wasn't exactly the praying type, yet discomfort prickled along the back of her neck as she peered through the grime-streaked window of the priestess's room. Corrupt priestess, Riya reminded herself, who was stealing from people. That made the impiety a little better.

Or at least she hoped it did.

Riya leaned in, standing on her tiptoes. Her bare feet were already numb and aching from the cold stone slabs that made up the interior of the temple. Someone had washed the courtyard after the last visitors had gone, leaving wet patches to dry. Patches Riya hadn't noticed until *after* she'd stepped in a puddle of icy water. She'd shrieked loud enough to rouse the goddesses themselves — or at least that's what Kavita had snapped as she dragged Riya out of sight of the entrance.

Somehow, Riya's quip, "At least now we know the temple really is empty," hadn't appeased Kavita.

Riya cupped her hands around her face to block the glare of the flickering torch behind her. The glass defiantly reflected her own dark eyes, and she pulled away, frustrated.

"It's no use, Kavs. I can't see a thing."

Kavita tilted her head to one side, a hand on her hip and a crooked smile at her lips. It was the Kavita standard just before she said something she thought was especially clever. "Did you expect we'd find an open door and a *thieves welcome here* sign? Or maybe you'd like to scream again and see if the goddesses want to lend a hand."

"Can you be serious?"

This was supposed to be a brief reconnaissance mission to find out whether the rumors were true — whether the priestess actually was stealing and selling the jewels and idols that the few pious citizens left in the city of Dvar were donating to the temple. But so far it had been neither short nor fruitful.

Kavita looked the very picture of boredom, leaning against the wall, flipping and twirling a knife between her fingers with enviable deftness. "Come on, Riya. This is a waste of time. We should be with the others."

Kavita had a point. The Ravens were thieves, not vigilantes; this wasn't what they did.

Things had been shifting in Ashoka for a long while now. Jobs were declining. The ports were empty more often than not. And then the maharani had raised taxes inexplicably, taking even more from citizens who had far too little — chipping away at the remnants of their purses, scraping away the last of their hope.

Many blamed Maharani Vira for the way their fortunes had turned, but Riya knew that the people of Ashoka had been struggling even before Vira ascended to the throne. Before Maharani Shanti had been killed. Before war had broken out in Ritsar and armies had been pulled from their training bases and sent to the Lyrian border.

Those who could had fled the country in search of better opportunities. But there were many who couldn't afford the journey — and many who didn't want to leave their homeland, in good times or bad.

That was who the Ravens helped, the ones the goddesses and maharanis had forsaken. They made sure the people had enough money in their pockets after the tax collectors came around — sometimes twice in the same month — even if it meant stealing it back from the maharani herself. That's where the other Ravens were: breaking into the carriage that transported the collected taxes to the Dvar Fort.

"Yash asked us to do this," Riya reminded Kavita.

That earned her an eye roll. "You volunteered," Kavita said. "The only one to volunteer, might I add."

"We help people."

"We help the poor," Kavita amended. "For all we know, the priestess is selling donations because that's the only way for her to pay the collectors. In case you haven't noticed, priestesses aren't in high demand these days."

"No job is in high demand," Riya said. "But she's deceiving people. They think their donations are going to the goddesses. To help . . . I don't know, ensure that their prayers are heard quicker."

Kavita snorted. "That's not how prayer works."

"That's not the point. Faith is all that some people have left. Shouldn't we help them preserve it?"

"Vaishali's bones, Ri."

"Look, you didn't hear that poor lady begging us to find out what happened to the lamps she donated."

"Oh, and you did?"

"Well, no. But Yash —"

Kavita smirked. "The rest of us aren't so swayed by his beautiful eyes and chiseled jaw."

Riya flushed. "This isn't about . . . *that*."

Kavita had been with the Ravens since she was a child, so she didn't get it. For Riya, it was different when Yash asked. He'd been the one who'd found her stumbling through the forest — who'd taken her in and given her a home. A purpose.

A familiar ache settled between her ribs at the thought of the Ravens. Kavita called it love, but Riya couldn't imagine that love would be so terrifyingly painful, so overwhelmingly intoxicating. They were her family, her entire life, and some days it felt as if there was nothing she wouldn't do, no line she wouldn't cross to keep it that way.

Some part of her still wanted to show Yash just how grateful she was. She was on his side no matter what. He could trust her — with his secrets, with his life. And maybe if she went above and beyond, he would finally see that she wasn't the helpless girl he'd rescued.

Riya huffed as she caught sight of Kavita's grin. "Can you focus, please?" Riya asked, wanting to change the subject.

Kavita's amusement faded into exasperation. "There's nothing to focus on. The door's locked with magic. Unless you plan to burn your fingers picking it, we should leave before the priestess comes back."

She wasn't wrong. Mayaka-forged locks burned to the touch if anything but the matching key was inserted. Trying to force their way in would be a painful waste of time. But maybe there was another way. If Riya recalled the layout of the temple correctly, the rooms on this side of the hall overlooked the courtyard. Which meant —

"There's a window on the other side."

Kavita groaned. "You're being stubborn."

"You mean passionate."

Kavita's head thudded against the wall.

"Come on," Riya urged. "We've come this far. If there's no window, I swear we can leave." Kavita didn't move. "*And* I'll buy you a full plate of khandvi."

It took a moment for Kavita to react to the mention of her favorite snack from her home province of Ravas. But then her fingers stopped moving, and she slid the dagger into the folds of the dupatta wrapped around her waist. She pushed away from the wall with an exaggerated sigh and gestured for Riya to lead the way. "I'll get the khandvi myself, thanks. Your taste in Ravasi food is abysmal."

"My taste is fine. You just want an excuse to flirt with the girls who run the stalls."

Kavita's dimples glinted in the dusty light. "Not all of us are lucky enough to be in love."

"I'm not — oh, Kausalya help me."

Riya made her way toward the small balcony opposite the stairwell. Below them was the back courtyard of the temple. Uneven stone slabs spread out across the square, weeds and grass sprouting from cracks left unattended through the years. In the center, behind a tulsi plant, was a neglected altar to a forgotten goddess. The iron gate they'd scaled to enter the temple was to the left, but the heavy chains coiled around the bars ensured that it wasn't a functional door. The real temple entrance was somewhere to the right, beyond the building that housed the altars to the three goddesses. Though perhaps *building* was a loose interpretation. It was nothing more than a sea of carved stone pillars that held up the pyramid-shaped gopuram tower.

The railing of the balcony pressed into Riya's stomach as she leaned over the edge. "Window." She pointed triumphantly.

"You win," Kavita said dryly.

Riya sized up the wall. It was weatherworn, with enough crevices to provide plenty of finger- and footholds. It would be easy to climb, even without the stone eagle perched helpfully between the balcony and the ledge below the priestess's window. She hoisted herself up onto the railing, a hand gripping the wall to steady herself.

In the distance, the glimmering lights of the Dvar Fort rose above the city — a glittering beacon visible from every street. It was magic that made those lanterns burn unnaturally bright. Magic the maharani and her Council hoarded in their quarry while her people struggled to survive in the streets.

Those lights were meant to be reassuring, a comforting reminder of the maharani's power and protection. To Riya, it was a constant reminder of all the ways in which the maharanis had failed Ashoka.

She took a deep breath, anticipation pooling in her stomach. And then she leapt.

She landed lightly, her hands wrapping around the eagle's head while her bare feet found purchase in the stone beneath the talons. She slid a leg onto the ledge, testing it before she swung herself onto it fully. Wind whipped strands of hair into her face as she ran a hand over the padlock that held the shutters together. No magic, thank the goddesses.

Riya slid the mayaka-forged silver hoop earrings out of her earlobes and unwound the circles into long, thin lock picks. Within seconds, the lock clicked open. Riya landed on the floor of the priestess's empty room with a soft thump. She whistled — two trills, like the chirp of a mynah bird. The Ravens' *all clear* signal. Seconds later, Kavita swung in after her, as quiet as a cat, closing the window and sealing them into the room.

Kavita withdrew a small rock from her pocket, bathing them in a soft orange glow. Riya surveyed the room. It was a bedroom and an office — and thoroughly impersonal on both counts. A single cot was flush against a wall, next to a wooden chest. On the other side, a rickety desk was covered in stacks of ledgers and books.

As Kavita drifted toward the desk, Riya made her way to the bed. Nothing under the mattress or wedged into the space between the cot and the wall. The chest was full of innocuous saris, petticoats, and blouses. She dropped to her knees and looked under the bed, sliding her arm underneath, waving it back and forth to see if it caught on anything.

"Nothing." Riya sneezed twice. "Unless you count dust."

"I think I found something," Kavita said.

Riya picked herself up. "What is it?"

Kavita was thumbing through the pages of a ledger. "What did that lady say she was missing again?"

"Uh . . . gold lamps with peacock ornaments on top." Riya peered over Kavita's shoulder. "Is that a list of who's donated to the temple?"

Kavita trailed the glowing stone down the list. "Found it. Two peacock lamps for Vaishali's altar."

"Is there a record of who she's selling them to?"

"Doesn't look like it." Kavita flipped through the rest of the pages. "Maybe there's anoth —"

The doorknob turned.

Riya dropped to the ground, pulling Kavita — and the ledger — down with her. Kavita gasped in shock as Riya clamped a hand over Kavita's mouth and another around the rock. Half a second later, the door swung open.

Torchlight flitted in from the corridor, bright enough that even the slightest motion would lengthen their shadows and give them away. They were too far from the window to escape that way, and if the priestess came around to sit at her desk, she would trip over them before she ever reached for a quill.

Dread coiled in Riya's stomach as she met Kavita's panicked eyes.

The footsteps grew louder. Riya catalogued every twitch of shadow, every swish of cloth. Wind rattled the shutters, and Riya bit the inside of her cheek. The window was unlocked — all it would take was the right gust of wind, and it would blow open.

Next to her, Kavita shifted imperceptibly, drawing her dagger. Riya pulled her hand away from Kavita's mouth, her movements slow and smooth as she reached for her own weapon. Familiarity surged through her as her fingers curved around the patterned metal hilt, a faint trace of magic still clinging to it from when her mayaka father had forged it.

The dagger was the only thing that remained of her old life. It had been her constant — and sometimes only — protector since she'd left home two years earlier. But even that did little to curb the fear surging through her frozen body.

But acting on fear was for amateurs. No, Riya had surprise on her side. She would wait until the priestess approached the desk and . . . angle in through the stomach and then up. Piercing her heart. Or lungs. It was certain death.

Or so she'd been told.

There was always a price to pay for taking someone's life — her father had told her that the day he'd given her the dagger. She'd thought about this so often over the years that she could recall his exact words, the precise inflections of his deep, somber voice.

You may not see it now, my dear Riya, but every act of violence bears a cost. Some things leave a physical scar. A cut. A burn. Those can fade with time. But some acts, like taking a life — those leave a mark on your soul.

And those never disappear.

But those rules belonged to another life, to another girl she'd left behind. A dagger in her hand and secrets in her heart. That was how Riya had secured her place among the Ravens. And that was how she'd escape the priestess.

The footsteps stopped. Riya held her breath, listening, waiting. Her heart thundered against her ribs, each beat seeming louder than the last.

The sound of shuffling parchment right above her made her start. Her fingers tightened around the dagger.

In through the stomach and then up.

More shuffling. The scratch of a quill. The dripping of wax. The stamp of a seal. Silence.

And then the distinct scraping of a box dragging against the coarse stone floor. Metal and stone clanged as the priestess rummaged through, slammed it shut, and then dragged it back.

The footsteps receded. The door closed, and they were once again plunged into darkness.

Relief flooded Riya. Her spine relaxed. Blood rushed back to her numb legs, tingling as she stood. She closed her eyes for just a second, her father's words still echoing in her ears.

Some acts, like taking a life — those leave a mark on your soul.

Her soul would remain unmarred for another day.

CHAPTER THREE

— RONAK —

OVER THE LAST eight months, Ronak had walked from the palace to the dungeons two hundred and thirty-four times. By now, memory guided his steps. Habit made him skip over the unfixed crack in the stone stairs and veer away from the scraggly thorns of the rosebush that leaned too far onto the path. He could probably close his eyes and still manage to make it there unscathed. But he didn't want that. He wanted to see everything. Remember everything.

Wind swirled around his shoulders, strong enough to carry away the stench that perpetually clung to the dungeons no matter how many jasmine vines the Council draped over the building. Two surly guards stood on either side of the metal gate that led down to the cells.

"Rajkumaara," they mumbled in unison, not bothering to mask the displeasure in their voices.

In another life, Ronak might be offended by the tone. His twin sister, Vira, probably would be — but then again, she'd always cared more about being liked. Ronak understood why no one wanted him visiting every night. His presence was a reminder of a fact that everyone in the palace seemed desperately to want to forget: the dungeons held another rajkumaara.

Ronak stood silently, letting the guards search him for any weapons before they allowed him to lift a flameless magic lantern from the wall to guide his way through the underground maze.

When Ronak was ten years old, he'd developed an interest in prisons. He'd found a book that described rooms full of ancient weapons magically forged to leech blood or sear flesh off the bone. It had thrilled and terrified him so much that for weeks afterward he'd holed up in the library, going through book after book of bone-chilling contraptions and the ways they'd used them on prisoners.

His fascination had been a short-lived phase — partly because the images were spawning nightmares and partly because Vira had discovered his interest and promptly informed their parents. But though the books had been relocated and the librarian fired, the pictures were burned into Ronak's mind. And the first time he stood outside these gates eight months earlier, he'd been certain that he knew exactly what to expect.

Ronak had torn through the stone halls, racing ahead of the guards, past rows and rows of cells built just as the books described — until he came up abruptly on Kaleb.

Knees drawn to his chest, arms wrapped tightly around himself, head hanging down . . . it wasn't the Kaleb that Ronak knew. And he'd learned in that moment that no number of books could have ever prepared him for the sight of his brother like this.

And two hundred and thirty-four times later, it hadn't gotten any easier.

Ronak approached slowly, hanging the lantern on a hook opposite Kaleb's cell. Kaleb was sitting on the floor, legs crossed, eyes closed. His black kurta seemed to swallow him whole.

There was no door or wall to separate Ronak from his brother — only dark metal shackles coiled around Kaleb's wrists and ankles, magically forged to keep him confined in his cell. A single metal bar on the floor, also imbued with magic, delineated the invisible barrier. If any part of Kaleb crossed the barrier, his body would be racked with enough pain to subdue an elephant.

Kaleb's eyes opened as Ronak reached inside his right pocket and withdrew a cloth-wrapped package of chapati, piping hot from the kitchen tava.

"You need to stop bringing me food," Kaleb said reproachfully even as he rose. "If the Council finds out, we'll both get in trouble."

"When was the last time any councilor bothered to step foot in here?"

They both knew full well that Ronak was the only one who ever visited. Ronak pushed the chapati over the metal barrier into Kaleb's hand. Though the magic only worked one way to keep the prisoners confined, it was forbidden for visitors to enter cells. Ronak had ignored that rule from the day the guards stopped shadowing him.

"Here, even the spies have spies. Remember?"

Ronak almost smiled. It was a favorite saying of their father's — one that Ronak more than anyone had internalized. He'd thought of it often in the two years since Papa had died.

As Kaleb sat back down and tore into the chapati and spicy mango pickle, Ronak also dropped to the ground, mirroring his brother's posture.

"Did you sleep well?" Ronak asked.

"Did you?" Kaleb returned.

"I'm not the one locked in here."

"No, you're the one wandering the streets of Dvar in the middle of the night."

Ronak ran a hand over the back of his neck, slipping his fingers beneath the simple gold chain. Kaleb watched his movement, and Ronak self-consciously dropped his hand. It had been Kaleb's first. Papa had given it to him many years ago, and it had passed to Ronak after his imprisonment.

"I'm not alone," Ronak said. "I have Jay."

"Right."

"What?" Ronak asked.

Once, Kaleb would have said nothing until he'd thought long and hard about the most diplomatic response. But now he held Ronak's gaze and said, "I know you don't want to hear it, Ro, but he's impulsive and careless."

Ronak pursed his lips. Jay and Kaleb were in the middle of a ten-year-old war that Ronak wanted no part of. Kaleb thought Jay was reckless; Jay thought Kaleb had no sense of adventure. And after a childhood spent mediating peace between his brother and his best friend, Ronak was tired of the role.

"He's been a *friend*. Perhaps you've forgotten, but there aren't many people lining up to befriend a rajkumaara."

Use him, sure. Everyone wanted to twist his supposed sway with Vira to their advantage. But Jay saw him as a person.

Kaleb looked up sharply. "You think I don't know how hard it is to make friends?"

"That's not what I meant."

"It's not friendship to insist that you follow him down whatever illegal path he's chosen now."

Ronak said nothing.

"Last I heard, it was chariot races. Before that, what was it? Ah yes, transporting *raw magic*? I was sure I'd lost my mind, because I know my brother would not be so foolish."

Ronak blinked in surprised. He purposely hadn't told Kaleb about that.

"So it's true." Kaleb shook his head.

Ronak looked away, but not before he saw the disappointment in Kaleb's eyes.

"What were you thinking?" Kaleb asked.

He hadn't known what it was—not until it was too late—but that wouldn't matter to Kaleb.

"There's a reason," Kaleb continued quietly. "A reason mayaka go through all that training. Papa raised you better than that. Or have you forgotten, now that he's gone?" Bitterness lined his words.

Of course Ronak hadn't forgotten. Kaleb had only ever had one dream: to follow in Papa's footsteps. He'd study at a renowned university, apprentice under one of the top mayaka forgers, and take over for Papa as the palace's mayaka. If Vira hadn't locked him up—hadn't sided with the Council despite knowing that Kaleb could never be involved with the death of the maharani—he would have completed his first year of university by now.

"How'd you find out?" Ronak asked.

Kaleb's lips quirked in a poor imitation of a smile. "You think you're the only one with spies, Ronak? I may not care for these court games, but perhaps *you've* forgotten that we were raised the same."

It took Ronak a moment to make sense of the words. Of course. The maidservant who'd found him throwing up in his chambers from raw magic poisoning.

Mayaka spent half a decade learning to work with magic, the training carefully overseen by the Mayaka Association. Prolonged exposure led to worsening symptoms—headaches, nausea, memory loss, paralysis, until it eventually led to death. It was why miners at the quarry worked in shifts of no more than six hours at a time, with frequent days off to recuperate. And it was also why they were outfitted with special clothes and gloves that covered their whole bodies—items Ronak hadn't known he'd need when he'd accepted the job.

"I just don't get it, Ronak. Why would you do it?"

For you, Ronak wanted to say. But he couldn't tell Kaleb—not until he had every part of his plan in place.

The will to fight drained out of him. "I don't want to argue, Kaleb."

Kaleb rose and made his way to a small clay pot of water in the corner. He washed his hands, then wiped them on the cloth Ronak had brought the chapati in.

"I worry about you, Ro," Kaleb said. "I worry you're focusing on the wrong things. Fun and adventure are well and good, but you're eighteen now."

Dread pooled in the pit of Ronak's stomach. "I know, Kaleb. Trust me."

The Council didn't approve of how often he visited his brother, and they disliked even more that he'd been digging into the past, trying to figure out who had framed Kaleb. It was only a matter of time before a councilor said the right words, offered the right incentive, and Vira would bend to their will. Then the Council would be free to send him to any province — any country — that could offer an alliance. What better way to be rid of Ronak than marrying him off to the highest bidder?

He was no more free than Kaleb. His prison was larger, more lavish, but he still felt the chains tightening around his wrists and ankles.

"Don't you ever dream of leaving all this behind?" Ronak blurted before he could stop himself. He stood up. "We could travel the world, explore other countries."

"Ronak."

"We could find a new place to call home." Ronak paced back and forth. "A secluded town somewhere in the mountains. Pristine lakes reflecting snow-covered peaks. I could paint all day. You could find a nice boy —"

"Dreams are for the free," Kaleb said flatly.

"You won't be locked here forever. Just think about —"

"I don't want to!" Kaleb's words reverberated in the air around them.

Ronak stopped moving, taken aback.

"I don't want to think about a life I'll never get to have."

"I didn't mean —" Ronak swallowed, staring hopelessly at the pain in Kaleb's eyes. "Kaleb —"

"I know." Kaleb exhaled. "I know, Ronak. But no one can run forever. At some point you have to stop and face reality."

For a moment, the only noise was the wind whistling outside.

"I should go," Ronak said. He reached for the cloth and tugged it gently out of Kaleb's grasp. "I'll see you tomorrow."

Kaleb had been right about many things. But he'd also been wrong. Ronak wasn't a bored rajkumaara testing the limits of his privilege. He was a boy trying to change his fate. There *was* escape from this life — for him and for Kaleb.

And Ronak was going to find it.

CHAPTER FOUR

— RIYA —

IT WAS A warm night, but Riya shivered as she looked up at the overcast sky.

The forest was unforgiving under the best of circumstances. Old hunting traps from long-abandoned settlements littered the ground. Wild animals roamed free, eagerly awaiting any prey that wandered too close. The Ravens knew the surroundings better than anyone. Carved trees and fallen logs that looked identical to unpracticed eyes were signposts to them, as clear as if they had words and arrows etched on them. But there were some nights when even the Ravens didn't dare stray too far from camp — nights when heavy downpours obscured their vision and turned dirt paths slippery with mud. Then the forest stopped being dangerous and became deadly.

Kavita stopped. "Do you hear that?"

Riya hoisted the box they'd taken from the priestess's room higher on her hip, tilting her head to one side. And then she heard it too. Voices.

Kavita cupped her hands around her mouth and sounded another bird trill, this one mimicking the three-note song of the koyal. It was a question: Who's there? A beat passed, and then another. There was no reply. Whoever was approaching wasn't a Raven.

As one, Riya and Kavita moved off the path and into the thicket just as three figures drew closer.

"Guards." Kavita pursed her lips as if she'd bit into a lemon. "What are they doing here?"

Guards were always around, circling market stalls, trying to sniff out counterfeit or smuggled goods hidden among the trinkets. They never found anything, of course. The real smugglers operated on the other side of town, in parlors luxurious enough to rival rooms in the maharani's palace. Still, the guards didn't usually venture into the forest.

Riya watched them through the space between two branches. The girl leading the way carried a flameless lantern flickering with magic. Another had her talwar drawn. But the third one looked to be entirely weaponless.

"—she'd just leave us here," the girl with the lantern was complaining. "Who cares if a few guards are maimed by beasts, right?"

The girl with the talwar shushed her. "She's the maharani. She can do whatever she wants."

The lantern girl scowled. "What about the dead body? You think she took it back to the fort?"

An uncomfortable chill scuttled down Riya's spine. The maharani had been in the forest?

"Dead body?" Kavita echoed under her breath.

The guards disappeared around a bend in the road, the wind snatching the rest of the conversation.

Riya bit her lip. "Do you really think she was here?" She tried to ignore the way her stomach twisted into a knot. "The maharani?"

"Who cares?"

But Kavita looked unsettled too, her eyes lingering on the empty path. Deaths in the forest were never a good sign. And that this one had the attention of the maharani was even worse.

✳

The Ravens' camp was nearly deserted. The only movement Riya could make out was Yash pushing a heavy tree trunk closer to the flickering fire pit. It always surprised her how strong he was, because looking at him, he was all bones and joints. He raised his hand in greeting.

Up close, Riya could see dark circles under his weary eyes. Loose strands of his usually tidy hair hung across his forehead, dipping into his lashes. Yash was so quick to smile, to laugh, that it was easy to forget that he was responsible for all of them.

Riya deposited the box of stolen goods at his feet. Kavita tossed the ledgers on top of it. Yash's brows furrowed in confusion.

"We found the stolen items," Riya announced. "And who she's selling them to."

He glanced back up at Riya. "Really?"

The priestess had been clever, hiding items in a mayaka-forged chest. They'd been thorough in searching the room, yet they hadn't found anything until they emerged from behind the desk and spotted a wooden edge peeking out from beneath the cot. It was a common hiding practice for those who could afford to hire a mayaka — making objects invisible except to those who already knew of their existence.

Magic only worked on inanimate objects, and forging those objects was a difficult practice. Riya had learned at a young age that she had little aptitude for it. It involved a lot of sitting still, clearing her head, and focusing on just one thing. Her mind had always raced far too fast to be pinned down the way her father wanted. But the worst part was, it was never the same each time. The amount of magic, the amount of power, the exact way in which an object was meant to work all changed based on how focused or well trained the mayaka was.

"That's the beauty of it," Papa always said. "Each item is unique. The magic is based on the individual forger."

Riya had never seen what was so great about that. As much as she'd hated her mathematics lessons, at least there was a correct answer. With forging, everything depended on the intention of the mayaka. You couldn't be truly certain of what the object was meant to do without speaking to the mayaka who made it. The priestess likely thought the box would remain hidden to everyone except her. She hadn't taken into account lurking Ravens who might unintentionally uncover its existence.

"Good work, Riya." Yash flashed her a smile, and Riya beamed, ignoring Kavita's snort of laughter. "Leave it inside, will you?"

Yash had sent her to find out if there was any truth to the rumors, but she'd done so much more than that. It would be only a matter of time until he recognized how indispensable she could be.

✳

The Ravens had two tents, made of thatched straw and old saris, propped up against a wall of trees. They were primarily for supplies: a small cabinet that housed their limited armory of stolen weapons, stacked wooden trunks full of spare clothes, and clay pots of carefully rationed food strung up along the roof between tree branches.

Riya deposited the box in the back corner near the armory, tucking the ledger away behind it. Maybe Yash would let her join him when they returned the lamps.

"What are you doing?"

Riya jerked up, nearly knocking her head against one of the pots. Varun — Yash's brother — stood at the entrance, a bow in his left hand, a quiver of red-fletched arrows hanging askew off his shoulder. His gaze bored into her, and Riya fought the urge to turn away. There was something unsettling about the way he looked at her, as if he saw more than he should.

"That's none of your concern." She walked past him, but he moved quickly, blocking her path.

"What do you want?" she asked, pulling herself up to her full height, refusing to let him intimidate her. But even then he towered over her. The air around him smelled faintly of tulsi which infuriated Riya. Thieves weren't supposed to have a signature scent. But she couldn't remember a time when he hadn't had an endless supply of tulsi leaves stuffed in his pockets.

"You were supposed to investigate, Riya. Not rob the priestess."

"I don't recall you issuing the orders."

He scowled. "What if the others find it? What if they sell those donations before they can be returned to the rightful owners?"

"They wouldn't if Yash told them not to."

"Right. Yash." His jaw tightened. "Open your eyes, Riya. Not everyone puts my brother on the same pedestal you do. It's getting pathetic how desperate you are for his attention."

Riya sucked in a breath, the words cutting deeper than she expected. She stepped closer to him. "What's pathetic is how often you involve yourself in matters that don't concern you. Are you so desperate to be relevant?"

She moved around him again, but Varun's grip on her forearm held her back. He leaned in close, his warm breath fluttering against her cheek. "You can deflect all you want, but you know I'm right."

"Touch me again, and I'll break your hand."

He let her go, but he didn't step away. Her arm burned with the imprint of his hand.

A throat cleared behind them, startling them both. Varun stepped back.

"Well, if you two are quite done," Kavita said dryly, "the others are back."

Varun walked away without another word. Kavita watched him leave, her expression unreadable.

"Don't," Riya said before Kavita could open her mouth.

"I didn't say anything."

Riya scowled. "He started it." She felt like a petulant child, especially when Kavita rolled her eyes.

"He has a point, Ri. You do tend to see the world the way you want to."

"What's that supposed to mean?"

Kavita sighed, then looped her arm through Riya's, tugging her forward. "Nothing. Come on. We're deciding what to do with the prisoners."

"What prisoners?" The Ravens didn't usually take prisoners.

Kavita's gaze darkened. "The others found the dead body."

Riya froze for a moment. "What? The one—"

"—the guards were talking about," Kavita finished.

The eerie cold returned to Riya. "And the prisoners?"

"More guards." Kavita's frown deepened. "I don't know why they bothered to bring them here. They should have just taken their weapons and cut them loose." She shook her head, disgusted. "You should see their swords. So much magic it nearly knocked me back. Yash estimates that they're worth at least several hundred tolahs. Maybe more."

"Really?" Those weren't the kind of weapons guards were normally issued. And they were certainly not the kind of weapons one brought into a forest full of notorious thieves. A sudden, horrifying thought hit Riya. But no. It wasn't possible. The maharani was gone. The guards had said—

Riya stopped walking.

The guards had assumed that the maharani had left with the dead body. But if the Ravens had the body . . .

"Where are you going?" Kavita called after her, but Riya was already rushing back into the glades, past the Ravens clustered around the fire, toward the far side of the clearing. The shapes came into view even before she slowed.

There were two of them.

A guard. And . . . her.

Riya's chest hurt as if someone were sitting on it, squeezing all the air out of her lungs, all the blood out of her heart. She couldn't breathe. She couldn't think.

This was wrong. All wrong. Vira wasn't supposed to be here. Vira wasn't supposed to know. But there was no escaping the truth. Riya's past had finally caught up with her.

Vira looked nothing like the statue of the arrogant young maharani they'd erected in the center of Dvar. No. The girl sitting in front of her looked like just that — a girl. Her hair was parted in the center and pulled back in a practical braid. Her ears and neck and arms were unadorned, yet there was something undeniably regal in the way she sat, even as she was tied to a tree, unconscious.

You don't have to tell us what you're running from.

Those were the first words Yash had ever said to her. The Ravens had never cared about her past. They didn't even care that she was reluctant to talk about it. After all, none of them had happy stories. The Ravens were made up of runaways and castaways, of survivors and scoundrels.

But then she'd gotten to know them. People who'd become her best friends, her family. And suddenly, keeping her past from them no longer felt freeing. It felt like a burden. She'd meant to tell them — she really had. *One more day*, she'd told herself. *I'll tell them tomorrow.* But countless tomorrows had come and gone.

Now her secrets were literally sitting in the glades, and she'd run out of time.

Vira had found her.

And Riya had to get her sister out of the forest before her entire world crumbled around her.

CHAPTER FIVE

— VIRA —

IT WAS THE headache that woke Vira — a dull throb, insistent in her temples. She couldn't remember falling asleep with the window open, but cold air was blowing through her room. It smelled fresh, of dirt and rain.

Vira groaned. The maidservants would be coming in any moment to usher her to the baths. But she couldn't move her limbs. She couldn't even open her eyes.

"Vira?"

I'll be up in a minute, Vira tried to say, but her lips weren't working.

A second later there was another insistent hiss of her name. "Vira. Are you awake?"

She groaned again and then cracked her eyes open a tiny sliver to brace against the bright morning light.

There was only darkness. She forced her eyes open. Confusion muddled her thoughts. Dirt. Leaves. Trees. She wasn't in her room. She wasn't even in the palace.

Slowly, like a layer of morning mist receding in sunlight, awareness returned to Vira's body. Cold made her skin ripple with gooseflesh. Then fear tore through her veins. She jerked forward — and was immediately wrenched back. Ropes wound tight around her torso, pinning her arms at her side, cutting into her skin the more she struggled.

"Amrit?" Her voice came out in a hoarse, painful rasp. The smoke. She remembered the way it had burned and made her cough.

"Vira. Thank the goddesses," Amrit said somewhere to her left. "Are you hurt?"

She turned, wincing as her neck protested the sudden movement. "No. Are you?" Rough tree bark scratched against her cheek as she took him in. He was tied to a tree trunk, his posture mirroring hers, but he looked unharmed.

"No." Amrit strained against the ropes. They didn't budge. From the look on his face, this wasn't the first time he'd tried to get free. "I didn't think it was possible for this night to get worse."

That wasn't funny, but Vira laughed — and then immediately regretted it as sharp pain burst in her throat.

"The Council is going to be furious," she said.

"We'll find a way out of this together," Amrit promised.

She mentally sifted through the information her Council had gathered about the Ravens. She couldn't recall any stories about them taking prisoners. She'd assumed they didn't hold captives, but now she couldn't help but wonder if there were no stories because no captive had survived. Panic rose within her again, but she suppressed it.

Panic is the enemy of logic. Emotional thinking cannot coexist with rationality.

And according to her mother, Vira was always thinking too emotionally.

She surveyed the area. They were in a large clearing surrounded by dense forest. Cloth sheets were strung up between tree branches on the other side of the clearing, sectioning off areas to create privacy and provide limited shelter from the elements. In the center, orange embers glowed within a fire pit. A real fire. Vira hadn't seen one of those in years.

And next to the flames lay their weapons. She had often wished it was customary in Ashoka to bury the dead instead of cremating them. Maybe then the talwar would have been trapped somewhere beneath the earth with her mother's bones instead of being another burden for Vira to bear.

Yet she couldn't tear her eyes away. The talwar was lying in the dirt like a cheap, abandoned trinket, and the sight twisted at something primal in her chest. A weapon in her hand and whispers in her head. That was all Vira had left of her mother.

"Glad to see you're awake." A tall Raven approached them, a lantern in one hand that he set down beside Vira. He crouched to examine her bonds, and his wavy hair fell into his tired eyes. He was younger than Vira expected. And he was unarmed save for a small knife at his waist.

"Are you hurt?" he asked.

"What does that matter? We're prisoners."

His eyes lifted to hers. "Prisoners, too, deserve kindness."

"Compassion doesn't make you less of a criminal."

"Criminal, huh?" The boy's mouth twitched as he rose to check on Amrit. "Judgmental words from a killer."

"We're not killers," Vira said.

The Raven gestured to Amrit. "No one gets scars like that without being well acquainted with weapons. And don't think I didn't notice the magic in your weapons. Or the expensive clothes on the dead boy. I don't know who you are, but I'd be a fool to believe you were just guards who stumbled onto a dead body."

"You'll find out soon enough just how well acquainted I am with weapons," Amrit snarled.

The boy laughed. "I like you." He glanced back at Vira. "Any chance you'd want to defect? We could always use a spy or two."

"Vigilante justice," Vira bit out, unable to help herself, "isn't true justice. Those who operate outside the law can never uphold it."

"Suit yourself," the Raven said with a shrug. "But I'll remind you that there would be no need for us if there wasn't a gap in the protection provided by your maharani."

"Yash?" someone called from the distance.

"Coming."

As the boy — Yash — left them alone once more, Vira replayed the exchange in her mind, lingering on the way he'd said *your* maharani. As if he didn't consider himself included under the rule of the crown.

She knew there were people who didn't approve of her as the maharani. Half the members of her Council believed they'd be a better ruler than she was. But the thought that there were those who believed they didn't need to answer to the maharani at all left an unsavory taste in her mouth.

Sometimes she couldn't help but wonder if her mother had meant for her to inherit a dying country. Her mother's legacy was safe, but she'd left Vira alone and unprepared to deal with the mounting problems. And it didn't matter what she did or how many mistakes she tried to fix — she still came out looking like the villain.

Vira automatically reached for the pendant around her neck before she remembered that her arms were tied. She exhaled, wishing desperately that things were different. That there was no looming war. That her parents were still alive. That she still had a sister to share her burden. That there was more magic.

She'd unearthed all of Papa's research, examining every clue he'd already found, tracing every lead that had led him nowhere. Hunting for something — *any*thing — he might have missed. But there was simply no more magic to be found.

"Harish isn't here." Amrit's voice cut through her thoughts.

He was right. The Ravens were keeping the body elsewhere. She and Amrit had to leave before the Ravens began asking questions — or worse, finding answers.

What would her mother do? She'd look for a weakness — and then she'd exploit it.

Vira turned toward the fire pit, her gaze landing on Yash. They couldn't get free of their ties, but maybe they could convince Yash to untie them. Slowly, the fragments of a plan began to come together in her mind.

She glanced over at Amrit. "I have an idea."

Amrit watched her with quiet intensity, the entirety of his attention on her. "What do you need me to do?"

"Nothing, except sit there and look concerned." Vira took a deep breath. And then she screamed.

Yash was beside her in seconds, his eyes wide. "What's wrong?"

"What did you do to me?" she demanded, fighting against the rope.

"What are you talking about?" He crouched before her again. She could see the plain metal hilt of the knife tucked into his side, inches from her bound hands.

"Please —" she breathed. "You have to tell me what was in that smoke."

"Nothing," he said, alarmed. "It was just to knock you out. You were out for no more than fifteen minutes."

"It did something to me. I'm seeing things." Vira fought against the ropes again, feigning urgency. "What did you do to me?"

"Stop. *Stop.*" Yash's face was suddenly pale. "*Shit,*" he muttered under his breath. "All right." And then he reached behind her to untie the rope. She felt it go slack around her shoulders and then lower around her arms.

Vira's fist flew out, catching him square in the jaw. The unexpected force sent Yash sprawling to the ground—but not before Vira grabbed the knife at his side.

Yash ran a hand over his jaw as he clambered to his feet.

Vira used the tree to push herself up. Her numb legs trembled as she stood, but she held the knife out.

Yash stilled. "How far do you think you'll get?" he asked. "You're outnumbered. Trapped in the forest. A storm's on the way. You'll die before you reach the main roads."

"I'll take my chances," Vira said.

"What did you do?" a new, horrified voice asked.

Vira wasn't sure which one of them the newcomer was addressing. She turned. And stopped breathing.

"Riya?" she whispered. Her mind was unable to make sense of what she was seeing. Bathed in the flickering light of a lantern she held in one hand and the sparkling glint of the talwar she gripped in the other, her sister looked like a goddess come to usher Vira into the afterlife.

"Riya?" Vira's voice was a parched rasp. "Is it really you?" She thought back to the desperate desires she'd conjured minutes earlier—for her parents, for magic. For her sister. But wishes didn't come true. That, Vira knew for certain.

Yash's eyes flicked toward Riya. "Do you know her?"

"She's my"—Riya licked her lips—"sister."

Yash's surprised gaze swung to Vira—then back toward Riya. She could see him piece it together. They didn't look all that different. Riya was shorter, her skin darker, her frame skinnier. But their faces betrayed the truth: the same eyes, the same nose, the same chin—all inherited from the maharani herself.

"Can I have a moment alone?" Riya asked.

Yash hesitated, eyeing the knife in Vira's hand. Vira lowered it, but she didn't let go. He nodded and then walked away — but not without a lingering glance back.

Vira took in all of her sister, the sight twisting something inside her. "You look just like Amma."

"Funny." Riya slid the lantern onto a low-hanging branch. "That's what I was going to say to you, *Maharani*."

They stood in silence for a long moment. Vira searched for words, sorting through the hundreds of questions that were rising inside her. *Why did you run? Why did you join the Ravens? Why didn't you come home?*

But all that came out was "Why?"

Expressions flitted across Riya's face, each passing too quickly for Vira to decipher. Riya held out the hilt of the talwar for Vira to take. "You need to leave." Her eyes slid to Amrit. "Free him, and go."

"Go?" Vira echoed. "Not without answers. You've been here all this time? In Dvar? Hiding out with outlaws?"

"The Ravens are my family."

"*I'm* your family." Vira stepped forward — and Riya took a step back. "Riya, please."

"You need to leave," Riya repeated. "You can't be here, Vira."

But Vira didn't move. "Would you ever have told us?"

Riya looked away, and the truth hit Vira like a blow to her chest. If Vira hadn't stumbled into the forest, she would never have found her.

Vira laughed mirthlessly. "You'd really have lived out the rest of your life a half hour from the palace and never bothered to come home? I know you're stubborn, Riya, but this —"

"Home?" Riya's eyes flashed. "You told the world I was *dead*."

"To protect you, Riya." If the world had known she was missing, anyone could have kidnapped her, held her hostage — extorted the maharani of Ashoka.

"Well, I don't need protection anymore." Riya dropped the talwar so it thudded at Vira's feet. "Get out before you make this worse for yourself." She turned on her heel.

"You can come back now," Vira blurted out.

Riya froze. "What?"

"Come back with me, Riya. We can tell everyone it was a mistake. That you'd been sent away for your health. Or that you were lost at sea. That —"

"No."

Vira fumbled in the pocket of her kurta, pulling out a scrap of paper no wider than her palm, half of it with hastily scrawled instructions to Amrit on where to meet her. She ripped it and held one half toward Riya. "It's mayaka-forged. If you change your mind —"

"I won't."

Vira lunged after her, grabbing her arm and shoving the paper into Riya's palm. "*If* you change your mind, I'll send a carriage for you. Please, just take it." Vira closed Riya's fingers over the paper, trying to ignore the terrible feeling in her gut that Riya would never use it.

"Riya?" someone called from afar.

"Go," Riya begged, wrenching her arm from Vira's grasp. "Now."

Riya whirled around just as another Raven approached. "Riya, what's going on? Yash said something about your sister —" The girl caught sight of Vira, looking between the two of them with curiosity and confusion. "You're letting them go?"

"We can't keep them here, Kavs." Riya turned to glare at Vira, as if it were her fault that she was tied up in the Ravens' campsite.

"If you're so unhappy with my presence here, perhaps you should tell your friends not to kidnap the maharani," Vira snapped.

"Vira!" Amrit said, giving her a furious look, but she couldn't bring herself to care just then.

The girl's jaw dropped open. "Maharani?"

Riya paled, and realization struck Vira all at once. The Ravens didn't know that Riya was the rajkumaari. She'd hidden that part of her past, as if it were something to be ashamed of. Anger and hurt rushed through Vira.

"Oh, yes," Vira said, shoving her talwar into its sheath. "My sister, your beloved *Raven*, is the rajkumaari of Ashoka."

CHAPTER SIX

— RONAK —

RONAK'S CARRIAGE STOPPED three blocks away from the Market District. He pulled aside the curtain hanging over the window and peered into the dark. He could spot Jay's wiry frame leaning against a lamppost, casually flipping a coin up in the air and catching it. In the lamp's glow the coin glinted gold, but Ronak knew it was actually silver, the elephant carved on either side worn from years of handling. The coin had belonged to Jay's grandfather — a token from the years he'd served in the maharani's elephantry. It had been a staple in Jay's life for as long as Ronak had known him, tucked in his pocket until he was bored.

"Wait here," Ronak instructed the driver, and then shoved open the carriage door, fighting against the wind.

"You're late." Jay pocketed the coin. "He'll survive if you don't visit one night, you know." His feral grin showed off his perfect white teeth.

"Jay," Ronak warned. He knew full well that Jay thought he coddled Kaleb too much.

"It would give others a chance to visit," Jay continued, ignoring him. "Like your sister perhaps."

Ronak was positive that Vira had never once visited Kaleb. "Family loyalty isn't exactly my sister's priority." She hadn't thought twice before choosing a room of power-hungry councilors over her own brother.

"She didn't execute him, though."

"Vira doesn't deserve a prize for not killing her innocent brother," Ronak said flatly.

Jay's smile dropped. "You're no fun today."

"We'll have plenty of time for *fun* when we're free of this wretched place." He looked at Jay out of the corner of his eye. "Or didn't you hear the news?"

Before he left, Ronak had received word from the Council that Harish, his sister's betrothed, had been found dead in the forest. He'd been due to arrive several days earlier. Ronak hadn't wondered why he was delayed — and frankly, he hadn't cared. But if he'd been killed . . . Ronak didn't need to attend Council meetings to know what that meant: Ashoka was in trouble.

No alliance. No armies. No money.

And worse, it meant that the Council would hasten an advantageous engagement for Ronak.

"I heard." Jay crossed the street toward the market. "And we'll deal with that. But you'd better stop sulking before we get there. I heard she killed a man because he didn't smile enough."

"What? Is that true?"

It sounded like Jay's idea of a joke, but Ronak's stomach tightened. He didn't know what to make of the fact that Ekta, their secret benefactor, had requested a face-to-face meeting after months of contacting them only through an intermediary.

And it didn't help that Ronak knew little about her beyond rumors. On paper, she was a cloth merchant, but she made her living in countless illegal ways, including auctioning off outlawed mayaka-forged artifacts and — apparently — transporting raw magic. Ronak supposed he could have found out more concrete information about her doings, but he hadn't bothered. She paid well, and that was all that mattered.

The Council refused Ronak free access to the royal coffers, and until he turned twenty or was married, any withdrawal required approval from them. If he wanted enough money to start a new life, he'd have to find some other way of getting it. But, as Jay had helpfully pointed out, Ronak had been trained for nothing beyond being a rajkumaara — and, seeing as he'd shirked most of those duties, not even a particularly good one.

The only thing Ronak had in his favor was access to a palace full of rare and dangerous magical items — many of which had been forged before the maharanis had begun issuing decrees that limited what mayaka could make. And many of these things were imbued with so much magic, they'd left a trail of bloodshed in their wake. *Cursed,* the stories called them, but Amma had always insisted it was something far more banal that made entire countries wage war over a single object: desire.

Jay had found a merchant willing to pay very well to get her hands on them. All Ronak needed to do was transport an unmarked carriage into the neighboring province of Vrindh and prove he was serious about doing business with her. Raw magic poisoning was a small price to pay for that.

"I'm just saying," Jay said with a carefree shrug and another flash of his teeth. With his wide eyes and wild hair, he looked the very picture of innocence. "If you want her money, you have to play by her rules."

The fog rolling in from the ocean curled around the edges of the stores, turning dim lanterns into soft yellow blurs. Performers squeezed into the breathing spaces between stalls: dancers and musicians, storytellers and protesters standing on makeshift stages to draw viewers. Vendors stood in the streets, calling out prices, trying to entice customers to consider what they were selling. Eight seyrs for a painted vase. Two tolahs for saris spun of the softest silk.

But the true allure of the Market District had always been mayaka-forged items. Beaded necklaces that allowed the wearer to revisit their dreams. Pots that automatically replenished anything cooked in them. Even weapons made with magic: chakrams that turned to flame, swords that could slice through stone, invisible arrows that didn't appear until they'd struck their mark.

Ronak remembered coming here as a child, clinging to his father's hand because it was impossible to walk through the packed streets without getting lost or shoved aside. There had been a long wait for everything — getting food, looking at wares, even the performances that he couldn't see unless he sat on Papa's shoulders to rise above the crowd.

But that had been then. Now, nearly a third of the stalls had closed permanently. Magical items were so costly, most couldn't afford them.

A mess of smells wafted over Ronak as they passed a group of food carts: decadent gulab jamun soaked in rose water, chopped mangoes and guavas dipped in salt and ground chilies, paper-thin dosas stuffed with onions and spicy potatoes. A flyer fluttered in the air, the paper slamming into Ronak's chest. He peeled it off.

What has the maharani done for you? the text proclaimed. Underneath was a drawing of Vira, copied from the statue outside the Maharani's Mandap in the town center. But this drawing had her face scratched out, replaced with the demonic features of a rakshasi. Beside it were details advertising a demonstration scheduled outside the Mandap in four days' time, protesting the maharani's latest tax hike.

Jay peered over his shoulder. "What's that?"

"Nothing." Ronak crumpled it and cast it aside, trying to dismiss the queasy feeling in his stomach. In the palace, it was easy to pretend that the world outside didn't exist, that any unrest was distant and amorphous. But here, walking among the citizens, it wasn't so easy to ignore.

"Another protest," Jay surmised.

These were getting far too common, attracting large crowds that gathered at the City Center and marched to the fort. The Council had no idea who was pasting the flyers all over town, so they'd tightened security and staffed additional guards throughout the palace.

Jay looked at Ronak with uncharacteristic seriousness. "Do you want to go?"

Ronak's jaw tightened. "No." He hadn't meant to end up at the protest last month. It had been a cruel twist of fate that had brought him and Jay there, and it had been a mistake to stay — one that Ronak intended to never make again.

"But last time —"

"Drop it, Jay."

"If she's here —" Jay pressed, but he stopped as Ronak glared at him. "All right. I'm dropping it."

As they left the Market District, the carefully cultivated mirage of Dvar fell away. Wide stone roads turned to narrow dirt paths. The smell of fresh ocean air was replaced by the stench of garbage that hadn't been cleared away for days. Laughter and music drifted down from pleasure houses as smoke and spilled ale lingered outside the rows of taverns.

The worst of those streets was one the locals called Spit Street. If Spit Street had once had another name, Ronak didn't know it. It was called that because the dirt was stained a permanent red from people spitting out their paan. There were no alliances here. Brawls were common. So were thefts. And every other week, a body washed up in the Dhaya River, naked and beaten beyond belief. Only a betel leaf carved into the stomach of the victim offered any clues as to its origins.

Ronak glanced over his shoulder as he skirted a puddle of what might have been dirty water but could just as easily be ale or urine. It was naive to call attention to his discomfort, but he was painfully aware that they didn't belong here. He could feel eyes on him, cutting into his back, maybe trying to determine if he was worth robbing.

"Ro." Jay put his hand out to stop Ronak from walking forward.

Ronak swatted at the sudden influx of flies. "What?"

He looked down and immediately saw *what*. A dead body, discarded with little care. Ronak couldn't swallow his gasp. The Lyrian boy looked so young, no more than ten or eleven. His skull was a mangled mess of blood and brain, his face distorted beyond recognition. But Ronak's own imagination filled in the boy's face with darker curls, all-seeing brown eyes, a smattering of freckles across his nose.

He's not Kaleb, Ronak reminded himself. *He's not Kaleb.*

But Ronak could no more stop the dark turn of his thoughts than the nausea that gripped his stomach.

"Keep it together," Jay hissed.

Ronak let Jay drag him into a dark alley between two buildings. He ran a hand over his face. "*Shit, Jay.* He was a child."

Jay said nothing. There was nothing he could say. They both knew the reality of the rising tensions after Lyria had invaded Ritsar for access to Ashoka's magic. This wasn't the first Lyrian death at the hands of his people, and it wouldn't be the last. But casualties were easier to swallow when they were a string of impersonal numbers. It was different staring at a battered body.

According to the Council news sheets, they were finding more Lyrian immigrants with their throats slit, abandoned on street corners, or dumped into the Dhaya River. It might be the Emperor of Lyria who was their villain, but he was a faceless entity, distant and untouchable on his marble throne a country away. It was his people — the innocent families who'd made a life, a home in Ashoka — who were paying the price.

"We don't have to do this," Jay offered kindly. "We can turn back."

But they both knew that turning back wasn't an option. Ronak couldn't chance giving up a meeting with Ekta. She was his one shot at escape, and he'd learned a long time ago that there was nothing he wouldn't do to be free.

CHAPTER SEVEN

— VIRA —

THE CARRIAGE SENT up a spray of mud and rainwater as it hurtled through the roads.

Vira pushed her hair back from her forehead; her fingers came away damp. Riya had shown them to Harish's body and guided them out of the forest just as it started to rain. The dried blood on Harish's kurta had run as it mingled with the water, staining Vira's numb fingers as she helped Amrit heave the body into the carriage.

It was only fitting, Vira thought as she wiped her hands on her kurta, that his blood had wound up literally on her hands. She hadn't been able to keep Harish safe. The least she could do was return his body to his family.

She sighed and pressed her forehead to the window, the lotus pendant of her necklace clutched tight in her fist. The world blurred behind the curtain of rain, but the lights of the palace rose like a lighthouse beacon, its magic fighting the suffocating storm clouds to signal the way home.

The night had wrung her down to the bones, and she could feel exhaustion threaten to overpower her even as her mind raced. Riya was in Dvar. Riya was a Raven.

"Did I make a mistake?" Vira asked when she felt Amrit watching her. "Inviting her back?"

"You did what any sister would."

But maybe that was the problem. She was thinking like a sister, not a maharani.

"How could she so easily turn her back on the ideals we were raised with?"

Her anger had faded, and now only pain remained. Her parents were gone. Her Council didn't support her. She had one brother in jail and another who didn't speak to her. Some part of her desperately wanted someone who'd share the demands of the crown with her.

They'd been trained the same way, faced with the same burdens, taught the same lessons — they'd even weathered the weight of their mother's disapproval together. Riya was the only one who could understand what it was like to be in Vira's position, and she'd run away without a backward glance.

Amrit leaned forward as the carriage approached the gates of the fort, his warm eyes locking onto hers. "Vira, I haven't seen my brothers in a long time. I'm not the same boy who left my home four years ago — and I'm sure they aren't the same people I left either. But it wouldn't matter. As soon as we saw each other again, I know it would be the same as it always was."

He hardly spoke of his family. Everything she knew of his past had been cobbled together, scraps saved and stitched in her mind. They were the same in this way — careful in what parts of themselves they gave to others.

"That's not the same," she said. His brothers hadn't run away. They hadn't hidden half a mile from their childhood home and never once considered coming back. They weren't Ravens.

"I know. But time doesn't erase the bonds of family." He absently ran a finger back and forth over the knuckles of his right hand — speckled with old scars she'd never worked up the courage to ask him about. "Don't give up on her yet."

Vira looked out the window as the carriage slowed in front of the palace entrance. A figure stood waiting outside.

"What will you tell them?" Amrit was looking at Harish, but she knew he was asking about Riya.

"Nothing." Not until Riya was actually coming home.

The carriage door flew open, and Councilor Meena stood on the other side, disapproval lining her gaze. Vira fought the urge to cower.

Meena was the head of the Military Affairs Ministry, Ashoka's most prized warrior, and she'd been the closest thing Vira's mother had had to a friend. Yet despite having known the older woman for most of her life, Vira had never grown fully accustomed to Meena's forceful presence. Proud scars littered the back of her four-fingered hands, trailing up her arms like jasmine vines. Her face was weathered and hard, filled with lines and blemishes that made her fearsome to behold. With her stiff back, strong shoulders, and sharp eyes, she was the kind of person that troops would follow into any battle, no matter how low the chance of return.

"A maharani cannot leave the palace alone." Meena's voice was as rough as gravel. Her eyes flicked to Amrit. "And you should know better than to let her."

Amrit's jaw tightened, the only sign that the words affected him. "My apologies, Councilor."

"It was my idea to go," Vira said. "Amrit was only following my orders."

Meena had received notice first that some guards had found a dead body that matched the description of Lord Harish. Vira's job was to wait in her room for more news to be delivered, but she hadn't been able to sit and do nothing — not when her tenuous alliance was at risk.

Meena's mouth was pressed in a thin line as her gaze drifted down to Harish's drenched body. "You brought him here?"

"What would you have had me do? Leave him in the forest for the birds and rats?"

Meena frowned at the sharpness of Vira's tone, and Vira once again resisted the urge to shrink back. She was Vira's most trusted adviser, but lately, Vira felt that Meena was trying to manage her too much. Meena was her elder, but she was the maharani. Her mother would never have apologized for her words.

Of course they don't want to take orders from an eighteen-year-old.

But Vira was saved the trouble of responding to Meena's remarks by the arrival of a trembling messenger.

"What is it?" Meena barked.

"Apologies for the interruption." He flushed and bowed clumsily, faltering under Meena's stare. "Maharani, you're needed in the Judgment Hall."

"Judgment Hall?" Vira echoed. "What for?"

"The guards found Lord Harish's killer."

✳

The killer's name was Surya. He'd been found with a bow and quiver of conical black-fletched arrows, fleeing the forest shortly after Vira and Amrit had been taken by the Ravens.

Vira stood at the small window of the viewing chamber on the upper level, arms crossed as she looked down into the Judgment Hall. Light filtered down from angled lanterns, bathing the shackled man in the center of the room in a golden glow. His face was obscured by dark hair that hung to his shoulders, but his posture was proud — back straight, chin lifted as he stared at the interrogator.

"Look at the arrogance in his stance," Vira spat. "He doesn't care."

Amrit stood next to her, watching the interrogation with creased brows.

Vira turned to him. "Is it true? Did you see it?"

"Vira."

One of the guards had said that the killer had a tattoo. She couldn't see it from her vantage point, but she knew what it looked like: three jagged mountain peaks. It represented his home in the Koranos Mountains. But of the many peoples who lived there, only one group used tattooing in their cultural practices.

They came in the dead of night, carrying spears and arrows tipped with a poison that the best healers in Ashoka hadn't been able to even identify. They filled their ranks with children they snatched from nearby villages, brainwashing them with twisted ideals, turning them into remorseless hunters. They had no country, no loyalties. They were greedy and bloodthirsty enough to do the bidding of anyone who paid them to do it.

Mercenaries, the Council called them.

But that was too kind a word for the people who'd killed her mother.

"You knew," she accused him. Amrit had pointed out the arrowhead. He'd warned her about the poison. "How could you not tell me?"

Amrit didn't say anything.

"What were you doing in the forest?" the interrogator asked the mercenary.

"Taking a walk." Surya didn't speak loudly, but the magic in the tiles below his feet carried his voice effortlessly up to where Vira stood.

Her fingers twitched. Ashokan custom dictated that the maharani observe the interrogation only from a distance. It was supposedly for her safety, but Vira wondered for a second if it wasn't for his.

There was a knock at the door. Neha, one of the guards in Amrit's trusted inner circle, entered with a cloth satchel. "This is everything the prisoner had on him, Captain."

Amrit took the bag and dumped out the contents on a small table in the corner. Vira turned back to the interrogation.

"Did you kill Lord Harish?"

"No."

Silence. "We found your arrows. They match the ones used to kill the lord."

The chains around Surya's wrists clattered as he shrugged. "Anyone can buy arrows."

"Vira?" Amrit held up a small scrap of paper. "You need to see this."

Vira crossed the room toward him, reaching for it.

Five hundred jhaus have been delivered. Once you dispose of Lord Harish and bring us his dagger, you will receive the remaining five hundred.

There was no signature. But in the bottom right corner was a stamp of two curved blades crossed over a lotus.

Vira's heart skipped a beat. It was the same image that was on her pendant, a symbol she knew as well as her own name. A symbol that few others even knew existed, belonging to a secret society as ancient as Ashoka itself.

She looked up to see her shock mirrored on Amrit's face.

"Neha? Bring us Lord Harish's dagger immediately," Amrit ordered.

"Yes, Captain."

They stood side by side in tense silence, the interrogation below fading to a dull drone in Vira's ears. The seconds ticked away painfully slowly until the door opened again, and Neha returned with Harish's weapon.

Vira waited until the door shut behind Neha before examining the dagger. It was thin and ornate, probably ceremonial, given that the hilt was covered in jewels. As she twisted it back and forth, she felt light magic flutter over her fingers like a gentle breeze. It was expensive and well made — but that wasn't reason enough to kill for it. She frowned as she passed her palm over the knife. And then did it again.

"What is it?" Amrit said, moving closer. She held the dagger out, and Amrit repeated her movements. "There's less magic on the blade itself."

"Who would put more magic into the hilt of their weapon?" Vira asked, turning the dagger upside down, running her fingers over the gemstones more deliberately now.

"Perhaps one who doesn't intend to actually use it as a weapon."

Vira pressed an oval sapphire, and with a tiny snap, the base of the dagger disappeared. Inside the hollow cavity were two small, rolled-up pieces of paper. The first one had three words written in Ashokan letters — but they didn't mean anything.

qigzbm ovv bevfrkiovr

Vira set it on the table and reached for the second paper, immediately feeling the persistent hum of magic along her fingers. The paper felt powerful. Ancient. She unfurled it. It was torn on two sides and was no bigger than the width of her palm. It had faded to a pale yellow, but the ink was still jet-black.

"Vira." Amrit's voice was hoarse. "Look."

In the top left corner was the same symbol: twin blades crossed over a lotus.

Vira's racing heart leapt into her throat as her fingers traced the lines. After all these months of studying Papa's research, reliving Papa's futile hunts, she couldn't believe what she held in her hands.

Another piece of the map.

This was a chance to change everything. To save Ashoka.

Vira's grip on the paper tightened as she looked down at the killer in the hall below. "I need to talk to him. Alone."

"I'll arrange it."

The tiniest spark of hope flickered to life in Vira's chest.

CHAPTER EIGHT

— VIRA —

WHEN VIRA WAS six, she'd first asked her father: *Where does magic come from?*

From the earth, he'd said.

It was the standard response — the accepted one — but it had never been enough for Vira. It wasn't until she was eleven that she'd finally gotten the answers she wanted.

She could remember the day clearly, sitting on the sun-warmed veranda overlooking the glittering ocean. Pockets of clouds drifted lazily across the sky, and the gentle breeze smelled of salt and the sea. Ronak had ditched his lessons, so it had just been Vira and her father.

"But how did it come to be in the earth?" Vira asked, mostly out of habit.

Papa surprised her. "Do you really want to know?"

Suddenly she was alert. "Yes."

"This story begins a long time ago, back when there were dozens of quarries scattered throughout all lands that would eventually become Ashoka."

Vira's eyes widened. She'd only ever known there to be one quarry, and they were sitting above it.

"Back in those days," Papa continued, "no single person owned the quarries. Magic was just another resource, such as gemstones or coal or wood."

"And anyone could just use magic however they wanted?"

"If they were trained," Papa corrected, giving her a pointed look.

"I know, Papa." Vira rolled her eyes. "No one is allowed near magic without proper instruction," she recited dutifully.

It was his most important lesson. There were three mayaka professions, all of which required many years of study: miners who excavated raw magic from the quarry, processors who converted it into a safe form, and forgers who wove the processed magic into objects. Papa was a forger. In another life, Vira might have followed in his footsteps.

"Good."

"So why did it change?"

"Because people realized how powerful magic could be. Before Ashoka was a country, it was full of individual cities that were constantly at war with one another, fighting over land or which goddesses to worship. One day, people realized that they could put magic into their weapons — just like we do today. And the next time there was a battle, those soldiers slaughtered their opponents.

"Word began to spread. Other countries — including Lyria — wanted a taste of this magic. Of the power it promised, the wondrous things it could do. So to protect themselves, the various Ashokan cities united under a common leader —"

"Savitri," Vira interrupted. She knew this part — about her distant ancestor, the first maharani of Ashoka.

"Yes." Papa smiled. "She cared deeply about the people, so she made some very important decisions that shaped our country. First, she put all the quarries under royal protection. This way, if any outsider intended to steal the magic, the royal guards could defend it.

"Second, she decided that most of the magic would go toward defense. She ordered the construction of the wall we still have around Ashoka today, and she had mayaka imbue it with magic. If anyone dared to scale it or even come too close, they would burn to death. The only way to enter or leave Ashoka is through one of eighteen gates, which were to be guarded at all times."

Vira frowned. "But then how does Lyria have magic?"

"That's also because of Savitri," Papa said. "She negotiated with other countries, vowing to share the magic in her possession in exchange for goods. But really, she did it for peace. She believed that if she gave magic away freely, others would not invade our lands to take it by force."

"But the most important decision she ever made was to protect the people from herself. Savitri believed that the power of magic could become too great for just one person, so she entrusted its protection to a separate, impartial group. The Kamala Society.

"Members of the Society were expected to work in the best interests of the *people* rather than any one person or country. An equal number of people were selected from each of the nine provinces of Ashoka, and they were trained as warriors, mayaka, and record keepers. And under the guidance of the Kamala Society, Ashoka enjoyed peace and prosperity for a while."

"For a while?" Vira echoed, frowning.

Papa sighed as he looked out toward the ocean. "Unfortunately, as Savitri predicted, the allure of magic was too much to resist. Leaders began to ignore the counsel of the Kamala Society, and provinces began to fight each other once more to try to control the quarries."

This was something Vira understood all too well as a rajkumaari — and future maharani — of the only country that possessed a quarry. "Why didn't the Kamala Society do something?"

"They tried, but when it became clear that magic would fall into the hands of those ill-equipped to handle such power, the Society made a difficult decision: to seal all the quarries. All the knowledge they held was burned, and one by one, the quarries vanished. From the land. From memory. From history."

"What?" Vira yelped. "What happened to the Kamala Society?"

Papa shrugged. "No one knows. Most members simply vanished. A few were captured, but they never divulged that which they had sworn to protect with their lives."

They sat in silence for a few minutes. "Come," Papa said, rising. "Our lesson has gone on too long, and your mathematics tutor will be waiting for you."

Vira's mind was reeling with questions as they made their way to the library. "If all the quarries were sealed, how come we have one?"

"We don't know. Maybe there was no one left to seal it."

Another thought occurred to Vira. "If the Kamala Society is gone, how do we know this really happened?"

Papa's eyes twinkled as he looked down at her. "I'll show you."

When they entered the library, he veered away from the reading room, where her next lessons awaited her, toward the gilded staircase that led to the upper level. The moment that Vira spotted him withdrawing a tiny golden pendant that hung on a chain around his neck, she knew where he was taking her. He inserted the coin into a cleverly disguised lock meant to look like it was a part of the pattern on the wallpaper. A trapdoor high above them opened, and a narrow staircase lowered, stopping at her feet.

"After you, my dear."

The room held the royal family's private collection of rare books and artifacts. Impenetrable suits of armor worn by former maharanis. Giant telescopes that were rumored to reveal the secrets of the stars. Vira's head spun as she tried to take in everything at once, even as Papa bypassed all of it and led her toward a glass box that was almost too small to be worthy of notice.

There was nothing inside except a small piece of paper ripped on two sides. Lines swirled over the page — some solid, some dotted, some leading past and through tiny labeled cities — until they reached the torn edges and stopped abruptly.

"Look here." Papa pointed to the top right corner. A lotus with twin blades crossed over it. "Recognize it?"

Vira gasped. She'd seen it before. It was the same symbol painted on the walls in the quarry and stamped on her father's necklace. Papa winked, as if they'd just shared a secret.

"That is the emblem of the Kamala Society."

Vira frowned at the indecipherable words scrawled across the pages in some twisted form of Ashokan she couldn't read. "But what is it?"

"This, Vira, is a piece of a map that's said to lead to the Ivory Key — the key that can unlock the sealed quarries."

Vira looked at Papa, realizing something. "Your trips!" she said excitedly. "That's what you're doing, isn't it? Looking for other pieces."

Papa nodded. "To protect the secret, the Kamala Society hid the key and then created this map so future members could find it if they needed. Then they tore the map into three, each part entrusted to a member. Your great-grandfather's aunt found this piece in an ancient library nearly two hundred years ago."

"What about the other pieces?"

"No one knows. But there are people looking for them." Papa removed his necklace and crouched down so they were at eye level. "The reason I'm telling you this is because one day we might need more magic. There's a belief among some people that there will be a savior who will unearth the lost quarries and lead Ashoka into a new age of prosperity and magic."

"A prophecy?" Vira asked cautiously.

"No, dear child. Something much more powerful. *Hope.*"

Vira stared at Papa's familiar eyes, the corners crinkling with age and laughter.

"Maybe," Vira said, licking her lips hesitantly. "Maybe I can be that savior?"

Papa's smile was radiant as he slipped the necklace over her head. "I hope so, my dear."

CHAPTER NINE

— RONAK —

THE DOOR TO the tavern was bright blue. Three men stood outside, reeking of the bitter betel leaves packed with spices and areca nuts that they chewed. Their gums were stained black, their teeth already showing signs of rot when they leaned over to spit the paan out.

Inside, it smelled of sweat and smoke. Ronak switched to breathing through his mouth as he followed Jay, shoving past cramped tables. The single source of light was from a chandelier lined with tiers of clay lamps hung high above the crowd. On the far end of the room, a woman stood on a dais singing a sultry folk song, accompanied by the tabla and the sarangi.

They made their way over to a door behind the dais that revealed stone stairs descending beneath the tavern, and the din of the main hall fell abruptly away as the door slammed shut. Ominous flickering shadows cast by scattered torches guided their way down. The staircase twisted twice before depositing them into a long, narrow hallway, and a nondescript black door with an ornate silver keyhole awaited them at the end.

Jay withdrew the key that had come with Ekta's invitation. The door clicked open and swung noiselessly inward.

The soft strings of a veena gently washed over the room, magically amplified from some unseen source. Unlike the drunk and rowdy crowd upstairs, the people in this room were polished, refined, and extraordinarily wealthy. Rich silk hung from every shoulder in the room, regardless of which province or country it came from. Servants carried trays of glass goblets filled with Lyrian grape wine — difficult and expensive to come by ever since trade had stalled.

Lacy curtains and wooden screens forged to keep out noise divided the room into its various sections. Card tables stretched out on one side of the parlor, and the other side was full of plush divans where couples sat close together beneath floating lanterns, talking, touching, kissing. Ronak looked away, flushing, as a young Ashokan man ran his fingers — then lips — over the curve of a Lyrian man's neck.

Jay eyed the room appreciatively — and then his brows furrowed in confusion. "I didn't think there would be so many people."

Ronak didn't know what he'd expected. A seedy office with crates of illegal magical artifacts? This room, full of luxury, indulgence, and casually flaunted wealth, couldn't have been further from that.

Ekta was seated at a low table tucked into a secluded alcove near the back of the parlor. As they approached the partially closed screen, Ronak could tell that she wasn't alone. Through the diamond-shaped holes in the wood, he could see two young men seated across from a figure in the shadows.

The bearded man on the right sat with his shoulders hunched, brows pinched in obvious worry. His taller, clean-shaven companion shifted uncomfortably, his gaze focused on his palms resting on the painted table. He mumbled something Ronak couldn't hear.

"It was too *dangerous?*" Ekta's voice was rich and deep, with all the polish of a noblewoman. But Ronak could hear the warning simmering beneath.

"You didn't tell us there'd be others looking for it," the bearded man protested.

"You were paid handsomely, weren't you?" Both men shrank back as Ekta leaned forward, twisting the ring around her smallest finger: a fili-greed gold band fitted with a glittering emerald. "So why don't I have my amulet?" She pried the emerald off.

The clean-shaven man swallowed visibly. "We tried —"

He froze as Ekta trailed a black-painted fingernail over the back of his hand. "Perhaps you didn't have the right . . . inspiration." Without warning, she jabbed the ring into his wrist.

"Ow!" He yanked his hand back, but not before Ronak saw two pin-pricks of blood well up. "What did you do to me?"

"Cobra venom." She snapped the emerald back into place.

Jay grabbed Ronak's shoulder. "*Shit*, Ro."

The man looked petrified, whimpering as he cradled his hand. But there was nothing he could do. Cobra venom was deadly. A single bite could bring down an elephant in a matter of hours. She'd just sentenced a man to a painful and horrible death in full view of an entire tavern with nothing but her jewelry.

Ekta turned to the second man. He looked like he would pass out at any moment. "My people have your sister," she said coolly. "You have two days to bring me my amulet, or she meets the same end as your friend here."

She flicked her hand dismissively. They fled.

Silence.

Ronak met Jay's wide eyes in the dark.

"They say the maharanis of old punished eavesdroppers by having one of their ears removed." Ekta's wrist reappeared, beckoning them forward.

This is a mistake, Kaleb would tell him. *Run.*

Jay continued to stare at Ronak. *We don't have to do this*, he'd said. *We can turn back.*

But Ronak stepped around the screen, shoulders squared, feigning confidence despite his racing heart. Jay, ever loyal, followed a second later.

Ekta looked nothing like he expected. Her cold eyes pierced him, her smile pretty and lifeless. She was the living embodiment of ink, as if she'd leached the dye from pages of forgotten texts. Her dark hair hung in waves over her right shoulder, and the open collar of her black kurta revealed a string of onyx glittering at her throat. The single bit of color came from the golden rings stacked on her fingers.

Ekta gestured to the two empty seats across from her. "Please."

It was a command. They obeyed.

Ekta reached for her wineglass, swirling it before raising it to her lips. She watched them over its edge, her kaajal-lined eyes lingering on Ronak — and then flicking toward Jay.

"You don't look like palace servants."

It wasn't a question, so Ronak said nothing. He couldn't stop staring at the emerald on her hand, wondering if there was any venom left, wondering if the other jewels were full of poison too. It was one thing to be told that someone was dangerous. It was another entirely to witness her commit murder firsthand.

Ekta followed his gaze, a slow smile curving over her lips. "Nasty little thing, isn't it? Supposedly it belonged to one of the generals of Maharani Chandrika." She lovingly caressed the emerald, and Ronak felt the blood drain from his face.

Chandrika — who'd ruled nearly four hundred years earlier — had been notoriously bloodthirsty. She'd expanded Ashoka's borders east and south, invading cities that had refused to join Savitri's quest for unification. Her victories had been the result of magical weapons so deadly, even scholars and historians weren't allowed access to any records that listed them. As far as Ronak knew, very few items remained from her time; most had been destroyed or were locked away by the Mayaka Association out of fear that they'd fall into the wrong hands.

"We have an artifact for you," Jay blurted out.

That seemed to amuse her. "Direct," she said, setting down her glass. "I admire that."

She held out her hand, and Jay nudged Ronak. Ronak reluctantly reached into his pocket. He had selected an ancient weapon from the palace because it was likely to fetch the best price, but he was suddenly having second thoughts about giving her more tools to wield against people. He withdrew the small, cloth-wrapped disk and slid it toward her, quickly snatching his hand back.

Ekta unwrapped it, revealing an iron coin that was exuding so much magic that even across the table, Ronak could feel the faint prickle caress his skin. It had fallen out of favor so long ago that Ronak didn't even know its name. It was the size of her hand, and when she flipped it over, two metal horns emerged out of the sides, tapering to a point sharp enough to slice through tendons. She turned it back, and they disappeared. Her eyebrows rose in impressed surprise as she repeated the movement.

"And resourceful," she added, wrapping it up again. "I admire that, too. It's not often that servants are so daring as to steal from the maharani herself." She leaned back in her seat and watched them carefully. "I wonder if you're bold enough to get me something specific."

So that's why she'd asked for a meeting. She was after something in the palace. Ronak's shoulders relaxed a bit. "What are you looking for?"

Ekta reached for her wine again. "Did you know the maharani was to be married to the son of the Viceroy of Onaar?"

Ronak blinked at the abrupt topic change. "No," he lied. "Why does that matter?" he asked, taking care to keep his voice measured.

A rajkumaara never betrays his emotions. He shows others only what he intends them to see. It had been one of the few lessons his mother had bothered to impart to him.

"It matters," Ekta said, "because her betrothed is dead."

"Dead?" Jay shifted uncomfortably.

It was starting to concern Ronak that Ekta seemed so well informed about what was happening in the palace. Vira's impending engagement had been kept from nearly everyone. Harish's father had promised armies and immeasurable wealth for the protection of Ashoka, but the Council had wanted to ensure that everything was finalized before making a public announcement. There was no way the Council had been careless enough to let news of his death slip.

"Murdered," Ekta clarified. "Which is a true shame, because he was on his way to meet me."

"Meet you?" Ronak echoed.

Ekta downed the last of her wine and leaned forward to rest her elbows on the table. "What do you know of the Ivory Key?"

This time Ronak couldn't hide his surprise. It had been Papa's obsession for as long as he could remember, his quest for an object that could unlock the lost quarries of Ashoka. It wasn't a secret that there were others looking for it — treasure hunters and historians piecing together archaic clues that never led anywhere. Ekta's interest in it wasn't entirely unexpected, but the thought of the Ivory Key in her hands was terrifying.

"Not much," Ronak said, trying to school his features back into practiced indifference. "Is that another artifact?"

"Ah yes. I don't imagine servants hear much about magical lore," Ekta said, her smile widening as though she didn't quite believe him. "It's a mythical object, one that's rumored to lead its possessor to more magic than anyone can imagine."

"That sounds immensely powerful," Ronak said. He could feel Jay watching him, but he forced himself to keep his gaze on Ekta.

"Indeed," she said. "It's said that there is a map that leads to the Ivory Key. Lord Harish — the maharani's betrothed — had one piece of it. And there's a rumor that the maharani has another."

"And that's what you want," Ronak said, piecing it together. Harish had been Ekta's way into the palace — her way to the second piece of the map. With him gone, she needed someone to get it for her.

"Very good." Ekta arched her eyebrows expectantly.

Papa materialized in Ronak's mind, standing in front of his research, his face flushed with excitement and wonder as he held up some new clue he'd deciphered, some new detail he'd learned about the Kamala Society. It was one thing to sell her banned items. Could he really give Ekta a piece of the map his father had spent his entire life searching for? A powerful weapon she could use against Ashoka?

But when it came to Kaleb, the answer was painfully simple.

"Two thousand jhaus," Ronak said, feeling as though he might throw up. Jay kicked him under the table. It was an obscene amount of money to ask for — more than enough for them to build a new life several times over.

If Ekta was surprised by the ask, she didn't show it. "You've seen what happens when I don't get what I want."

"You'll have the pieces," Ronak promised.

Her smile changed into something more genuine — but no less ferocious. "Then we have a deal."

CHAPTER TEN

— RIYA —

RIYA SAT ON the roof of the abandoned astronomical tower, her arms wrapped around her knees, watching the first rays of sunlight dance over Dvar. From her perch high above the forest canopy, the Dhaya River was a blue thread weaving between the clustered districts of the city.

She could make out the dark line of the Granites hugging the distant coastline — so named for the expensive stones merchants had imported from the Maravat province to construct their villas. The painted buildings and open porticos of the Garden District were a stark contrast. Here, courtyards were full of harp players and ghazal singers. Vast prayer halls drew large crowds of immigrants who worshipped other goddesses and gods. And unassuming storefronts served the most decadent dishes: hearty breads fresh out of the oven, slathered with olive oil and fresh herbs; thick vegetable stews ladled over rice flavored with dried fruit and threads of saffron; deep-fried dough balls dipped in honey and rolled in chopped nuts.

Across the river, mist curled around the pristine white buildings of the City Center. But the safety it promised was nothing more than an illusion; the wide, well-lit roads funneled unsuspecting travelers directly into the side streets and alleyways of the Temple District. And Riya knew all too well that there were no goddesses there, only pickpockets and street gangs looking to take your money — but would just as easily take your life.

And of course, the Dvar Fort, rising above it all, watching, but never protecting.

Come home.

Riya closed her eyes. Vira's offer was tempting — more than it had any right to be. And Riya was a fool for even considering it.

Wasn't she?

She had a home, a family, a purpose. And yet with two words, Vira had sent cracks spidering through the walls Riya had built up within herself.

Footsteps startled her. She turned around, panicked. She wasn't ready — not until she knew what she was going to say to the Ravens. What she was going to do.

She'd slipped out of the glades well before dawn, tiptoeing over the sleeping forms of the other Ravens. They'd given her space, given her a whole tent in which to process her emotions. It was a luxury not even afforded to Yash, and that only made Riya feel worse. She'd lain awake for hours, listening to the rain, letting her anxieties fill the space until she could no longer bear the suffocation of her own thoughts.

Her pulse quickened as the footsteps grew louder, followed by the sound of bones clattering down the stairs — the remnants of animals left behind by the falcons who'd built their nest inside the tower.

And then a soft swear.

Riya's heart leapt into her throat. She recognized that voice. "Yash?"

But it wasn't Yash. It was Varun. The last person she'd expected to come looking for her. His presence caught her so off guard that for a moment, all she could do was stare. He looked different in daylight, the soft hues of dawn chasing away the sharp lines and jagged edges she associated with him.

Riya turned away, sitting at the edge of the roof. The sun had moved higher into the sky, orange rays cresting over the ocean, bathing the city in crimson and gold. But she no longer found the view comforting.

The maddening scent of tulsi washed over her as Varun dropped down to sit beside her, looking out at the city. She wondered what he saw. Dvar was his home now, but it wasn't where he'd grown up.

"Why are you here?" she blurted out.

"Did you sleep?" he asked quietly.

It wasn't what she'd expected him to say, and she felt inexplicably on guard. "What do you care?"

"It was just a question, Riya." He turned toward her then, his eyes roaming over her face, studying her. She wanted to look away, to shield herself from his scrutiny. But this felt like a competition somehow. And she didn't want him to win.

"Why are you here?" she repeated.

"Can I see your hand? Your right hand."

"Stop evading the —"

"If you show me, I'll explain," he cut in.

Bewildered, Riya looked down at her hand, then looked up again, and found that he was still watching her. In the end, her curiosity won out. She warily held it out. He took it, wrapping his fingers around her wrist, his touch surprisingly gentle as he flipped her hand over so it was palm up. He held her gaze the whole time, his callused fingers sliding over the soft skin of her inner wrist, skimming her pulse point. She suppressed a shudder.

"You know," he said, dragging his eyes down to her palm, "they said that the lost rajkumaari had a birthmark on her wrist in the shape of a star." His thumb grazed her wrist again, brushing the dark brown, star-shaped smudge.

Riya snatched her hand away. "You knew."

"Your posh accent. Your expensive dagger. Your rich clothes." He gave her an apologetic shrug. "It wasn't that difficult to piece together."

Riya could feel tears threatening, and she turned away before Varun could see. He'd known all along. All this time she'd fought to protect something that had never been a secret. A sudden thought entered her mind. "Does Yash —"

Varun's jaw tightened. "No. I never told him."

Riya gaped at him. He'd kept her secret. "Why not?"

"Do you remember the night when we found that Lyrian wine?" His voice was still soft, and betrayal filled her. His strange kindness, his quiet words and gentle touches were all a lie — an illusion cast to disarm her. Distract, then attack. It was how the Ravens worked. And like a fool she'd fallen for it.

"No."

But she did remember. The way the smoke from the fire pit mixed with the sweet fruit. The loud singing and unabashed dancing as the Ravens let go of all worries for a few hours. But most of all, she remembered the moments late into the night when a few of them had sat around the dying fire letting the happy haze of alcohol drag them toward impossible dreams.

"We could make our own coins," Kavita had said. It was getting harder to steal enough to help the people. With the raised taxes, people had less money, so they were spending less. But fewer profits meant that vendors couldn't keep their employees. And as people lost their jobs, they spent even less.

"We can't, Kavs," Riya had said. Coins had magic in them for that very reason — so no one could forge them.

"We can steal magic," Kavita had said with a hand wave, as if it were that easy. "Raw magic," she clarified. "Yash can process it."

Breaking into the carriages that transported raw magic from the quarry to the Mayaka Association was impossible. The routes changed every time, with decoys and armed guards in place to thwart anyone who would dare try.

"It won't work," Varun had said. He was sitting on the ground, his back against one of the tree trunks, lazily tossing a ball in the air. "We'll never steal enough. Magic wanes with use, so we'll have to keep replenishing it."

"Magic wanes based on *how* it's used," Riya had corrected without thinking.

Varun's eyes had snapped to hers.

"She's right," Yash had agreed, speaking up for the first time. "Coins have magic to keep them from being forged, so they use it up only when someone is trying to forge them — copying the design or melting it down." He frowned as he scratched the back of his neck. "Actually, I don't know what the mints specifically have the mayaka protect against. They don't teach that at university. Understandably."

"Or maybe they don't teach that to first-year dropouts," Varun had muttered under his breath.

"So it's doable?" Kavita had asked, her eyes shining with excitement.

"Maybe." Yash had shrugged. "If we could get information about when the raw magic is being transported."

"We'd need a spy in the fort," Varun had said.

Riya's stomach roiled, pulled back to the astronomical tower. She hadn't thought much of it that day, but she could recall the way his eyes, dark and serious, had watched her the whole time.

All at once she knew exactly why he was here, why he'd sought her out. Why he'd kept her secret: in case it ever came to this.

"I won't do it."

"You have to, Riya."

"You can't make me leave!" Her voice rose, carrying through the forest. Birds fluttered out of the trees, startled by the sudden sound.

"I'm not. I'm only —"

She didn't care what he was *only* saying. "I'm a Raven," she insisted. "Not a rajkumaari." He couldn't take that away from her.

"Then it's your obligation." Varun's voice was a growl, his eyes flashing with irritation. "Go to the palace. Help us steal the magic. Prove that you're one of us."

Riya felt her own rage simmering, and she took comfort in the rush. They were back in familiar territory. But in her heart she knew he was right. This was the only way to prove she belonged here, in the forest. The only way to protect the people.

If he were someone else, she might have said *I'm afraid.* Afraid the Ravens would abandon her. Afraid her siblings wouldn't want her. Afraid of leaving behind her friends, her chosen family.

If he were someone else, she might have said *I don't know how to do this alone.*

But he wasn't, so she swallowed those words.

The sun had risen, and the city was fully awake. Soon the dewdrops that dotted the flowers in the forest would vanish and humid heat would chase the morning chill out of the vibrant city streets.

She squeezed her eyes closed. There was nothing she wouldn't do to stay a Raven. "I'll go," she whispered.

When she opened them, Varun was gone.

✳

The Ravens were crowded around the fire pit, reaching for the piping-hot tumblers of chai that one of the boys was handing out. Quiet conversation mingled with the songs of the mynahs and koyals.

Riya leaned against a tree trunk, watching them. It was a familiar scene, but for the first time, she felt like an outsider, there to observe instead of participate. She knew that things had changed irreversibly — in the way the others didn't quite meet her gaze, in the way they stopped talking when she walked by.

She'd contacted Vira after toying with the crumpled paper for an hour. She'd barely felt the magic in it, and she had no idea if her words would even reach her sister, but Vira's response had come immediately, offering to send a carriage at once. Riya was actually going back.

Kavita walked toward her, holding two clay tumblers of chai.

Riya smiled faintly. "Thanks." She blew on the layer of fat that was starting to form at the top and raised the cup to her lips. Warmth spread through her body with the first sip.

"Kavs." Riya sighed. "I'm sorry I never —"

"We don't have to do this," Kavita said stiffly.

But they did. "This isn't how I wanted you to find out."

"Were you ever going to tell me?"

The same question Vira had asked. "Every day, I wished you knew, Kavs. But . . ." Riya trailed off, trying to find a way to speak things she'd carried in her heart, all the while knowing that no answer would ever satisfy her.

"But you weren't going to tell me," Kavita finished.

"I don't know," Riya said truthfully. "I thought that part of my life was behind me."

"Varun said you were leaving."

Riya looked at Kavita, memorizing her thick eyebrows and sun-darkened skin and too-wide mouth that was curved up in laughter more often than not. She couldn't imagine not seeing Kavita's face every day, not hearing her make terrible jokes.

"It's just a job," Riya said helplessly. If she said it enough, maybe she'd start to believe it.

"A job," Kavita said flatly.

"It's what we need, Kavs. What Dvar needs. I'll find the raw magic transport route. We'll lay a trap to steal the magic. And then I'll come home. It's that simple." It had to be.

Kavita stared at her. "It's not just a job, Riya. You're *leaving*."

Riya exhaled, frustrated. "I'm coming back. I swear it."

Kavita downed the rest of her chai. Riya followed suit. Kavita held out her hand for the empty cup, but Riya wasn't ready to hand it over just yet.

"Kavs, please." She'd lost everyone else. She couldn't lose her best friend too.

"What do you want me to say, Ri? You want my blessing? You've already made up your mind."

"I don't know how to do this without you," she said.

"Yes, you do."

"No, I don't. I need you," Riya begged.

Kavita shook her head, hurt evident in her face. "How could you keep this from me, Riya? How?"

Riya felt herself on the verge of tears for the second time that morning. "Because of how you're reacting now. Every day, we take a stand against the maharani. We steal, we lie. We fight against everything she does. Would you have trusted me if I'd told you she was my sister?"

Kavita pried the tumbler from Riya's hands. "I guess we'll never know."

CHAPTER ELEVEN

— VIRA —

SOMETIME DURING THE hour when Vira had finally managed to sleep, Riya had changed her mind. The words appeared exactly as Riya had written them on the scrap of magical paper Vira had given her.

Send a carriage. I'll come back.

The piece of paper was crumpled beyond recognition, worn soft from her anxious fingers, but Vira couldn't seem to set it down. Some tiny, irrational part of her feared that if she let it go even for a second, Riya's hasty cursive would disappear.

Back, not *home,* Vira had noted on one of the thirty times she'd reread it. Things had changed so much from when Riya had last been in the palace. Their parents were gone. Ronak was distant and angry. Kaleb was . . . well, he wasn't speaking to her either. Maybe Riya was right not to call it home.

Vira rubbed her tired eyes and sat up in bed. She hadn't slept well in months, but the night before, she'd slept even worse than usual, tossing and turning fitfully before giving up as sunlight streamed in from her east-facing window. Her maidservants would be arriving at any moment with her morning chai, and in just a few hours she would have to brief the Council about Harish.

Her stomach knotted in dread. She wished she were just a rajkumaari again, that the burdens and worries of the maharani fell on someone else's shoulders. But that line of thought never led anywhere, so Vira forced herself out of her bed and into the adjoining receiving room.

It still felt strange being in this space that she'd associated with her parents all her life. Most of the rooms still lay untouched, decorated just as Amma had left them. But this one — the smallest and simplest of all in the maharani's suite — Vira had converted into an office of sorts.

It was sparsely furnished with items from her old chambers. A chipped wooden table sat in the middle, surrounded on four sides by well-worn divans and soft cushions. An ancient almirah was tucked into the corner beside double doors that opened onto the veranda that wrapped around the suite. She unlatched the doors and flung them open, breathing in the cool ocean air.

Vira withdrew the necklace from beneath the collar of her kurta and pressed the lotus pendant into the magical lock that Kaleb had forged for her after Papa's death. The almirah clicked open, revealing stacks of bound journals, bundles of letters, and rolled-up maps of Ashoka. All the notes Papa had ever made on his various quests — the lost city of Visala, the missing compositions of the great bard Rasika, the treasure of the *Swarna* shipwreck, the sacred scrolls of the Eternal Library, and of course the Ivory Key. She reached for the note the killer had had on him, as well as the map piece and encoded message she'd taken from Harish's dagger.

Vira had tried to keep up Papa's search. He'd had many contacts — mayaka historians and treasure hunters and Kamala Society scholars he'd befriended over the years. They'd occasionally pass along word of new findings, a new clue or discovery sparking a flurry of investigation and travel. But once the world knew of his death, the letters had stopped. There were no more rumors for Vira to follow.

Until now.

She was the first person in centuries who had another piece of the puzzle. A twinge of pain hit her all at once. *I wish I could talk to you, Papa.* Vira closed the door and exhaled, but the heaviness lingered in her chest. Her father had never given up hope that they would find the Ivory Key.

She lowered herself to the divan. Things had gotten complicated. Harish knew about the Ivory Key. She had no idea who else did — who might come after her if they found out what she had. She trailed her finger over the Kamala Society's stamp. For so long she'd wanted proof of the impossible, some shred of evidence that the Society had survived these five hundred years. But the Kamala Society she'd read about was full of noble people doing the right thing. Whoever was behind this was willing to commit murder.

She had to move quickly and discreetly, but she had no idea where to even begin looking for the last piece of the map. Papa's journals held maps scrawled with possibilities carefully stitched together by studying history. Some places he'd searched himself, but there were many others he'd never had the chance to visit. And unlike Papa, Vira didn't have the luxury of traveling whenever and wherever she wished.

Her eyes landed on the encoded message. It had to be related to the Ivory Key somehow. Why else would Harish have stored it in his dagger? She stared at the letters, willing them to rearrange in front of her. She'd never had the patience for decryption — not like Papa or Kaleb. It would take time.

But in the meantime, there was one other lead to explore: the mercenary. She had a feeling he knew more than he was supposed to. And she intended to find out just what that was.

＊

The councilors started talking the second Vira stepped foot inside the meeting room.

"—Lord Harish—"

"Is he really dead?"

"Maharani, the alliance—"

All twelve present members—the directors of the six ministries and viceroys from six of the nine provinces—rose as Vira walked to the front of the room. Three seats were conspicuously empty. Two of them belonged to the councilors who'd walked out after the Battle of Ritsar. The third should have been Ronak's, but it was empty because he refused to formally claim the title of the Viceroy of Dvar.

Vira put up her hand as she took her position at the head of the table. Silence didn't fall immediately as it would have with her mother, but the noise quieted to hushed whispers.

"He's dead," she confirmed. "And the killer has been apprehended."

The room erupted into chaos again.

"How could this have happened?" asked Kunaal, the bespectacled councilor from Ravas, his voice rising above the din. "Where was his convoy?"

"They turned up this morning," Mandeep, the head of the Foreign Relations and Trade Ministry, said unhappily. At twenty-eight, she was the youngest councilor. Vira liked her. She was the only ally Vira had in the room most days. "They had no idea that Lord Harish was dead."

The Council had insisted that they keep the alliance secret until all details were finalized. Two months earlier, when Vira traveled to Onaar for the quick and efficient engagement ceremony, it had seemed prudent to exercise caution. Now she was regretting the secrecy. To maintain cover, Harish had journeyed with a small retinue of five soldiers as his personal guard. Apparently they'd made camp in the forest half a day's journey from

Dvar. Unbeknownst to them, Harish had slipped away after dark. They'd woken up, confused about the loss of their lord, and, after a fruitless search, decided to travel the rest of the way to Dvar.

"We must execute the killer at once," Arjhun, the representative from the Domestic Affairs Ministry, said. "We have to show Onaar we're not taking this lightly."

"We should send the viceroy the killer's head."

"Or better yet, send the killer himself—let the viceroy dole out the punishment."

There was a chorus of agreement, and Vira felt her stomach twist with worry. They couldn't execute him—not until she found out just what he knew.

"The assassin can wait," Vira said. "We need to salvage our relationship with Onaar and find another alliance."

"The viceroy won't renegotiate," Kunaal said.

"Not unless we're willing to give him something he really wants," Mandeep added.

The alliance had been hard enough for Vira to secure, but this was a second slight against the viceroy. He would look weak if he allied with her after this. And she would look weak if she caved to his demands for lower taxes in his province. They couldn't rely on Onaar any longer.

"We return Lord Harish's body to Onaar, and we send our heartfelt regrets," Vira said, trying to emulate her mother's authoritative manner of speaking.

"You think that will suffice?" Meena asked, her tone mild.

"It will," Vira said. It had to.

There was silence.

"Very well," Meena said. "I'll handle it."

Vira's head jerked toward her in poorly concealed surprise. It wasn't like the older woman to support her. She warily nodded her thanks, even if she registered in the back of her mind that there was a reason for it. Every one of these councilors had their own agendas, and they constantly pushed her to support their cause.

"Maybe we don't need an alliance," Gayathri—the councilor from Adhura—said. "Lyria hasn't made a move in months."

It was true. Lyria hadn't attempted another attack, and it worried Vira. It was no secret that the emperor was angry that her mother had cut off trade, that Vira hadn't renegotiated. And he'd made it clear that he would stop at nothing to get his hands on the magic he thought was being denied him.

The Council had haphazardly blockaded the borders around Ritsar. They'd sent all the troops they could spare—including the personal guards of several councilors—to guard the new wall, outfitting them with mayaka-forged weapons. But according to Meena, they were down to the last dozen crates of those, too. Without another source of magic, the new border would soon fail to hold back Lyria.

"Perhaps . . ." Mandeep trailed off. She slid a piece of paper out of a stack in front of her and looked hesitantly up at Vira.

"No," Vira said. Even from afar she could make out the pearlescent gleam of the wax stamped with Lyria's seal.

This was Lyria's third attempt at contacting her. The first letter had come a month after they'd invaded Ritsar. Vira had been desperate to avoid all-out war—desperate enough to meet with the emperor's envoy. But he hadn't come to negotiate peace. He'd come to offer her a deal: surrender Ashoka and its quarry to Lyria and in exchange Vira could keep her throne. A maharani, even if it was in name only.

It was a deal that Vira would never accept.

"So what?" Kunaal demanded, pushing his spectacles up the bridge of his nose. "We wait for Lyria to invade?"

"The Viceroy of Onaar can do as he pleases because his province doesn't border Lyria," said Aman, the soft-spoken Viceroy of Maravat. "But it's the people of Ravas and Maravat who will suffer when Lyria invades."

"And we're still in need of money," said Keerthi, the head of the Revenue and Finance Ministry.

That wasn't news. The same concerns and arguments came up at every meeting.

The maharanis of old weren't foolish. There was only one quarry, and it was a finite resource. And so they'd proposed a plan to phase it out of Ashokan culture. Reduce the amount of magic in coins. Limit the magic used at the borders during times of peace. Discourage citizens from relying on it for everyday use — in their kitchens and homes, in their clothes and jewelry.

Magic was synonymous with Ashokan culture, but it was a good plan, and it would have probably worked. But . . . it had never gone into effect. Vira didn't know which of her ancestors was to blame — which one had decided that she didn't want to be the maharani to curb the amount of magic in circulation. And now Vira was left with a nearly empty quarry, shouldering the brunt of the former maharanis' choices.

"An alliance for the rajkumaara," Meena said. Her voice was soft, but the room immediately fell silent. Vira tried not to quiver under the weight of everyone's sudden attention. "You hesitate because he's your brother, but a country thrives when all its citizens perform their respective duties. And a rajkumaara's duty is to secure the political or financial support the maharani needs."

"She's right," Keerthi agreed. "Your focus should be on protecting Ashoka. Let the rajkumaara get us the money we need."

Vira didn't respond right away. This wasn't the first time Ronak's name had come up, but she'd done what she could to spare him. The Viceroy of

Ishvat had never been their primary focus. Onaar was larger, and could provide them with more troops and resources, but Ishvat was the next best option. And though the Viceroy of Ishvat had left the palace eight months earlier, his daughter Preethi had remained, electing to stay with her cousin Archana.

Preethi had been closer to Riya, but she'd been Vira's friend once, too. And she was a good choice. She was well-mannered, exceedingly clever, and had political ambitions. Vira was certain that her father would negotiate if it meant that his daughter could be a rajkumaari.

But . . . duty or not, Ronak wasn't going to take it well. He hated being told what to do. And he hated that he couldn't control as many aspects of his life as he wished. But that was the price to pay for being a rajkumaara. The good of the country mattered more than family — more than choice.

"All right," Vira said, relenting. "Write to the viceroy. I'll tell my brother."

Meena gave her a curt nod and a rare smile, and Vira felt a sense of unease wash over her. Approval from the Council was not easily won.

"One more thing," Vira said as the councilors began to rise. She'd practiced the words, but now that it was time to say them, it was harder than she expected. "As you know, my sister, Priyanka, disappeared two years ago."

A tense silence fell over the room.

"Maharani, you mean she *died* two years ago," Arjhun corrected uncomfortably.

"We all know my sister didn't die — despite what my mother told the world." Vira took a deep breath. "She ran away. But I've asked her to return. And she's accepted."

Whispers snaked between the councilors.

"How do we explain her return to the people?" Kunaal asked finally.

"Make something up," Vira said. "That she was lost at sea or was taken ill and sent to family members."

"This isn't wise," Meena said. There was a slight wrinkle between her brows, and Vira knew that any goodwill she'd cultivated was gone. "Especially amidst such uncertainty."

"Perhaps not," Vira agreed, rising. "But my sister is already here. Make the necessary arrangements."

CHAPTER TWELVE

— KALEB —

THERE WAS A new prisoner.

Whispers had been circulating for hours among the guards. Kaleb usually ignored them, but this convict was different. He was a murderer, but that wasn't what intrigued Kaleb. It was the other word guards muttered under their breath.

Mercenary.

Like the one who'd killed his mother. Like the one he'd been accused of conspiring with.

Something strange coiled in the pit of Kaleb's stomach. It had been so long since he had felt anything but numbness that it took him a moment to name the feeling. Hope.

He was ashamed of it. He had no right to such a dangerous feeling, but he couldn't squash it. And no matter how much he told Ronak that he never dreamed of life outside the dungeons, it was all he could think about most days.

Sometimes he felt like he had too much of his father in him. Papa had spent his life being disappointed, meeting failure after failure on his quests, but he'd never stopped looking beyond his circumstances and seeing something better on the horizon.

Kaleb pressed his palms into his eyes as he leaned back against the wall of his cell. It had been a long time since he'd thought of the day he'd been imprisoned, but suddenly he couldn't block it from his mind.

Kaleb had always known that he was too Lyrian for some people. There was a long history of travel and immigration between the two countries, but every once in a while, a stranger who learned that his birth mother had been Lyrian would pry into his upbringing, asking pointed questions about his knowledge of Ashokan customs or demanding proof that he was Ashokan *enough*, whatever that meant. He couldn't recall being bothered by the implications of those comments as a child. It hadn't mattered to his family, so it hadn't mattered to him either.

But that was then. Things changed when Lyrian troops broke through the border and his mother — the only one he'd ever known — had been killed at the hands of hired mercenaries.

Kaleb had never known his birth mother, Alena. She'd died a week after he was born, and Papa, after four months struggling alone in a foreign land, had packed up his life and returned to Ashoka. He always spoke of Alena with respect, but Kaleb learned early on that though Papa had admired his Lyrian wife, he'd never loved her.

Going to Lyria had been a duty, and staying a necessity. Tensions between Ashoka and Lyria were already strained, and what Ashoka needed was for someone to better relations with them. Papa had been free to spend his childhood researching obscure myths and traveling in search of lost treasure. But as the son of the Viceroy of Adhura, he was bound by duty. He'd had no choice but to do what his father ordered.

So Papa had left behind Shanti — the rajkumaari he loved, whose life was tethered to Ashoka — and moved to the capital of Lyria. Five years later, widowed, with four-month-old Kaleb in tow, he'd come back to Ashoka, expecting to return to a quiet life. But Shanti, now the maharani, was still unwed. And she still wished to marry him.

Kaleb had never faulted his father for not loving Alena, for not loving Lyria. Papa had shared his memories freely when Kaleb asked. He'd taught Kaleb the Lyrian customs he'd picked up, and he'd even promised to take Kaleb to Lyria one day, to show him around the city that had been his home for so many years and introduce him to Alena's family. But it never came to pass.

A year after Papa's death, Alena's sister had written to Kaleb for the first time. He hadn't told anyone about the letters — not Vira, not Amma, not even Ronak. There was no real reason for him to keep it a secret, but the letters had unearthed complex feelings in him and he'd wanted the time to parse them out. He'd felt a strange sort of guilt that until his aunt invited him to visit, he'd never considered what it would be like to travel there on his own. He had aunts and cousins. Family he knew of but had never met, and he'd never even thought of getting to know them.

Vira's guards had come for him mere hours after Shanti's death.

We found the letters, the Council said. *We know you plotted her death.*

Kaleb hadn't understood what was happening until they'd shown him the letters from his aunt, full of tiny pinpricks beneath specific letters. Together they strung sentences of coded messages, seemingly passed back and forth for months, asking questions to confirm his mother's movements, to confirm the plot to hire mercenaries to kill her. And it looked like he'd been answering with detailed information about his mother.

He'd sworn he'd had nothing to do with it, that anyone could have added the pinpricks. But the letters were addressed to him. It didn't matter how much he insisted that whoever had truly orchestrated the assassination was still out there. They had a Lyrian boy in their midst they could conveniently pin it on, and the Council refused to search for another culprit.

Ronak had tried to investigate on his own, but it had been months since the trail had gone cold — led to a literal dead end. If the servant

Ronak tracked down had known anything, he'd taken that knowledge with him to his death.

It felt like the ground had crumbled under Kaleb's feet that day, and he wasn't sure that he'd ever recovered.

But now, one of the mercenaries was in the palace. Kaleb had a new lead. And he was finally going to get his answers.

✳

The fort's bells chimed nine times, and Kaleb pushed himself to his feet. He heard the jangling of the keys down the corridor long before he heard the quick footsteps of Aaliyah, the mayaka who oversaw the dungeons. Her face softened, as always, when she saw Kaleb. She'd been Papa's apprentice; they'd trained together once, a lifetime ago. But she didn't say anything as she lifted one of the keys on the chain that hung around her neck. She crouched to insert the key into one end of the metal rod on the ground in front of his cell, and all at once Kaleb felt the wall of magic in front of him disappear.

With a silent nod at him, Aaliyah stepped back. Kaleb waited until she left before he stepped out and made his way to the courtyard in the back. His shackles — lightweight iron bands that fit snugly around his wrists — stayed on. There was another metal bar woven with magic at the front entrance, in case any of them decided to run. That one stayed locked at all times, the magic in it replenished daily.

It had stopped raining sometime in the middle of the night. Water shimmered off every surface: rippling atop benches, dripping down from trees, coating the tiled walkways. Kaleb inhaled the crisp, fresh air.

The handful of other prisoners were already there, talking among themselves or playing cards on the tables in the center. Others were reading novels they'd bartered for with the guards or exercising in the corner. And they all ignored Kaleb.

During the first few months Ronak had encouraged him to make friends. Kaleb hadn't said anything, but what he'd wanted to say was *With who exactly?* The palace dungeons didn't hold many prisoners. Petty criminals were sent to one of the jails in Dvar, and those who committed violent crimes were usually executed. Few people needed the additional security of being within the fort itself: mayaka caught experimenting with dangerous magical artifacts, a spy from one of the island nations in the southern sea, a former librarian who'd stolen a collection of priceless books.

And even if Kaleb could overlook the fact that they were all criminals, none of them had any interest in befriending the rajkumaara of the country that had locked them up.

The new prisoner was sitting cross-legged, his eyes closed, on a bench underneath neem tree branches that hung over the compound walls. They were in an empty part of the courtyard, away from the guards and other prisoners, but Kaleb ignored the three unoccupied benches and selected the one opposite the mercenary.

He was younger than Kaleb had expected, and much more slight in stature. Kaleb didn't know what mercenaries looked like, but he'd assumed they would be tall and muscular brutes. This boy was disciplined with his mind. Kaleb, too, started each day meditating, and it was disconcerting to discover that he had something in common with a killer.

The boy's eyes opened. "You're the rajkumaara," he said.

"Do you have a name?" Kaleb asked.

"Surya." He uncrossed his legs and shoved the sleeves of his kurta up, revealing the dark lines threading across his forearm — a tattoo of jagged mountain peaks. He leaned forward. "Those guards haven't taken their eyes off us. Tell me, Prince, should I fear for my life?"

Kaleb glanced toward the guards at the courtyard entrance, and sure enough, they were watching. "Between the two of us, only one has committed murder."

"Is that so?" Surya looked amused. "Then maybe it's *you* who should be afraid."

Ronak always said that Kaleb lacked a sense of self-preservation, but he was in no physical danger. The magic in their shackles prevented prisoners from getting too close to each other, but there were other things to fear. If the Council found out that he'd been talking to the mercenary, that would further prove his guilt in their eyes. But he couldn't let it go — not when it was his only chance at freedom.

"What do you know about my mother's death?"

His directness seemed to take Surya by surprise. "You mean what do I know about who hired us."

"You know as well as I do that it wasn't me."

Surya watched him for a moment, sizing him up. There was an edge to his gaze — sharp intelligence lurking beneath a veneer of indifference — and Kaleb had the impression that he was deciding how to respond. "You want your freedom," he said finally.

"Yes."

"And what will you do once you're free?"

Kaleb hesitated. He didn't know why Surya would care about such a thing, but in the end he decided on honesty. "I just want to go back to my life."

It was apparently the wrong thing to say. Surya's face was suddenly devoid of emotion. His gaze bored into Kaleb's. "You'll never have your old life back. You can leave these shackles, but those people in the palace? They'll never forget what you did. Even if it's a lie."

Kaleb drew back as if he'd been struck. That wasn't true. It couldn't be true. It was different for him. "I don't expect you to understand."

"Oh, I think I do. You think your family will protect you?" His lips twisted into a cruel smile. "Tell me, Prince, what have they done for you besides lock you up?"

Kaleb's jaw tightened. "That's not how family works. You don't keep score."

"You're so quick to defend those who don't see your value." Surya shook his head, and Kaleb had the oddest sensation that he'd failed some kind of test. "I'd start with your sister's Council."

"I need more than that," Kaleb pressed. "A name. Or — or some kind of identifying feature."

He already knew that the order had to have come from someone powerful. Any member of the Council could have wanted his mother dead — could want Vira dead — but Kaleb was trapped in here, and there was little Ronak had been able to find out about the actions of individual councilors without arousing suspicion.

"There's a reason most people communicate with us only via code. It's all I know." Surya folded his legs once more, and his eyes fell shut. Kaleb had been dismissed.

CHAPTER THIRTEEN

— RIYA —

SOME PART OF Riya had believed that a familiar face would greet her at the palace entrance.

The bards always sang of the celebrations held when a rajkumaari returned from war. Dancers led the procession of chariots, tossing flower petals along the path. Villagers crowded the streets, clamoring for a glimpse of the returned warrior. And when she finally reached the palace, the maharani was waiting with a garland of roses to welcome her home.

But Riya wasn't a soldier, and it had been a long time since she'd called the palace home. And so no one awaited her. Not Vira. Not Ronak. Not even that surly guard who'd accompanied Vira into the forest.

Instead, she'd been delivered to one of the side entrances and left at the back stairs like a questionable package or a clandestine lover.

You should have known better.

Amma had always said that. Young rajkumaaris didn't make mistakes. They knew better. And it seemed that after all these years, Riya still hadn't learned her lesson.

The north tower rose high above her, its trellis-covered stone walls blocking her view of the rest of the fort, but she recognized the sounds: the carts of produce being rushed in, the gardeners pruning the hedges, guards training in the arenas below. She could hear the roar of the waves as they crashed against the long, straight walls that surrounded the fort complex. Riya's heart thumped uncomfortably with each passing second. It felt all too familiar — yet totally different.

"Rajkumaari?"

Riya turned to see a young guard approaching. She was dressed in the standard red and black uniform, but there was a distinguishing gold band that encircled her upper arm, denoting that she was a member of the maharani's personal guard. She bowed deeply despite being at least several years older than Riya. "I'm here to escort you to your chambers."

Riya didn't need an escort to find her own room, but she followed the guard, clutching her single bag of belongings. The halls were bustling with maidservants, guards, and messengers. Riya instinctively shrank back, trained by the Ravens to avoid notice. But after a few minutes she realized that no one was sparing her a second glance. Dressed as she was in her threadbare clothes, she didn't look to be anyone of note — certainly not any member of the royal family.

The palace looked the same as it always had, the cold stone warmed by embroidered tapestries and heavy carpets and wasteful magic. Everything from the sconces to the banisters to the ornate doorknobs was covered in a thin layer of gold, glittering in the midmorning light that streamed in from open windows and artfully designed courtyards. Chandeliers cascaded from the painted ceilings, their shimmering crystal tiers held together by the sheer willpower of a horrendous amount of magic.

Nothing had changed, yet everything felt . . . *off.* Or maybe she was different. It seemed inconceivable now that this had been her home for so many years, and it seemed unfair that just being here was enough to make her feel like a child all over again.

She was so lost in her thoughts that when the guard opened the door to her bedroom, the very sight of it snatched her breath away.

Everything was just as she'd left it. The broken latch on the window she'd used to sneak out to meet her friends. The telescope in the corner — a present from Papa, who'd taught her to identify the constellations. The mirror, the bedposts, even the tables were swirling with memories — as if she'd stepped back in time into a perfectly preserved memory.

Minutes later, three maidservants arrived to whisk her away toward the private baths. She should have known that this had been Vira's plan: scrub off all traces of the common people before anyone saw her. It was what Amma would have done, Riya realized bitterly.

The square pool in the middle of the room was large enough to fit at least three other people, but this was part of the rajkumaari's suite; she'd be the only one to use it. As soon as she stepped inside, she could feel the magic wash over her. All the palace baths were constructed the same way, their tiles forged by mayaka to keep the water at a perfect temperature for hours on end. It wasn't an unpleasant sensation, but it made her uncomfortable nonetheless.

Rose petals and lotus blossoms floated on the water. Incense burned in the corners, the perfumed smoke mixing with the whorls of heavy steam. Small basins of various herbal scrubs for her hair and body sat at the edge of the pool.

She couldn't remember the last time she'd taken a bath that wasn't a quick plunge into the stream that cut through the forest. She hadn't minded it much, but hot water was a luxury that Kavita had dreamed about.

She'll come around, Yash had said when he'd helped her board Vira's carriage. *Just give her time.*

Riya hoped he was right. She didn't like the way they'd left things.

After the bath, the maidservants poked and prodded at her, taking measurements for the kurtas and lehengas that would fill the rosewood almirahs by the end of the week. One of the women returned with a bottle-green lehenga made from Ravasi silk. The full skirt and matching blouse were printed with elaborate roses and hemmed in zari. It was one of her old outfits, two years out of fashion. It didn't fit quite right, but Riya let the girls dress her in it, using the heavy gold dupatta to mask where the blouse was too loose around her shoulders and waist.

When they were done, Riya gaped at herself in the mirror. Her skin shone from the sandalwood and turmeric they'd rubbed all over her face. Her neck and wrists and ears were adorned with heavy gold that made her slouch. Thick strokes of kaajal outlined her eyes in black. Even her wild hair was tamed, slicked back with scented oil into a neat braid.

She looked like Vira.

✻

Once the maidservants left, Riya pulled out her bag. It didn't have much in it, but she dumped the items out onto the bed. The dagger Papa had given her. A few spare plain kurtas. Yash's lock-pick earrings. A stack of mayaka-forged paper.

She'd seen a pot of ink on the writing desk, so she scratched out a quick note to the Ravens saying that she'd arrived at the palace. After waiting a few moments for a response, she felt silly. She couldn't expect them to sit around staring at a piece of paper all day waiting for a magically transmitted message.

According to the clock in the room, she had an hour before she was due to appear in front of the Council. Vira's carriage had come with a sealed note full of instructions on what to say about her two missing years. Riya should have known that her return would hinge on approval from

Vira's Council — on if she could prove that she really was Priyanka, the rajkumaari miraculously returned from the dead.

It was for your protection, Vira had said. Riya didn't believe that for a second. It was to protect the royal family's image. It was better for the maharani to have a dead daughter than one who'd run away from her.

Riya thought she'd made peace with her anger long ago, but it came flooding back so quickly — as fresh and painful as the day she'd run away — along with every insecurity and fear she'd tried to bury. She felt as if she were back in her mother's room, both of them saying things they couldn't take back. They'd argued so often over the years — about the way Amma treated everyone around her, the way she could change the world and chose not to, the way Riya didn't understand being a ruler. Papa had always stepped between them, but after he died, they hadn't had anything to stop them.

Spoiled, her mother had called her. *Naive. Child.*

Selfish, she'd shouted back. *Irresponsible.*

Then leave, her mother had snapped. *If you hate it here so much, leave. You won't last out there in the real world for even a single day.*

So Riya had left, determined to prove her wrong. But now her mother was also gone, and the sense of vindication never came.

Find the magic quickly, Riya told herself. *Find it and go home.*

She needed to access the quarries, where she would be able to find the ledgers that tracked the mayaka transport. There were several entrances from the fort, but each one required a special key. The Council had one, locked away in a secure, magical vault that she had no hope of breaking into. The other two had belonged to her parents.

Amma's key would have gone to Vira. Papa had given his key to Kaleb, who'd been poised to take over as the palace mayaka once he finished his training. But with him imprisoned, it would likely have gone to Ronak.

Riya exhaled deeply, her stomach knotting with unexpected nerves at the thought of seeing her brothers. She'd never been particularly close to Ronak, but Kaleb had been the one person she'd never meant to leave behind. It had come as a blow to the gut the day Kavita told her that the maharani's killer had been caught, and that it was Kaleb. Riya hadn't believed for a second that he could have anything to do with Amma's death.

She desperately wanted to see him, but something held her back — fear, maybe, or cowardice.

I'll say goodbye this time, she promised herself. Just not yet.

She glanced up at the clock once more. The sooner she found the magic, the sooner she could go back to the Ravens. It was time to pay Ronak a visit.

CHAPTER FOURTEEN

— RONAK —

A YEAR AFTER Papa's death, Ronak had ordered all his belongings to be brought up to the minuscule rooms in the south tower. His father had used the space as an office and personal library, but it was never meant to be lodgings. It was always cold. During heavy storms the tower seemed to sway with the wind. And even the mayaka-fortified windows couldn't manage to keep out all the rainwater and dust, or the occasional mynah bird.

Ronak didn't really know why he'd insisted on the move. His old rooms had been perfectly adequate. Spacious, full of light, with a picturesque veranda facing the ocean. But there was something compelling about the tower and its seclusion from the rest of the palace. Sometimes, as he stood looking out the windows at the waves crashing against the walls of the distant lighthouse, he felt that he was the only person in the world.

And it didn't hurt that the narrow spiral staircase that led to his room was deterrent enough for him to avoid human contact for days if he wished. In fact, he couldn't remember the last time anyone other than Jay or the servants had visited his chambers.

Which was why he woke with a start at the intense *tap, tap, tap* on his door.

Maybe he could pretend he was asleep. No guard or servant would wake him, and Jay would have simply barged in. His head pounded from the smoke he'd inhaled on Spit Street, and the last thing he wanted was whatever awaited him on the other side of the door.

But the knocking persisted. He forced himself out of bed and yanked open the door. "What?" he barked.

Vira stood in front of him. "Is this how you greet your visitors?"

Ronak stifled a groan. He *definitely* didn't want whatever it was that she needed him for. "Personal visits are beneath your station, aren't they?"

"And yet here I am. Can I come in?"

Ronak reluctantly stepped back, letting her in. She'd already dressed for the day in a dark green chiffon sari embroidered with tiny gold flowers. She'd paired it with enough antique jewelry to compensate for the relative simplicity of the fabric. It was the kind of thing their mother would have worn, Ronak thought, and it looked strangely out of place on her.

Vira shut the door behind her, sealing them into the small, circular space. She'd been there before, of course, but she looked around the room anyway, her eyes narrowing as if it were her first time there. Anything he wouldn't want her to see was carefully hidden, but Ronak looked, too, just to make sure.

Curved shelves lined the length of the wall, full of Papa's old books and memorabilia. Canvases of half-finished paintings gathered dust behind an abandoned easel in one corner. More books and scraps of paper were scattered across a large desk — chaos to foreign eyes, perhaps, but Ronak had an order to the mess.

Vira pulled open one of the heavy curtains that hung over the four windows. Ronak flinched away as bright sunlight streamed in, illuminating the unmade bed in the center of the room.

"You kept that?" Vira sounded surprised as she looked at the sole canvas that hung between the window and a bookshelf.

It was a colorful imagining of Visala, Ashoka's once great founding city, the famed home of the first maharani, Savitri. The painting was old and faded — and more than likely inaccurate given the dearth of information about the long-lost city.

Once, Ronak had soaked up everything he could about Visala, voraciously reading every account Papa had found detailing its wonders. Visala had been another ancient mystery — like the Ivory Key — that Papa had tried and failed to solve. Ronak knew better than to waste time on treasure hunts by now, but Papa had loved the painting, so Ronak hadn't been able to bring himself to take it down.

He crossed his arms over his chest. "I assume you didn't come here to talk about Papa's obsessions."

Vira turned to him, her face oddly solemn. "He *was* obsessed, wasn't he?"

"He was," Ronak agreed. And it was no secret that Vira had inherited his infatuation with things best left buried in history and lore. He wondered if Vira knew what her dead fiancé had had in his possession. A tiny flash of guilt pierced him, but Ronak pushed it away. Vira had made her choices.

And Ronak was making his.

"Why are you here?" Ronak prompted when Vira didn't say anything else.

"A country thrives when all of its citizens perform their respective duties," Vira said, sliding seamlessly into the role of maharani.

Ronak snorted. "And which councilor do I have to thank for putting those words in your mouth?"

"Yours" — Vira continued as if he hadn't spoken — "is to help us forge an alliance."

Dread pooled in Ronak's stomach. He'd known this moment would come, but he hadn't thought it would be so soon. "I'm not interested."

"That's not up for discussion."

Ronak smiled blandly, walking forward until he stopped in front of her. Vira had always been the tall one between them, but he'd grown so much in the last few months that she had to tilt her head back to look him in the eyes. "We'll see about that, won't we?" he said.

"Don't," she said, as though she could see right through him. "Whatever you're thinking. Don't do it. You can't get out of this. The Council *will* try you for treason."

"Well, then, I suppose I won't have to try so hard to visit our brother. Not that you'd know anything about that."

Vira glared at him. "Do you think this is funny?"

"A bit, yes."

"It's not."

For a moment, Ronak couldn't help but wonder just how they'd gotten here. They'd been close once, able to trust and rely on each other. But as he looked down at her, all he could think was that the distance between them felt as wide as a chasm.

Vira inhaled deeply, as if to compose herself. "The engagement ceremony will happen in three weeks' time."

Ronak's smile dropped. "Three weeks?" That wasn't enough time to free Kaleb, to get out of Ashoka.

"Circumstances have changed. Or did you not hear about my dead fiancé?" She hesitated, and then added, "It's Preethi."

Ronak stared at Vira. "Preethi," he echoed in disbelief. "You cannot be serious."

He knew her — not well, but enough to know that they had absolutely nothing in common. She was competitive and ambitious, but clever enough to charm others into getting what she wanted. She loved to be the center of attention, thriving when there were dozens of admirers watching her every move. But worst of all, she'd made it abundantly clear that she actually enjoyed court life — that she wanted to serve on Vira's Council and participate in all the mundane duties that came with it.

"It's a political alliance, Ronak."

"No," Ronak said forcefully. "I won't do it." He refused to sign his life away — a life he'd barely lived, full of experiences he hadn't yet had.

"I did what I could to stop this," she said, lowering her eyes almost as if she felt guilty. "But this is the only way, Ronak. I'm sorry."

"You expect me to believe that?" Just as he'd predicted, a councilor had said the right words, and Vira was bending to their will.

She looked back up at him. "I don't expect you to do anything except marry the girl."

✳

Jay had learned from his brother, Kunaal — who served on the Council — that Vira intended to send Harish's body back to Onaar for the proper cremation rites by the next morning.

"Don't panic," Jay had said when he stopped by to tell Ronak the news. "We'll get it before they leave."

But panic was all Ronak could do as he paced the length of his room. They had a short window during which they could sneak in to search the body and find the map piece for Ekta. And now that his timeline had moved up, he needed Ekta's money.

It wasn't only that. He barely had a plan to break Kaleb out of the dungeons. It would be easy enough to bribe the guards to look the other way once he had Ekta's money, but getting Kaleb out of the shackles would be impossible without a mayaka — specifically the mayaka who oversaw the palace dungeons. And bribing Aaliyah wasn't an option, not when she'd trained under Papa.

Ronak fell back on his bed, wishing he could talk to his brother. Kaleb would know how to circumvent the constraints they faced. But Kaleb had made it perfectly clear that he intended to stay in jail until Vira saw fit to release him — which Ronak knew would never happen.

There was another knock at the door. Ronak sat up, reaching for the small book he kept beside his bed, which wasn't a book at all. It was hollowed out, the pages glued and cut to make a secret hiding compartment. He'd dumped out the contents after Vira's visit — results of his investigation into Kaleb's framing, his emergency stash of coins, notes on ways to free Kaleb — and now he shoved them all back in. He hadn't had visitors in weeks; having two in one day set him on edge.

The person knocked again, louder this time. "Ronak?"

He looked up, frowning. There were very few people in the palace who called him by his given name. He closed the book and made his way to the door.

Ronak's stomach plummeted in shock. "Riya?"

"I heard you lived here now." She smiled a little ruefully, not quite meeting his eyes.

She looked so remarkably like Vira. She was shorter, and she didn't have that air of haughtiness, but everything else was much the same: the hair, the clothes, the jewelry, even the kaajal around her eyes. Ronak stared at her, unable to get any words out. How was she here? *Why* was she here?

And why had no one told him?

Riya bit her lip. "Can I come in?"

Ronak numbly stepped back. "What are you doing here?"

"Vira didn't tell you?" There was genuine surprise in her voice. "Oh, I assumed —" She stopped herself.

Vira knew. She'd known when she came to see him, and she hadn't told him. Every time he thought Vira couldn't possibly disappoint him further, she still somehow found a way.

Riya glanced at him for permission before she walked around the edge of the room, trailing her fingers over the spines of Papa's books, surveying the area much like Vira had. "This suits you."

She'd probably spent as much time in this room as he had, doing her lessons on the faded rug beside Papa's desk while Ronak drew, both of them hanging on to Papa's every story. But that had been a lifetime ago.

"Why did you come back?" Ronak blurted out.

"Vira asked me to." Riya fiddled with the bangles stacked on her wrist. "So we can be a family again."

"Family," Ronak echoed. "You expect me to believe that?"

She looked up in surprise.

"I saw you, Riya. I saw you at the protest last month. With those rebels."

Riya's face drained of color. "Ronak —"

His mind kept flashing back to that moment over a month ago when he and Jay had ducked into the crowd. It had been a shortcut, an easy way to cut across to the Market District to meet Ekta's intermediary. But then he'd seen her. She was one of the protesters, there with a group of rebels. *Ravens*, someone had called them.

He remembered how often she'd fought with Amma — how their last fight had sent Riya racing off into the night. They'd always thought she'd come back, but she never had. She'd left them without sparing a second glance, and now she stood in front of him as if this were a common occurrence. It was all too much.

"You walked away from this life," Ronak said, his voice thick with emotion. "From us. And now you're telling me that you don't have some secret agenda?"

He could read the guilt on her face. They stood in silence for a long moment, studying each other. She seemed worlds away from the fifteen-year-old he'd last seen. Who'd shared his passion for the outdoors, for the adventure and games that Kaleb was too cautious to play and Vira was too stuck-up to entertain. This girl who stood in front of him was a stranger.

"Whatever it is you came back to do, leave me out of it." Ronak turned away. "The door, sister, is where you left it. Don't forget to shut it on your way out."

CHAPTER FIfTEEN

— VIRA —

Papa used to say that smell was a powerful key to memory, but Vira didn't anticipate the sharp sense of dread and regret that slammed into her when the guards pulled open the door and stifled dungeon air washed over her.

Kaleb hadn't fought. He hadn't argued. He'd just lowered his gaze and held out his hands to be shackled when she'd sentenced him. And this was the closest she'd stood to him in eight months.

Coward, a voice inside her muttered. That voice wasn't wrong. She hadn't gone to see him, because she couldn't bear the thought of looking into his eyes and seeing resentment. Hate. Anger. Emotions that she'd put there.

"Maharani?" The confused guards were still holding the gate open for her. Vira picked up the skirts of her lehenga and stepped inside.

The mercenary's cell was in the back. Vira walked quietly and deliberately, her eyes trained on the ground. Feeble light and humidity streamed in from windows high up in the walls, but there wasn't enough warmth to combat the strange kind of cold that lived here.

If Surya heard her approach, he didn't show it. He lay on a straw pallet, his arms folded beneath his head. The sleeves of his kurta were rolled up to his elbows, but the tattooed skin was hidden from view by his hair.

His head twisted finally, and the side of his mouth twitched. "A visit from the maharani. I must be blessed indeed." He sat up and lifted his right arm to rub the back of his neck, revealing the tattoo on his upper arm.

Vira's breath hitched.

Surya's eyes followed her gaze, and he smirked. "Is this why you came? To find out if it was me who killed your rani? Your *mother*."

"Was it?" Her voice was raw.

"No." Surya's smile was almost cruel. "That honor was given to my father."

Honor. He didn't know the first thing about that word.

"There is no honor in murder." Rage burned low in Vira's stomach. "And *father* is a lofty term for the man who kidnapped you."

Surya walked forward, his movements as deliberate as a cobra stalking its prey. "Don't speak of things you don't understand, Rani."

There was ferocity in his gaze, protectiveness in his voice, and pride in his stance. For a man who had removed a young boy from his family. A man who had turned him into the killer who stood before her. That wasn't a father. That was a monster.

"And what of things *you* don't understand," she spat. "Like the Kamala Society."

An emotion passed over his face that she couldn't read. "A story for children."

"We both know it's not."

Surya raised a brow. "Do we, now?"

They studied each other. He wasn't much taller than she was — or much older. But there was something in the way he carried himself, in his stiff back and wide stance and careful speech, that lent him an air of authority. His features, too, were striking: a crooked nose, deep-set eyes, a scar that cut through one eyebrow. Two onyx studs in his earlobes winked through the curtain of dark hair. He looked like a soldier, like someone who thrived in battle, who'd command the respect of entire armies, and Vira hated him in that moment.

"I am the only thing keeping you alive. My Council wants to see you dead — and your head shipped to Onaar. I can protect you, but only if I have reason to." Inexplicably Vira stepped closer to him. "You seem clever enough not to die simply to spite me."

"What are you proposing exactly, Rani?"

"A deal," Vira said, forcing the words out. "Your life in exchange for the information you have."

Surya laughed. "There's a reason the mongoose and the cobra aren't friends. One will always kill the other."

"I'm prepared to take the risk."

"Then you're a fool."

"I've been called worse."

Surya stared at her for a long moment. "Freedom. That's my price."

"You're in no position to bargain."

"Oh. But I think I am." A slow, wolfish smile stretched across his face. He, too, stepped forward, and Vira was too aware that all that stood between them was a thin metal bar and a wall of magic. "You came here, Rani. You need me." His eyes sparkled with a challenge. "I don't fear death. And *you* seem clever enough not to lose simply to spite me."

He knew he was right. And she knew he wouldn't bend. Against Amrit's counsel, she'd been prepared to offer him protection, but she would not let a murderer — and a mercenary — run free through her city.

"Fine," she said. "Your freedom."

A corner of his mouth twitched — almost as if he knew she was lying. But he merely crossed his arms over his chest. "What would you like to know?"

"Who hired you?"

"You already know that."

"Why did the Kamala Society want Harish dead?"

"I think you already know that, too."

So he knew about the Ivory Key.

"He would have been a terrible rajah, by the way. Your lord planned to betray you. And he was far too quick to give up his plan in exchange for his life."

"And you killed him anyway."

Surya lifted one shoulder. "I never pretended to be anything I'm not, Rani."

No. He hadn't. "What were you supposed to do once you'd killed him and taken his dagger?"

"There was a contact I was supposed to meet at an inn outside Dvar. Don't bother to look. He's long gone. The Kamala Society doesn't care what happens to me." He smirked, as if enjoying a private joke. "They were the original mercenaries, you know."

"And the last piece of the map?" Vira prompted.

Surya's amusement faded. "Our deal, Rani. Free me, and I'll take you to it."

Vira's heart skipped a beat. He knew where it was. "I'll free you once I have my information."

"Then you'll be waiting a long time. You think you'll crack his code?"

Vira looked up just in time to see Surya's eyes widen slightly. He'd mis-stepped. He'd given something away he hadn't intended. The encoded message led to the last piece of the map.

It was her turn to smile even as her pulse raced and her knees threatened to give out. "I guess I have everything I need."

"You'll wish you hadn't done that," he said. "You'll need me sooner or later, Rani. And you'll regret this."

"No. I don't think I will." She turned and walked away.

✳

Amrit was waiting outside the dungeons. Midmorning light seemed to wash away his shadows, painting him with softer brushstrokes. Vira let her eyes trace over him, from the curl of his exceptionally long lashes down to the curve of his lips. He'd probably slept even less than she had, but somehow he looked refreshed, his eyes lighting up as he saw her. It really was unfair that some people were so effortlessly beautiful.

He offered her a smile and a paper-wrapped parcel and then nodded toward the stone stairs that led back to the palace.

"What's this?" Vira unwound the parcel as they walked. Perfect diamonds of mango and coconut burfi, topped with a smattering of crushed pistachios and saffron threads. Her breath caught in surprise. She didn't know if she'd ever told him that this was her favorite dessert.

He didn't say anything until she looked up at him. "An apology."

"What?"

"Yesterday, I didn't act as a guard would to his maharani," he said. "I acted as . . . as a friend. I should have told you about the mercenaries in the forest. I'm sorry, Vira."

"Oh. Thank you," she said, feeling some strange, heavy emotion stir within her. She hadn't given it another thought since they'd left the interrogation room. But he had. He'd considered what she'd said and how he'd acted.

Some days Amrit was all duty and sage advice. On other days — when he offered her smiles and sweets and sorries — it was harder to forget that he was a boy, too.

"Your sister is meeting with the Council," Amrit said.

"It's going well?" She'd wanted to greet Riya personally, but she'd needed an audience with Surya while the Council was occupied. *She'll understand,* Vira told herself. This was more important.

"As well as it can. And how was your talk with the prisoner?"

Vira recounted the conversation as she followed Amrit up a set of stairs. Warm sunlight bathed the fort in a soft gold haze. Around them servants hurried by with baskets of flowers and vegetables. Off-duty guards lounged on the grass, trading gossip and homemade snacks. Chattering children breezed past Vira, running up and down the stairs in what looked to be a game, but Vira knew was a training exercise.

"So the encoded message will lead us to the final piece," Amrit said when she finished. "Do you trust him?"

"I don't know." Catching Surya, interrogating him, getting him to divulge everything she wanted to know — it had all been too easy. But she couldn't figure out what angle he could possibly be playing.

"Any luck with the code?"

"Not yet. You?"

He shook his head. "I haven't had the time."

That was the problem. Neither of them did. Vira hesitated. "I don't want to involve other people, but . . ."

"Who is it?"

"Kaleb." She bit her lip. It was unfair of her to ask him this, but he'd understand. He was the only one who would.

As they passed through an open courtyard, Vira veered away from the path toward a balcony that overlooked the training arena. A group of shirtless men were running laps around the edge of the oval grounds. In the center, two girls carrying wooden talwars and shields circled each other slowly. A crowd had gathered around them — cheering, suggesting moves, hissing when one of the girls landed a blow.

"Remember those days?" Amrit asked, coming to stand beside her, resting his elbows on the railing.

"I try not to."

It had been ages since she'd been down in the arena, running drills or sparring with the guards. There, it hadn't mattered that she was the future maharani. She was just a girl with a talwar and a shield who had to prove her worth. But real life wasn't like that. In real life, labels were attached before you had a chance to earn them. With a small sigh Vira pushed away from the balcony. It was best to leave the past alone.

But Amrit called her back. "Have you thought about returning to training?"

She suspected that he knew why she hadn't, but it was one thing for him to speculate and another to admit that she was a failure on so many counts.

"I have nightmares," she said before she could overthink it.

Amrit was quiet for a minute. "From Ritsar?" he asked.

She nodded. "And from when . . . she died."

Ashoka hadn't had a war in centuries. Everything Vira had known about it was theoretical, things she'd studied in history books, in strategy games she'd played — and lost — against her mother. Until the Battle of Ritsar.

War had never *needed* to be a concern, not when every month, when magic was mined and processed, the bulk of it was sent to reinforce the borders. It wasn't until later that Vira learned, in the wake of diminishing magic, that her mother had decided to forgo fortification in certain areas that were blocked by natural borders, such as the Koranos Mountains, and Lyria had somehow discovered the weakness. And when her mother hadn't wanted to rewrite the trade agreements, the emperor had chosen to invade Ritsar instead of negotiate.

Riders had arrived in Dvar, pleading for help. Vira's mother had prepared to lead the defense to win back the fallen Fort of Ritsar, but she never had the chance. Lyria had hired assassins to ensure that she would never make it there. The mercenaries had waited and watched as her mother left the Dvar Fort — and in the few seconds that Shanti was alone, they'd slit her throat.

"I'd be surprised if you didn't have them," Amrit said. "But you did your best, Vira."

"Maybe." But that didn't change the fact that Ashoka had lost Ritsar because of her. Without her mother, the command of the army had fallen to her, and she'd let her grief, her pain, her fear take over. She'd retreated — abandoned her people.

The Council had put up new borders outside of Ritsar, fortified with all the magic and troops they could spare. But now other parts of the border were failing, too. With the Viceroy of Ishvat's help they would have the resources to protect the country for several months — maybe a year, if they were lucky and Lyria didn't attack again. But without magic, Ashoka wouldn't last much longer than that.

"It's easy for others to judge," Amrit said. "For outsiders to think they'd know what they'd do in your place. If you'd stayed and fought, maybe Ashoka would have Ritsar. But what of the cost?"

Maybe he was right. Maybe it didn't matter that her mother might have made a different choice. She wasn't here; Vira was the one who had to face the consequences.

"I feel like I'm fighting my mother's ghost." Vira laughed dryly. "And it's not a fair fight."

Amrit smiled sadly. "That's the thing about battling ghosts, Vira. The living always lose."

Below them, the girls were done sparring, and two others took their place. As Amrit watched the guards, Vira watched him.

He'd rolled his sleeves up to his elbows. She could see a burn mark on his left forearm — a mark he traced absently. Vira found herself pulling out the small treasure chest in her mind in which she stored the sparse details of his past.

He'd been raised somewhere in the north. He had three brothers. His father had been the one to train him in combat — and when he turned fourteen, he left his family to travel, picking up fighting styles from around the country until he'd come to Dvar to train the maharani herself.

"Does it hurt?" she asked.

Amrit looked down at his arm, as though surprised to find that he was touching the mark. He pulled his sleeve back down. "No. It hasn't hurt in a long while."

"Some scars hurt even after they heal."

Amrit's smile faltered for a brief moment. "Memories only have power over us if we let them."

She touched his arm gently. "Sometimes talking about them can help loosen their hold."

But Amrit only smiled again and drew his arm away from her. "Come. We should return to the palace."

CHAPTER SIXTEEN

— RIYA —

RIYA'S MEETING WITH the Council went far better than she expected. Vira had been conspicuously absent, but Riya recounted her sanctioned lie anyway — that she'd run away to stay with distant cousins in Adhura. Riya didn't know if the Council bought her story, but after an hour of questions they'd let her leave. Just like that, Priyanka, the rajkumaari of Ashoka, was resurrected.

Riya self-consciously kept her gaze trained on the ground as she exited the meeting room. Now that news of her return had spread, she could feel people's eyes on her everywhere she went. The workers were too well trained to be caught openly staring, but other occupants had no such qualms.

The eastern wing, where the Council held its meetings, was reserved for visitors and members of the Council who traveled from far-off provinces. It wasn't uncommon for them to bring their families — children they were training to replace them or were trying to marry off to eligible suitors.

The royal wings had only a few suites, all spaced apart to allow each member of the family their own private areas. But in the eastern wing the hallways were narrower, the rooms smaller, and there was vivacity in the air. Riya could make out muffled laughter coming from behind closed doors, the delicate strings of a veena as a boy practiced in an empty room, even a heated game of carrom tucked away on an open veranda.

Riya had practically lived here, spending more time in her friends' rooms than in her own. Those girls were likely still here, and Riya was hit with a sudden curiosity to see them — to see what her life would be like now if she'd stayed. On a whim, she veered right, through a courtyard filled with lush plants and a gurgling fountain and up two flights of stairs, until she reached an open terrace overlooking the rose garden.

Four girls sat on floral-patterned divans. Half-eaten platters of deep-fried kachoris and twisted murukku and tumblers of rose milk had been pushed to the edges of a square table, making room for the chessboard in the center. It was such a familiar scene that Riya's breath caught.

She'd been there the day they claimed this spot as their own. She'd been there as they dragged the divans out of an unused room, begging Kaleb to infuse magic into the silk to protect it from the elements. She'd been there as Indra attempted to teach them how to play chess day after day while Archana pretended to care and Preethi flirted with whichever pretty person happened to cross her path.

One of the girls turned around just then — and did a double take. "Vaishali's bones. *Riya?*"

Three sets of eyes were suddenly on Riya, and she felt her face flush. She waved, battling unexpected nerves.

Preethi's hands flew to her mouth, and then a second later she was on her feet. She let out a shriek of excitement, throwing her arms around Riya, nearly toppling them both over.

"I heard you were back. I couldn't believe it," Preethi said, her voice muffled. She pulled back and grabbed both of Riya's hands in hers, looking at her with wonder and shocked elation. *"You're back."*

"I'm back," Riya repeated weakly.

Then Archana and Indra were there too, hugging Riya, and emotions overwhelmed her. She hadn't spared a second thought to any of these girls for the last two years, but standing here wrapped up in them — in their familiar scents of orange peel and cloves and jasmine — it was as if she'd never left.

Riya let the girls drag her over to the divan, press a cup of chilled rose milk into her hands, and pepper her with questions.

"You have to tell us everything!"

"Where have you been?"

"When did you get back?"

Riya sipped the rose milk, using it as a buffer to gather her thoughts. She studied them over the edge of the terra-cotta tumbler. They looked the same as ever.

There was Preethi: dark brown eyes, mole on her angular chin, thin white scar stretching across her temple from a childhood injury. She'd always been confident, but there was an intimidating ease to her now — as if she knew exactly who she was and what she wanted. Her waist-length hair cascaded down in gentle waves, and six tiny gold rings and diamond studs glittered down her earlobes.

Indra, a chess champion, sat to her left, wearing a simple off-white cotton sari that she'd pleated in a strange style, almost like a dhoti, over a maroon velvet blouse. She'd styled it artfully with a thin gold belt around her waist, and Riya felt a pang of jealousy. It was the kind of thing that would look absurd on her, like a child playing at being an adult, but Indra had always managed to turn the most eclectic pieces into an elegant look.

On Riya's other side sat Archana, Preethi's cousin. Her thick, curly hair was pulled back in a loose braid. Her feet and hands were lined red with alta, and she was still wearing the loose-fitting kurta pants and pleated half-sari she wore to dance practice. Beside her was a thick tome, the page marked carefully with an ancient cloth bookmark made from one of her grandmother's old handloom saris.

"Come on, Ri," Preethi prompted. "Where did you go?"

It was one thing to lie to the Council, but it was another to lie to these girls who'd known her for most of her life. Who'd shared secrets with her and comforted her after fights with her siblings. But . . . they'd also never understood why she'd clashed with her mother so much. They'd never cared about the world outside the palace — the world beyond politics and parties and petty problems.

"I went to Adhura." Riya lowered her lashes, studying the curling designs carved into the weatherworn table. "I got into a fight with my mother, and . . . I ran." She took a deep breath. "I thought about coming back," she admitted honestly. "But then the longer I stayed away, the harder it was to come back. And then my mother —"

"Told the world you died," Archana finished bluntly.

Riya smiled wryly. "Told the world I died." She finally looked up. "I'm sorry I didn't tell any of you where I was going."

But the girls were already shaking their heads. "What matters is that you're back now," Preethi said, reaching across the table to clasp Riya's hand again.

"Though, Kausalya help me, we need to get you a whole new wardrobe." Indra wrinkled her nose as she eyed Riya's out-of-fashion clothes.

"You haven't changed at all," Riya said, laughing in surprise. "None of you."

"That's not true," Archana said. "Indra's engaged."

"Really?"

"We're going to be married in the spring. I wanted a longer engagement to make sure all the arrangements were perfect, but Neha just wanted to get married." Indra rolled her eyes, but Riya could see the happiness radiating from within her.

"She's a guard here," Preethi explained. "One of your sister's, actually. She started a few months after you left."

"Though of course we didn't find out about it for months," Archana cut in, giving Indra a pointed look.

"When will you let that go?" Indra turned to Riya. "I didn't think my mother would approve of anyone who wasn't a soldier. I was waiting until I knew for certain she wouldn't have Neha shipped off to the farthest corner of the world. But I'm pretty sure she likes Neha more than me now."

Her mother was Meena, the councilor. Riya had been terrified of her as a child, desperate to avoid her stern glances and strict demands at all costs. It was strange to think of her as a doting mother preparing for a wedding.

"Preethi's engaged, too," Archana said. "I, however, am very happy to be alone."

Riya turned to Preethi in surprise. She didn't think Preethi had much interest in marriage at such a young age.

Preethi looked down, uncharacteristically reticent. "Yes. Well. I wasn't sure you'd heard."

"You're going to be sisters!" Archana blurted out.

Riya's mouth parted in shock. "You're engaged to Ronak?" She certainly hadn't heard that.

"It's not official," Preethi said. "The ceremony's not for a few weeks. But yes."

"I'm thrilled for you," Riya said, meaning it.

Riya couldn't wrap her mind around the idea of Ronak having a wife — of him being a *husband* — but in some ways, Riya supposed that they were well suited. Preethi was clever and charming and cunning, able to persuade practically anyone to do what she wanted. Ronak, too, had a

way with words when he wished it. The problem, though, was that most often he didn't. She couldn't recall the two of them ever having spoken much,
but two years was a long time for her to be away.

It was an advantageous match, to be certain — for both of them. Preethi would get to wed a rajkumaara and cement her place in history, which
had been her lifelong dream. "Don't you want people to know your name?"
she'd often asked Riya when they were younger, shaking her head in bewilderment when Riya didn't seem to care. And it was no secret that the
Viceroy of Ishvat had walked out of Vira's Council along with the Viceroy
of Onaar. Riya didn't know what Vira had promised Preethi's family — or
what they had promised Vira in return — but that was always the way of
royal marriages.

Her conversation with Ronak was still in her mind, filling her with
unease. That he knew about the Ravens had thrown her, and now she had
to find a different way into the quarry. It was frustrating knowing that he
had the very key that she needed. It was forged to be invisible, but she'd recognized the gold chain. She did not expect him to give it up willingly, but
it wasn't going to be easy to steal it if he didn't want her anywhere nearby.

But maybe, with Preethi's help . . .

Riya sipped her rose milk as the girls continued chattering, catching
her up on all the court gossip: who was angling for what promotion, who
had fallen out of favor with the Council, who'd been caught having an affair
with whom. She'd forgotten that this was what palace life was like, always
trying to impress someone, always fearing that the smallest slights would
result in consequences. Even Vira, who'd been guaranteed the position of
maharani, had spent so much time trying to impress the Council, desperate to be seen as the dutiful, responsible daughter.

I might need their political backing one day, Riya, she'd said over and
over. *You just don't get it.*

Riya didn't get it. But maybe she would have if she'd stayed. Maybe this was what her life would have become: days spent trying to figure out which people to use to get what she wanted.

But this *was* her new life now, she realized with a jolt. She wasn't a Raven — not within these walls. She was a rajkumaari. And if leveraging other people's ambitions was what it took to get her the answers she needed in order to leave, that's what she would do.

CHAPTER SEVENTEEN

— RONAK —

THE MORGUE WAS on the lowest level beneath the palace, at the end of a long, narrow corridor lined with unlit lamps and locked doors.

"Walk faster," Jay muttered. "I don't like being down here."

If Ronak was in a better mood, he would have found it funny. Instead, he just lifted the lantern higher.

Despite what the eerie shadows suggested, there was nothing sinister here. The hallways were cramped because the floor had originally served as lodging for servants. When one of his ancestors expanded the fort complex, separate quarters had been constructed for the workers, and the rooms here were abandoned. Now they were filled with useless objects: waist-high silver lamps, stacks of carved sandalwood chairs, and crates full of ornate brass sconces — things someone had meant to catalogue and restore but had never gotten around to doing.

Out of habit Ronak reached out and trailed his fingers along the papered wall. He'd spent hours down here as a child, running around with Vira, scouring the halls for clues that marked secret passages hidden by the Kamala Society. They'd never found any, but the memories still pressed into him, achingly vivid. He let his hand fall away, allowing the cold reality of his present circumstances to chase away the warmth of nostalgia.

On the other side of the iron door at the end of the hall, Harish's body was being prepared for travel. Jay reached it first and tried the door. It was locked.

"Hold this," Ronak said, handing Jay the lantern.

Ronak withdrew the gold chain from under the collar of his kurta, pulled it off over his head, and dangled it in front of the keyhole.

The necklace, which had belonged first to Papa and then Kaleb, had been forged to open the doors that led down into the quarries. Ronak believed that to be its only purpose until, several months earlier, he'd discovered that it also worked on doors within the palace — but not all. Several locks had proved to be impervious to its magic, including Vira's chambers and the vault where the Council stored the country's money. He'd wanted to ask Kaleb about the limitations, but Jay had pointed out that he'd have to explain why they'd been trying to break into those rooms in the first place.

Jay let out a sigh of relief as a long, thin golden key slowly materialized. "Thank the goddesses."

Ronak unlocked the door and replaced the chain around his neck. By the time they entered the morgue, the key had once again disappeared.

Jay found the mechanism that controlled the lanterns in the room, and magic flared to life around them, bathing the room in crackling yellow light. Ronak had only ever been there to privately pay respects to each of his parents and grandparents, so it felt strange being there with Jay instead of his siblings. The room looked just as bare as he remembered. To the right, a set of double doors led to separate baths used by priestesses to wash the bodies. To the left were cabinets full of medicinal salves and tinctures used by healers before funeral rites were performed. The single coffin sat in the center of the room on a raised platform.

"Let's get this over with," Jay said.

Even before they approached the body, Ronak could feel the magic emanating from it. The casket had been forged to protect Harish's body on the journey to Onaar. The lid was propped open, and Ronak could see that the body had been washed and was now covered with fresh silk cloth, hiding the arrow piercings that had supposedly killed him. Harish lay flat on his back, eyes closed, hands crossed over his chest.

"Did you ever meet him?" Jay asked.

"Briefly."

Not all councilors brought their families to the palace, so Harish had visited only once, three years earlier. He'd spent the entirety of his trip getting drunk and shamelessly flirting with anyone who happened to look his way. The only reason their paths had even crossed was because Kaleb — who'd been enamored with Harish's friend Faisal — had dragged Ronak to every party the Council had thrown that week.

It was hard to reconcile that proud and vain boy with the one who lay before him now, and for a fleeting moment Ronak wished he knew some prayers to say.

"I can't imagine how Vira must be feeling," Jay said quietly.

It hadn't occurred to Ronak to consider Vira's emotions, so he merely shrugged.

Harish's items were lying on a table beside the coffin. Two black-feathered arrows. His clothes — covered in blood, dirt, and rainwater. His shoes. A few gemstone-studded rings. A small booklet with mayaka-forged pages. It wasn't uncommon for people to carry small books like this on long journeys. It was a way to communicate secretly — the pages could be ripped out and burned once a message had been received.

But there was no dagger.

Jay reached for a set of notes left by the healer who'd prepared the body. On the first page was a list of his effects. "There's supposed to be a dagger," Jay said, tracing his finger down the list, then turning the pages. "Shit. Ro. Look at this."

The healer was evidently very meticulous and had made note of what happened to the dagger. A guard by the name of Neha had taken it on the maharani's orders.

"Vira has it." Ronak's stomach sank. She'd somehow known what was in the dagger and had gotten to it first.

"What do you want to do?" Jay asked.

It seemed almost inevitable that he and Vira would end up on opposite sides yet again, but this was his only shot at freedom. Ronak refused to let her take one more thing from him.

"We get it back."

✳

The Council had prepared a lavish feast to welcome Riya, followed by a concert in the gardens. As they left the morgue, Jay had pointed out that it would be the best time for them to get the second map piece from the library. The dinner was limited to handpicked guests, but everyone was invited to the concert — scholars, families of the councilors, even guards and servants, as long as enough members stayed at their posts. It was a good plan, but Ronak had anxiously paced the length of his room for three hours until it was time for him to meet Jay.

"That's great, Ro. Look angrier," Jay said when he found Ronak in the garden. "Would it kill you to act as though you liked people?"

"I don't," Ronak said. "And I see no reason to pretend."

Jay rolled his eyes. "You know there's a problem when you're one of the most influential people in the room and everyone is steering clear of you."

"They only *think* I'm influential," Ronak said. But he unwrinkled his forehead — if only because it was easier to avoid notice if he performed the role of the bored, spoiled rajkumaara people expected to see. "Kausalya help me. How long is this going to take?"

It was nearing ten o'clock, and the garden was still only half full. Guests were slowly filtering out of the palace in small groups to take their seats on the blankets and cushions that had been set out on the grass. The musicians were already seated on a raised platform at the front, tuning their instruments to the drone of the tambura. Next to them, two young mayaka were setting up magical amplifiers that allowed concerts and speeches to be heard all through the fort.

"Be patient," Jay said. "Vira just got here."

Ronak turned toward the section at the front reserved for the maharani and her guests, where Vira was sitting alone.

"We could get the dagger now," Jay added.

"How?" Ronak asked. "My key doesn't open Vira's room."

"No. But maybe there's someone who we can ask for help." Jay nodded toward the palace entrance, where four girls were making their way down the wide steps.

Ronak's jaw tensed. "Absolutely not."

"She's a thief."

"She's not an option." He wasn't involving Riya, not when he had no idea what angle she was playing. "I told her to stay out of my life, and I'm not going to drag her back into it."

"You did what?"

"She ran away," Ronak said.

"And? That's exactly what you're planning."

"It's not the same," he said. Everything he was doing was _for_ family. Riya had run to escape them. It was different.

As if sensing his presence, Riya turned toward them. Her gaze locked with Ronak's, but her face betrayed no emotion. Ronak looked away first.

He recognized those girls — they were the same ones she'd spent all her time with before she left. And one of them was Preethi. He tugged at the collar of his kurta. It suddenly felt too tight, like he couldn't breathe.

"You've known her forever," Jay said, following the turn of his thoughts.

He had. They'd both practically grown up with her. "That doesn't mean I want to marry her."

Jay scratched the side of his jaw. "You might like her."

Ronak snorted. "I doubt that."

"Maybe, if you bothered to get to know her, you'd find you have some things in common."

There was an odd edge to Jay's voice that gave Ronak pause. Jay believed that everyone had hidden depths if you looked hard enough.

Sure, they'd known each other since they were children, but Ronak couldn't recall the last time he'd spoken to Preethi. He stayed away from the Council, and because he didn't like large crowds, he didn't attend most palace parties either. And after Riya's disappearance, they'd had very little reason to interact.

But, if Ronak was being honest, it wasn't about her. It was what she represented. Responsibilities, politics, duty — all the things that tethered him to the palace. All the things he intended to escape.

The gardens fell silent as the first notes of the violin reverberated around them. The concert was starting.

"Let's go," Ronak said.

As the singer improvised the first notes of the raga, Ronak and Jay slipped into the library, through the trapdoor, into a secret room, and lifted the piece of the map out of the case for the first time in two hundred years.

CHAPTER EIGHTEEN

— KALEB —

MOST NIGHTS, KALEB didn't mind his prison. But most nights it was only silence that waited for him on the other side of the walls. The single window — a circular hole high up fitted with iron grates — was letting in more than air. It was letting in memories.

His cell flooded with the somber notes of the singer. *Familiar* notes. Kaleb remembered listening to the same song — one of the epics composed by the renowned bard Rasika, hummed slightly off-key in the mayaka lab as he'd worked with Papa. The singer was embellishing the notes in a way that his father never could have managed, but Kaleb's chest tightened all the same.

Concerts in the gardens had always been his favorite. He recalled sipping rich badam milk by lanterns that hung down from tree branches, swatting away the mosquitoes that hovered around the magical flames. He remembered flirting with the sons of whatever councilors or visiting dignitaries happened to be around, his nights full of fleeting touches and stolen kisses beside the moonlit pond. He could picture lying on the grass beside Riya, tracing constellations in the air long after everyone else had departed for the night — and later, after Riya was gone, doing the same with Ronak.

But that was a life he would never get to go back to, and the sooner he let go of any fanciful notions of freedom, the happier he would be.

Kaleb's head fell back against the cold stone wall.

Riya was back. He'd heard the rumors from the guards first — and then had it confirmed by Ronak.

Kaleb had never given up faith that she'd come home. But he'd assumed that when it happened, he'd be welcoming her, helping her settle back in. But he was locked in here, and she hadn't even come to visit him.

Maybe she thinks you're guilty, the voice in the back of his head whispered. She wouldn't, the rational part of his brain assured him. But he couldn't ever completely ignore that voice no matter how hard he tried.

Kaleb squeezed his eyes closed, wishing he could shut out the noises, the smells, the memories.

Most nights this was much easier.

His eyes flickered open at the sound of footsteps. Relief coursed through him. He'd tried to dissuade Ronak from his daily visits, but Kaleb had never admitted just how much they meant to him. They were what had kept him grounded, day after day after day otherwise spent in isolation. Kaleb owed his brother a life debt.

But it wasn't Ronak.

It looked like a scene from one of Ronak's paintings. A golden goddess stood at the entrance while two guards held flickering lanterns behind her. The lanterns lowered, revealing Vira's elegant face and a shimmering floor-length kurta.

Kaleb wrapped his arms around his knees and laced his fingers together.

Eight months, he'd waited for this visit. He'd conjured scenario after scenario of what she would say to him, what he would say to her. Eight months, he'd dreamed of what it would be like for her to free him from this wretched place. Yet now that the moment was here, he felt . . . empty.

"Leave us," she said to the guards.

"I'm surprised you didn't want a bodyguard," Kaleb found himself saying. "You know, to make sure I don't orchestrate the death of yet another maharani."

"I suppose I deserve that." Vira hesitated. "I need your help."

The small shred of hope he'd carried in his chest vanished. She wasn't here as his sister. She was here as the maharani. Kaleb's laughter rang bitter and hollow. "And here I was naive enough to think this visit was about *me*, not you."

He knew he was pushing her. If he wanted to get out, this was not the way to do it. He should be playing to her weaknesses, preying on her arrogance. He should be begging to solve her problems in exchange for his freedom. Instead, all he could summon was anger, burning hot and furious in his heart.

"We are on the verge of war, Kaleb." Vira toyed with the bangles at her wrist. "And it's your duty to contribute to your country."

Your country. He licked his lips, wishing the words didn't hurt as much as they did. "So now Ashoka is my country."

Vira blinked. "What?"

"Months ago I was Lyrian, because it was convenient."

She dragged in a deep breath and looked away. "I didn't — I mean —" She exhaled. "Your mother was Lyrian."

She said it simply. As though that was enough to justify locking him in the dungeon.

"And Papa was Ashokan."

His mother might have chosen his name, but he'd grown up fluent in the language of his father's people, dressing in the clothes of his father's people, practicing the customs of his father's people. He'd grown up believing he was Ashokan through and through — until the day it wasn't enough.

"Kaleb . . ." She leaned back against the wall, her eyes closed. "I'm sorry I didn't visit."

He didn't know if she was apologizing because she meant it or because she thought that was what he wanted to hear. It was dizzying thinking this way, questioning actions and second-guessing motivations — things that came naturally to Ronak. To Vira. This wasn't him. Mind games were for politicians, not mayaka. And unlike Vira, this wasn't the person he'd ever wanted to become.

The anger fled his body, and Kaleb felt deflated. "I don't know what you want me to say."

"That you'll help me." She produced a small journal. Kaleb recognized it as Papa's when she held it out toward him.

Kaleb wanted to tell her he wasn't interested. But a part of him was curious to know what had changed — what Vira so desperately needed help with that she'd come to see him after all these months.

"What is this?" he asked.

Vira glanced over her shoulder and then lowered her voice to a whisper. "I found another piece of the map."

Kaleb froze. She didn't need to say what map. There was only one that would make her take out Papa's journals. That would make her come here. He rose. "You're serious."

She nodded. "And I have a lead on the third piece."

The Ivory Key. Papa had always believed that Vira would find it, and she actually had. He'd never felt Papa's absence so deeply as he did just then — a pain he could see mirrored in her eyes. He wanted to offer her comforting words, but things had changed so much he hardly knew what to say to her.

She withdrew a scrap of paper tucked inside the cover. "It's encoded.

I've tried everything, but I can't figure it out." Vira bit her lower lip. "Can you take a look?"

A part of Kaleb wanted to immediately agree. Papa would have done anything to get his hands on this knowledge — and once, Kaleb would have, too. But his dreams of becoming a trained mayaka had disappeared with his imprisonment.

Yet he felt the dim flicker of hope within his chest again. "What do I get in exchange for helping you?"

"What do you want?"

Surya's words rang in his ears. *You'll never have your old life back. You can leave these shackles, but they'll never forget what you did.* He ignored them. "I want you to clear my name."

Surprised flitted across her face, and then a look of anguish. "Kaleb . . ."

She wanted his help, but she wasn't going to free him. She hadn't even expected him to ask. Kaleb dragged in a ragged breath, hit with the sudden, painful realization that Vira didn't know him at all. He tried to recall some past time where she'd simply understood him, but he couldn't. Maybe in his months of imprisonment his imagination had simply conjured up some version of her who empathized with him, who knew what he wanted and what he stood for.

Don't say anything. Don't say — "She was my mother, too, you know."

Vira opened and closed her mouth. Then, a moment later, "What do *you* want me to say, Kaleb?"

"Do you truly think I did it? That I conspired to kill her?"

"No."

"Then clear my name."

"Kaleb, it's not that ea —"

"Then, no."

"No?"

Eight months ago, he would have done anything she asked. Anything to ease the burdens she carried. She was still only a young girl, forced to carry the weight of the country on her back. But she'd shown her gratitude by locking him up, putting her trust in a Council of strangers over him. And now she'd lost his faith.

Kaleb was resolute. "That's my price, Vira. You came to me asking for help. If you want it, you have to clear my name."

Vira twisted her bangles as she considered his words. "All right," she said finally. "It'll take some time, but I'll bring it up with the Council."

"Then I'll help you."

"That's all it would take?"

Kaleb tried to pretend those words didn't sting. "That's all it would take." He took the journal from her.

"Thank you." She lingered for a moment. "Kaleb, I —"

"Vira?" Ronak was walking toward them, carrying a lantern in his hand, his brow furrowed in confusion. "What are you doing here?"

Vira stepped away from the cell. "Just leaving." She gave Kaleb a small smile.

Ronak silently watched her walk away. "Why was she here?"

"It's nothing," Kaleb said.

But it took Ronak no time to spot the journal Kaleb was still holding in his hand. "And what's that?"

Kaleb tossed it on his pallet. He'd need to wait until daylight to look at it anyway. "It's . . . something Vira needs help with."

"You're *helping* her? After everything she's done?"

"Ronak, I don't want to argue."

"I don't either," Ronak said, though it was clear he was angry. "What are you helping her with?"

Kaleb shook his head. "You have to ask her." Despite being twins, Vira and Ronak had always had their differences, and Kaleb had no desire to get in the middle of their feud.

"Really? After everything, you're going to take her side?"

Kaleb rubbed his forehead. "I'm not taking anyone's side. I'm tired, Ro. I don't want to do this."

"Fine." His brother reached in his pocket to withdraw the chapati he brought every night. And then he reached for the lantern. "We'll talk about this later."

"You're not staying?" Kaleb asked, surprised. Ronak always stayed.

"Not tonight." And then Ronak walked away with the only source of light, leaving Kaleb to eat alone in the dark.

CHAPTER NINETEEN

— RIYA —

RIYA FOUND HERSELF falling into an uneasy routine as the next few days passed. With the Ravens, no day had been like another, but in the palace there was consistency.

A day after her arrival, the Council had saddled her with a task to keep her busy: planning Ronak's upcoming engagement ceremony. She'd intended to spend her mornings finding ways to secure magic and return to the Ravens, not choosing between two identical swatches of silk. *This is why I left,* she found herself muttering under her breath each time one of the Council's aides showed up at her door. It was all useless — a waste of time and money and resources. But Vira was too busy and Ronak refused to participate, so the task had fallen to her.

In the afternoons, one of the girls invariably showed up and dragged her to play chess on the veranda or watch the performers the Council had invited to the palace. Riya protested at first. She wasn't here to plan parties or rekindle old friendships. She was there to find magic. But she'd made little progress finding a way into the quarry, and she quickly realized that the girls were far more adept at navigating the Council's humongous list of specific requirements.

"They're *clearly* different," Indra had said, her mouth dropping open in horror when Riya had complained about the silk swatches, and then she'd promptly claimed the task.

Archana, too, was proving to be useful. She had her own political aspirations, and as the second of four children, she had competition to overcome if she wanted any hope of replacing her father on the Council. She'd taken over all the logistics concerning performances, using her bharathanatyam contacts to hire the best dancers, musicians, and storytellers from all over Ashoka.

Two days after her return, Riya had her monthly bleeding, along with pain that made her stomach seize up. She spent three days in bed, complaining to anyone who would listen — which, as it turned out, wasn't very many people. Apparently not even the title of rajkumaari was incentive enough to put up with her dramatic suffering.

One of her maidservants had taken pity on her and brought extra helpings of rasmalai. Preethi and Archana, on the other hand, were less indulgent. They'd dragged Riya out, insisting that a long walk around the grounds would help her feel better. It *had* helped, but Riya refused to admit that aloud.

She knew that the palace thrived on scandals and rumors, but she'd severely underestimated the sheer volume of gossip that spread through the halls each day. Her shocking return was old news in a mere four days, shoved aside in light of a new arrival to the palace: a handsome young scholar.

"We should go see him," Preethi had said on one of their walks, a glint in her eye. She'd never been able to resist a pretty face.

"You're engaged," Archana pointed out.

"It's just looking." Preethi rolled her eyes and dropped the subject, but she'd remained sullen the rest of the day.

Since the first day of Riya's return, Preethi hadn't seemed thrilled about the engagement. Between Preethi's reluctance to talk about it and Ronak's unwillingness to have anything to do with planning his own celebration, it was starting to become clear that it wasn't a love match, as Riya had initially thought. Getting involved in her friend's — and brother's — personal lives was also not why she was back, so she stayed out of it.

But without Preethi's help to get her closer to Ronak, her plan to steal the key from her brother had hit a snag, especially given that Ronak barely emerged from his room. He'd never enjoyed large gatherings, but apparently he didn't even dine with the rest of the palace anymore. She'd seen him only once, in the garden where the Council had hosted a concert, and he'd pointedly looked away from her. Vira did show up to meals, at least, but she barely glanced in Riya's direction as she took her seat at the head of the room, flanked by councilors or guards. Riya had thought she looked like Amma that day in the forest, but that was nothing compared to Vira in the palace, dressed in overpriced silk and layers of jewelry that Riya could sell for enough money to feed half of Dvar for months.

She'd updated the Ravens twice more, but she'd still had no response. She considered writing again, just to have some outlet for her thoughts, but pride had stopped her from sending a third message — not until she had some kind of assurance that the Ravens were even reading them. She hadn't realized how much she'd miss them — not just Kavita, but all of them. There had always been people in the glades to keep her company.

It was loneliness, Riya realized with a jolt as she lay in bed one night, staring at the crescent moon outside her unlatched window. Her family wanted nothing to do with her. Preethi and the other girls were too concerned with frivolities to share her worries. And now the Ravens were keeping their distance, too.

She had no one to talk to. She truly was alone.

✳

A week after her arrival, Riya finally heard from the Ravens. Though she hadn't heard anything in days, the first thing Riya did every morning was check the sheet of forged paper. And every morning it remained empty of any words aside from her own. Until today.

Her heart leapt into her throat as she saw Kavita's handwriting.

Ten o'clock this morning. Library.

She didn't know what to make of it, but she paced her room, eyeing the clock every few minutes until it was half past nine. It was early, but she couldn't wait any longer, so she slipped out, practically running down the halls until she burst into the library.

Riya cast her eyes around the room. It looked the same as always. Bookshelves lined every corner, save for the windows, from the plush carpet up to the high, vaulted ceiling, spanning multiple stories. Ladders stood next to each case to help reach the books on the topmost shelves. The center of the room was filled with tables for studying the manuscripts, each outfitted with a small, magically forged glass orb to amplify ancient texts.

"Can I help you find a book?"

Riya spun around to see the librarian at the front desk eyeing her sternly over the edge of her gold-rimmed glasses.

"I'm just . . . looking," she said.

The librarian snorted and then lifted a stack of books. "If you're going back there, you might as well take these to him."

Riya didn't fully understand her meaning until the woman shoved the stack into Riya's unsuspecting arms. Riya staggered back.

"Two aisles down and to the left," the librarian said, returning to the heavy tome in front of her.

Riya followed the librarian's directions, confused, until she abruptly came upon a group of girls.

"Archana?" Riya said, surprised to see her huddled behind one of the shelves, half hidden from view.

Archana shushed her and pulled her into the group.

"What are we looking at?" Riya whispered.

"The new scholar, of course," Preethi said, pointing him out.

Of course. "She dragged you into this, too?" Riya asked Indra, seeing her on Preethi's other side. Indra just shrugged.

Riya watched the scholar in question carefully flip a page of a manuscript. They could only see the back of his head, so Riya had no idea what she was supposed to be entranced by exactly. "All right," Riya said, pulling away. "I have to go. But feel free to keep ogling."

The scholar chose that moment to turn around. Riya dropped her stack of books on Archana's foot.

Archana yelped. Indra winced. Preethi clasped a hand over Archana's mouth.

It was Varun. Varun was the scholar.

"Riya," Preethi hissed, but Riya couldn't move. She had no idea what to do. Run? Hide? Eviscerate him in front of everyone? But before she could do anything at all, Varun rose. Her brain told her to flee, but her legs refused to cooperate.

He stopped in front of her. "Rajkumaari." A moment later, he bowed — as if it were an afterthought. "I have the books you wanted to discuss."

"What?"

"Over there," he said slowly. His voice was even, but she could read the flash of irritation that crossed his face.

Preethi nudged her forward, and when Riya didn't move, she gave Varun a charming smile. "She'll be with you in just a moment."

His eyes narrowed, but he walked back to the table. Indra picked up Riya's books and pushed them into her hands, but Riya could only gape after Varun. What had just happened?

"Discussing books!" Preethi said. "That's brilliant. I wish I'd thought of that. All right, I know he's attractive, but —"

That snapped Riya out of the spell. "He's not *attractive.*"

Archana's eyebrows shot up. "Um, were we looking at different people? Because —"

"I have to go," Riya said.

Riya's stack of books landed with a thud on the table where Varun was seated. She could practically feel Indra's wince from across the room as heads swung in their direction.

"What are you doing here?" Riya hissed.

"You didn't think I'd let you come back alone, did you?" He glanced up from the book in front of him. "You've adjusted to palace life well."

"What?"

"Sit down, Riya," he said coolly. "You're drawing attention."

Riya wanted to remain standing just to spite him. But he wasn't wrong. Gritting her teeth, she dropped into the seat opposite him.

His eyes darted to the girls, still lingering behind the bookshelf. "Why are they staring at you?"

"They're staring at *you.*"

A flicker of doubt crossed his face. "At me? Why?"

"They think you're —" Riya cleared her throat. "Interesting."

Varun's gaze was guarded. "What's that supposed to mean?"

"Don't ask me. I haven't the faintest idea why anyone would think you were."

"Well, get rid of them," he said. "We can't talk freely with an audience."

"You're the scholar," Riya said. "You find a way."

His jaw clenched, and then he stood up again. "Follow me."

She glanced over her shoulder at the girls and then followed him toward the back of the library, through the aisles, until she could no longer hear the rustle of pages or the shifting of silk or the occasional soft cough from the other scholars in the room. Varun pushed open the door to one of the few private reading rooms.

"What are you doing here?" she asked as soon as the door shut behind them. "How did you even get in? You're not qualified." Only a few scholars from Ashoka's top universities were allowed access to the maharani's personal collection.

"I interviewed for the position," Varun said. "So? What did you find?"

"You interviewed?" she echoed, incredulous.

"Yes, Riya," he snapped. "I interviewed. I told your sister's Council just what I intended to research during my time here, and they let me in. Are you satisfied now?"

No. She had a million other questions. "Yes," she lied.

"Good. Now let's talk about you."

Riya reluctantly recounted her days — about the problem she'd run into getting the key that would lead her down to the quarry to find the details the Ravens needed.

"So you have nothing," Varun said when she finished.

Riya bristled. "I'm working on it."

"How, exactly?" He raked his eyes up and down her body. "Dressing in fancy clothes and wasting our tax money?"

Riya's fingers twitched, and she tamped down the violent impulses rising within her. "You sent me here. You told me to come back and find the magic. I'm *working on it.*"

She didn't wait for his response before she yanked open the door and stormed out. He caught up with her a few aisles over.

"Riya, wait. I didn't mean —" Varun's fingers snaked around her forearm, pulling her back toward him. Riya, caught off guard, slammed into his chest. The faintest scent of tulsi lingered in the air as she tilted her head back in surprise. Varun towered over her, his mouth parted in matching shock. His dark eyes met hers, swirling with some strangely overwhelming emotion she couldn't name.

He leaned forward.

There was a gasp. They spun around to see Archana, Preethi, and Indra in the aisle right behind them, their eyes wide.

Riya yanked her arm out of Varun's grip and stepped away from him, smoothing her kurta. "We were looking something up," she blurted.

Preethi nodded. "Right."

"Anyway," Riya said brightly. "I should go."

She turned and calmly walked through the library, ignoring the fact that her heart was racing as if she'd run the whole way. The girls caught up to her halfway to her room. "Riya, wait!"

"I didn't know," Preethi said earnestly.

"What?"

"About you and the scholar!"

Riya stared at them, bewildered. And then she realized how it must have looked, her hand in Varun's, standing close enough for their chests to touch. She could feel her face flush. "It's not like that —"

"It makes so much sense now," Preethi went on. "The way he was looking at you. The way *you* were looking at him. Did you meet him in Adhura?"

"Wait, did he come here so he could be closer to you?" Indra asked.

Riya's mind was still reeling. It was basically the truth, and it wasn't as if she could tell them why he was really there, so she just nodded.

"That's so romantic!" Archana was practically swooning. "Pree! Give her your bangle."

"Oh, yes!" Preethi yanked a bangle off her arm and thrust it at Riya. "We'll have the palace mayaka make you one, but for now you can use mine."

"Bangle?" Riya asked with a blank stare.

Preethi winked. "Love letter."

Riya jerked back. *"What?"*

Indra held it out so Riya could get a closer look. Magic emanated from the silver bangle in waves, making the pads of her fingers tingle. There were grooves in the metal, small enough to look like a simple pattern, but there was something strange about them . . .

"Are these letters?"

"Yes!" Indra said excitedly. "You paint over it with some ink and roll it across some paper to reveal the message." Indra pointed to three notches on the underside of the bangle. "Those indicate how many turns you do. Three notches means the letters will change three times."

"We all have them," Archana explained. "It was Indra's idea."

"Neha's actually," Indra corrected. "We used it for months to secretly communicate before we told people."

Riya couldn't handle this. Love letters? Magical bangles? It was all so frivolous and wasteful, and she desperately wanted the conversation to end.

"Thanks," she said, snatching the bangle out of Indra's hand and stuffing it into the pocket of her lehenga with absolutely no intention of ever using it.

✳

When Riya returned to her room, a note was waiting for her. It had been slipped under her door, written on heavy paper and stamped with the maharani's red wax seal. Riya opened it and scanned the contents.

Vira was inviting her to dinner. Apparently her sister had finally remembered her existence.

Riya tossed the note onto the nearest table and collapsed on the divan, pressing the heels of her palms into her eyes, not caring that it was likely smearing the kaajal. Varun was in the palace, watching over her, and that complicated everything. She needed to find a way into the quarries fast and get out quickly.

She could feel the bangle pressing into the side of her thigh, and she pulled it out. The idea that she and Varun would ever exchange love letters was truly laughable, but she couldn't deny it was clever to use something so innocuous to trade messages. Of course people in the palace would have such a brilliant idea and then waste it on romance and gossip.

She sat up as a knock sounded at her door. She wanted to ignore it, but there was a guard stationed outside, so whoever was there would know that she was in fact inside. She forced herself to answer.

"Ronak?"

He stood on the other side, looking uncomfortable. "Can I come in?" His hair was curling around his neck, still wet from a recent bath. She stepped aside to let him in. He scanned her room much the way she'd done to his. There wasn't much to see; she'd left it largely impersonal, the same as it had been years earlier. "I need your help," he said.

Riya's eyebrows shot up. "What happened to 'Whatever it is you came back to do, leave me out of it'?"

"I . . . I might have been a little hasty."

Riya's brows rose. Ronak didn't admit mistakes, ever. "Apologies usually include the word *sorry* in them somewhere."

"I'm sorry," he ground out. An awkward silence lingered between them, and then he cleared his throat. "I need you to steal something for me. It's a dagger. It would be in Vira's room."

Riya blinked at him. "You want me to steal from Vira?"

"Isn't that what you already do?"

"So it's all right to be a rebel as long as it works in your favor, is that it?"

His jaw tightened. "Are you interested or not?"

Her eyes landed on Vira's invitation. "Maybe. Why do you want this dagger?"

"That doesn't concern you."

Riya eyed him. He was desperate enough to come to her, which meant she could ask him for something in return. "Your chain," she said. "That's my price."

She held her breath, but he didn't look surprised. "Fine. Is this what you came back for?"

"I told you," Riya said. "I came for family." That wasn't a lie. They just happened to be talking about different families.

"Right. Then why haven't you gone to see Kaleb?"

"That's irrelevant."

"You can't pick and choose what's relevant, Riya. No, I think you haven't seen him because you knew you couldn't lie to him. You'd have to tell him about the Ravens. Tell him that you're not intending to stay."

Riya said nothing, hating that he was right — that he'd found the one thing she didn't want to face.

"It's probably a good thing," Ronak said. "It would probably break his heart to learn where you went."

"Stop it, Ronak."

He didn't turn around. "Once I have the dagger, you'll have your chain." The door slammed shut behind him.

Riya exhaled. All she had to do was steal a weapon, and she'd have access to the quarry. Varun would leave her alone, and she could finally leave the fort once and for all.

CHAPTER TWENTY

— VIRA —

VIRA ANXIOUSLY PACED the length of her private dining room. Riya was late.

She'd intended to see Riya as soon as she'd returned, but things kept coming up. Harish's body. Negotiations with Preethi's father, the Viceroy of Ishvat, who'd arrived in the palace two days earlier. Another protest in Dvar. It was only now, a week after Riya's arrival, that Vira had a free night to dine with her sister. Except it seemed that her sister wasn't coming.

There was a knock at the door. Vira lunged for the handle. But it wasn't Riya. It was Amrit.

"Sorry for interrupting."

"You're not interrupting anything." She threw open the door. "You might as well join me. She's not coming."

"Give her time," Amrit said.

Vira doubted that time would change much. "What is it?" she asked. Amrit didn't visit her room unless there was something important she needed to know.

He had a grim look on his face. "The piece of the map in the library is gone."

"What? How can it be gone?"

Hardly anyone knew it was there — and no one except the two of them knew she had another piece.

"The librarian didn't see anyone in the area," Amrit said. "I'm having my guards look into it. Discreetly of course."

Only a handful of people had access to that special room. Members of the Council. Ronak. But Ronak had no interest in Papa's treasure hunts, and the Council had made it perfectly clear that they thought the Ivory Key was nothing but a foolish fantasy. But one of them had the piece of the map. And they weren't exactly people who could be searched easily without alerting the entire palace to what Vira was looking for.

Panic clawed at her throat. She'd been so close to the Ivory Key — to find a way to protect Ashoka forever. "Maybe I should have taken Surya's deal," Vira said. "He could have led us directly to the last piece by now."

"No," Amrit said. "You did the right thing. We can't trust him."

"But now I'm out a map piece," Vira snapped. She exhaled. It wasn't Amrit's fault. He didn't deserve her anger. "I'm sorry. It's just —"

"I know." He held out the necklace to her — the one with the lotus pendant that she'd lent to him to access the secret room in the library. Vira took it from him, fumbling with the clasp when he stepped behind her, saying, "Let me."

Vira felt oddly self-conscious as she swept her hair to one side, feeling his fingers brush against the back of her neck.

"Sorry I'm —" Riya burst into the room, then stopped as she saw Amrit. "Late."

Vira felt Amrit step away as he bowed respectfully to Riya. "I was just leaving, Rajkumaari." He gave Vira a reassuring smile. She could read the meaning behind it as if he'd spoken aloud. *Enjoy dinner. I'll handle this.*

But how could she relax when her only means of protecting Ashoka was slipping through her fingers?

"A bit young to be a captain, isn't he?" Riya asked, looking in the direction of the door.

Vira pursed her lips. "Where were you? You're half an hour late."

"I lost track of time. I'm sorry."

"Doing what?"

"I was with friends," Riya said. "It's been a week, Vira. I'm sorry I'm not sitting around waiting for you to decide I'm important enough to make time for."

Friends. Vira felt an unexpected pang of jealousy. It had been a long time since she'd had friends.

"Oh." She sat down and reached for a tumbler of water. "Well . . . I'm glad you're adjusting to being back." The words sounded stiff to her own ears.

Riya dropped into the seat across from her. "Why'd you ask me to come here?"

"To talk. To see how you were settling in."

"I don't mean *here*. I mean the palace."

Vira frowned. "Because you're my sister, and I want us to be a family again."

"Family? Vira, you didn't tell Ronak you found me. You didn't tell me Ronak was engaged to Preethi. You say you want me here, but you spent the whole week ignoring me."

"Because I was busy," Vira said defensively. "I'm the maharani, Riya. I have a whole country to think about."

"That's exactly what Amma used to say."

Because she was the maharani, too, Vira wanted to snap. But she held her tongue as she rang for their meal. "Let's eat."

They sat in silence as the maidservants appeared with platters of rice tossed with jeera and peas, kadhi with fried onion pakoras, slow-roasted eggplant cooked in a spiced tomato sauce.

"And what about Kaleb?" Riya asked after the maidservants left. "How could you imprison him, Vira? He's family, too."

Vira couldn't look her in the eyes. "I don't expect you to understand."

"How could you ever believe he'd have anything to do with Amma's —"

"It has nothing to do with that." It wasn't about his guilt or innocence. It had been a calculated move — one that was necessary for the people to maintain trust in her leadership. There was proof, even if Kaleb claimed it was manufactured. And she felt guilty over her decision every day. "I don't want to talk about this."

"I thought you invited me here *to* talk," Riya said.

"You don't know what it's like to be in my shoes, Riya. The decisions and choices I'm faced with every day. It's easy for you to sit there and tell me you'd have done things differently. You don't have to worry about keeping an entire country safe."

"I *do* know," Riya said. "Because I've been doing it. Half the citizens in Dvar would starve if not for the Ravens."

"The Ravens are thieves," Vira spat. "You can delude yourself into believing your cause is noble, but you're criminals."

Riya scoffed. "I thought you'd be different. You *promised* you'd be different. But you're just like Amma. You dress exactly like her. You talk exactly like her. And it's all the same empty promises and lie after lie."

"Stop it, Riya," Vira snapped, hating the way the words cut into her. "How can you sit there and act like Amma and Papa didn't give you *everything* in the world? Do you know how distraught Amma was when you were gone?"

"Then why did she tell the world I died?"

Vira exhaled, frustrated. She wanted to start the night over. She'd asked the cooks to prepare all of Riya's favorite dishes, and they hadn't even touched the food.

What would Amrit say? *Try to see it from her perspective.*

"Maybe it was a mistake," Vira blurted out. "Maybe . . . maybe Amma was wrong to tell the world you'd died. Even if she really thought she was protecting you. But you were wrong too, Riya. You can't just run away from your problems — or because you didn't like something Amma did. Amma and Papa weren't like other parents — you have to know that. They had bigger problems to worry about, and they did the best they could with us."

Riya looked at her sharply. "Did they, though?"

"I have to believe that," Vira said.

"Maybe if they were better parents, we wouldn't be like this." Riya stood up. "I'm going to go wash my hands."

Vira opened her mouth to say that she'd had the cooks make rasmalai, but Riya was already walking toward the basin in the adjoining room. She came back a few minutes later, declined dessert, and left without another word.

✳

Amrit's note came ten minutes after Riya left. Vira recognized his handwriting at once, much neater than hers, with his letters slanting slightly to the right.

Meet me in the training arena. Eleven o'clock.

It had been a long while since they'd trained the way they used to. It had been a long while since Vira had trained at all. She glanced up at the talwar — her old talwar, mounted on the wall. She hadn't touched her mother's weapon either, not since that day in the forest. Amrit had often told her that she had different strengths, but every time she looked at it, it reminded her that this was yet another way that she failed to live up to her mother's reputation.

But part of her wanted the distraction — wanted something else to worry about. Her dinner with Riya hadn't gone well, and the weight of Riya's judgment loomed over her.

The fort was practically empty when she made her way down. There was something magical about seeing the grounds like this, after the rest of the palace had gone to sleep, when the noises of nature weren't washed away by the bustle of crowds.

Amrit was already there when she arrived, bathed in the glowing light of the lanterns that surrounded the arena, surveying the weapons in the cabinet. He glanced at her over his shoulder and flashed a grin that sent a flash of nerves through her. He pulled a talwar from the wall and handed it to her, hilt first.

"Maybe we should practice with the wooden swords first," Vira said. This was too fast. She'd thought she'd have more time to think, to prepare.

"Those are training weapons."

"Is that not what we're doing here?" she asked mildly.

But Amrit only gave her a knowing look. "The longer you stay away, the worse the fear becomes."

Maybe he had a point. She took the talwar. It was lighter than her own, plain and impersonal. Maybe she could wield it. She slashed it through the air, testing the weight.

"We'll start easy," Amrit said, holding up a shield.

Vira lost count of how long she practiced these basic, mindless drills, striking the small shield in Amrit's hand as if she were a child again. But there was something comforting about that, too. And when the drills were over, it was almost easy to step back into sparring.

Amrit tossed the shield to the ground and stood before her, weaponless.

"No talwar?" she asked.

"Not today." He grinned again and cracked his neck.

Vira frowned, and then it dawned on her: today was about getting her used to wielding a talwar again. Her heart tripped. That had always been his strength — meeting her where she was, adapting his teaching methods to suit her needs.

"Ready?" Amrit asked.

Vira didn't answer. Instead she spun and slashed, the metal arcing through the air. Amrit ducked easily, stepping out of the way as she went in for a second attack. They went back and forth — with her striking and Amrit ducking and weaving out of reach, as if he could predict just where and how she'd strike next.

"Break the rhythm," Amrit reminded her.

Right. It was easy to fall into a rhythm, almost like a choreographed dance. But you landed strikes when you broke the pattern.

"You're thinking too much," Amrit said. "Clear your mind."

And then he was on the offense. He kicked, aiming for her head. Vira dodged his leg — but not his fist, which went straight for the hand with her blade. But she was prepared. She loosened her grip on the weapon. Instead of the talwar going flying as he'd intended, it dropped right into her waiting left hand. Vira spun around, putting distance between them again. She grinned, tossing the weapon back into her right hand.

"Good," Amrit said. Despite the full hour they'd been doing this, he'd barely broken a sweat.

Vira felt ragged in comparison, panting as she wiped away the hair that had fallen out of her braid. "Again."

This time she struck first. A kick to the shoulder to throw his balance off. As he jerked back, she slashed her talwar upward through the air. Amrit was quick enough to dodge the blade — but his kurta wasn't so lucky. It ripped, gaping open at an odd angle. But before Vira could apologize, he threw a punch. Vira ducked his fist, spinning around to attack low from the side. Amrit blocked her. She turned back the other way, cutting down at an angle — but he stopped her again, grabbing her wrist. And this time he was successful in disarming her. Vira's talwar fell to the floor as she staggered back, panting.

Amrit grinned as he ripped the kurta fully, dropping the tattered cloth on the ground and kicking it off to the side. He picked up her talwar and held it out to her. "Again."

But Vira was frozen, staring at his shirtless torso. She'd seen them before, his scars, but it had been months, and the sight caught her off guard. Flickering light filtered into the arena, dancing golden over his dark skin.

Vira was no stranger to scars, but these had always been more than that. The burn on his forearm. The pale thin line that wrapped around his upper arm like a bangle. A grotesque knife wound that sliced over his ribs and down into his stomach. On his shoulder were four matching puncture wounds, like a bite mark. They were all from different weapons, different times.

When she dragged her eyes back up, his eyes were dark. "You've seen them before."

Vira swallowed, taking an involuntary step toward him. "You never told me how you got any of them."

"You can ask," Amrit said, his voice rough. He let go of the talwar. It landed on the ground between them.

She could. But would he tell her the truth? Her eyes trailed down to the burn mark—and his followed. She could see the way his jaw tensed, the way his gaze shuttered even before she said anything. "How'd you get that one on your shoulder?"

"One of my brothers." Amrit ran his fingers over the marks softly, almost lovingly.

"He . . . bit you?" Vira asked, mildly horrified.

Amrit laughed, though it wasn't remotely funny. "No. He hit me with a bagh nakh."

Vira's horror only grew. It was called a tiger's claw for a reason, and it was a favorite weapon of northwestern assassins. They'd been outlawed for centuries. "On purpose?"

Amrit frowned thoughtfully. "You know, I never asked."

Vira stared, aghast, not sure if he was joking. What kind of relationship had he had with his brothers exactly? She and her siblings certainly had their share of childhood scuffles and scrapes—pranks gone too far, competitions taken a violent turn—but they'd never done anything to purposely hurt one another. Or maybe it was just that they had learned to do their wounding verbally, eviscerating one another with sharp blows to the soul, unearthing weaknesses like rare gems to treasure and hoard—and ultimately exploit.

"This one"—he pointed to the thin scar around his upper arm—"is from an urumi." A highly dangerous flexible blade that the wielder treated like a whip. "And this"—he lifted his pant leg to show a dark scar on his calf where it looked like part of his flesh had been gouged out—"is from an aruval." A hooked blade popular in the southern provinces of Ashoka. "Well . . . a snakebite, *then* the aruval."

Vira gaped at him. "Are those all from your brothers?"

"No." But he didn't elaborate.

"Oh." She stood there for a moment, not knowing what to say before stepping back and putting distance between them. Amrit picked up the talwar and held it out to her.

"Again."

CHAPTER TWENTY-ONE

— RONAK —

WHEN RIYA ASKED Ronak to meet her in one of the suites in the eastern wing, she'd neglected to mention that she was actually inviting him to a party. Ronak heard the music echoing through the halls even before he approached the door, realizing too late that the very room Riya had specified in her note was the one it was coming from.

He lingered outside, feeling a wave of discomfort wash over him. He shouldn't have been surprised. After all, the people who resided here were the bored children of councilors who had too much money and not enough oversight. And with additional guests already arriving for his engagement, it was only expected that there would be entertainment.

But it had been a long time since Ronak attended one of these informal gatherings, and he felt wildly out of his depth.

Just get the dagger and leave, he told himself. It would take no more than five minutes, and he could be on his way to see Ekta.

He took a deep breath and pushed open the door. Ronak's eyes immediately found the raised dais in the center, where someone was belting out a drunken tune better suited to a bawdy tavern than the palace, accompanied by a number of mismatched instruments. It was someone's living area, but the space had been cleared and all furniture shunted off to the sides. Groups of people in exquisitely designed sherwanis and lehengas sat in divans clustered around the musicians, sipping drinks from copper tumblers and tapping their feet to the music. Others lingered off to the sides of the room, conversing over the din or loitering around tables piled high with snacks and sweets. Only a few lanterns were lit, leaving the vast majority of the room shrouded in darkness and lending it an air of intimacy despite the crowd.

He cast his eyes around for any sign of Riya, and not finding her, he made his way toward an adjoining room. As he walked through the arched doorway, a girl walking in the opposite direction knocked into his shoulder.

"Oh, sorry," she said — and then her eyes widened. "Rajkumaara!" She bowed clumsily.

"It's all right," Ronak said even as he saw heads turn in their direction. He'd hoped to avoid notice, but everyone would know he was here within minutes.

The second room was quieter and just as dimly lit, with more divans clustered around low tables. A quick scan showed that Riya wasn't here either, but he spotted Jay in a dark corner, a drink in his hand, laughing at something someone beside him was saying. Ronak sighed in relief.

"Thank the goddesses," Ronak said, dropping into the seat beside him. He felt Jay stiffen as he swiped his drink. "I was —"

Ronak froze. The two other people seated across from Jay were Preethi and her friend Indra.

An awkward silence fell over the table as Ronak downed the remainder of Jay's tadi in one go. Palm wine wasn't nearly as potent as Lyrian grape wine, but Ronak was grateful for the sour taste of it.

Jay cleared his throat. "I, uh, didn't expect to see you here," he said.

Ronak kept his gaze on the empty tumbler. "Riya asked me to meet her here."

"Well, you know Riya," Preethi said, laughing a little. "She's never on time."

"She'll be here soon," Indra added.

There was another uncomfortable pause. Ronak bit the inside of his cheek. He didn't want to stay there, but if he left, he would only be inviting strangers to come talk to him about Vira or the Council or the engagement.

Ronak looked up as Preethi rested her elbows on the table and leaned forward, a dazzling smile on her lips. "Jay tells me you're an artist. I can't say I remember that about you."

Jay talks too much was what he wanted to say. Instead he plastered a vapid smile on his face. "It's a more recent hobby," he said, glancing around the room once more for any sign of his sister. "Do you paint?"

"Not at all, but perhaps you can teach me sometime?"

"I'm going to get a refill," Jay said, abruptly standing.

"I'll come—" Ronak started to say, but Jay had already disappeared into the crowd.

"Oh, I see Neha," Indra said, eyes brightening. "I'll be right back." She also rose, holding up the skirts of her lehenga as she crossed the room toward her fiancée.

Ronak turned back to find Preethi watching him. "You don't want to get married," she said.

Ronak's brows rose in surprise. He hadn't expected her to broach the topic directly. "No," he admitted. "But that's a general stance," he clarified. "It has nothing to do with you specifically."

"I didn't think it did." She looked amused. "But it's your duty as a raj-kumaara."

"It is."

"So I propose we make the best of it."

Despite himself, Ronak was intrigued. "What do you mean?"

"You have no interest in politics," she said, her voice even. "I do. I'll take your seat on the Council as the Viceroy of Dvar, and you'll be free to live your life just as you do now."

Ronak laughed dryly. "Except that we'll be married."

She met his gaze squarely. "Ronak, I have no illusions about us falling in love. We're different people with different lives. That doesn't need to change. But we were friends once, weren't we?"

He turned away. It wasn't a bad offer, and if he intended to stay, he would have considered it. But he didn't.

"Pree—"

"Think about it," she insisted. "You don't have to say anything now."

He exhaled. "All right," he promised, even though his answer wouldn't change.

"There you are," Riya said, approaching Ronak. She stopped when she saw Preethi across from him, her brows furrowing in confusion.

"Took you long enough," Ronak said, standing. "Come on."

"What were you doing with Preethi?" Riya asked as she followed him into a secured corner behind two wooden screens.

"It wasn't planned. Do you have it?"

She withdrew the dagger, which she'd tucked into the waistband of her lehenga, carefully draping her dupatta so it hid the weapon. It was just as ostentatious as he expected, covered in gemstones and doused in magic. He shoved it into his pocket.

"Your turn," she prompted.

Ronak pulled the gold chain over his head and dropped it into her waiting palm.

"Be careful," Ronak couldn't help but say as Riya walked away. "Whatever you're doing with that. Just . . . be careful."

She looked at him over her shoulder. "I can take care of myself."

"Right."

Ronak rubbed the back of his neck as she walked away. It already felt bare, but he would get used to that soon enough. It wasn't as if he would be needing the keys to the palace for much longer. All he had to do was deliver the dagger to Ekta, and he would be free.

✳

The night was surprisingly warm, which meant that Spit Street smelled worse than normal. Out of the corner of his eye Ronak could see a figure lying on the ground. He quickened his pace, telling himself it was someone who had fallen asleep after too much to drink. It wasn't another dead body.

"Slow down," Jay muttered.

Walk fast, but not too fast. Make eye contact, but not too often. Be confident, but not too much. Those were the rules on Spit Street: never be *too* anything.

The dagger burned in Ronak's pocket, knocking against the side of his leg as he walked. He'd rushed to his room to examine it moments after Riya had given it to him, but his elation had been short-lived. It had taken him only a few minutes to open the hilt of the dagger, just as Ekta had instructed. But there was nothing inside. The small thread of hope he'd clung to — that Vira didn't know what the dagger was — vanished. Vira had discovered the piece of the map and was keeping it elsewhere.

He'd hurled the dagger at the door, but it had done little to help, aside from making a dent in the wood. Ekta wouldn't pay him if he didn't deliver both pieces, and there was no way Vira would give up hers.

"Ronak, I said slow down!" Jay hissed. "What's wrong with you?"

Ronak shook his hand off. "Nothing."

"It's not nothing," Jay said, grabbing Ronak by the shoulder.

"I'm fine." A piece of paper — that was all that stood between him and freedom. Between him and an arranged marriage he didn't want. And now that was gone too.

"Pull yourself together before you get us killed. We just need to buy some time."

But time was the one thing they didn't have.

Ronak forced himself to take a deep breath. And then another. "I'm fine," he repeated.

Jay scanned his face and then pulled away, looking serious. "You better let me handle Ekta."

✳

Ekta sat at the same table as the last time, nursing a goblet of wine. This time she was alone. And this time she wore a bright red sari draped over a long-sleeved lace blouse. A heavy choker of rubies encircled her throat. She still wore the assortment of rings on her fingers, but today she'd added a simple gold bangle — a two-headed snake coiled around her slender wrist. The bright color of her dress caught Ronak by surprise, but perhaps it shouldn't have. After all, in nature, red was the color of danger.

"Boys," she drawled, looking up from beneath long black lashes as they approached. "I thought maybe you weren't going to come back."

Ronak didn't know if that was her idea of a joke, but he didn't dare laugh.

"We have a map piece," Jay said, pulling it out of his pocket and unfolding it. He'd taken it from Ronak outside the tavern. He set it down, and all Ronak could think was that it looked so strange on this table in the middle of a tavern, when it hadn't been taken out of its glass case for hundreds of years.

"*A piece?*" Ekta used her index finger to drag the scrap toward her. "You were supposed to bring me two."

"We hit a snag," Jay said, crossing his arms. "We need more time to get it."

Ekta looked up sharply. "A snag?"

"The maharani has it in her personal chambers," Jay clarified. Ronak hadn't wanted to tell her that, but Jay had argued that Ekta wouldn't grant them any leeway if they didn't have a compelling reason for the delay.

"That doesn't sound like much of an issue." Ekta speared Ronak with her gaze. "Seeing as she's your sister."

Ronak's heart stopped. She couldn't know who he really was. This changed *every*thing.

The amusement on Ekta's face made the hair on the back of his neck stand on end. "It's your fingers," she said. "They're too clean to be a servant's. And you are not as clever as you think."

"We just need another week," Jay said.

"No," Ekta said, sliding the piece of the map back toward them. "We're making a new deal. You're going to get the Ivory Key for me instead."

"What?" Ronak asked, unable to hide his shock.

"Word on the street is that the mercenary who killed Lord Harish was hired by the Kamala Society. I have no intention of attracting their attention. I imagine that once she has the final piece of the map, your sister intends to follow it to the key. So you will give this to your maharani. You will make sure you're on this expedition. You will find the Ivory Key. And then you will bring it to me."

Ronak stared at her. "You cannot be serious." This was not what he had signed up for. It was, in fact, the exact opposite of what he needed, which was to get *away* from his family. He had no desire to follow in Papa's tragic footsteps as a failed treasure hunter.

Ekta rose, and Ronak was struck by her imposing height. The pleats of the sari pooled at her feet like spilled blood. Ronak stood rooted to the spot, his face inches from hers. She smelled of amber and jasmine and something else — a sickly sweet, intoxicating scent that burned through Ronak's nose. She grabbed his chin, her nails digging into his skin as she lifted his face.

"You," she said, "are in no position to negotiate. Do you think it was a coincidence that you came to me? Do you think your friend simply stumbled onto my name when I take so much care to hide it?" Her amusement grew. "I needed a fail-safe in case Harish didn't deliver on his end of the bargain. I know where to find you. I know who you care about. And you can be certain that if you don't get me what I want, I will make sure that your brother meets a fate far worse than anything you can imagine."

There was nothing but promise in her gaze, and fear flashed through Ronak. His brain stopped working, and all he could think about was Kaleb, needing to protect Kaleb, needing to keep him away from Ekta at all costs.

"We need —" Jay began to say, but Ronak cut him off.

"I'll do it." Jay glared at him, but Ronak ignored him. "I'll do it. I'll bring you the key."

CHAPTER TWENTY-TWO

— RIYA —

THE EASIEST WAY to access the quarry was through the old mayaka lab that Papa had used. Riya waited until midnight, made sure that Ronak's chain was carefully hidden in her pocket, and slipped out of her room. She clung to the shadows as she made her way across the full length of the palace to the southern wing.

She hesitated as she walked past the library. The scholars' sleeping quarters were just around the corner. Varun would be furious that she'd gone to the quarry without him, but she didn't particularly feel like seeing him just then. Besides, this was *her* mission for the Ravens. She didn't have to involve him just because he'd taken it upon himself to spy on her.

The mayaka who'd replaced Papa had relocated her workshop to the eastern wing, wanting to be closer to the clientele she served, so when Riya pushed open the door to the workshop, everything was covered with cloth sheets. But she could still see Papa's handprints all over the carved wooden animals on the supply shelves, the faint smell of neem and salt water in the air, the paintings of famed historical cities on the walls. There was a time she'd practically lived in this room, finishing assignments for her tutors in the back while Papa and Kaleb tinkered with magic.

The door to the quarry was hidden behind one of the shelves that spanned from floor to ceiling. She couldn't remember exactly where the mechanism to open it was, so she had to search two shelves before she found the tiny lever. She pressed it, and the cabinet slid smoothly to one side, revealing a metal door.

Riya took a deep breath and pulled out the chain, using the magical key to unlock the door. She pushed it open.

Cold air washed over her as she stepped out onto what looked to be a platform. Magical lamps flared to life, lighting a path all the way down into cavernous depths. On one side were stacks of heavy white kurtas and dupattas — specialized to protect miners from raw magic poisoning. Riya grabbed the set at the top and pulled them on, wrapping the thick dupatta around her head to protect her face.

On the other side of the platform was a small carriage that she recognized from one of Papa's old books. Kaleb had once tried to explain the mechanics of the contraption — the cables and pulleys and magic used to lower people to the quarry. She'd never understood it, but she stepped inside and pulled the lever. The carriage lowered slowly. Riya gripped the side tightly, looking over the edge — but she saw nothing but endless rows of magical lights.

The carriage finally stopped, depositing her inside a cave. She disembarked, looking around in confusion. To one side was an office, with a desk and bookshelves that contained rows and rows of ledgers. Riya pulled the newest ledger off the shelf and flipped through the pages. There was nothing about the transportation of raw magic, but she paused as she saw employment records. There were only eight mayaka miners currently working in the quarry.

She stared at the number, wondering if she'd misread it somehow — or if there were accounts missing. Papa had told her that miners came into the quarries only twice a week, to limit exposure to raw magic. Anything longer, and they'd start experiencing side effects. If there were only eight miners, they'd be coming in almost every day. It didn't make sense. How were these miners not sick? Why hadn't the Council hired more?

She reached for other ledgers from previous years. Last year, there had been twenty-four miners. The year before, sixty-three. But these numbers were still far fewer than the hundreds she remembered from her childhood.

Riya stowed the books and walked deeper into the cave. Though she'd never been allowed to visit as a child, Papa had shown her drawings of the quarries. She walked through the large cave, searching for the ladders and explosives and tools used by miners to unearth the magic. Where was everything? And where was all the gold magic glittering within the rock?

She hesitantly lowered the dupatta. She couldn't feel any magic.

She made her way to a second cave — and a third. But there was still no magic, no tools. It wasn't until she approached the fifth chamber that Riya heard anything at all — voices. She froze. She hadn't expected anyone to be here past midnight, but as she inched closer, she could see two miners sitting on the floor with their backs against the rock. One of them had a ball that she was aimlessly tossing against the opposite wall. Neither of them wore the protective gear Riya had put on.

"This is the last time, Sana, I swear," one of the girls was saying.

"You always say that, Kamini," Sana said. "But next week you'll beg one of the others to take your shift."

Kamini sighed. "Honestly, I don't even know why they bother sending us here. It's not like there's any magic left."

The words pierced Riya's lungs like shards of ice. *What?*

"Kamini!" The other girl's voice was sharp.

"Sorry," she muttered. "I know I shouldn't complain, but I didn't spend all those years training to be a mayaka to just sit here."

"It's a job, and we get paid well," Sana snapped. "It's more than a lot of people have these days."

They continued talking, but Riya stopped listening.

It wasn't true. It couldn't be true. Maybe she'd heard wrong.

But . . . in her heart Riya knew that it was.

This was how Lyria had been able to invade Ritsar. And this was why Vira was raising taxes: to pay for troops at the borders. This was why the people of Ashoka were suffering — and why Vira wasn't doing anything about it.

Pain tore through her heart — followed by anger. There was no magic left, and Vira had kept it from people. Everything Riya had fought for was for nothing.

✳

Riya paced the hallway outside Vira's room, waiting for her sister. She had no idea when Vira would even be back, but after spending the morning seething in her room, Riya couldn't stand to stay there any longer.

She could have gone straight to Varun — to the Ravens. In fact, she'd mentally composed about eighty different notes to them. But every time she sat down to put the words into ink, she'd backed out.

I just need to hear it from Vira, she told herself. Then she'd go to the Ravens.

She had turned to walk back down the hallway when she saw her sister approaching.

Vira paused. "Riya?" She opened her door. "What are you doing here?"

"Is it true?" Riya followed Vira inside.

"What?"

"Is. It. True?" Riya demanded. "Ashoka has no magic?"

"Riya!" Vira slammed the door shut. "What's the matter with you?" she hissed.

"Oh, good. At least it's not just me you're lying to."

Vira pursed her lips. "Your friends have big mouths."

"My friends have nothing to do with this. Did you really think you could keep this from me?"

"Of course not." Vira made her way to the vanity, yanking off her rings and bangles, depositing them on a small golden plate.

"Magic doesn't disappear overnight, Vira. You must have known about this for months." Riya met her sister's gaze in the mirror. "Don't you ever get tired of all the lies? All the deception?"

"That's enough, Riya." Vira closed her eyes and breathed deeply before turning around. "Listen to me. You have every right to be angry, but you don't understand the full picture."

"I understand enough."

"Telling the truth will result in chaos," Vira said.

"That's ridiculous."

"Is it? Think about it, Riya. People will be fighting, trying to hoard what little magic is left. Our country will be under siege, armies running through our streets, looking to take the last of the magic that remains."

"And you think the same won't happen when the magic does run out?"

"I have a plan to fix it." Vira turned back to the mirror and pulled off her earrings. "I'm going to get the Ivory Key. And then I'm going to find the lost quarries."

"The Ivory Key?" Riya's surprise morphed into irritation as she realized that Vira was serious. "That's not a plan, Vira. That's a fantasy. You saw what it did to Papa."

"It's not the same. I found another piece of the map."

That silenced Riya. She gaped at her sister.

Vira rose from the vanity. "And I have a lead on the last piece."

"Really?"

Vira had actually done it. She'd found the rest of the map that Papa had devoted his whole life searching for.

"Ashoka is built on magic," Vira said, walking toward Riya. "We can invent a new currency or do without magical trinkets, but we can't survive without magic in our weapons and borders. What else would you have me do, Riya?"

"Not this!"

Vira hesitated. "You could come with me. We could find the key together."

"No," Riya said. Papa's obsession had consumed him, and Riya had sworn long ago that she wouldn't let it do the same to her. She'd thought Vira felt the same when she'd locked away Papa's maps and journals after he died.

"Remember our treasure hunts?" Vira asked, a pleading edge to her voice. "Papa would give us riddles and puzzles and we'd run around the fort trying to find the next clue."

"You mean *I'd* run around the fort," Riya corrected, "while you sat in your room hoarding the clues."

"We always made a formidable team. We beat the boys every year."

"Because Kaleb isn't competitive and Ronak's a sore loser." Riya shook her head. "This isn't the same thing, Vira. If we fail, we don't lose toys. We lose a country."

"Then we don't fail."

"It's not —"

"Riya, I've considered this from every angle. This is the only way." Vira stood in front of her, taking Riya's hands in hers. "Come with me. Help me."

Riya searched Vira's face. "And what will you do with the magic when you find the key?"

Vira shrugged. "We can figure that out later."

"There *is* no later. Don't you get it, Vira? People are *dying*."

"You think I don't know that?" Vira's eyes suddenly widened, as though she were struck with a realization. "Wait. That's why you came back, isn't it? What was your plan? Steal magic from the quarry and return to the Ravens? What were you going to do with it?"

Guilt flashed across Riya's face before she could stop it. She looked away. "We were going to make more coins," she admitted. "So at least a few people would have something after your tax collectors came around."

Vira laughed. "That's absurd, Riya. If it were as easy as putting more coins into circulation, don't you think we'd have done it? Don't you think *Amma* would have done it?"

"How could we have known?" Riya demanded. "All we see are people losing jobs, people starving. We see a maharani who stopped trade, who keeps raising taxes."

Vira smiled humorlessly. "You think I wouldn't jump at the chance to tell people the truth? That I like people questioning my judgment? Calling me a rakshasi and protesting in the streets? But a maharani doesn't always get to do what she wants."

Riya had vacillated between disbelief and anger since she'd visited the quarry. She'd come here expecting Vira to deny the claims. She'd expected to fight her sister — to have Vira confirm what Riya had always known: that the maharani and her Council were greedy, that they were hoarding resources, indifferent to the suffering outside the fort.

But that image was so far from the truth. And Riya had no idea how to process it.

Vira watched her carefully. "You want more magic, Riya? There's none for you here. But there might be somewhere else."

✳

Riya sat on a jhoola in the rose garden behind the palace, letting the wooden plank rock her back and forth. She'd loved sitting on the swing as a child, watching the ocean for hours, the fragrance of fresh roses wafting over her. But even the sight of the sea shimmering under the setting sun couldn't quell the turmoil within her.

She'd been certain that the Ravens were making a difference. That once they had the magic they needed, everything would be different. And maybe making coins and magical artifacts would help a few families . . . but what of the rest of Dvar? The rest of Ashoka?

Vira had been right to laugh — it was a foolish plan. And the realization made Riya feel hollow. Two weeks ago she'd known exactly who she was and what she stood for. Now she had no idea.

It was unfair that there weren't any clear-cut answers. That there was no way to know what choice would lead to the outcomes she wanted. As a child, she'd hated it when Amma and Papa had told her what to do; now she wanted nothing more.

She wished she could talk to someone about all this, and it wasn't just anyone she wanted to talk to. It was Kavita. But Kavita still hadn't responded to any of Riya's messages.

Riya turned at the sound of footsteps along the path. Varun was walking toward her, his hands tucked into his pockets, wind blowing hair into his eyes.

"How'd you know I was here?" she asked.

"One of those girls you spend all your time with said you were here."

Of course. She should have guessed. They'd largely left Varun alone after that first day in the library, but they hadn't stopped peppering her with questions about him — his childhood, his hobbies, his scholarly interests. Riya had been bewildered to discover that she couldn't actually answer most of them despite having spent every day with him for nearly two years.

Varun scowled. "You missed our meeting."

They'd agreed to meet in the library every other day to exchange any information they found. Varun spent most of their hour together idly flipping through some old text and telling Riya what a poor job she was doing being a spy. Riya spent it wondering how many gold candlesticks she could hide in his sleeping quarters before someone noticed and fired him for theft.

"I wasn't feeling well," she lied. Truthfully, she'd been avoiding him. She didn't know how to tell him that there was no magic left.

He approached her slowly, his demeanor shifting. If it were anyone else, she might have thought he cared. "Are you all right?" he asked.

Riya bit the inside of her cheek. He wasn't Kavita, but he was a Raven. "Can I ask you something?"

He looked wary, but he sat beside her. "What is it?"

"Why'd you and Yash found the Ravens?"

If he found the question surprising, he didn't show it. "It was the only way we knew to help."

"But it wasn't," Riya pointed out. "Yash told me that your mother housed refugees and immigrants. Why not continue that?"

Varun looked at her sideways and then exhaled, his shoulders relaxing. "Because it always comes down to money. There was never enough for the people who needed it, so we learned to steal it from those who had too much."

"Do you think that's the best way to help?"

"Where is this coming from?"

"I just . . ." She sighed, frustrated. "Never mind."

"I think doing something is always better than doing nothing," Varun said after a moment. "I . . . I don't know if I'll be a Raven forever," he admitted. "But right now, it's a way for me to make a difference in someone's life. Even if it's only a few families."

"But if there was another way?" Riya asked. "Where we could help everyone?"

"Then I'd do that in a heartbeat."

Varun looked so earnest that Riya had to look away. She'd never seen him like this. They sat in silence. She could hear workers setting up a dais for yet another concert — a renowned singer invited to perform for the maharani.

"Have you . . . talked to anyone?" Riya asked, unable to help herself. "Since you've been here?"

Varun's jaw clenched. "You mean Yash?"

Riya frowned. "I meant Kavita." She hesitated and then admitted the whole truth. "We haven't spoken since I left."

Varun studied her. "She's hurt," he said finally. "And probably more than a little angry. Give her time. She won't be upset forever."

"But what if she never forgives me?" Riya blurted out. She looked down, fiddling with the edge of her dupatta. It felt odd being so vulnerable with Varun, of all people, but there was no one else she could talk to about this.

"She will."

"How can you know that?"

"Because I did."

Riya's eyes snapped up, but Varun didn't meet her gaze. She didn't know what to say to that. Their relationship had never been honest or open. They'd fought more than they talked. But sitting here with him, both of them having shared tiny pieces of themselves, it almost felt like they could be friends someday.

CHAPTER TWENTY-THREE

— KALEB —

KALEB HAD ALWAYS loved ciphers. They had been his favorite among the puzzles Papa made them do every year, competing to win some prize or other. They were entirely based on pattern recognition and logic, and it was the one thing Kaleb had always been better at than Riya or Vira.

But it had been years since he'd looked at one, and he was rusty. It was taking him far longer than expected to crack the note Vira had left him with.

qigzbm ovv bevfrkiovr

Nineteen letters. That was all that stood between him and freedom.

He hadn't heard from Vira since the day she'd visited more than a week ago, but he clung to the hope that she would keep her word. Ronak had been cold to him all week, refusing to ask Vira about the nature of their deal and unwilling to accept Kaleb's silence on the matter. But the idea that he'd be able to leave the dungeons at all still felt so tenuous that Kaleb couldn't bear the thought of getting Ronak's hopes up, too.

Kaleb shuffled through the dozens of failed attempts before he found the sheet he was looking for. There were rows and rows of letters. The topmost listed the Ashokan alphabet in order. Below it, the Ashokan alphabet again, but the letters shifted over one position. They continued that way, each subsequent row adding an additional shift until he'd reached the end.

It had been easy to tell that it wasn't a simple substitution. The two *v*'s in a row had seen to that. If they were encoded using a single shift, the two *v*'s would have corresponded to the same letter in the plain text, but no matter how he decoded it, it still remained gibberish.

So Kaleb had moved on to testing polyalphabetic substitutions. Usually there was a keyword, and each letter was encoded using a different shift based on that word. But without knowing the key — or even how long the key was — it was a painfully slow process.

He cracked his neck and adjusted his sitting position before bending over the notes again. His mind kept returning to the same three letters: *ovv*. Papa had always broken his encoded messages in arbitrary places, inserting spaces randomly to throw them off so they could not rely on the number of letters in a word to simply guess the phrase. But what if *ovv* was actually a three-letter word?

Kaleb thought for a moment, and then wrote out *the* right above *ovv*. He worked backward, looking at what shift would have been needed in order to convert *the* to *ovv*.

v to turn *t* into *o*.

o to turn *h* into *v*.

r to turn *e* into *v*.

Kaleb looked at those letters of the potential key — *vor* — and then added in two more letters.

I V O R Y

He laughed in shock, wondering if the key to decrypting the message truly could have been so simple.

qigzbm ovv bevfrkiovr
inside the dwaramatha

Kaleb was staring at the words, shocked that his solution had worked, when he heard footsteps in the hallway.

"You promised you'd stop working so much."

Kaleb jerked up. "Riya?" He scrambled to his feet, not caring as Papa's journal and all his work tumbled to the floor. "You came."

"I'm sorry it took me so long to visit." Riya's voice was heavy with emotion. "You shouldn't be in there. I know you'd *never*—"

Kaleb felt something unknot in him. "It's all right," he said.

She looked so different—but exactly the same in a way. Familiar but changed. It was the way she held herself, he realized. She'd never been shy, but there was a new confidence in her stance: her straight back, her quiet calm, her steady gaze.

He wondered what she saw looking at him now, locked in here.

"Can we sit?" she asked.

She didn't wait for his response before swishing the heavy skirts of her maroon lehenga out of the way and sinking to the floor. Kaleb followed suit on the opposite side of the barrier.

There were a thousand questions he wanted to ask her, but he couldn't stop himself from blurting out the one that had kept him awake at night for months.

"Why didn't you talk to me?" he asked. "Two years ago."

Riya let out a breath of laughter. "You never ask the easy questions, do you?"

Kaleb didn't say anything as he waited for her to find her words.

"I was angry," she said, fiddling with a silver bangle on her left wrist.

"Amma and I had another fight, and things just got out of hand. I think a part of me knew that if I told you, you'd have stopped me."

Riya took a deep breath and then told him about the Ravens — about how she'd found them, why she'd come back, about Vira's offer to look for the Ivory Key. And when she was done, Kaleb told her about everything that had happened since she left. The letters. The imprisonment. Ronak's failed attempts to clear Kaleb's name. His own deal with Vira.

By the time they were done talking, the sun was lower in the sky. A ray of bright orange light filtered in through the high window, forcing Riya to throw a hand up to shield her eyes.

"I still don't get it," he said honestly. "Why the Ravens?"

"I didn't go looking for them specifically," she said. "I just wanted to prove Amma wrong, prove that I could survive outside the fort, live without her. But I couldn't. I had no friends, no money, no food. Another day, and I would have come home. It was pure chance that the Ravens found me." She shook her head, as though she still couldn't believe it. "They took me in and gave me a home. And after learning about how they stole to protect people, I couldn't just come back to the palace and pretend I hadn't seen citizens suffering right outside our doors."

"And what about now?" he asked. "Do you regret coming back?"

Riya laughed again. "I don't know," she admitted. "Maybe? Being here has made me question a lot of things I never expected to."

Kaleb smiled wryly. "I know the feeling."

There was a lot he'd taken for granted. A lot he'd never questioned until he'd been forced to. He'd never been angry with Riya for leaving, but he hadn't understood it either. Kaleb hadn't really looked beyond the fort in any meaningful way. In his mind, his life would always be tethered to the palace and to his family, and leaving either behind had simply never occurred to him. But hearing about Riya's life with the Ravens pressed against an ache deep within his heart — something that had maybe always been there but only become painfully evident these last few months when he had no obligations to occupy his thoughts. He wasn't sure he'd ever be brave enough to simply walk away, but he had to acknowledge that there was a whole world outside these walls — outside his family — that he wanted to experience.

"Do you ever feel like you're being untrue to yourself? Like . . ." Riya selected her words carefully. "Like you're torn between two facets of who you are, and you can't reconcile them?"

"You mean being Ashokan and Lyrian?"

"I don't know if I've ever asked you about that. About what it was like growing up."

He considered her question. "I don't know that it's ever felt irreconcilable to me." It had been a fundamental fact of who he was his entire life. "But honestly, I never felt like my identity was complicated until others made me feel like it was."

"Until you were old enough to understand what those around you were saying," she said.

"Exactly." He looked at her curiously. "Where is this coming from?"

She looked down at her hands again. "These last few years, being a Raven, I thought I knew who I was and what I believed in. But now I can see things from another perspective." Riya bit her lip. "And I'm scared that I'm losing part of myself."

"I don't think anyone loses any part of themselves just because they embrace another aspect of their identity. I'm not any less Ashokan if I embrace my Lyrian family — just like growing up in Ashoka doesn't erase the parts of me that are Lyrian."

"But what if the people around you only see you in a particular way?"

Kaleb shrugged. "You can't control how people see you, Riya. Believe me, I've tried." It had taken him a long time to learn that he simply wouldn't be Ashokan or Lyrian enough for some people. It wouldn't matter what he did or said — they'd made up their minds, and he could never meet the arbitrary standards they'd set. "Identities don't always fit in neat boxes, and the people who want to put labels on you will always do so regardless."

Riya finally looked back up, and a small smile crept over her face. "When did you get so smart?"

Kaleb laughed bitterly. "I'm not smart at all." If he'd been smarter, he wouldn't be here, imprisoned for a crime he didn't commit.

"I truly am sorry I didn't come earlier," Riya said.

"Why didn't you?"

"For the same reason I didn't tell you I was leaving. If anyone was going to change my mind, it would be you."

"And have I?" Kaleb asked.

"I don't know yet."

"I think you do." He watched her with a measured look. "You've already picked a side, Riya. If you wanted to leave, you would have told the Ravens. You'd already be back in the forest. But you came here."

"But I came here," she agreed.

CHAPTER TWENTY-FOUR

— VIRA —

INSIDE THE DWARAMATHA.

Vira stared at the note in her hand. Kaleb had actually managed to figure out the code.

Her heart beat rapidly as she sat on the divan in her office, flipping through Papa's journals until she found it. *Matha* referred to a monastery and *Dwar* had been the old Ashokan spelling of Dvar. Papa hadn't thought it a location of much importance, so he hadn't made any notes, except that it was somewhere within the Swapna Forest.

And it held the final piece of the map that Vira needed.

Amrit still hadn't had luck tracking down the library piece. They'd agreed that it was best that no one else — including the guards — know what they were searching for, which of course made it all the more difficult.

Vira was frustrated at the notion that every time she made any kind of forward stride, there was a new setback. This was the closest anyone had been in *centuries* to unlocking the secrets of the Kamala Society.

Focus on the last piece.

The Council had insisted that she meet with the Viceroy of Ishvat for the third time that week. It was what she should have been focused on — ensuring that Ronak's engagement went off without a hitch. But instead Vira had ignored Meena's counsel and skipped her obligations for the day. Finding the Ivory Key was more important.

Vira looked up when there was a soft knock at the main door of her suite, and then she heard the handle turn. She'd told the guards stationed outside that she wasn't to be disturbed by anyone except Amrit and that he could let himself in. She made her way out to the receiving room.

"I think I have —" She stopped when she realized Amrit wasn't alone. Riya was there too. "What are you doing here?"

"I want to help," Riya said. "With the key."

Vira searched her face for any sign of insincerity even as she felt a sense of relief fill her. "All right," she said. "Because I know where the last piece is, and it's in the forest."

✷

When Vira told her about the monastery, Riya had claimed to know exactly where it was. But it still took them over an hour of walking through the forest before they came upon the ancient ruins.

"Are you sure this is it?" Vira asked. It didn't look like much of it had survived, and what remained was quite large, the stone walls stretching deeper into the forest than Vira was expecting.

Riya's nostrils flared. "Yes, I'm sure." She stepped over a broken-down wall and forged ahead.

"It's definitely a monastery," Amrit agreed as they followed her. He pointed to the stones that disappeared between the trees. "That would have been the outer wall of the compound. Typically, only forts and mon-asteries have them, and it would be pretty useless to build a fort in a forest. And over here you can see the remnants of what would have been lodgings for the monks, the uniform rooms all surrounding an open courtyard." He pointed to an area where grass and weeds had grown uninhibited.

Vira frowned. "And you just . . . *know* this?"

"You don't have to sound so surprised, Vira," he said dryly. "I have interests."

"In monasteries?"

"In architecture." Amrit turned to find Vira staring at him. He shrugged a little. "In another life, I would have very much liked to design buildings," he admitted. "I know it's silly."

Vira watched him a moment longer, trying to reconcile that Amrit — one with drawings and dreams — with the one before her. "It's not silly."

"It's just as well," he said with a wry twist of his lips. "I doubt we'd have met if I had become an architect."

"Yes, we would have," Vira insisted. "You, the best architect in all of Ashoka, come to design a building for the maharani. It would be just as we are now."

"The best architect?" He glanced up at her, his smile surprisingly bright. "What would you have had me design?"

"Oh. Something ostentatious, of course. Definitely featuring at least half a dozen statues of myself."

Amrit laughed as they trudged through the overgrowth. It didn't look that different from the forest around it, having been open to the elements and wildlife for so long. Animal droppings littered the ground, and water dripped down the side of stone walls that looked like they'd once held frescoes and paintings.

"Things seem to be better between you and your sister," Amrit noted, watching as Riya made her way to the single building in the center that had remained largely intact — a shocking feat considering the rest of the monastery.

"Maybe," Vira said, self-consciously running her hands over the kurta she'd chosen for the day. It was made of a lightweight silk and cotton blend, and it was well suited for traipsing through the forest. But she couldn't deny a part of the reason she'd worn something so unassuming was because of what Riya had said during their dinner.

She hadn't intended to emulate her mother's style so closely, but it had been easier in those early days — after Amma died and Vira had unexpectedly become the maharani — to dress just like her. To armor herself with beautiful silk and expensive jewelry and hope that no one saw how terrified she was underneath it all.

"Here," Riya called. "I think this is it."

"This was probably the meditation hall," Amrit said as they approached a heavy door made of wood.

It would have taken a tremendous amount of magic to preserve the wood in the forest for so long, but when Vira touched the door, she felt no sign of it. There was no handle, so Riya pushed. It didn't move. Amrit joined her, using the weight of his body to shove against the door.

"I didn't think we'd be breaking down doors," he said with a frustrated huff. "We don't have the right tools for this."

But Vira's eye caught on something. A tiny etching on a part of the wood that looked darker than the rest: twin blades crossed over a lotus. Vira trailed a finger over the mark — then gasped as the wood shifted in front of her eyes, dissolving and disappearing completely until it revealed a square opening slotted with wooden blocks.

"How did you do that?" Amrit asked.

Vira didn't answer. Her eyes were wide with awe. There were sixteen blocks, each with a number painted on it, from one to eight.

"It's a puzzle," Riya said unhappily.

Vira exchanged a glance with her. Papa had once shown them a puzzle very much like this. She stared at the blocks, willing herself to remember how it had worked. The one Papa had given them had only nine blocks, the square stretching three blocks across and three down. And they all had to add up to fifteen.

Two of each. Sixteen blocks. Four rows and columns. And if she added up all the numbers, one through eight, twice, and then divided by four . . .

"Eighteen!" Vira said.

"What?" Amrit asked.

"Each row has to add up to eighteen," Riya explained, her mouth set in a tight line. "Kausalya help me, I always hated these."

Amrit still looked bewildered as Vira and Riya pried eight blocks from the door and lined them up on the ground in two rows.

1 2 3 4

8 7 6 5

"See how each pair adds up to nine?" Vira gestured at the remaining blocks left on the board in the door. "So do those. Now we just need to find the right combination. It all has to add up to eighteen — forward, backwards, up and down, diagonally."

They pulled the remaining blocks from the door and arranged them on the ground. Vira muttered to herself as she added and moved the blocks around. Amrit and Riya watched, occasionally pointing out an incorrect sum. It took them ten minutes to work out the math, and then they had all sixteen blocks arranged.

1764

8235

3582

6417

"How do you know how to do this?" Amrit asked as Vira slowly slid the blocks back into the door.

"I do have interests, you know," Vira said, using Amrit's words. But then she smiled lightly as she slotted in the third row. "It was our father. He was always obsessed with puzzles, codes, riddles, hidden treasure. He was certain we'd find the Ivory Key, and he wanted to prepare us to face the Kamala Society's obstacles."

"Every summer, when it was far too hot to go outside, Papa would hide something in the fort and then give us clues and puzzles to solve," Riya added. "We got pretty good at them."

Vira missed him terribly then, her heart flooding with too many emotions. She reached for the pendant he'd given her. They were supposed to find it together — the map, the key, the quarries.

I'm doing it, Papa. Just like you always hoped.

She put the last block in place and stepped back. Nothing happened.

"Are we supposed to do something else?" Riya asked.

As if the door had somehow heard her, a smaller panel melted away on one side of the door — and from within it emerged a metal handle. Vira tugged on the handle. Although the door had been shut for centuries, it opened smoothly and silently. Vira stepped inside, squinting as her eyes adjusted to the dark room. "Maybe —"

Something landed on her. She screamed and shoved it off. It crashed to the floor.

And then she saw what it was. A skeleton.

"Vira!" Amrit said.

A skeleton. Had fallen on her.

She was going to be sick.

"Vira." Amrit's fingers found hers, tugging her toward him, pulling her close so she was pressed against his side. She was shaking. "You're all right."

She somehow forced herself to nod. "We need light."

Amrit nodded, but he also looked shaken. Vira tried not to dwell on that. It took a lot to faze him.

"Here," Riya said from behind them, pulling out from her pack one of the flameless lanterns they'd brought with them. She lowered the light so it illuminated the skeleton.

"This is becoming a bad habit of ours," Amrit muttered. "First Harish, now this."

Vira laughed, her breath shaky. "Let's hope there's not more." She looked up, half expecting to find a host of other skeletons floating in the air. "Any chance you've got a secret passion for archaeology as well?"

"It looks . . . old?" Amrit guessed. So that was a no.

"Come on," Riya said, already moving away.

It was an empty square room with large windows in each wall that had once let in light. Now they were darkened by the overgrowth pushing against the outside, trying to break into this unclaimed space.

"There's nowhere to hide anything here," Amrit said.

The door had been marked with the Kamala Society's symbol. Maybe the hiding place would be, too — a way for someone who knew what they were looking for to piece it all back together. "We need to look for another symbol," Vira said. "Somewhere on the walls maybe?"

"How about the floor?" Riya asked.

Marble tiles stretched over the entire room, and as Vira looked closer, she realized that each was painted with a lotus. They spread out, slowly making their way through the room, studying every tile.

"Found it," Amrit said. He was crouched over one tile close to the wall. This one was different. It had two swords crossed atop the flower — easy to miss if you weren't looking for it.

Vira dropped to her knees and pressed her palm against the tile. There was a click, and then the tile rose above the others. Vira lifted it with trembling fingers.

Inside the hollow space were two things: a gold-plated oval mirror and a clothbound journal. Vira lifted them up.

The glass had an odd red sheen to it as it reflected their three anxious faces. Vira ran her hands over the elaborate leaves and feathers and animals carved into the frame, and then she turned it over to find an inscription.

May this always remind you of your greatest treasure — N

"Who's N?" Riya asked, but Vira could only shrug as she set the mirror aside.

Amrit brought the torch closer as Vira flipped through the pages of the journal. It was written in Ashokan, but a form that was outdated, old and formal, like the epics her tutors had made her study. And tucked into its very center was what they'd come to find: the third piece of the map.

Vira's hand shook as she ran her fingers over it. The same Kamala Society symbol. The same bold lines. And she was the first person in five hundred years to hold it.

"We actually did it," Riya said, shaking her head in disbelief.

Vira laughed, a little giddy, a little breathless. They'd done the impossible, but it wasn't enough. She slipped the map between the pages of the journal again, tucking that and the mirror into her bag. With a final search to make sure there was nothing else hidden beneath the tile, Vira slid the tile back into place. It closed with a soft click.

"We should go," Vira said, rising. "Once we get the last piece —"

"I thought this was the last piece," Riya said, frowning.

"It would have been. I have this one and the one from Harish's dagger. But the one Papa had — the one that was in the library — went missing a few days ago."

"Only a few people have access to that room," Amrit said. "We'll find it soon enough."

"Harish's dagger?" Riya asked. And then she closed her eyes as though realizing something.

"What is it?" Vira demanded.

"I know who has it."

CHAPTER TWENTY-FIVE

— KALEB —

IT WAS DUSK when Aaliyah, the palace mayaka, released Kaleb from the dungeons. Apparently it took less effort to free him than it had to lock him up because in a matter of minutes, the shackles were gone and he was following a guard through the fort. He rubbed the backs of his wrists uncomfortably, trying to ignore the stares and whispers that trailed behind him. It wasn't often that prisoners were released, so this wasn't unexpected. But even without the plain black kurta denoting his status as a criminal, everyone in the palace knew his face and his alleged crime.

You're free, he reminded himself. *That's all that matters.*

It still didn't feel real. Vira had actually kept her promise. She'd let him go even if she hadn't issued a formal pardon yet. She needed the Council's approval for that, which meant he'd have to argue his innocence in front of them — but that was more than he'd been afforded eight months ago. All he had to do until then was keep his head down and resume his old life.

But the pointed glances and hushed conversations only grew more noticeable as Kaleb stepped foot inside the palace. He was used to curious looks. After all, being a rajkumaara — even one who'd spent most of his time in the library or the mayaka lab — meant that he'd grown up in the public eye. But there was something different about the way people looked at him now, almost as if they were afraid of him.

You can leave these shackles, but those people in the palace? They'll never forget what you did. Even if it's a lie.

Kaleb shoved Surya's words aside and kept walking until he reached his rooms. He'd been gone less than a year, but when he pushed open the door, the sight felt strangely unfamiliar. Everything was just as he'd left it, but judging by the dust that coated most surfaces, it was obvious that no one — not even a servant — had bothered to step foot in the room since his imprisonment.

The guard cleared her throat. "I, uh — Sorry, Rajkumaara. I should have had someone check the room."

"It's fine," Kaleb said.

"I'll send someone to clean."

A few minutes later, two young boys showed up at his door, looking positively terrified. Because he had nowhere else to go, he'd lingered off to the side uncomfortably, watching them work and pretending he didn't hear their hushed conversation.

"I can't believe they're allowing a killer to live in the palace."

"No. Didn't you hear, the maharani cleared his name."

"That doesn't mean he didn't do it."

They'd worked quickly and left as soon as possible, without saying anything directly to him. But their whispered words burrowed deep within him. Maybe this was how it would always be — constantly wondering if the people around him thought he'd truly conspired to kill his own mother.

He had never had many friends, not like his sisters. He had Ronak, and he had his work — and that was all he'd ever needed. But as he stood in his empty room staring at the remnants of his old life, he was hit with the sudden realization that he didn't even have that anymore. Ronak was getting married. There was a new palace mayaka — one who, unlike Kaleb, was properly trained. And Kaleb hadn't gone to university as he'd planned, so he didn't have his studies to occupy his time either.

He sank into one of the divans, lowering his head into his hands. The world had moved on without him. He hadn't left his mark in any meaningful way, and the life he'd wanted to return to simply didn't exist anymore.

✳

When he'd dressed and eaten a quick meal, Kaleb went to see Ronak. He climbed the stairs two at a time, pushing open the door to his brother's room. "Ronak?"

No response.

Kaleb looked around the room. Nothing had changed in the months that Kaleb had been gone. The perpetually drawn curtains, the messy desk, the armoire door left open, the faint scents of sandalwood and neem that clung to everything: this was definitely Ronak's room. The familiarity of his brother's space tugged at Kaleb's heart.

He made his way to the piles of half-finished paintings. How had his brother seen the world in the last eight months?

Before he could help himself, he was rifling through the canvases.

Peacocks strutting through overgrown grass, a ghost of a temple in the background. The palace lake, an empty rowboat drenched in pale moonlight. A boy sitting in a cell, his arms wrapped around his knees, his head hanging down.

Kaleb sucked in a breath, unable to look away. The Kaleb in the painting looked so young. So broken. Was this how Ronak saw him? Was this who he had become?

He let the paintings fall back against the wall with a thud.

His eyes landed on a stack of books on the bedside table, and he sat on the bed, running his fingers over the spines. Ronak had always managed to find the most outlandish tales in the library, staying up all night to devour adventures in far-off lands and then recounting all the details to Kaleb the next day.

For most of their lives Kaleb had ignored him, sure that Ronak was wasting his time on stories when he should have been focusing on his studies. But in the dungeons, things had changed. With nothing to do and no one to talk to, Kaleb had clung to the tales in those books, begging Ronak for story after story.

Kaleb reached for one of the books, but when he opened it, he found it wasn't a book at all. The inside was hollowed out, the rectangular space filled with folded scraps of paper and a pouch of coins. He blinked in surprise. He knew he ought to put the items back. It was not his business whatever Ronak was doing, whatever he was hiding.

But then he saw his own name scrawled on one of the papers. Kaleb pulled the papers out, unfolding them. They were plans — to bribe guards, to threaten the mayaka, to free him. And beneath that was something else. The piece of the map that led to the Ivory Key. Kaleb looked at it in confusion. Ronak had been the first one to declare Papa's quests foolish — the first one to stop participating in Papa's silly puzzle games. It didn't make any sense that he had this, why it wasn't still locked up in the library.

"What are you doing?"

Kaleb jumped. But it was too late to hide the evidence. Ronak stood at the entrance to the door, watching him with anger. His expression morphed to shock. "Kaleb?" He glanced at the door, then back at him. "How are you here? You're free?"

Ronak rushed forward, throwing his arms around his brother. Kaleb instinctively hugged him back, but his eyes remained on the bed, on the pieces of paper outlining details he'd never known. There were a few lines that Kaleb never crossed. He didn't keep secrets from his brother, and he certainly never lied to him. Ronak, however, didn't seem to share those principles.

"Were you ever going to tell me?" Kaleb asked.

Ronak pulled away, confused, until he followed Kaleb's gaze. He snatched the book away, shoving everything back inside it. "Of course I was."

"When? The night you broke me out of the dungeons?"

The defiant look on Ronak's face was answer enough. "You would never have agreed to it."

He should have known. All that talk of escape and finding new lives — he should have known it was more than just talk, more than wishful thinking on Ronak's part.

"I told you I didn't want to talk about leaving, Ronak. You didn't listen to me." Kaleb rose. "You speak of escape and freedom, but all it is is running away. What are you so desperate to avoid? What do you think you will find out there that you can't find here?"

Ronak shook his head. "I don't know. But we'll have choices."

"We have choices here, too," Kaleb said. "And you've found a way to make plenty of choices in the pursuit of freedom — despite your belief that our titles only imprison us."

"That was different," Ronak snapped. "I was trying to save you."

"Perhaps you should have asked me whether I needed saving."

"Don't you get it? Running is the only way for us to keep our lives. To be able to make our own decisions."

"And what kind of life can we hope to have when people still think the worst of me?"

"People will think what they want, brother." Ronak gestured to himself. "They think the worst of me, too."

"This is different, Ro. No one is calling you a murderer."

Ronak's voice was hoarse when he spoke. "You would rather stay here and be Vira's puppet than seize a new life that you can call your own?"

"Of course not. But we can't start a new life as fugitives."

"There are places in the world where no one will know. No one will care."

"*I will care.*"

Silence rang out.

"I get to make my own choices, Ronak," Kaleb said. "Even if you don't like them."

Ronak's eyes narrowed. "Why did Vira free you? Why now?"

Kaleb stared his brother down. He hadn't planned on saying anything, but the words burst out of him. "Vira asked me for help in finding the Ivory Key." He pointed to the book in Ronak's hand. "So do you want to tell me why *you* have a piece of it?"

But before Ronak could answer, Vira stormed in through the open door, fury in her gaze.

CHAPTER TWENTY-SIX

— VIRA —

VIRA STRODE INTO Ronak's room, Amrit and Riya on her heels. "Where is it?" She shouldn't have been surprised. Of course he would stop at nothing to keep her from getting what she wanted.

She stopped as she realized that Kaleb was also there. He'd bathed and dressed in one of his old kurtas, and for a moment everything felt so normal—as if this were an everyday occurrence. Except she could see the effects of the months of imprisonment in the way the clothes hung too loose on his frame, in the dark circles under his eyes.

"Kaleb!" Riya threw her arms around him, pulling him into a tight hug. Vira tried not to feel jealous of their warm greeting.

Ronak looked bored as he faced Vira. "Where is what, sister?"

"I'm not in the mood, Ronak," Vira snapped. "The map that leads to the Ivory Key. I know you have it, and I know you had Riya steal the dagger from me." That hurt, too, but Vira was too angry with Ronak to worry about Riya's betrayal just then.

"Well—"

"It's in the book he's holding," Kaleb said, sounding tired.

Ronak didn't stop Kaleb as he reached for the book, withdrew the piece of the map, and handed it to Vira.

All at once her anger faded to a dull throb, and all she could think about was that the three pieces of the map were united. It seemed fitting somehow to do this here, in Papa's old study, all of them together.

A hush fell over the room as she sank to the floor in front of the bed. Riya tugged open one of the curtains as Vira laid out all three pieces on the floor, their torn edges lining up.

Amrit crouched on the floor beside her. Riya knelt on her other side. Kaleb sat on the bed behind her, and Ronak stood in front of them all. And they watched with bated breath as all at once the three pieces fused back together, as if the map had never been torn.

The lines on the map around the temple were shifting, changing, rearranging, until they formed a map of Ashoka as it had looked five hundred years ago. Somewhere in the northwestern part of Ashoka was a lake. In the middle of the lake was a temple. And above it, the symbol of a key.

The key to unlocking the quarries.

"We find the temple, we find the key," Vira said.

"We need a map of present-day Ashoka," Amrit said.

"I have one," Ronak said, moving items around on his desk and pulling out one of Papa's old maps that had been rolled up in the corner. He spread it out on the floor next to them. Vira watched as Ronak's finger traced back and forth.

"It's somewhere here," he said, pointing.

The realization hit Vira like a blow to her stomach. Ritsar. The land she'd lost to Lyria.

"It's not there," Riya said. She pointed to the border, and then the temple, slightly more north. "It's in the mountains."

That was even worse.

"That's mercenary territory," Kaleb said.

Despair threatened to overwhelm Vira. She put a hand on the ground to steady herself. The very land she'd lost was what she needed to protect the rest of the country.

"We'll find a way to get there," Amrit said. "I promise."

Vira's heart was heavy with success and failure, with discovery and loss.

Kaleb pointed to the edge of the journal that was poking out of her bag. "What's that?"

"We found it with the map," Riya said, pulling it out. "And this mirror, too."

Kaleb took the journal while Ronak reached for the mirror, examining it just as Vira had in the monastery.

"'May this always remind you of your greatest treasure,'" Ronak read. "What does that mean?"

"I don't know," Riya said. "The treasure is probably the key."

"It says *your* treasure, not *the* treasure," Amrit noted.

"How would a mirror remind you of treasure?" Ronak asked.

"Vira, did you look at this?" Kaleb asked.

She turned at the sound of confusion in his voice. "No — why?"

Kaleb turned the book around and pointed at two words. *Maharani Savitri.* The first maharani of Ashoka. Their distant ancestor.

"Listen to this. 'The first phase is complete,'" Kaleb read. "'Maharani Savitri is already establishing the new' —" Kaleb frowned. "I don't know this word. 'The new' . . . *something*. 'Now everything rests in the hands of the ambassadors. I know them to be difficult' — no, fierce? — 'warriors and deeply loyal, but I cannot help but fear for their safety. Savitri would caution me to trust, to believe. I wish that came as naturally to me as it does to her.'" Kaleb lowered the journal. "I think whoever wrote this lived five hundred years ago. They knew Savitri."

No one knew much about Savitri, or what the world had been like half a millennium ago. Since the capital had been relocated from the Maravat province south to Dvar, the records in the palace stretched back only three hundred years. And here in their hands might be the only surviving record from a time period forgotten even by the history books.

"Can I keep this?" Kaleb asked, flipping through more pages.

Vira nodded. She didn't have the time — or patience — to read old Ashokan, and there could be something useful within the pages. "Tell me if you find anything interesting." She picked up the map and reached out to Ronak for the mirror. "It's probably best that I keep these until we figure out a plan."

"Wait." Riya grabbed Vira's hand. "Look." She pointed at the mirror. In the mirror, the back of the map wasn't blank. Instead, there was red writing on it.

"Bring it closer," Vira said, and Ronak — for once in his life — obeyed without question. It took a moment for Vira to make out the words. "'When the equinox sun sets, the mirror will illuminate your path.'" She turned the map over and held it to the mirror. The front, too, had writing on it, right above the temple. "'The only way out is through.'"

"The equinox sun?" Riya repeated, frowning. "That means we have to be at the temple in less than two weeks."

"Eleven days," Ronak corrected.

Vira exhaled. That didn't give them a lot of time. "We have to leave —" She looked up at Ronak. His engagement ceremony was in a week.

"The day after the ceremony," Ronak finished.

"That doesn't give us much time," Amrit said. "We can't go directly into Ritsar. There are too many troops stationed there. So our best bet is to go here" — he pointed to the east of Ritsar — "and cross into the mountains."

"We still have the border walls," Riya said.

"I'll take care of crossing the border," Vira said. "But that still leaves us walking through mercenary territory."

"And I'll take care of that," Amrit said.

"Papa had a lot of tools stashed away, from all his trips," Kaleb added. "Up in the library, but also in his personal collection."

"I'll work with Kaleb to sort through that," Riya said. "We'll need some other things, too. Kaleb can forge them for us."

"I'm coming with you," Ronak said.

Vira looked up in surprise. "What?" She didn't think he cared about any of this. "Why?"

"I'm part of this family, too. Papa started this. If you're all going, I'm coming with you."

Vira opened her mouth, but Kaleb spoke first.

"You didn't seem to care much about that half an hour ago."

"I've changed my mind, brother." Ronak didn't face Kaleb. "I didn't think I had to consult you."

"That's unfair," Kaleb said. "I'm doing what I have to —"

"I had a *plan*." The words tore out of Ronak as he whipped his head around to finally look at Kaleb. "A plan to get you out of there."

"A plan I wanted no part of."

A plan to get you out of there. Out of the dungeons. Out of Vira's grasp. The pieces slotted together, and realization dawned on Vira. "He agreed to help me," Vira said. "That's why you're so upset? That Kaleb chose me —"

"I did not choose anyone," Kaleb said, cutting in. "And I can speak for myself, thanks."

But Vira's words had their desired impact. Ronak's jaw tightened. "What do you know about that temple?" he asked. "Do any of you even know what it's called? Or the significance of the equinox? Or where to go once you're *in* the temple? Because I do."

None of them answered.

"You need me," he said. "You might know more about magic or solving puzzles or picking locks" — he pointed at each of them — "but none of you know nearly as much about the history of Ashoka."

"He's right," Riya said after a pause.

Kaleb had followed in Papa's footsteps as a mayaka. Vira had taken on his obsession with treasure. Riya had inherited his sense of justice and action. But it was only Ronak who had fallen in love with Papa's true passion: uncovering the past. It was Ronak who'd devoured every book, every myth that Papa had ever put in front of them. It was Ronak who was here in this room now, living in Papa's library, surrounded by all of Papa's stories.

Vira had believed that Ronak hadn't cared about the Ivory Key, or any of the quests Papa had set out on. But maybe it was just that he cared about it differently.

"All right," Vira said. "We'll find it together."

"What will you tell the Council?" Amrit asked.

Vira exhaled. "I don't know. I'll think of something."

"The anniversary of Papa's death," Kaleb suggested. "It's in two weeks. That's our way out of the palace."

"We can say we're all going to Gauri Mahal," Riya added. "They can hardly say no to that."

It was a good idea. Gauri Mahal was a smaller palace in the north — less fortified, used mainly in the spring, when they traveled there to celebrate the start of the new year. They hadn't gone there in years. The Council would be incredibly unhappy about it.

But for once, Vira didn't care about the Council. "I'll arrange it."

✳

Three days later, Amrit was waiting on Vira's balcony when she returned to her rooms. She walked forward slowly, through the open doors at the far side of her room, to where he was standing, elbows resting on the marble railing, long fingers twined together as he looked down into the depths of the ocean. She came to stand beside him, inhaling the salty air. She could hear the waves crashing against walls of the fort below, the only sound in the otherwise still night.

"I hope it's all right that I let myself in," he said, turning slightly.

"You're welcome here anytime. You know that."

"How was the meeting?" Amrit asked.

"As exhausting as always."

The Council had insisted that she attend to the Viceroy of Ishvat personally, welcoming Preethi's parents and sisters into her family. Vira had argued for a smaller engagement ceremony, but the Council had overruled her, insisting that the viceroy be allowed to invite whoever he wished. Most of the visitors were staying in Dvar, but the palace still felt stiflingly full with additional guests and the flurry of engagement preparations.

"Did you tell them about the journey?" he asked.

Vira sighed. The conversation had gone about as well as she'd expected. "The Council doesn't want me to go to Gauri Mahal."

They'd cited protests, or the possibility that Lyria would finally make a move, but that was all the more reason for her to go. The best protection was finding more magic.

"And will you listen to them?"

Her mother would probably have agreed with the Council. She'd have focused on the ceremony, on Ronak. But Vira couldn't think about anything else — not when the Ivory Key was within her grasp.

"No," she said. "We'll proceed as planned."

He nodded. "All right."

Vira watched him for a moment. He'd never been talkative, but lately he'd been coming around more often — stopping by to visit her, to ask about her day or share a story about his. She'd gotten used to that version of him, and now she had no idea what was going through his head. She didn't like it.

"Is everything all right?" she asked.

He smiled a little. "Yes, of course. I was just . . . thinking."

"About?"

"Our journey."

"I have been, too," Vira admitted. "Maybe . . . maybe we should consider Surya?"

"Surya?" He pushed away from the railing, turning to face her.

"We need a guide who is familiar with mercenary territory. One who can help us evade capture. One who is invested in finding the key."

"We can't take him, Vira." His mouth was set in a grim line. "There's too much at risk."

"There's not," Vira said. "I've thought this through. We can keep him shackled. We can find a way to make sure he doesn't escape."

But Amrit shook his head. "It's too dangerous. What happens after we find the key?"

She shrugged. "I don't know. We'll figure it out then. We need his knowledge."

"I'll make sure we get there safely. Trust me."

"It's not about trust, Amrit. It's about guarantees. It's not just myself I have to worry about, but everyone else — Riya, Kaleb, Ronak."

"I promise that I'll keep all of you safe," Amrit said earnestly.

"How can you promise that?"

Amrit opened his mouth. And then closed it. Something unreadable flickered in his expression.

Shadows had always lived in his eyes. She'd known there were parts of his life that he wasn't ready to share with her — that he might never be ready to share with her. But somewhere along the line, the walls she'd put up around herself had simply vanished with him. She'd told him things she'd told no one else. About her panic attacks, about her mother, about the fears she couldn't outrun.

And she was starting to fear that he didn't return that trust.

"You ask me to trust you, Amrit, but I don't know if you trust *me*. You know everything about me. And I can count on both hands all that I know about you."

"You know more about me than anyone else," he said. "Vira, you know everything that matters."

Vira said nothing.

"Where is this coming from?" he asked. His eyes were wary, confused, almost a little hurt.

"From me, Amrit." She suddenly felt exhausted. All she wanted was to climb into her bed and hide from the world.

"There are some things that are not . . ." He huffed, running a frustrated hand through his hair. "There are some things I can't share, Vira."

"I can handle it. Whatever it is."

"I know you can. But I don't know if *I* can."

"What does that mean?"

More silence.

"I'm not asking for much. Just something." Vira sounded like she was begging. Maybe she was.

"We've been up here for too long," he said. "I should go." He pushed away from the balcony.

"Amrit, wait," she called after him, but he was already walking out of her room.

CHAPTER TWENTY-SEVEN

— RIYA —

RIYA WAS ACTUALLY enjoying Ronak's engagement party.

Her body was weighted down by heavy gold jewelry that covered every inch of her. Colorful bangles were stacked up her arm, and even her ankles hadn't been left bare, encircled by bell-laden anklets that jangled with every step. But she couldn't remember the last time she'd laughed so much.

She'd had fun with the Ravens, of course, but it was different making fun of councilors with Indra or sneaking extra helpings of sweets with Kaleb. She didn't think she'd missed this, but she had — and it was her last chance to enjoy palace life before she returned to the Ravens with the Ivory Key.

"Can you believe Preethi's *engaged*?" Archana asked, dropping into the empty seat at the table they'd claimed hours earlier. But while Riya and Indra had stayed there, Archana had spent the time dutifully checking in on Preethi. Riya felt a spark of guilt that she hadn't done the same for Ronak, but he'd made it clear that he didn't want her around.

"Hmm," Jay said, gesturing to a nearby servant to refill his tumbler of palm wine. Riya didn't know why he was there and not attending to Ronak, but he'd inserted himself into their group several hours earlier.

"It still doesn't feel real," Indra agreed, adjusting the pallu of her sari.

She'd selected one that was scandalously sheer, revealing the elaborate embroidery of her full-sleeved blouse.

"You danced beautifully, Arch," Riya said.

Archana beamed. She'd choreographed and performed a dance with
her other family members. She looked stunning too, trading in her simple
dance practice clothes for a stone-studded anarkali that flared every time
she moved.

Riya stole Kaleb's untouched tumbler of tadi. He raised his eyebrows,
and Riya shrugged. "It's not like you were drinking it."

He'd stayed by her side most of the night, not speaking much, looking around as though he still couldn't believe he was free. He'd loved these
kinds of events, she remembered, and it made her sad to see him so uncharacteristically reserved.

Archana suddenly grabbed Riya's arm. "Wait. Is that Varun?"

"What?" Riya whipped her head around. She found him immediately,
standing next to a pillar on the walkway, glaring at the crowd.

"Who's Varun?" Jay asked.

"He's a scholar," Riya said miserably. What was he doing here?

"A very young and attractive scholar," Archana clarified, as if that made
it any better.

"Attractive?" Jay leaned forward, looking in the same direction.

"Go talk to him," Indra urged. "He looks out of place, poor thing."

"Who's this scholar?" Kaleb asked, craning his head. He looked more
interested in this than anything else they'd discussed so far, and the last
thing Riya wanted was for her brother to meet Varun.

"You're right." Riya stood and drank the last of the tadi in her glass. "I
should go talk to him."

She felt their eyes on her back the whole time as she made her way toward him. He turned as she approached, and his eyes traveled down the length of her body. He was dressed in a dark silk sherwani, looking far too much like he belonged in this world, and Riya didn't like it.

"You've been avoiding me," he said by way of greeting.

She'd skipped her meetings with him that week, citing preparations for Ronak's engagement. She'd half expected him to show up at her door and demand updates, but he'd left her alone.

"I saw you yesterday," she said mildly.

"And you walked away before we could talk."

"Not here." She subtly nodded toward where Archana, Indra, Kaleb, and Jay were unabashedly staring at the two of them.

Varun's eyes flicked to them. "I thought you took care of it."

"I can't help that they think we're —" She stopped herself. She'd had too much tadi. It was making her careless. She'd almost said *they think we're in love.*

His eyes narrowed. "They think we're what?" His voice dropped to a whisper. "That we're Ravens?"

"No!"

"Then what?"

"It's nothing. Look, can we do this later?" She wasn't in the mood for a drawn-out argument with him.

"So you can go back to enjoying yourself with your friends?" he asked. "I'm sorry to inconvenience you by reminding you that you're here for a reason."

Vaishali's bones. "Fine," Riya said, relenting. She couldn't avoid him forever. She grabbed his forearm and pulled him deeper into the garden, walking between hedges and rosebushes until the sounds of laughter and music dimmed.

"Well?" she prompted once she verified that they were alone. "What did you want to talk about?"

"I think there's something wrong with the quarry."

Her heart skipped a beat. "What do you mean?"

"There's something off about the guards stationed at the entrance. They're too relaxed."

"The fort is well protected, Varun. And not a lot of people go into the quarry on a daily basis."

"But that's the thing, Riya," Varun said, his eyes shining as if he had stumbled onto something important. "*No one* goes there. And in the last month, not a single shipment has arrived at the Mayaka Association. I don't think they're taking any magic out of the quarries."

"That's absurd," Riya said. "I've been there. Everything is perfectly fine."

Varun looked taken aback. "You went into the quarry?"

"Yes. Ronak took me. They're probably just behind on the shipment because of the rains." The lies tumbled from her lip with startling ease.

His eyes bored into hers. "You went to the quarry?"

She nodded.

Varun crossed his arms over his chest. "That's funny. Because I *also* went to the quarry. And imagine my surprise to find that it was entirely empty."

Riya's stomach plummeted. How had he gained access? Who had taken him? But it didn't matter — Varun had been there. He knew just how much magic was left.

And he knew that she had lied to him.

"How long have you known?" His voice was deadly quiet.

Riya swallowed. "Two weeks."

"You've known for two weeks." Rage simmered in his voice.

"I have a plan."

"A plan?" he echoed. "What's the plan?"

Riya bit her lip. "I — I'm sorry, I can't tell you."

"You can't tell me?" He sounded incredulous. "You can understand why I'd doubt you."

"No, I really can't." She turned to face him, unable to stop herself from saying the words that had plagued her for days. "You told me to come here and prove to you that I'm a Raven. And then you showed up a week after I did. You didn't even give me a chance."

"Because you're not taking it seriously." He was in her space, looming over her, his dark eyes burning into hers. "I see you every day, Riya. Flitting from social engagement to social engagement. Laughing with those girls over chai and sweets. *Wasting time.*"

"That's what's expected of a rajkumaari!" she blurted out, hating how much she sounded like Vira. "Of course that's not what I want to be doing, but it's what the Council expects me to do. I can't defy them outright if I intend to keep my cover. Isn't that the reason you do research in the library?"

"That's different."

"It's not." She pulled away from him. "I'm handling this, Varun. I just need some time."

"You've had plenty of time," he said coolly. "You could have talked to me about this days ago, and you chose to lie. Tell me now. Or I walk out of here and you no longer have a home with the Ravens."

Riya froze. "You can't do that."

She could have dealt with this days ago. She could have accused him of theft and gotten rid of him, but she hadn't. And some part of her couldn't help but wonder if that was on purpose. Maybe she'd wanted him to find out. To take the choice away from her.

"You told me you were a Raven, not a rajkumaari. So which is it?"

"I —" Riya swallowed. She didn't know.

Varun shook his head, disgusted. "That's what I thought. You're out."

Suddenly feeling like she wanted to cry, Riya wrapped her arms around herself, leaning heavily against a nearby tree trunk as Varun walked away from her.

CHAPTER TWENTY-EIGHT

— RONAK —

RONAK WAS NOT enjoying his engagement party. It wasn't as though it was actually for him. It was for the Council and the string of influential wealthy people they'd invited. But he was the one who was forced to sit on an elaborately decorated throne and smile as stranger after stranger came up to offer the pair their congratulations.

Next to him, Preethi didn't show the slightest bit of exhaustion. She'd been there just as long as he had, covered head to toe in gold and ruby jewelry, but her smile had never wavered. She leaned over to him, her bangles brushing the sleeve of his kurta. "That's Councilor Aman's wife, Jasleen, and son, Ranvir," she said under her breath.

Ronak adjusted the garland of flowers around his neck and sat up straighter. As much as he'd wanted to ignore her, he'd realized it was easier — and faster — to get through the night with her whispering details to him. Unlike him, she took her duty seriously and learned who everyone was, inquiring thoughtfully about their interests or their children.

As Preethi talked to Jasleen, Ronak looked around the gardens for any sign of his siblings. He hadn't seen any of them since the formal ceremony in the morning. Ronak had been wakened at the crack of dawn, dragged to the baths, and placed in front of the fire pit next to Preethi. Smoke from the coals had twined with incense and made Ronak cough as the priestess chanted mantras to invoke the goddesses. He'd received blessings first from Vira, as the maharani, and then Kaleb as his elder brother. Ronak had made a commitment he had no intention of honoring. And then it was over.

In the back of his mind it had occurred to him how strange it was that it was Vira's feet he'd touched, not his mother's, but the thought passed as quickly as it came. It didn't matter who was on the throne — he would still only be a string of numbers to them, his worth reduced to the number of resources that would trade hands with this alliance.

"Would you like to eat?" Preethi asked. "I can have one of the servants fetch us plates."

Ronak turned around, surprised to realize that Aman's family was gone and the crowd had dwindled, drawn to the feast that had been laid out. He awkwardly fiddled with the collar of his kurta. It would be the polite thing to do, but he didn't much feel like eating.

"Maybe another time," he said.

"Another time," she agreed amicably. She hadn't pressed him for an answer to her earlier offer, but he could see the question in her eyes every time she met his gaze. He felt bad — he did. But he was leaving the palace behind as soon as he had the Ivory Key, and she deserved someone who would stay.

He gave her a small smile and walked away from the dais. The gardens, for what it was worth, were decorated beautifully. Tiny lanterns with flameless magic light were tied up on strings, crisscrossing in the air. Divans had been set out on the grass and pavement, allowing small groups to gather. On the far side of the garden, separated by a wall of rosebushes, there were silk tents with tables carrying delicacies from across the provinces of Ashoka — deep-fried vada soaked in vegetable sambar; crisp kachoris topped with potatoes and chutney; makki ki roti served with spiced saag; coconut stew ladled over steamed idiyappam; kulchas and stuffed parathas fresh from the tandoor. There was an entire table dedicated to sweets: halwa with dried fruit and nuts, bowls of kesar rabri with creamy malai, rows of kala jamun drizzled with cardamon and rose sugar syrup, stacks of milk peda and coconut burfi.

Ronak stopped in his tracks as a figure stepped into his path. He would recognize Ekta anywhere, but the shock of seeing her here made his mind screech to a halt.

"Congratulations, Rajkumaara," she greeted him. On anyone else, Ronak would have believed the smile to be sincere. She wore bottle green today, her velvet sari accessorized with muted gold necklaces and bangles that were fashionable when his grandmother had ruled. "How are you enjoying your party?"

"It's great," he lied. "I'm having a wonderful time."

That made her laugh. "I'm not a politician. You don't have to lie to me."

"What are you doing here?" Ronak asked. He wasn't in the mood to trade veiled barbs in plain view of everyone in the garden. And though they were on his turf, it still somehow felt as if she had the upper hand. She wasn't out of place here. She spoke and held herself like a noble.

"I have a vested interest in you, Rajkumaara. A good businesswoman keeps a careful eye on her assets." She laughed again. "Oh, don't sulk. It's rather unbecoming of a rajkumaara."

It was the kind of thing his mother would have said — or Vira, for that matter — and it irritated him even more. "Why are you here?" he repeated.

Ekta looked at him and then answered with surprising seriousness. "I was invited. I grew up in this world, you know. Not one of the nobles, of course not, but close enough to know the power they wield." She looked almost wistful, but Ronak knew better. "See, you and I aren't so different. We were both unhappy with the circumstances of our birth, and there's little we wouldn't do to change it." Her gaze sharpened once again. "I trust you remember the terms of our arrangement."

"I remember," Ronak said.

"Very good." She smiled. "It would be awfully rude of me to take up too much of your time. If you'll excuse me." She brushed past him, and the cloying scent of her perfume washed over him.

"What are you doing?"

Ronak turned to see Riya standing behind him, watching him with a troubled expression on her face. She looked different from the last time he'd seen her—less like Vira. It was her hair. It was loose around her shoulders, hanging to her waist in waves. She'd parted it to the side and pinned half of it back with a gold peacock clasp.

"Trying to get out of this incredibly dull party," Ronak said.

"That's not what I meant. I meant with *Ekta*."

"Who?" Ronak asked, feigning ignorance.

"I'm serious, Ronak," Riya said. "I heard you. An arrangement? What were you thinking?"

"Were you spying on me?"

"Ronak, listen to me. She's not someone you want to mess with. Even the Ravens keep their distance from her for a reason."

"I have it under control."

Riya opened her mouth to say something else, but then she thought better of it and just shook her head. "Fine. But don't say you weren't warned."

She walked away too, and the sense of dread within Ronak grew. He knew full well what he'd gotten himself into. This was the price he had to pay for his freedom. It was so close, he could practically taste it. Jay was ready to embark on any adventure. Kaleb was no longer imprisoned.

All he had to do was get the Ivory Key, and once he had a way out, a proper plan, he'd be able to convince Kaleb it was the best thing for them. The three of them would be able to disappear to some foreign land, never to worry about Ashoka or its problems anymore.

Ronak cast his eyes around the garden again, looking for any familiar face. He couldn't see Kaleb anywhere, but he found Jay sitting alone at a table.

"Enjoying your evening?" Ronak asked as he sat next to him.

"Absolutely," Jay said, not looking at him as he raised a glass to his lips.

"Ekta's here."

"What?" Jay glanced at Ronak, then sighed as his gaze drifted toward the food tents. "Great. Just what we needed."

Ronak frowned, unsure of what to make of Jay's strange mood. His friend wasn't often sullen or moody, and he didn't know how to deal with Jay when he was like this. "Are you all right?" he asked.

"I'm fine." Jay stood — and then lost his balance momentarily, grabbing the back of the divan for support.

Ronak's brows furrowed. "Are you drunk?" he asked, shocked. Jay didn't drink much, and Ronak could count the number of times he'd seen him like this.

"No." He began to walk away, and Ronak hurried to catch up with him.

"Jay, we should —" Ronak put a hand on his shoulder to stop him, but Jay whirled around, knocking Ronak's arm away.

"Stop it, Ronak. I'm fine."

Ronak stepped back, alarmed at the sharpness of Jay's tone. "Vaishali's bones, Jay. What's gotten into you?"

"You think I wanted to be here? To see you get engaged to her?"

"To her?" Ronak repeated, blinking in confusion.

"You don't even want to marry her. You're leaving." Jay's eyes were full of anger and hurt, and Ronak felt a sudden sense of realization that this wasn't about him. It was about Preethi.

"Do you . . ." he asked uncomfortably. "Are you and Preethi —"

"No! I —" Jay ran his hands through his hair and then down his face. "Yes? Maybe. I don't know, Ronak. *Shit.* This wasn't how I was going to tell you."

"Oh, so you *were* going to tell me?"

"I would have told you before you left Ashoka."

"Before *I* left?" Ronak asked. Jay's eyes widened in surprise — like he'd said something he hadn't meant to — and all at once his meaning was horribly clear. "You're not coming." Ronak felt like he was falling off a cliff.

Jay shrugged helplessly. "I have a life here."

"I don't understand." They were supposed to leave together. That was what they'd always worked toward. "Everything we did, every deal we made with Ekta was so we could be free."

"So *you* could be free. I helped you because you're my friend, Ronak. But you never asked me what I wanted."

"And what you want is Preethi and a life in the palace." Ronak's voice sounded strangely detached to his own ears — as if it belonged to someone else. "You lied to me. For *months.*"

Jay's eyes closed a little. "Ronak, I . . ."

"You said you wanted to travel," Ronak accused. "That you wanted to meet people from all over, to hear their stories and catalogue them."

"I do!"

"But you don't want to leave."

"Because we have time for that, Ro. I just . . . I don't feel ready to leave this life behind. To leave these people behind."

Ronak just stared at Jay, suddenly aware that they were still in the middle of a garden where hundreds of people could hear them. "You're not yourself," he said, shaking his head. "We'll talk when I'm back from my trip." He pulled away, but Jay's voice stopped him.

"I'm not changing my mind."

Silence stretched between them. It had never been like this. In all their years of friendship, Ronak couldn't remember a time when he'd felt so angry or hurt or betrayed. When he'd felt so distant from his best friend.

"I have to go," Ronak said, backing away.

"Ronak, wait. I don't want to leave things —"

Ronak didn't turn back as he walked away.

CHAPTER TWENTY-NINE

— VIRA —

THE PALACE GARDENS were breathtaking, Vira noted with a tinge of awe. The beaded pallu of the gold sari the maidservants had draped on her trailed behind her as she walked to the edge of a terrace overlooking the gardens. Her bangles clinked as she rested her elbows on the stone railing and savored the beauty of the decorations.

She could see the Viceroy of Ishvat in the crowd, surrounded by his wife and daughters, laughing heartily at something one of the other councilors said. She was relieved that the Council was pleased, and that the viceroy would return, bringing with him money and troops. Vira should have been down there with them, but her official duties for the night were over and she wanted a few minutes to herself.

She inhaled deeply, taking in the scents of roses and jasmine and hyacinths. The gardens glittered below her, bathed in the pearlescent light of hundreds of gilded lanterns strung between the coconut trees and hanging from branches. Real flames danced in open fire pits. Smells of roasted spices and ghee-laden sweets wafted from rows of tables piled high with food from all corners of Ashoka.

She could see Riya among the dancers in the middle of the garden, the full skirts of the gold and white lehenga twirling around her ankles as she spun and laughed with her friends. Just a few years ago Vira had been down there with them, out of breath and flushed from dancing too long. She couldn't believe how quickly things had changed.

Vira turned at the sound of footsteps.

"It's stunning, isn't it?" Amrit came to stand beside her. "It'll be a night to remember."

His eyelashes looked longer than ever, casting flickering shadows over his dark eyes. Stubble from a few days of not shaving sharpened his jawline. He was wearing a sherwani she'd never seen before. It was the deep blue of the open ocean, with embroidery slithering down the length of his torso like a golden serpent from legends of old.

There was beauty to savor in people, too.

He quirked his lips into a confused smile. "What?"

Vira shook her head, turning her gaze back to the garden. "You're right," she said.

She hadn't seen him since they'd argued about Surya. They'd talked — notes passed through impersonal messengers — but it wasn't the same when she couldn't hear his reassuring voice, see his small smiles and expressive eyes.

"It's different from your engagement," he said quietly.

"Very," she agreed, her mouth dry. Her ceremony had been brief and impersonal, attended only by two councilors and Amrit. It felt like a lifetime ago now, even as she realized that if Harish were alive, she would be down there getting married instead of standing here with Amrit.

But the key would change that.

If she had more magic, she wouldn't need to marry for troops or resources. She could wait to marry someone she loved.

Her heart skipped a beat as she turned to face him. "Hi." A million stars twinkled above them, and she could see them reflected in his eyes.

"Hi," he replied. "We leave tomorrow. Are you ready?"

"Yes." Anticipation pooled in her stomach. "It's finally hitting me how dangerous this could be," she admitted. "The mercenaries, Ritsar, a temple full of magical obstacles . . . There's a chance we might not return."

No one understood why she was doing this — why she had to do this. But she didn't know who she was if she wasn't the maharani who brought back magic. She'd given up so much for the Ivory Key. She'd hung all her hopes on it, and the notion of failure terrified her.

Vira had learned at a young age that death was a part of life, certain and inevitable. But when it came to her own mortality, she'd always assumed she would amount to . . . *something* before she died. She didn't want to be known forever as the maharani who lost Ashokan land. The maharani who'd lost magic. The maharani who'd disappeared chasing a myth.

Amrit looked startled by her admission. "Vira, I promise, I will not let you die on this quest."

"I know."

He was quiet for a long while. "I'm sorry," he said finally. "For the other night. I . . . I shouldn't have walked away from you like that."

Vira licked her lips. "No. I'm the one who's sorry. I shouldn't have pried."

Maybe she didn't need all his secrets. Maybe this was all of him that she would get to have — and maybe she was fine with that if the alternative was not having him at all.

He exhaled deeply. "I've spent so long being alone, I think I've forgotten what it's like to confide in someone."

"I know that feeling," Vira said, her voice heavy. He was the only one she had ever been able to easily talk to.

"I want to tell you *everything*," Amrit said. She'd never seen him like this: eyes wide, desperation clinging to his hoarse voice, his eyes holding hers as if she'd vanish if he looked away. "Every minor, mundane detail of my life."

Vira shivered. "Then tell me."

"I don't know how."

The honesty in his words nearly broke her. "You don't have to tell me everything, Amrit. And certainly not all at once."

He turned, the sharp angle of his profile silhouetted against the white glow of the moon. "I think . . . I wish." His eyes closed. "Wishes are for fools. My father used to say that."

Vira was certain that if her mother had ever shared her opinion on wishes, it would have been the same. "I don't think it's foolish." She swallowed. "Tell me one of your wishes, and I'll tell you one of mine."

"Wishes are also dangerous things."

"Something else your father told you?"

"No. That I learned on my own." He sighed deeply again. "You asked me how I could promise to keep us safe. It's because —" He stopped himself, his brows furrowing as if he were trying to find the right words. "My family died when I was seven."

"What?" He'd spoken often of his family — of sparring with his brothers, lessons learned from his father.

"The family I was born into, I mean," he clarified.

"Amrit. I'm so sorry." Vira couldn't help but put her hand on his. He didn't pull away.

"It was a long time ago." He smiled, a little strained. "I told you I was from the north, but I was actually born in Vrindh. My parents were farmers, and they worked on land owned by some rich family. And when I was six, they were approached by a man who claimed there were better opportunities in the north — a chance for them to own their own land for just a few hundred jhaus. It was all the money they had, but he said they would make it all back tenfold in the years to come, so they accepted the offer. And a month later, we moved.

"As soon as we arrived, it was clear that something had gone wrong. The land my parents had bought was land that belonged to someone else — another rich lord. They were mortified, and they'd spent all their money, so they begged the landowner for work. But he cast us out on the spot. He said he didn't hire people who weren't clever enough to not get scammed."

Vira's heart ached. "Oh, Amrit." She squeezed his hand.

"We couldn't afford the journey back, but the only home we could find was even farther north — in a village at the base of the Koranos Mountains." He turned to look at her then, and Vira could see the depth of the sorrow in his eyes. "A year later, they were both gone. My mother died first, and my father a few months later. I was orphaned by the time I was seven."

It was no wonder he didn't want to talk about this, and Vira suddenly felt horrible that she'd pressed him. "You don't have to —"

"I want to tell you," he said. "I was lucky enough to be taken in by another family, a few towns over. A family who treated me like I was one of their own, and that's when I learned that family isn't always about blood. Sometimes your family is made up of the people who raised you, who taught you to protect yourself, who taught you valuable lessons."

"They were lucky to have you," Vira said.

His smile grew a little more real, and then he flipped his hand over, threading his fingers through hers. She didn't know when it had become so easy for them to stand this close together, to touch each other with such familiarity.

"I grew up in those mountains. Sparring with my brothers, running

227

through the jungles." He pointed at his ankle. "That snakebite? That happened there. And it was my father who used the aruval to take the fang out before I lost my whole leg."

He turned toward her fully then, taking her other hand in his. "I don't know what lies on the other side of the border, Vira. I don't know what will happen with the mercenaries. But I know the land. And I will do everything in my power to protect you. To protect your entire family."

Vira tilted her head, looking up at Amrit. It wasn't always easy to read him, but in that moment she could see with startling clarity that his eyes held one thing: promise.

And whatever happened, whatever fate awaited them on their journey, the one thing she knew with absolute certainty was that he would always keep her safe.

"I trust you," she said simply.

✳

The knock at the door came while Vira was sipping her morning chai. It was early—she'd woken with the sun, butterflies swimming through her stomach at the thought of journeying to the Maravat province. Vira rose and pulled open the door. To her surprise, it wasn't Amrit but Meena.

"Good morning, Maharani."

"Councilor." Vira opened the door wider. "Please come in. Would you like some chai?" she offered.

"No, thank you. This will be a quick visit." Meena lingered at the door, but her eyes drifted to the trunks, packed and ready to be loaded into the carriages. Vira intended to carry only a small bag with her into the mountains, but they'd all packed suitcases in order to keep up pretenses. Her maharani's talwar rested on top of the stacks, still in its cumbersome sheath. "I've come to urge you to reconsider. It isn't wise for you to leave Dvar now."

"I'm needed with my family," Vira insisted. "It's the first time the four of us have been together. Kaleb deserves to be there with us, to honor our father."

It wasn't a lie. The anniversary of Papa's death was coming up, and normally that would involve a ceremony officiated by a priestess. But finding the Ivory Key was the best way Vira knew to honor her father.

Meena didn't look pleased by her answer. "Your mother would know that a maharani doesn't have the luxury of attending all family ceremonies."

"I'm not my mother."

"No, you are not," she said, not waiting for Vira to dismiss her before she walked away.

Vira had walked right into that trap, but for the first time, guilt didn't consume her. She wasn't her mother. But why did she have to be? Her mother was gone.

This was what Ashoka needed.

Vira would save Ashoka, but she would do it her own way.

Without thinking about it, she made her way into her bedroom and yanked the talwar down from its mount on the wall opposite her bed. She wasn't her mother, but she was still the maharani.

When Amrit knocked on the door, Vira was sliding her own talwar into its sheath.

"Vira are you—" His eyes landed on her mother's talwar by her feet — and at the unadorned hilt of her old talwar at her side. The one he'd spent hours and hours training her to use back when she'd been the rajkumaari and he a trainer in the arena. A smile flitted across his lips. He cleared his throat. "Are you ready?"

Vira smiled back. "Let's go."

CHAPTER THIRTY

— KALEB —

As their carriage jostled along the sand-dusted roads of Ashoka, Kaleb sat with his eyes closed. He'd slept poorly the night before, and his eyes ached. It was dark and it was quiet, but as much as he willed the rocking motion and gentle hum of magic to quiet his mind and lull him to sleep, his thoughts kept drifting back to Surya's words from weeks ago.

You'll never have your old life back.

He'd been so sure that was a lie, but everything about Ronak's engagement party had proved the mercenary right. Kaleb had spent the evening uncomfortably lingering off to the side, pretending he didn't notice the wary looks other guests shot in his direction when they thought he wasn't looking. The only person who'd spoken to him was Riya. And after she'd disappeared with her friends, Kaleb had also left, tired of being simultaneously ignored and scrutinized. He didn't think anyone noticed his absence.

"Stop moving," Riya snapped at Ronak.

Kaleb cracked his eyes open. After sitting in silence for so long, any sound seemed too loud.

Ronak pushed her arm away. "Then stop digging your elbow into my side."

"There's nowhere else for my elbow to go." Riya shoved him back.

"Enough," Vira said sharply.

Kaleb sat up, pressing his fingers into his temples and abandoning all hope of sleep. "Are we there yet?" He didn't remember carriages being so tiny — or family trips being this vexing.

For what seemed like the hundredth time since they'd left, Riya lifted the curtain covering the window. Kaleb blinked away from the sudden stream of sunlight.

"Stop doing that." Vira slapped Riya's hand away. "Nothing has changed since the last time you looked, *thirty seconds ago.*"

"I'm just trying to make sure we're going in the right direction."

"And since when are you an expert on the roads of Maravat?" Vira asked coolly.

Ronak snorted. Riya shot him a dark glare but dropped her hold on the curtain. Kaleb let his head thump against the back of the seat.

Kausalya help me. This was going to be a long journey.

✳

It was evening by the time the Koranos Mountains stopped being blurs in the distant horizon. Patches of orange and purple bruised the twilight sky as the carriage slowed, then stopped altogether. Kaleb let the curtain fall back over the window as Amrit pulled open the door and brisk, dry air filled the stuffy carriage.

Vira rubbed her eyes as she sat up. "We're here?" She reached for her dupatta, which had slipped away during their journey, and draped it properly across her shoulders.

"There's an inn at the end of the road where we can wash up," Amrit said, offering Vira a private smile. He looked surprisingly alert for someone who had driven a carriage through most of the day, and Kaleb tried not to resent him for it.

As if sensing the direction of his thoughts, Vira's gaze turned to Kaleb. "Did you sleep at all? You look terrible."

"Thanks," he said dryly.

"I didn't mean it like that." Vira looked as if she wanted to say something else, but then she shook her head and exited the carriage.

Kaleb ran his hands over his face and through his hair. He was sure he did look awful. Unlike other academics, he'd never been fond of late nights. On the rare occasions he'd been forced to eschew sleep, he knew he wore his fatigue clearly the next day. His skin turned pale, his eyes were bloodshot, and it took at least three cups of chai for any semblance of energy to return to him. He sincerely hoped this inn would have some very strong, very spicy chai.

Riya yawned and stretched in the seat across from him. "Ignore her," she said. "You look great."

It was a lie, but it made him smile anyway. Riya had always been quick to come to his defense, to take his side no matter the argument.

Next to her, Ronak stirred but didn't wake, his brows knit together as though he were dreaming of unpleasant things — perhaps his family. Riya nudged his shoulder, but he swatted her hand away.

"Go," Riya said to Kaleb, stifling a second yawn. "We'll meet you there."

Kaleb disembarked. Despite the late hour, the tiny village — if the collection of several dozen homes along the single street could even be called that — was still bustling with activity. A group of women walked past him, balancing clay pots atop their heads. A produce vendor pushed her cart up the sloping street, calling out prices in strangely accented Ashokan for varieties of prickly gourds, stalks of sugarcane, and freshly harvested bundles of moringa. They all stopped to stare at the newcomers — first at Vira and Amrit and then at Kaleb as he followed.

Something nagged at the back of his mind, and it took him a moment to recognize what it was. The produce cart, the milk jugs, the pots of water — none of it had magic.

"Where are we exactly?" he asked as he caught up to Vira and Amrit.

"Inhadh," Amrit answered.

Kaleb had never heard of it, but he wasn't entirely surprised. According to Papa, there were hundreds of minuscule towns like this dotting the foothills of the Koranos, clustered around the rivers that streaked down the mountains.

"Do they not have magic?"

"Lower your voice," Vira hissed, looking uncomfortably over her shoulder.

But Amrit looked unsurprised by the question. "They use it differently here." He nodded discreetly toward an approaching alley. "Look."

The path was narrow, barely wide enough to fit two people walking side by side, and it ended abruptly at a small temple. He'd seen temples like these before, honoring one of the lesser-known goddesses or saints, tucked into the sides of buildings or in hollowed-out tree trunks.

But this one was different. There was no goddess here. Instead, where an idol would have been, there were rotating obsidian spheres floating in the air, moving in concentric circles. The largest one was in the center, covered in powdered vermilion, ash, and turmeric.

"They're planets," Kaleb said in awe. He knew there were plenty of people in Ashoka who worshipped other goddesses and gods, whose rites and customs differed based on which province or country they were from, but he'd never seen anything like this before. He took a step toward them, pulled by some unseen tether, but Vira's hand on his shoulder tugged him back.

"A lot of these mountain towns don't worship goddesses directly," Amrit explained, "but rather interpretations of them. Supposedly, this temple has been here for more than four hundred years."

They were too far away to feel the prickle of magic, but Kaleb knew it was there; keeping stones of this size suspended in midair for so many years required a lot of magic. And some very talented mayaka. No one in Dvar spent much magic on the goddesses these days, but once, temples had been at the heart of Ashokan civilization, and priestesses were the first mayaka. It was odd to see this vestige of a bygone era tucked away here.

✳

The inn was at the end of the street, larger than the homes they'd passed, but not much grander. Cracks spidered through the plaster, revealing the stone slabs that made up the external walls, and through the rusted metal of the gate Kaleb could see overgrown foliage tipping over onto the walkways. A single fading sign proclaimed that it was an inn, written first in Ashokan and below that in Lyrian.

"I didn't think there would be an inn in a town so small," Riya said when she and Ronak caught up with them.

"They were for traders," Ronak said as they approached the door. "Back when the main trade routes passed through the mountains rather than the sea." Vira gave him a surprised look, and Ronak scowled. "What?"

Vira just shook her head, but Ronak's scowl deepened anyway.

The inside of the building was in far better shape than the exterior suggested. Simple wooden benches lined either side of the foyer, and evening light streamed in from large west-facing windows. As the five of them approached, two servants who were scrubbing the grime off the windowsills stopped, dropping their rags into a bucket of water.

"We're looking for the innkeeper," Amrit said, and one of the servants pointed toward the door at the far end of the room. "Wait here." Amrit disappeared through the door, returning a few minutes later with two large metal keys. "There are baths out back, and the innkeeper will prepare us a meal," he said, handing one key to Vira and the other to Kaleb. "We can rest here, but it's best if we make it into mercenary territory by sunrise."

Kaleb nodded, his stomach turning to lead as he took the key. Crossing mercenary land had felt like a distant and abstract concept when they'd discussed their plan days ago, but now they were fast approaching it, and it was starting to strike him just how real the dangers of this quest were.

Vira and Riya followed Amrit, but Kaleb put a hand out to stop Ronak.

"Can I talk to you?" Kaleb rubbed the back of his neck, waiting until the others were out of earshot. "What are you doing here? Really?"

All real emotion vanished from Ronak's face, replaced by the passionless smile he used to charm his elders and vex Vira. "Protecting my country, brother. Isn't that why you're here?"

"You know that won't work on me."

Ronak's jaw tightened, and he looked off to the side. "What do you want me to say, Kaleb? What answer can I give that will make you stop doubting me?"

Kaleb bit the inside of his cheek. They both knew there wasn't any answer. "Are you planning to run?" he asked instead.

"No. Are you satisfied?"

"Ronak, I just —" Kaleb stopped himself. He couldn't tell whether Ronak was lying, and that frustrated him. Once, he'd believed that his brother would never lie to him. And here he was, wondering if Ronak had ever told him the truth. "Fine. Let's go."

"No. Say it." Ronak couldn't resist prodding. "You've said plenty to me already, brother. What's one more thing?"

Ronak turned to face him, piercing Kaleb with his intense stare. His hair was a mess from his restless hands, and his mouth was curved into a cruel smile. He looked strangely youthful — strangely wild. Kaleb didn't want to talk to him when he was like this, so he backed away without another word.

"Don't act like you don't have your own agenda," Ronak called after him.

Kaleb ignored him. That wasn't news. They all had their own agenda. Still, he couldn't shake the lingering feeling that something had snapped irreversibly between them.

CHAPTER THIRTY-ONE

— RONAK —

RONAK SQUINTED AT himself in the dirty mirror that rested against the wall in one corner of the sparsely furnished room and ran his hands through his still-wet hair. Without magic in the bathing pools to keep it hot, the stove-heated water had quickly turned tepid in the cold mountain air. Ronak had stayed in it just long enough to scrub himself clean, but a chill clung to the air even indoors here, making him shiver.

Kaleb hadn't said a word to him since they'd talked in the foyer, but he'd left a wool coat out for Ronak — one of the matching ones they'd packed from Papa's old almirah. Ronak shrugged it on over his plain maroon kurta, wishing Kaleb's silence didn't irritate him so much. The heavy material felt uncomfortable, weighing him down and restricting his movements in a way he was unaccustomed to, but it was necessary this far north.

He scanned the room, checking that Kaleb had carefully hidden both their bags, and then he let himself out, locking the door and following the narrow hallway back the way they'd come. The others were already seated around a low, circular table in the dining hall, talking in hushed voices even though only one other table was occupied. Ronak slipped his shoes off and lowered himself onto the divan between Vira and Kaleb.

"It's better to go east," Vira was saying, pointing somewhere on a roughly sketched map that Ronak couldn't make out.

"East is *away* from where we need to be going," Riya argued. "It'll take longer to double back, and we only have two days before the equinox."

"But it's safer," Vira hissed back. "We can handle a few soldiers, but not a whole battalion."

Ronak frowned. "Soldiers?" They'd picked this town for crossing the border because it was just far enough from Ritsar that they could avoid the soldiers who were protecting the new border there day and night.

Amrit nodded toward the other occupied table. Now Ronak could see that all three people seated there were dressed in the same red and gold outfit. One of them turned just then, and Ronak caught sight of Ashoka's crest emblazoned on the soldier's chest.

Vira had propped her left elbow on the table, using it to hide her face. The soldiers weren't paying them any attention, and even if they were, without her rich clothes and heavy jewelry she would have nothing more than a passing resemblance to a maharani they'd seen only in portraits or from a distance. Still, it wasn't good.

"What are they doing here?" Ronak asked.

Vira's jaw tightened. "Apparently, a month ago, the Council decided to deploy additional soldiers to patrol the northern border."

After Harish died. "Apparently?" Ronak repeated. "You didn't know?"

Vira gave him a look of annoyance. "Clearly not —"

"Amrit knows the area," Kaleb cut in. "Perhaps we should let him decide."

Riya pursed her lips as Amrit — predictably — looked at Vira. It took all of Ronak's self-restraint not to roll his eyes. Whatever their personal relationship, she was still his maharani. But Amrit didn't have a chance to answer before a server approached their table, pouring ice-cold water from a copper jug into the tumblers set out in front of them.

Vira snatched the map off the table. "We'll discuss this after we eat."

Somehow Ronak didn't think there was much up for discussion, but he kept silent as more servers appeared with platters of local dishes: lotus stems, coated in besan and fried with garlic and onions; kachoris stuffed with black gram paste; pumpkins cooked in a sweet and tangy gravy; channa roasted in yogurt and raw spices; and chapatis slathered in ghee and served with pickled citrons, raw mangoes, and boondi raita.

"We should go east," Amrit said once they were left alone. "Vira's right. We can't risk being detained." He hesitated, and then added, "But it does mean we won't reach mercenary territory until midday."

"So our options are lose half a day or walk through the night," Riya said, ripping into her kachori. "Great."

"How many soldiers are there?" Ronak asked.

"We don't know," Amrit admitted. "According to the innkeeper, there are those three who come here frequently, but there are other inns a few miles away."

"How could you not know what your own Council is doing?" Riya snapped. "We could have prepared for this."

Vira gritted her teeth. "They were doing what they felt was best for Ashoka."

Ronak snorted. "They keep secrets from you, and still you protect them. If only you gave your family the same consideration."

"Ronak," Kaleb warned, but Ronak ignored him.

"You think I haven't protected our family?" Vira's eyes flashed. "I make the hard choices, Ronak. While you're free to do whatever you wish, I'm the one who weighs the options, who makes the tough calls in times of danger. And against my better judgment, I shielded you for as long as I could."

"I'm still engaged, aren't I?"

"Only because my betrothed *died* — or did you forget that?"

"Maybe we should discuss this elsewhere," Amrit said.

Ronak ignored him too. "You certainly didn't stop your Council from locking up our brother."

"Leave me out of this," Kaleb said. And then he paused, turning to Ronak. "Is that what you think you're doing? Protecting me?"

"Someone has to."

"Making decisions on behalf of others isn't protection. People get to make their own choices." Kaleb blinked at him. "I thought you of all people would understand that."

"That's different." Everything Ronak had done was what he needed to do to survive. Vira and the palace had nothing left to offer him — to offer either of them — and he didn't understand how Kaleb couldn't see it as well.

"How exactly is it different?" Riya asked. Of course she'd jump to Kaleb's defense. Ronak was getting tired of his family taking any side that wasn't his.

"Stay out of things that don't concern you, Riya. You made your choice two years ago when you abandoned us."

She lifted her chin defiantly. "So? I'm back now."

"Well, maybe you should have just stayed away," Ronak snapped, irritated. The entire table fell stiflingly silent. Riya dropped the chapati on her plate and turned away — but not before Ronak saw the hurt flash across her face. *Shit.* "Riya —"

"I thought you were right," Riya said. "That Vira was this horrible sister who ruined your life — ruined Kaleb's. But that's not true, is it? You push away anyone who ever cares about you, and then you act like it's their fault for leaving." Her voice dripped with venom. "And if I were you, *brother*, I wouldn't be so quick to judge. After all, I'm not the one hiding secret ties to a criminal empire." She rose from the table and stalked out of the room.

"Criminal empire?" Vira demanded. "Ronak, what did you do?"

He didn't say anything. Out of the corner of his eye he saw her shake her head in disgust before she, too, walked away, Amrit on her heels.

"You went too far," Kaleb said quietly, and then he was also gone, leaving Ronak alone at the table with four half-eaten dinners.

CHAPTER THIRTY-TWO

— RIYA —

RIYA WAS AWAKENED at the crack of dawn by Vira shaking her shoulders. Her eyes felt heavy, but she forced them open as she pushed herself up. The room had stayed cold all night despite the extra blankets Vira had piled on the bed they'd shared, and she'd slept poorly despite being exhausted from their long journey. She stretched her neck, wincing at the stiffness from the uncomfortable inn mattress. Maybe Varun was right. She'd grown too accustomed to the luxuries of the palace.

Amrit was already dressed and armed, sitting on the second bed in the room, rifling through one of the packs. Riya followed Vira into the washing room, splashing her face with hot water and braiding her hair away from her face. It felt odd not to be laden with any jewelry, aside from her simple silver lock-pick earrings, but it was odder still seeing Vira dressed so simply — like that day in the forest.

"This suits you," Riya said, realizing that Vira had mirrored her, parting her hair to the side instead of down the middle the way Amma always had. Vira had been dressing less like their mother lately, and Riya had noticed that she'd brought her old talwar instead of Amma's. It felt significant somehow. Vira self-consciously ran a hand over her bare neck, but she smiled a little.

The boys were waiting in the dining hall, dressed in Papa's wool coats. Ronak didn't say a single word to her, but more than once Riya caught him staring in her direction. She clenched her jaw and kept her gaze trained on the table in front of her. She hadn't come back for family — for anything other than magic. She'd made a mistake. She'd lied, and it had cost her a place among the Ravens. But as soon as she had the Ivory Key, she had every intention of using it to fix things between them.

But . . . Ronak's words had hurt more than she'd expected.

Riya didn't feel much like eating, but she forced herself to drink a cup of strangely spiced chai and picked at the kachoris the innkeeper set out for them. Amrit carefully verified that all their supplies were there, making sure that the waterskins they'd found among Papa's things — forged to filter out any unsafe particles without needing to boil the water — were filled and that the innkeeper had packed them enough food to last them for a four-day trek through the jungle. It wasn't until Riya caught Amrit checking their belongings a third time that she realized he was nervous.

She didn't think any of the others had noticed, but his anxiety worried her. Her siblings weren't used to traveling like this, and they had an uncertain journey ahead of them. It would fall to her and Amrit to ensure that they all made it there and back.

It was still dark as they made their way through the town and then turned away from the main roads toward the forested area that separated Inhadh from the next village.

"This way," Vira said, squinting at one of the maps she'd copied over before leaving Dvar. "I think."

It turned out that they didn't need the map. They felt the magic before they saw the border wall.

"Wait here," Riya said, stopping the others.

"Why?" Vira demanded.

"You're too loud," Riya said flatly. "It would be better if Amrit and I went first to see what we're up against."

"We're not loud." Vira scowled as Kaleb chose that moment to yawn and Ronak stepped on a twig. "Fine," she relented. "Be quick."

Riya and Amrit crept forward, the push of magic growing stronger with each step. As the wall came into view, they hid behind a tree, peering around the edge of the trunk. This was different from the border wall near Dvar. It wasn't as ornate, but it was no less ferocious, standing more than fifteen feet tall and made of solid, smooth gray rock. There were no cracks, no damage from the elements, not even vines crawling over the surface. It certainly didn't look like it had stood there for five hundred years.

There was only one soldier walking along the length of the wall. Riya pulled a watch out of her pack, keeping time as she and Amrit silently moved through the trees, following the guard's path.

"Good news," Riya said as they rejoined the others fifteen minutes later. "There's only one soldier."

"Great. So we can just knock him out," Ronak said.

"Bad news," Amrit said. "The patrol paths overlap."

"Someone will notice if he doesn't show up," Riya said. "We'll have to search in ten-minute bursts." It wasn't ideal, but they had no other choice.

Vira pulled out a gold coin the size of her palm. It had seals stamped on either side: a war elephant on one and Ashoka's crest on the other. "Spread out," she ordered. "We need to figure out where this goes."

It was a fail-safe, a holdover from when the borders had surrounded each major city rather than Ashoka as a whole. It was a secret way for healers to bring in injured soldiers after battles, for generals to be able to discreetly move troops without using the gates. Each one-mile section of the border had a secret door that could be unlocked with a special coin.

Very few people knew about it because the only remaining key was in Vira's hand, preserved for generations in the treasure trove above the library. But it also meant that no one knew for certain where the coin was to be insert-ed to open this wall.

"It can't be on the wall itself," Kaleb said. "No one would be able to get close enough."

Vira nodded in agreement. "We'll check the ground first."

Riya kept time while the others fanned out. After ten minutes she called them back, and they moved to the next section of the wall. By the time they'd searched the entire mile-long stretch, the sun was starting to crest over the mountains.

"We're missing something," Riya said, frustrated. They had turned over every piece of rock, rifled through the shrubbery, but there was no place they could possibly insert a coin. If they couldn't get through the border, their whole journey would fail even before they started.

Ronak stood staring at the wall, his arms crossed across his chest. He'd been standing there for nearly twenty minutes. "I've read every biography of Savitri that Papa has, and if there's one thing they all agree on, it's that she wasn't the type to leave things to chance. The point of this coin is for emergencies."

"You think she'd have left a marker to identify it quickly?" Kaleb asked. He glanced at Vira and then at Riya.

"It's a possibility," Vira conceded.

"It would have to be on something she knew would survive," Amrit pointed out. "Something that wouldn't be moved or destroyed."

"Like the wall?" Ronak asked. He crouched and then pointed, and Riya saw what he meant.

There were notches along the base of the wall. All of them the same length — except for one, which was longer. Not by a lot, but enough to notice if you were looking for it. And directly in front of it was a tree. At the base of the tree, covered in moss and lichen, was a stone slab with a hole just wide enough for a coin.

Riya brushed the foliage away and held her hand out to Vira for the coin. As soon as Riya inserted it, a portion of the wall dissolved into an arched gateway, the magic within the wall waning. *Thank the goddesses,* she thought.

"Quickly," Riya said, glancing at her watch. "We only have a few minutes."

Amrit went first, then Vira, Kaleb, and Ronak. Riya wasn't sure how long the door would stay open after she removed the coin. She'd have to run just to be safe. She took a deep breath.

"What are you doing?"

Riya whirled around to see a soldier staring disbelievingly at the hole in the wall. It wasn't the soldier they'd seen patrolling the area, but a different one — one of the ones from the inn.

"Shift change," she muttered. They'd forgotten to account for that.

The soldier was rushing toward her, his shock having worn off, reaching for his weapon. She didn't have much time. She wrapped her dupatta around her nose and mouth and reached for one of the three identical spheres she'd had Kaleb design before they left. It was a variation of what the Ravens used — smoke from the special plant in the forest that could knock people out.

Riya smashed it. As smoke enveloped him, the soldier began to cough and then collapsed to the ground. Riya yanked out the coin and ran through the door seconds before it sealed shut.

CHAPTER THIRTY-THREE

— VIRA —

VIRA HATED BEING in the jungle. As the sun rose higher in the sky, the air turned hot and humid, and her clothes and hair kept sticking to her skin. There were explorers who'd mapped the flora and fauna of the Koranos Mountains, and Vira had spent the days before their trip flipping through tomes to see what they might encounter, but reality, she was finding, was nothing like the beautiful images of waterfalls and exotic plants painted in those manuals. She swatted the dragonflies hovering around, the drone of their wings irritatingly close.

"I hate this," Kaleb muttered, grimacing as a black and green butterfly the size of Vira's palm landed on his shoulder.

"It's just a butterfly." Riya gently brushed it away.

"It's bigger than any butterfly has the right to be," he said darkly. His shoulders remained tense. "And their wings are terrifying."

Ronak snorted, but Vira secretly agreed. The jungle had far too many insects for her taste. Beetles scurried up tree trunks, disappearing into holes too small to see. Spiders spun glistening webs between tree branches, lying in wait for whatever prey they could ensnare. Even the ground wasn't safe, the dead leaves crawling with little black leeches that latched onto unsuspecting victims.

Vira had been to the forest dozens of times, but she hadn't considered

how different a jungle would be — how much difference the forest's prox-
imity to civilization would make. Everything was wilder here, tucked away
from the prying hands of humans.

It was nearing noon, but the canopy was thick enough to keep most
light out. A few rays of sun dappled through the leaves, pouring down like
fine grains of sand to illuminate twisting roots and tangled vines. Fallen
trees hindered their paths, forcing them to scramble over the large tree
trunks, long since colonized by invading species. Even the animals were
far easier to sense here: the strange hooting of birds, paw prints in the still-
damp dirt, the occasional rustling above as some unseen creature swung
from branch to branch.

Amrit guided them through the thicket, carefully tracking a path that
would be easiest for them to follow. Riya kept glancing down at Papa's com-
pass, which was hanging around her neck, making sure they were walking
west now, right into mercenary territory.

Vira's legs ached, and resin coated her palms as she crawled over what
felt like the eightieth fallen tree. They would need to stop soon to refill their
water, to rest and eat before continuing, but Amrit and Riya showed no
signs of slowing down.

Riya had always excelled at anything that had an element of physicality — dancing, fighting, swimming. Her time with the Ravens had further
honed those skills, and she looked at ease as she trailed Amrit, glancing
behind occasionally to make sure they were all following. Vira stayed close
by, driven by some inane desire to prove to Amrit that she could keep up
with him. But it was clear that she wasn't the only one struggling. Ronak
had fallen so far behind that Vira couldn't even see him around the bend in
the path. Kaleb, too, was struggling to breathe, leaning heavily against the
log as he took a long swig from his nearly empty waterskin.

"Wait," Vira called.

Amrit turned around at once, concerned. But Vira pointed farther down to where Ronak was just appearing.

"We need to stick together," Riya told Ronak.

"We need to rest," he countered.

Riya pursed her lips and, to Vira's surprise, glanced at Amrit.

"A little bit farther," Amrit said. "And then we can stop."

Vira caught up to Amrit. "What's going on?" she asked in a low voice.

Amrit didn't look too happy, but he pointed to a tree trunk. There were scratches on it — three large claw marks covered in dried blood. "Leopard," he said. "They drag their prey up into the trees."

Vira blanched. She couldn't see the remnants of whatever poor monkey or deer the leopard had killed, but suddenly it seemed all the more imperative that they keep moving. She drank more water and summoned the last of her energy to keep pace with Riya and Amrit, glancing behind to make sure her brothers were still there.

They heard the gurgling of water first, and then the trees began to thin out as they walked down into the valley. They followed the sound, which grew louder until the rapidly moving stream cut right through their path. A log served as a makeshift bridge, but water poured out through the cracks in the wood like a small waterfall.

"We'll rest on the other side," Riya said, looking visibly relieved. She went first, scurrying across the surprisingly sturdy bridge, and the others followed.

There wasn't much cover here, but they sat on the bank in a circle and ate the carefully rationed food Riya doled out. The chapati was a little hard and dry, but Vira forced down two pieces smeared in mango and lemon pickle, washing it down with a lot of water. Vira also splashed her face with water, and the cold seemed to revive her a little.

"We're on the edge of mercenary territory," Amrit said, spreading one of their maps on the ground. He pointed to where he guessed they were and then drew a path with his finger for where they were heading. "This is Ritsar. And all this is mercenary land."

"All of it?" Kaleb asked, warily eyeing the large expanse Amrit had delineated.

"Well, we don't know," Vira said. They had no idea where the mercenaries even originated from — or how they entered Ashoka. Anyone the Council had sent to find out had disappeared. Her stomach knotted as she looked at the trees ahead of them. It was hard to see much beyond darkness.

"And we also don't know what lies ahead," Riya said.

"Great," Ronak muttered. He dusted himself off and rose. "Let's go, then."

❈

It grew colder once again as the sun sank behind the mountains. Vira wrapped her dupatta tighter around her shoulders, swatting away mosquitoes. The jungle here was even thicker, slowing their progress. They'd had to stop and hack away at multiple knots of vines as they pushed through. Twice, Vira had jumped — once when the earth moved right where she'd been about to step as a tiny snake slithered out of the leaves, and a second time when she'd caught the glossy eyes of tiny venomous lorises watching from the canopy. She had stifled her startled screams, but it hadn't stopped Riya from glaring at her for being too loud.

"We have to stop," Amrit said unhappily as the last of the sun disappeared.

They pulled out magical lanterns, which only attracted more insects — moths drawn to the light, more mosquitoes, even a grasshopper that landed on Kaleb's hair and scared him so much he'd tripped over his feet and crashed to the ground.

"There's nowhere to stop," Vira said. They were in the middle of the wilderness. There was nowhere to sit, nowhere to light a fire, not even a stream to refill their water. Anything — any*one* — could stumble on them here. They had no protection and certainly nowhere to rest comfortably.

"I know," Amrit said. "But soon it'll be too dark to see anything."

They walked until they found a slightly wider clearing, bordered on one side by a fallen log, with just enough room for the five of them to sit. They sat in silence around the small lantern as they ate.

"I'll take the first watch," Amrit said, then outlined shifts of two hours for each of them. He disappeared through the trees, one hand on his talwar.

Vira didn't think she was going to sleep much, but she sat with her back against a tree trunk, sliding the lantern closer to her and opening Papa's journal. Riya lay down on the ground, curling up in a ball with her pack as a pillow and her coat as a blanket. Next to her, Kaleb also closed his eyes, and within minutes his breathing turned even. Vira turned as she felt Ronak's gaze on her.

"I suppose being able to sleep anywhere is the one benefit of being imprisoned for a year," Ronak said.

He hadn't said much since they'd left Inhadh. Riya had refused to explain her comment about criminal empires, and it was starting to worry Vira. She couldn't help him if she didn't know exactly what he was mixed up in.

But she bit the inside of her cheek to stop herself from responding, returning her attention to Papa's journal. She must have fallen asleep at some point, too, because she was wakened by Kaleb for the last shift. She yawned and closed the journal, setting it atop the tree trunk before pushing herself up.

"You don't really need to patrol," Kaleb said, his eyes already closing. "Just stay alert."

Vira did as ordered, but everything remained quiet until dawn broke. Birds chirped in the distance, and soon the sky was light enough to wake the others. Vira felt her anxiety grow as they prepared to continue walking. They only had a little more than a day to reach the temple before the equinox sunset, and they hadn't made nearly as much progress as they needed.

She had expected that the jungle would be easier to navigate on the second day, but they'd barely slept in days, and it felt like they were moving even slower. She reached for the waterskin in her bag, which she'd been carefully rationing — and then froze.

"We have to go back," she said, stopping everyone in their tracks. "Papa's journal. I left it behind."

Riya gave her an incredulous look. "What?"

"We might need it," Vira said insistently. "I have to go back."

Amrit nodded. "Just wait here," he said. "Vira and I will go. We'll be back in twenty minutes."

Riya looked unhappy, though neither of the boys seemed to care. It was faster going back, following the path they'd already worn with their feet. They reached their camp in minutes, finding where Papa's journal had slid off the log and onto the ground. Vira dusted it off and tucked it away securely in her bag.

"We're not making good time, are we?" she asked Amrit as they walked back to the group.

"We'll make it," he said with a confidence that Vira wasn't sure he truly felt. He was worried. She didn't know how she'd gotten so good at reading him, but she could sense his mood.

"What if—"

There was a rustling between the trees. Amrit moved faster than Vira could think, whirling around with his weapon raised.

"Stay behind me," he whispered as he stalked forward, twisting away from the path they'd taken. Vira followed him, trying to match the silence of his movements. But there was nothing there.

"An animal," Vira said.

"Probably," Amrit agreed. "This way." He nodded toward the way they'd come.

Vira took a step—and then tripped. Amrit caught her by the elbow just before she pitched forward into the dirt. Then there was a snap, and the ground moved beneath her feet.

She let out a strangled cry as she and Amrit were scooped up into the air. Amrit's talwar clattered to the ground, and he groaned as Vira's elbow collided with his jaw. Then they were hanging in midair, suspended between two trees, the ground spinning beneath them.

"Hunting trap . . ." Amrit panted.

Rope bit into Vira's back, her arms, her shoulders. Her legs were tangled with Amrit's, her body pressed so tight against his she could feel his heartbeat. Feel the heat of his body pressing against her chest, her thighs.

She twisted—and Amrit's hand collided with her stomach. Their foreheads smacked together. Amrit groaned again. Vira stilled, letting her breath even out, willing her heart to stop thundering. She was practically on top of him, pinning down one of his arms. Their other arms were tangled together, trapped between them.

Vira felt her face heat. She'd never been this close to him—this close to *anyone.* Amrit's gaze lifted to meet hers, and all Vira could think was that she'd never known that his eyes weren't black, but the darkest of browns.

"Well," Amrit breathed, and Vira felt his breath flutter against her lips. "This is . . . not ideal."

Her hair was falling out of her braid, framing her face as she looked down at him. "How do we get out of this?" She didn't know why she was whispering.

"I think I can cut us out if I can reach my knife." He sounded out of breath, his chest rising and falling too quickly.

Vira nodded. "I think . . . I can do that."

She twisted away from him and put her right hand on his chest — right over his heart — to push herself up. Her back pressed against the net, just far enough for Amrit to pull his right arm free. But instead of reaching for his knife, Amrit tucked her hair behind her ear, his knuckles brushing against her cheek. Lingering. She froze. Her face burned where his fingers had trailed across her skin.

Vira's gaze dropped to his lips.

There were some things a maharani didn't get to want.

Amrit swallowed. "Vira." His voice was so soft. "I —"

"Well, well," a voice called from below. "That looks quite comfortable."

Vira jerked back, turning her head to look through a hole in the net. It was a figure dressed entirely in black. He carried a bow. And a quiver of black-fletched arrows.

And he had one of them nocked and aimed directly at the two of them.

The mercenary cocked his head, studying them. And then, impossibly, he lowered his bow. "On second thought," he said. And then he fired at the tree trunk.

"Wait —"

There was a snap. Time froze for a horrifying second — and then they fell. They tumbled to the ground, limbs still tangled. Vira winced as she tried to sit up, shoving the net away. She'd landed on a rock. Not sharp enough to break skin, but she was certain it would leave a bruise against her lower back.

"Are you all right?" Amrit crouched beside her, one hand on her elbow, another at her shoulder, helping her up. Vira could only nod. Her body ached everywhere.

The boy had another arrow pointed at them as he watched them with a dark smile.

Amrit raised his empty arms, palms outward. "We just want to pass through," he said. "We have no business with your people."

"If you want to pass through our territory, you *will* have business with us."

It was the same kind of arrow Surya had used to kill Harish. Even if the arrow didn't hit true, there would be no surviving the poison that tipped it. Vira glanced at Amrit. They didn't have a lot of options.

There was more rustling — and then voices. Vira's heart leapt into her throat as the mercenary's eyes widened. He had counted on them being alone.

"Cover your face!"

Riya's voice sounded somewhere to Vira's left. The mercenary turned and let his arrow fly — but it was too late. Riya's orb shattered in front of him. Vira shoved one end of her dupatta at Amrit and pressed the other against her nose and mouth as smoke engulfed the mercenary. He coughed, and a few seconds later he collapsed into a heap on the ground.

CHAPTER THIRTY-FOUR

— KALEB —

EVEN UNCONSCIOUS AND tied to a tree trunk, the mercenary looked dangerous. Kaleb kept his distance as he studied the boy. He looked around the same age as Surya — maybe younger — but much more like what Kaleb had imagined mercenaries to be: burly, muscular, menacingly tall.

Behind him, the others debated what to do with him.

"We must be close to their hideout," Ronak said.

"Which is all the more reason to leave quickly," Vira pointed out. "We can't risk being followed. We don't have an endless supply of smoke."

Kaleb hadn't had time to forge more than a handful of items, and his sisters had agreed that making the smoke was the best use of his time. And now they were already down to the last one.

"We can't just leave him here." Riya crossed her arms over her chest. "There are wild animals, Vira. Leopards. He will die."

Vira gave her a look. "How is that any different from what the Ravens did to us? There are wild animals in the forest, too."

"They were with you the whole time. You weren't in any danger." Riya gestured to the bag in Vira's hand. "Besides, we wouldn't be in this situation if you hadn't left Papa's journal behind."

"We only have ten minutes before he wakes up," Kaleb said, stepping between his sisters. He didn't like abandoning the mercenary either, but he wasn't sure he saw another choice.

"We should interrogate him," Ronak said. "Maybe he can help clear Kaleb's name."

"I already tried that," Kaleb said. "The mercenary in the dungeons didn't know much."

Both Vira and Ronak turned to Kaleb in surprise.

"You spoke to him?" Vira asked.

"And you think he told you the truth?" Ronak followed up.

"I did," Kaleb said. "And I do think —"

"If we plan to run, we have to do it now," Amrit cut in, giving Kaleb an apologetic look.

"There's no harm in asking again," Ronak insisted.

Kaleb bit his lip. Maybe it wouldn't hurt to see what this one knew — if there were more details that Surya had kept from him. Something that could help convince the Council once and for all that he was innocent. But it was a risk. There was no guarantee they'd get anything useful out of him. "We're here for the key," he said finally.

Ronak's lips flattened, and Riya gave him a reproachful look.

"We're near one of their traps." Kaleb shrugged, pointing to the loose net still on the ground. "I'm sure someone will come looking for him soon, before any animals find him."

Vira turned to Amrit. "You're sure the knots will hold?"

He nodded, and then tugged on the ties again for good measure. "There's no way he's getting free," he promised.

"Then let's go."

With one last glance at the mercenary, they all followed Vira out of the clearing, back toward the path they'd been on.

✳

Progress was slow, and though pitifully little sun managed to make it to the jungle floor, Kaleb was sweating by the time they stopped for lunch. He was sure he smelled horrendous, covered in dirt and bugs and sweat. He hoped they'd be able to bathe in one of the rivers, but apart from a small waterfall they'd used to refill their waterskins, they hadn't encountered much water.

Kaleb sat on a log while Riya handed out more carefully rationed chapatis and pickles. He couldn't help but recall every night in the dungeons — the same food Ronak had brought to him. He glanced at Ronak, who was sitting alone, apart from the rest. Kaleb sighed and made his way over. He was tired of fighting. Ronak scowled at him but didn't move away.

"You know, this was my favorite part of every day," Kaleb said, holding up the half-eaten chapati in his hand. "When you came to visit."

"What?"

Kaleb looked out toward the distant horizon. "It's hard to explain how time passes when you're imprisoned. Every day is the same — the same routines, the same food, the same people. It feels like no time passes even as you *feel* it passing. But you coming to see me every day. Bringing me food. Telling me stories. It was the best part of each day."

"Don't," Ronak said, his voice rough. "Don't talk about it like that."

Kaleb turned, startled by the anger in his voice. "Like what?"

"Like you've already forgotten what it was like." Ronak's entire body seemed to be shaking with fury. "Like you've already painted the memories over in your mind. I lived those months, too, Kaleb. I know it's not the same, but I remember what it was like. You didn't want to talk about *anything*. You refused to even entertain hope that you would leave, that you wouldn't die in that dungeon. What was I supposed to do? Let you keep believing that you didn't deserve to live? To have a real life —" His voice broke.

The words hit Kaleb in the gut. He'd kept the outside world at a distance, tried to convince Ronak — and himself — that he'd never get to leave. That had been his way of protecting himself.

But who had protected Ronak?

Vira and Ronak hadn't been close in a long time — long before Kaleb had been accused of treason, even long before their parents had died. But things had changed. There was venom in their words now, hardened hatred forged into verbal blades meant to cut. To scar. Kaleb couldn't recall things being so bad between them even a year ago. Or maybe he'd just been willing to overlook Ronak's growing anger because of his own hurt.

✳

By the time evening fell, their progress had slowed even more. The foliage had grown a little thinner, but the area was full of traps set by the mercenaries. Riya had spotted a symbol carved into a tree trunk beside the trap Vira and Amrit had fallen into, and once they noticed that, it was easy to see that every few hundred feet there were more markings on tree trunks and rocks. They were forced to constantly stop and search for any tripwires or hidden weapons. Magic could be easily detected, so the mercenaries had cleverly eschewed using it.

Which was why, when Kaleb felt the familiar prickle of magic, he stopped mid-stride.

"Do you feel that?" he asked. It was faint, but it was definitely there — and it was not coming from anything they'd brought with them.

Vira looked out into the jungle unhappily. "I think we're getting closer to the mercenary settlement."

"What if we don't make it there by the equinox?" Ronak asked. It was nearing dusk, the warmth of the sun an already fading memory as it dipped lower in the sky. They hadn't made it as far west as they needed, and they would once again be forced to camp in mercenary land.

"We will," Vira said. But they all knew they'd have to cover a lot of ground quickly if they wanted any hope of reaching the temple by sunset the next evening.

"We need to keep moving," Amrit insisted.

"We need to look around," Kaleb said. The insistent prickle of magic was growing.

"It's too dangerous," Ronak said.

"Kaleb's right," Riya said. "If we're close to the mercenaries, we need to know."

Vira took a deep breath and then nodded. "We shouldn't split up. We'll all go."

They followed Riya as silently as they could, letting her pick the path through the wilderness. Kaleb was the most sensitive to magic, so he directed Riya toward the source. He could tell they were approaching something large, and it worried him.

"Careful," Amrit warned, steadying Ronak as his foot caught on a knotted root. Kaleb carefully stepped over it, looking up at a humongous tree wrapped in black vines. The vines were everywhere, Kaleb noted, looping over branches, stretching from tree to tree, trailing down like curtains.

He didn't know how long they'd walked before Riya stopped abruptly.

She pressed a finger to her lips and inched forward, pushing aside two large leaves. Through the gap in the foliage, Kaleb could see that it was far worse than they'd thought.

The mercenaries didn't just have a campsite. They had a fort.

It was a ferocious beast that looked old as the mountain itself, its walls crawling with more thorny black vines. The foundations were cracked as tree roots burst through the stone. Parts of buildings had crumbled due to erosion and the elements. The top turret had broken off entirely, leaving the circular tower open to the sky. The only reason it had survived was the sheer amount of magic that held it together, allowing it to weather the forces of time and nature.

This had been Surya's home. This was where the man who killed their mother had been trained. Kaleb could see movement in the distance, two people dressed in impersonal black kurtas walking along the crenelated battlement. One carried a talwar and the other a gada — a metal staff topped with a heavy, spiked ball that had fallen out of fashion so long ago, Kaleb wasn't sure he'd ever seen one.

Riya let the leaves fall back, blocking the mercenaries from view. "This is really bad," she whispered once they'd backed up far enough from the edge of the fort. "We can't stay here."

"It's nearly night," Kaleb said. Without enough light, they couldn't be sure that they were evading all the traps. But if they lit their lanterns, there was a chance they'd alert the mercenaries to their presence. "We should make camp."

"We could get ambushed," Riya said. "I say we take our chances in the jungle and keep walking."

"We could get ambushed anywhere," Ronak pointed out. "If we have to fight, it would be better if we can pick the location and prepare."

"Riya's right," Amrit said. "There's still light now. We can go south, away from the mercenaries. There should be fewer traps there, and we can navigate it better."

"South is farther away from the temple," Kaleb pointed out. "We'll have more ground to cover."

"But we'll move faster without the traps," Riya said. "Vira, what do you think?"

Vira, who'd remained uncharacteristically silent, just shook her head. "I don't know. I can't think. I just—" She pressed the heels of her palms into her eyes. "Let's keep going," she said finally, taking a deep breath and lowering her arms. "I trust Amrit and Riya."

Ronak pursed his lips but said nothing. Kaleb glanced at the hidden fort one last time and followed the others. The sky was rapidly darkening, making it harder to navigate the tangled roots that erupted through the ground. Kaleb followed Vira, stepping where she stepped—until she lost her balance.

Vira tipped backward into him. She reached for the closest tree trunk to steady herself, but it was too late for Kaleb. His foot went through the ground. For a split second, shock made time freeze. And then he fell.

He grabbed for the nearest vines as the ground beneath him crumbled. But they unfurled under his weight and he was falling again, thorns slicing through his palms. It was a short fall, and he landed on the ground, a circular hole of light above him.

He winced as he shifted, testing his body. His shoulder and ankle ached from the landing, but nothing felt broken. His palms, however, were covered in blood, stinging where the thorns had pierced his skin.

"Kaleb?" Vira peered down through the hole, her face blocking the meager light.

"Throw down a rope," Riya ordered.

The others went through their supplies before Kaleb remembered. "I have it," he said.

"Toss it up," Amrit said, reaching down for it.

Kaleb sat up, groaning, and reached for his bag. His hands felt suddenly hot — as if they were burning — and when he looked down, there were purple welts where the bloody cuts had been. He stared at his hands, blinking as his vision blurred.

"I think something's wrong." Was that his voice? It sounded so strange and garbled.

"Kaleb?" someone called. "Kaleb? What's happening?"

It was hot. So hot. He was just. Going to close his eyes. For a moment. And then he would —

The world went dark.

CHAPTER THIRTY-FIVE

— RONAK —

RONAK PANICKED.

"Wait —" Amrit put his hand on Ronak's shoulder, but Ronak had already jumped. It wasn't a far drop, but he landed badly, wincing as his knee banged into the ground. He ignored the pain shooting up his leg as he scrambled over to where Kaleb lay on a bed of dirt and grass.

"Kaleb?" Ronak shook him. "Kaleb!" He shook him harder, but it had no effect.

Ronak pressed a hand to Kaleb's forehead. His skin felt clammy and hot to the touch, as if he had a fever. But when Ronak scanned him, he looked unhurt except for the cuts all over his palms. Purple threads twined over the back of his hands, winding up his forearms.

Ronak's mind was on the brink of shutting down. He couldn't think beyond the fact that Kaleb was hurt. "I think he's poisoned. I don't know what to do. I don't —"

"Ronak," Amrit snapped. "*Ronak.* Toss me the rope."

Ronak reached for Kaleb's bag, dumping all its contents on the ground. He grabbed the coil of rope and threw it up into Amrit's outstretched hand.

A moment later the rope dropped to the floor and Amrit rappelled down. He crouched on Kaleb's other side, examining his hands.

"We have to do something," Ronak insisted. "We have to —"

"Hold out his hands," Amrit ordered. He dug through his own bag and withdrew a small metal tin that held a green, earthy-smelling salve.

"What's that?"

"A mix of herbs. It's supposed to work on most poisons."

"*Most?*"

Amrit didn't respond as he scooped some out with his fingers and spread it generously all over Kaleb's cuts, first on one hand, then the other. Somewhere in the back of his mind Ronak registered that Vira and Riya were also sliding down the rope, but all he could do was stare uncomprehendingly at his brother's unconscious form. He couldn't wrap his mind around the idea of losing Kaleb.

Please work.

For a few painful minutes, nothing happened. And then the purple stopped spreading up through Kaleb's veins.

"Look," Amrit said, pointing to where the poison was slowly receding. "It'll take a little while, but he's going to be all right." He wiped his hands on his kurta and rose.

Ronak sat back on his heels, a sharp sense of relief rushing into him. He turned to see Vira beside him. She held Ronak's gaze for a shocked moment, alarm and fear plainly visible on her face, before her eyes flicked to Kaleb.

"Don't," she said before Ronak could say anything. "I know what I did. I know I made a mistake. Just —" Her voice was raw, trembling, as if she were on the verge of tears. "Don't."

Ronak sat in stunned silence, watching his sister kneel beside Kaleb. He'd wanted this from Vira for months — a sign of remorse, a sign that she cared about them at all. And now that he had it, Ronak had no idea what to do with it.

He stood abruptly, walking away from Vira.

Amrit and Riya were examining the vines that dangled down through the hole. "He grabbed them when he fell," Riya said. "Don't touch them," she added when she saw Ronak approach.

"Where are we?" Ronak asked. Now that he was looking around, he realized that Kaleb hadn't fallen into a dirt hole, but into some kind of stone man-made structure — one that clearly hadn't been occupied in centuries.

"I don't know," Amrit said. "But it looks well hidden. We can make camp here."

The sun had set fully, and the only source of light was the lantern that Riya held, but Ronak could tell that they were at one end of what seemed to be a large room that extended endlessly. He took out a second lantern from his bag and walked into the darkness.

"Where are you going?" Vira called after him, but Ronak ignored her.

The glow of the magic wasn't very strong, but it was enough to illuminate the dark gray tiles that curved and wound through the cavernous space like a walkway. Yet there was nothing for the tiles to curve around. Still, Ronak followed the path, his footsteps echoing until he reached a wall.

He stopped. But the walkway continued all the way up to the edge of the wall — almost as if it would keep going on the other side.

"Ronak?" Riya's voice reverberated from somewhere behind him.

"Here." He held his lantern higher to throw light on more of the wall. It was plain. There were no markings, no carvings, not even any sign of erosion over time.

"What are you doing?" Riya asked, sounding annoyed. "We can't afford to get separated."

Riya hadn't spoken to him since they'd argued at the inn, and when she had to, her tone remained clipped and direct. He'd tried to forget her accusations, but they kept circling through his mind. She was wrong. He didn't push people away. They left *him*. Ronak would do anything for his family, but his parents, Vira, Riya, Jay, even Kaleb . . . they'd all chosen something else — some*one* else — over him.

Still, Ronak felt his chest tighten with regret. They wouldn't have survived the jungle without her. It had been so easy to see her slip back into palace life as though she'd never left at all, but out here, he could tell how much her time with the Ravens had changed her. Her gaze was sharper. She made decisions quicker. There was no hesitation when she acted.

She's so much like Amma, he thought with a jolt of surprise.

But the words of his half-formed apology were stuck in his throat.

"There's something strange about this wall," he said instead, putting a hand on it. It was faint, but he could feel magic brush his palm.

"The wall?" she asked skeptically.

But she trailed behind him as he walked alongside the wall, not sure what he was looking for, not sure why this place was unsettling him. He'd traveled the full length of the wall before he saw the metal lever wedged into it on the right side of the room. As soon as he approached, he could tell that it was forged with a lot of magic.

He tugged on the lever. It didn't budge. He set his lantern down and then threw the full force of his weight behind it, pushing with both hands until it finally moved. There was a rumbling sound, and the wall they'd been standing in front of suddenly — inexplicably — began to dissolve. It took several seconds for the magic to work, the stone disappearing from the end closest to them all the way to the far end, and the two of them stood side by side, wide-eyed.

Rows of chandeliers cascading from the ceiling flickered to life one by one as they watched, illuminating a city below them. Three flights of stairs led down, and from this high up, Ronak could make out multistoried buildings with wrapped verandas and painted shutters, vanishing into the distant horizon. A wide main road cut through the center, intersecting with smaller roads that twisted around buildings and fountained courtyards.

"What is this?" Riya asked, a hand pressed to her mouth in shock.

All at once everything resolved, and Ronak knew exactly where they were standing. It was a fort — one lost to time so long ago that its history was steeped in lore. It was said that this fort had magic so powerful it had been constructed with the ability to rise and sink beneath a mountain. It had never been conquered, but simply vanished one day. It was said to house treasure so valuable that hordes of people had died in pursuit of it.

Yet here it was, buried under mercenary territory for more than five hundred years. The founding city of Ashoka.

"This is Visala."

✳

"Vira, I need to see Papa's jour —" Ronak stopped talking when he saw that Kaleb was awake and sitting beside Vira and Amrit. "Kaleb!"

"I'm fine," Kaleb said, smiling weakly at Ronak.

Ronak's relief was sharp as the two of them joined the others on the floor. All the poison had left Kaleb's fingers, and his breathing was steady once more. Red welts remained, but they were no longer bleeding. His skin looked sallow in the dim light, and his hands trembled as he drank from a waterskin, but other than that, he really did look fine.

"Are you sure?" Riya dropped to her knees in front of him, her eyes full of concern.

"I'm sure," Kaleb said. "Why do you need Papa's journal?"

Ronak didn't answer as he snagged it from where it was peeking out of Vira's open bag, frantically flipping through pages of Papa's notes and annotated maps. He knew it was in there somewhere. He'd sat in his father's office with him the day Papa had meticulously copied the map that now hung in Ronak's room, wanting it for reference on his travels.

"Found it." Ronak turned the journal so it faced Vira and Kaleb and set it on the ground between two lanterns. He had the book open to a drawing of a fort complex.

"Found what?" Vira asked. She glanced down, then back up at Ronak. "Visala?" She frowned. "I don't understand."

"Ronak thinks this is where we are," Riya said, her arms crossed over her chest, her raised brows signaling her doubt.

"What?" Kaleb reached for the map. "That doesn't make any sense."

"It does," Ronak insisted. "Look, we're here," he said, pointing to the northeastern corner of the drawing. "And all this" — he pointed to the center section, then to the direction he and Riya had come from — "is what's out there."

"Visala is supposed to be in ruins," Vira said.

"Well, maybe not if the stories are true," Amrit chimed in. "That the fort could be raised and lowered at will beneath the mountains." Vira turned to him in surprise, and he shrugged. "Interests," he said with a small smile.

"Visala is somehow connected to the Ivory Key," Ronak said. He tugged the journal back toward him and turned a few more pages until he found a second map, this one providing a broader picture. "Look."

Visala remained in the center, but Papa had noted four other locations: a fort to the north, two forts to the west, and a monastery to the southeast. The note beneath it, scrawled in Papa's hurried handwriting, read *According to one source, Visala had a network of ancient tunnels that could be navigated when it was lowered underground to provide quick escape. The source lists three forts and a monastery, but fails to name them or offer any addi-*

tional descriptors. Unfortunately, without knowing the distance these tunnels span, it would be quite impossible to narrow down these locations to specific monasteries or forts to search.

"This could be our way out," Ronak said, tapping the tunnel that led to the west.

Vira exchanged a glance with Amrit. "We don't know which fort it leads to. None of these are named."

"But we do," Kaleb said after a short pause. "There are only two forts to the west of here that would have been around five hundred years ago."

"The forts at Ritsar," Amrit said.

Emotions flickered over Vira's face, but she tamped them down. "The Lyrians have one of those forts, and the other is in ruins. It's too big a risk."

"Kaleb's hurt. The jungle is hindering our progress. This will be safer and easier to cross," Ronak said.

There was only silence for a few minutes as they considered their options.

"The northern fort," Kaleb said, looking at Ronak. "Do you think it's the one the mercenaries are using?"

Riya looked at him sharply. "You think they know about this place?"

"I'm not saying that," he said.

"No, but maybe you're right," Vira said. "We could never figure out how they were getting into Ashoka. If this *is* Visala — and if Papa was right and there's a tunnel that leads to a monastery somewhere . . ."

"It could be in the mountains on the other side of the border," Amrit finished.

"There must be another entrance here," Ronak said, lifting one of the lanterns and standing. If he had to guess, they were in an antechamber of sorts. He made his way to the wall closest to the hole they'd fallen through. It didn't take that much time for him to find a second lever.

"Don't," Vira said, putting her hand out to stop Ronak from pulling it. "We don't know what's on the other side."

"If the mercenaries know about this place, we're not safe here either," Riya pointed out.

"Ronak's right," Kaleb said. "Going through Visala is probably our best option."

"I won't make this decision for all of us," Ronak said. "But I think I can get us through Visala to Ritsar." He turned to Vira. "Do you trust me?"

Ronak's stomach twisted with unexpected nerves as Vira held his gaze for a long moment. "I trust you," she said finally. "We'll go through Visala."

CHAPTER THIRTY-SIX

— VIRA —

THE FORT COMPLEX was large — easily several times the size of the Dvar Fort, and far more elaborately constructed. There were hundreds of buildings, sectioned off and separated by arched gates and sprawling courtyards and colonnaded walkways.

This was what Papa had spent so long looking for. This was what he'd spent so many years researching, so many years teaching them about. It seemed almost unfair to be here without him.

"Isn't it strange to think that people lived here once?" Kaleb sounded bewildered as he looked up at a row of what had clearly been houses — as if he couldn't possibly reconcile what he was seeing with the stories of his youth. As if he couldn't understand how their ancestors had walked these streets, touched the same marble pillars, or rested on the same iron benches.

Vira understood. Most places felt inhabited. There were stray animals or lamps burning in open windows or fading rangoli left on porches to be swept up in the morning and redrawn. This abandoned fort had none of that. It was all perfectly preserved, as picturesque as if they'd stepped into a painting. It didn't even look like it had been defeated. It was as though one day, every single inhabitant had simply packed up and walked away. There was no treasure, no money or gold or jewels. There was nothing left behind. It was too clean. Too silent, a stillness that only came from a lack of life — a city inhabited by ghosts and memories.

Vira followed Kaleb through a scalloped arch into a different part of the fort, where Ronak and Riya were arguing over Papa's journal. Ronak had never looked so much like Papa as he did just then — his eyes lit up in excitement, brandishing the journal, spouting facts about historical findings. Riya, on the other hand, didn't have patience while Ronak frequently paused to examine architecture and admire murals. She wanted to forge ahead with ruthless efficiency. As Kaleb stepped between them, Vira found herself hanging back. It was odd not being the one in charge, and she didn't quite know what to do with herself.

"Did you sleep well?" Amrit asked, coming to stand beside her.

"Well enough." They'd made camp at the edge of Visala. Without having to worry about wildlife or the elements or secrets traps, they'd actually been able to rest for the first time in days. None of them had protested when Riya woke them up at the crack of dawn to continue their journey to the temple. "You?"

"Well enough," he echoed. She could hear the smile in his voice. "Your brother looks better."

He did. All traces of poison were entirely gone, except for the gruesome red lines remaining on Kaleb's palms. But Vira couldn't shake her sense of guilt. She'd brought them here. She was responsible for what happened to each of them. She'd known it would be dangerous, but it was different experiencing it.

It was different seeing Kaleb hurt.

She felt shame course through her once more. It hadn't seemed so bad then, doing what the Council wanted — doing whatever she could to keep the peace, even if it meant imprisoning her own brother. She thought she'd been protecting Ashoka, but Kaleb was her brother. He'd been there for her every time she needed him, and the moment he'd needed her, she'd turned her back on him.

"Thank you for helping him," she said to Amrit.

She couldn't begin to imagine what would have happened if Amrit hadn't been there. If he hadn't had the salve. Vira knew pitifully little about plants, but even she'd been able to tell that there was something strange about those vines. They were pitch-black, and they looked sickly, almost as though they were rotting. She wondered for a moment if this was what the mercenaries used to poison their victims, but the thought faded as quickly as it had come. No healers in Ashoka had a cure for whatever the mercenaries used.

"I'm only glad it worked," he said.

After nearly three hours of walking, they finally reached what Ronak proclaimed to be — according to Papa's map — the center of the fort. Ronak had been right — the distance they'd crossed was far greater than anything they would have managed in the same amount of time in the jungle. But there was also a part of Vira that couldn't help but be terrified that they'd made a huge mistake, that they were trapped here with no exit. And with every passing hour, they had even less time to reach the temple before sunset.

"Where's that light coming from?" Riya asked when they stopped to eat. "There aren't any chandeliers here."

"Outside." Ronak pointed to the curved section of the wall near where they were sitting. "Those are windows."

"Windows?" Vira asked, confused.

"Here." He rose, beckoning for the rest of them to follow him. "Put your hand on this section." Vira did. It felt like stone. "Now put it here." He gestured at a location a few feet away.

When Vira moved her hand, she immediately felt a wave of magic wash over her. As soon as she put her hand there, the stone melted into glass that gave her a clear view of the mountainside. When she removed her hand, the glass turned back to stone.

"An illusion," Vira said, awed. She turned to Ronak, surprised. "How did you know that?"

Ronak shrugged, almost a little embarrassed, and pointed at the ceiling. "I noticed that the chandeliers always disappeared closer to the outer edges."

"No wonder the city was never found," Amrit said. "From the outside it probably just looks like part of the mountain. Your ancestors were really clever."

They were. They'd thought of everything. Defense, escape routes. Even underground, they would have been able to withstand any siege for months.

"I feel like we ought to say something about Papa," Vira said, feeling strangely sentimental as Riya pressed her palm to the stone and it once again revealed the lush vegetation of the Koranos Mountains. "This was his dream, after all."

"One of his dreams," Ronak corrected.

"If it had been up to Papa, he would have unraveled every secret Ashoka has to offer," Riya added.

"You know, the last time we were all together was when he died," Kaleb said quietly. "It seems fitting that this is what brought us back together."

"I was at Amma's cremation too," Riya admitted. She pulled her hand away, letting the wall turn to stone. "I hadn't planned to. It was the only time I ever lied to the Ravens."

"You were?" Vira asked, astonished. She hadn't expected that.

Riya shrugged. "I don't know. I fought with her. I was angry with her. But I guess . . . I guess some part of me thought that I would see her again someday. She was still my mother, and I wished I'd gotten to say goodbye."

None of them had had that chance.

"She wasn't perfect," Ronak said. "Papa, too. They cared about us in their own way, but . . ." He looked down at Papa's journal in his hand, smoothing his fingers over the cover. "Maybe if they'd been different, it wouldn't have been so easy for the four of us to be torn apart."

They stood in silence for a while, feeling the truth of Ronak's words.

He was right. Papa had been too obsessed. Amma had been too busy. They'd done their best to prepare their children to face the world, but in the end, they'd left the four of them largely alone.

"Maybe it's all right to hold on to the parts of them we loved and let go of the rest," Kaleb said finally. "We're not them. We don't have to be defined by their choices or values. We get to make our own destinies."

Vira glanced at Amrit. Maybe Kaleb was right. They did get to shape their own futures. She didn't have to be bound by the rules that had defined her mother. She was going to be her own kind of maharani, and she would save Ashoka in her own way.

*

"We're almost at the palace," Ronak said, looking down at Papa's map, then back up. "I think."

According to the map, the palace was the last building they would encounter within the city, which meant they were nearing an exit. Vira couldn't stop the nervousness coiling in her stomach. If Papa's source had been right and there were two forts that connected to Visala, they could only assume that they were the twin Forts of Ritsar.

"Are you all right?" Amrit asked, touching Vira's shoulder.

"I'm afraid," she admitted. She looked ahead, where her siblings were well out of earshot, and lowered her voice anyway. "I turned my back on them. I abandoned an entire city to Lyria." She took a deep breath. "My mother used to say that regret was a useless emotion."

Good or bad, a maharani's choice affects the fates of entire nations, Amma would say. *Once you've selected a course of action, you must proceed with conviction — as if that was the way it always was and always will be.*

"You can't simply wish away your emotions, Vira." Amrit frowned. "It's never easy to face the consequences of our actions, but you're not the same person you were eight months ago."

She wasn't. But Ritsar remained the site of her greatest failure, and she would have to live with that forever.

"Vira?" Riya's voice echoed through the empty space. "You need to see this."

Vira picked up her pace, turning around a bend in the path until she abruptly came upon a wall. "What is this?" It looked like nothing she'd ever seen — an opaque crystalline barrier that cut right through the middle of a building and stretched to what looked to be the full length of the fort from floor to ceiling, from wall to wall.

"It's magical," Amrit said, running a hand over it.

"Magical?" Vira mirrored his motion. She could feel it too — the faint wave of magic exuding from it.

"We should have been able to sense it from much farther away." Kaleb looked unsettled. "Something this big and powerful would —"

"I think this is the palace," Ronak cut in, looking down at Papa's map. "A part of it, anyway."

"Give me that." Vira snatched the journal away from him. It wasn't a very detailed map, but it had been fairly accurate in guiding them.

"That would be the courtyard we just crossed," Ronak said, coming to stand beside her and look over her shoulder. "And this is where we are."

He was right. They were at the edge of the palace. And with their path blocked off, there was no way they'd be able to exit.

"So this is a dead end?" Vira asked. She could hear the frantic edge to her voice.

"There's a way out," Riya said, returning from where she'd followed the barrier to one end of the fort. "I found another lever."

"Can you tell where it leads?" Vira asked.

Ritsar was a city that spanned two hills. At the peak closest to the Ashokan border was the Syena Fort, which had burned down nearly two hundred years earlier and now lay in ruins. Atop the second hill, closer to Lyria, was the Simha Fort, which had inspired the lion crest of the entire Maravat province. That fort had fallen to the Lyrians eight months earlier.

Riya shook her head. "Apparently, for all their brilliance, no one thought to mark the exits."

"There might be another way out," Kaleb said, examining a section of the wall thoughtfully. "I think there's a door here."

Now that he'd pointed it out, Vira could make out a faint rectangular outline. And when Kaleb passed his hand over where a doorknob would have been, one simply appeared. He waved his hand again. It vanished. He repeated the motion a third time, and when it reappeared, he gripped the handle and turned it. It opened silently, revealing a dark, narrow corridor.

"Wait here," Vira told the others before pulling out a lantern and following Kaleb. It wasn't a long path, and within a few minutes they'd reached the end — another flat rectangular door. But this one had no handle, and no matter how many times Kaleb or Vira ran their hands over the wall, none appeared.

"What's the point of having a door?" Riya huffed when they returned.

"Double security?" Ronak suggested. "Maybe you need someone on the other side to open it."

They let the useless door fall shut — the doorknob still visible — and followed Riya toward the other entrance she'd found. Amrit made his way to the lever, but Vira stopped at the wall perpendicular to the exit, looking at a mural of two girls facing each other, a wizened priestess standing behind them.

Both girls wore matching saris of gold silk, and it was evident that they were sisters — they shared the same eyes, the same nose, the same bow-shaped lips. One girl wore a ruby set in gold on a chain around her neck, which looked for a split second just like the mirror Vira had found in the monastery back in Dvar. The other girl had four stacked necklaces, each with a different gemstone: one white, one blue, one green, and one purple. Along the bottom, a white ribbon of text named the girls as Savitri and Niveda. Vira knew the story of Savitri, Ashoka's first maharani. Yet the priestess was placing the crown atop Niveda's head.

"Niveda!" Kaleb snapped his fingers suddenly. "I knew I recognized that name." He pulled out the journal that Vira had found in the monastery. "There are over a dozen mentions of her in here. Whoever wrote this knew her well."

"But who was she?" Riya asked, confused.

"It looks like *she* was the maharani," Ronak said, gesturing at the mural.

But none of them knew what to make of that.

"We should go," Amrit said. He had already pulled the lever, revealing another antechamber.

✴

The tunnel ended after they'd walked for nearly half an hour. There was another lever in the wall. Vira held her breath, one hand on her talwar, as Ronak approached it. She desperately hoped they wouldn't find themselves in the middle of the Simha Fort, now occupied by Lyrians.

A moment later, the wall dissolved, revealing a set of stairs. Amrit walked up them first, gently pushing open a trapdoor — then throwing it open entirely. "The Syena Fort," he said, and Vira exhaled.

Amrit held out a hand to help Vira up, and the first breath of fresh air overwhelmed her lungs. After being trapped so long underground, she'd forgotten what it was like for air to be clean and crisp.

"I think this was the kitchen," Ronak said, looking at the partial ruins in awe. The building was mostly intact, though the stones were charred black and overrun with wildlife.

"We need to keep going," Riya said. "We can examine the architecture on our way back."

The fort complex wasn't very large, and it wasn't difficult to cross, given that most of the buildings had been partially or fully destroyed. Vira picked her way over broken walls and dense overgrowth, slashing at weeds with her talwar — until the fort abruptly ended. Where the outer wall once stood, there was nothing but a sharp drop down a cliffside.

All at once her heart seized. This was the city she'd lost.

They were atop a hill — one of two that made up the city of Ritsar. Vira could see the city spill out before her.

"Vira?"

She couldn't focus on anything but the past. Ghosts rose around her. Stories flashed before her eyes. She pressed her eyes closed, but the ghosts didn't live in Ritsar. They lived in her mind.

Someone's hand was around hers. Warmth. "Breathe," Amrit whispered.

She forced herself to inhale. And then exhale. Another breath. And then another.

"All right?" Amrit asked quietly.

Vira nodded. She didn't trust herself to speak just yet as she studied the city. It looked different, far less vibrant than it had been. Some of the buildings destroyed in the battle had begun to be repaired, but others still lay as piles of wood and stone.

Across the hill, Vira could see the Simha Fort. It was among the oldest forts in Ashoka, surviving countless raids over the centuries, until the Lyrians had captured it.

"Look. There it is." Ronak pointed, pulling Vira's gaze away from the city and toward the valley between the two hills.

The temple. It was right in the middle of a pristine blue lake. Vira could see the jagged shapes of the two gopuram towers. She could see the single bridge that stretched from the edge of the lake to the temple entrance.

They'd finally found their destination.

CHAPTER THIRTY-SEVEN

— RIYA —

THE TEMPLE COMPOUND was larger than Riya had expected. The dark gray stone of the gopuram towers loomed over them as they walked across the narrow stone path that connected the temple with the banks of the lake. It was quiet — eerily so. The water on either side of them was still, with no breeze to disturb it. Even the wildlife seemed to be holding its breath. Every step they took, every word they uttered seemed too loud here.

"It has an odd construction for a temple," Ronak said as they approached the gate. "Most notably the well."

The gate had been latched, but someone had broken through it, so the chains trailed on the ground, scratching against the stone floor as they pulled it open.

"What do you mean?" Amrit asked as they entered the front courtyard. Perpendicular to them was an elevated pillared walkway that seemed to wrap around the entire central courtyard.

"Come look," Ronak said. They climbed up the five steps to the walkway — then back down to the central courtyard. In the center of it were more steps, leading directly down to the lake below. "Usually, wells were constructed near temples, but not inside them. Supposedly there were once crocodiles here."

"Crocodiles?" Riya asked suspiciously. "That sounds like a myth." Elephants or cows she could understand. But no one kept crocodiles in a temple.

"Maybe not." Kaleb pointed as something made the water ripple. Two dark shapes were definitely moving under the water.

"Probably some fish," Vira said unconvincingly.

Ronak looked shocked. "I . . . I meant centuries ago."

"Let's maybe not invoke more ancient obstacles," Vira said.

"I didn't think you were superstitious," Riya said, and Vira shot her a glare.

"Where do we go?" Amrit prompted Ronak. The sun was dipping lower into the horizon, but it wasn't quite setting yet.

"Western temple," he said. "Western *facing*," he amended as Amrit began to walk to the left.

Riya looked up at the gopuram towers, each carved with rows and rows of goddesses and beasts. The entrance to the building was an open doorway with a single golden step they had to cross.

Small altars to minor goddesses were embedded in the walls of the pillared building, but each of the three main goddesses had her own altar in a small room. To the right was Devyani's, guarded on either side by stone peacocks. To the left was Kausalya, which had two roaring lions instead. And directly across from them was Vaishali's, which had an elephant on either side, its trunk raised.

"In here," Ronak said, pointing at Vaishali's room.

The right door had a broken hinge, and it sagged heavily against the stone. As Riya drew closer, she could make out Vaishali's obsidian face. The jewels that should have hung around her neck and adorned her ears and wrists were gone, probably taken by thieves. But somehow, dressed in a threadbare cotton sari, a torch in one hand, holding out her palm to guide souls forward, she looked even more ferocious than if she'd been fully decorated.

"What's supposed to happen when the sun sets?" Kaleb asked Ronak. "You said there was something special about the equinox."

Ronak walked behind Vaishali's statue, where there was a second room. Riya reached for a lantern, but Ronak stopped her. "Look." He pointed to a single stream of light striking the back wall from a source high up. And slowly, as the sun lowered, Riya could see that it was illuminating a small stone goddess carved into the stone.

"It's said that the sun hits the entirety of this carving only twice a year, on the equinoxes," Ronak said. "People used to travel great distances to come here and see this."

"Look at the shape," Riya said, realizing that the alcove the goddess was carved into was a perfect oval.

"It looks to be about the same size as the mirror you found in the forest," Kaleb said.

Vira pulled out the mirror from her bag and pressed it into the wall. It fit perfectly, covering the goddess entirely.

"The sun will set in a minute," Amrit said, looking down at a watch in his hand.

They stood in tense silence, waiting as the sun sank lower. As soon as light hit the center of the mirror, they were surrounded by red light. Riya turned away at the sudden brightness, shielding her eyes.

"Look," Kaleb said.

To the right, on one of the stones that made up the wall, was a glowing red symbol: twin blades crossed over a lotus. Then another one appeared on a different stone below it. Then on the left wall. And then behind them. They turned, looking in every direction as eight of these symbols emerged.

A moment later the sun's light vanished, but the stones remained lit.

"Do we press one of them?" Ronak asked.

"All of them," Kaleb suggested. "At the same time."

But Vira was thinking. "No. One person can't touch eight stones at once. It has to be a pattern."

"The order in which they appeared," Riya said.

"That one was first," Amrit said. "Then that."

"That was third," Riya said.

Slowly, they pieced the order together. "Are we sure?" Vira asked. When they nodded, she walked to the first one. As soon as her hand touched it, it moved back into the wall. She moved slowly, pressing them one by one, until all had disappeared.

With a startling rumble, the rest of the stones in the room began to shift and grind and dissolve. Riya stepped back, watching as the wall to the right of the goddess disappeared, revealing a narrow stone hallway.

"Do you feel that?" Vira shivered. Next to her, Ronak did the same, rubbing his arms as if to rid himself of gooseflesh.

"Magic." Kaleb exhaled. "And it's strong." Riya could feel it too, a prickle that crawled along her skin as she walked closer to the wall.

As soon as they all stepped in, the wall closed behind them.

"The mirror!" Vira said, turning back. But it was too late. There was no door, no gap. Nothing indicating that this wall was anything but immovable stone.

"'The only way out is through,'" Ronak recited, recalling the words on the map.

There was no turning back.

"Stairs," Amrit said, pointing to the end of the hallway.

Riya leaned over the railing to look up. "How high does this go?"

"Doesn't matter," Vira said, and she began to climb.

They walked in silence, winding up the spiral staircase. A few more twists later, Riya could make out a sliver of light filtering through an open window that was at least double her size. She paused beside it for a moment, and as she moved away, her hand knocked over a clay lamp. She jerked her hand back as cool oil leaked onto the ledge, and she wiped the oil that was on her hand on the edge of her kurta.

"It's just a lamp," Ronak said, righting the toppled lamp. "During festival times, they'd light them so the entire gopuram was lit up."

"Still," Riya said, her eyes on the darkened stone where the oil was seeping into the crevices. "It's odd that they're filled with oil. They wouldn't have been lit in years."

"Maybe."

"Stop dawdling," Vira called down from several flights above them.

"Let's go," Riya said, letting go of her kurta. But her finger continued to prickle where the oil had touched it, almost like it was made of magic.

CHAPTER THIRTY-EIGHT

— RONAK —

RONAK HAD STOPPED counting how many windows they'd passed or how many times the staircase turned, but his legs burned with exhaustion. Which was why it felt like they came upon the door abruptly.

"We're here," Vira said, breathing heavily.

She pushed the door, and it opened easily and silently. Like the wall at the foot of the stairs, the door sealed them in as soon as they had all crossed the threshold. A moment later, stone chandeliers flared to life and flames erupted along a ledge built into the side walls of the large, rectangular room. Large tiles alternated in color between gray and white, like a chessboard, extending across the length of the floor. Across the room was a door that looked identical to the one they'd just entered. Statues lined the walls: twelve identical archers standing in front of each row of tiles, each carrying stone bows aimed at the sky. Their gemstone eyes glittered dangerously in the firelight.

Riya started to step forward, but Vira held her back. "Wait. This has to be an obstacle."

Kaleb tilted his head to one side. "Something feels . . . *off* about those archers."

Ronak followed his gaze. They looked like any other statue in the Dvar Fort, but they were made of plain sandstone rather than expensive marble.

"Well, we're not going to know what happens unless we do something," Riya said.

"She's right," Ronak said. He stepped on one of the white tiles. Then the gray one directly in front of it. He glanced back and lifted his shoulders. "It seems fine."

Riya followed. Vira hesitated, but when Amrit stepped forward, she did too. They walked cautiously, one step at a time, one tile, then another.

Kaleb stopped. "No. Remember all those stories Papa would tell us? We're missing something. Something *important*."

"Like what?" Ronak stepped onto a gray tile.

"Ronak!" Kaleb's yell made Ronak jerk back — just in time to see the stone archer at the end of the row move, pointing an arrow directly at Ronak. And then the statue fired.

Ronak dove backwards, but not quickly enough; the stone arrow ripped through the flesh of his thigh. He crumpled to the floor, gripping his leg in agony.

"What was that?" Riya asked. In the blink of an eye the statue had returned to its position, bow pointed at the sky, as if it hadn't moved.

"Statues aren't supposed to do that." Vira's voice shook.

"Ronak!" Kaleb was in front of him, prying his hands away from his right leg. Ronak sat up, wincing through the pain. His palms came away sticky with blood.

His kurta was already torn where the arrow had pierced it; Kaleb ripped it wider and then exhaled in relief. "It's not that deep. You were lucky. It just grazed your thigh."

"Real lucky," Ronak said, gritting his teeth through the pain.

"Don't!" Kaleb shouted.

Across the room, Amrit froze. "I just want to look at the arrow." He pointed to where it had embedded neatly into the wall on the far side of the room.

"No. No one move." Kaleb stood, looking at the way they were scattered over the first five rows, all of them standing on various rows, various tiles. "The tiles probably have magic to tell when one of us steps on it. And we just found out what happens when we step on a wrong tile."

"So what? We just stay here?" Vira asked.

"No," Riya said. "We figure out the pattern." Her eyes narrowed as she scanned the area.

Ronak groaned. Kaleb was right, the cut wasn't too bad, but Ronak had no idea if he could walk — or how far.

Vira unwound the dupatta from her waist, balled it up, and tossed it. It unwound halfway through its arc — but not before Kaleb grabbed the end and snatched it out of the air. Ronak attempted to clean the wound with the ripped part of the kurta before Kaleb wrapped it tightly.

"Do you have more of that salve?" Vira asked Amrit. He shook his head, giving Ronak an apologetic look.

Kaleb held out his bloodstained hand. Ronak grasped it and pulled himself up.

"Can you walk?" Kaleb asked.

Ronak tested his weight on the right leg. It hurt. "I think so," he lied.

He looked around at the two tiles through which his blood had seeped — and the one Kaleb was standing on. Ronak frowned. There was something off about Vira's placement. She was the only one who wasn't on the diagonal the rest of them were on. "Vira, tell me how you walked there."

Vira outlined her path. Three steps forward, then veering right. "What are you thinking?"

Ronak rubbed his jaw. His blood-covered fingers smelled metallic. He wiped them on his kurta again, but it made no difference. "I'm not sure. Riya?"

Riya traced the steps she'd taken. Followed by Vira, Kaleb, and Amrit. They'd all walked different paths, most of them straight through contiguous tiles without consequence. It was Ronak who had stepped off the pattern . . .

"What if it isn't a logical pattern?" Kaleb asked. "What if it isn't mathematical, or something so complicated, but rather . . . an image."

"Image?" Riya echoed.

"Like the symbol of the Kamala Society," Kaleb suggested. "They seem to love putting that on everything."

"He has a point," Riya said. "It didn't matter where we stepped back there, because it was all the base of the flower and it was fine. But when Ro stepped here, it wasn't on one of the blades or a petal."

"Which means we need to be more careful the closer we get to the end, because there's more open space and fewer tiles that would cover the design," Ronak added.

"He might be right," Amrit said, pointing at the base of the statues toward the farther end of the room. "It looks like the bases on those are more worn than the ones near the front. Which means they've moved more over the years."

Vira stared at him. "You think other people have come here over the years? It can't be. Their bodies would be here."

"Maybe not," Kaleb said, pointing at the floor. Ronak's blood on the tiles had vanished, as if the stone tile had absorbed it.

Ronak's eyes traced along the tiles, mentally scaling the image so that he could visualize it spread over the room. "Vira, step back one tile and then to the right. No, wait." Her feet hovered above the tile, freezing in place. "Sorry. Back one more and then to the right."

Vira glared at him as she obeyed the command.

"Then right again," Ronak said. "Now diagonally to the right."

It felt as if all the air had been sucked out of the room, all of them holding their breath as Ronak slowly guided her forward.

"And now is the tricky part," Ronak said. As far as he could tell, the image ended where Vira stood. But she was still several tiles away from the plain stone that made up the border around the tiles. "You'll have to jump."

Vira looked back at him. "You're joking."

Ronak shook his head. "I don't think there's anywhere you can go without getting shot. You'll have to get to the concrete."

Vira muttered something too quiet for him to hear — but he was pretty sure he could guess. But then she bent her knees and launched herself into the air. She landed on the stone with a thud, the momentum propelling her as she crashed into the wall, heaving a sigh of relief and collapsing.

Ronak exhaled too. "Who's next?"

CHAPTER THIRTY-NINE

— VIRA —

THE DOOR AT the other end of the room opened to nothing.

Vira recoiled from the sharp drop that awaited her. Maybe she shouldn't have been surprised. Papa had often joked that the Kamala Society liked to send unsuspecting intruders plummeting to their death. She just hadn't expected it to be quite so literal.

The sun had fully set now, and the barest hint of purple coated the sky. Looking across the temple to the second gopuram on the other side of the courtyard, Vira guessed that they were about halfway up the tower. Right in the middle was the courtyard they'd walked by — and in its center the pond of water with the two crocodiles.

"How are we supposed to cross this?" Riya asked, leaning out of the doorway to look below and then twisting to look at the upper part of the gopuram.

"Rope?" Amrit suggested. Wind whipped against his face, blowing his hair into his worried gaze.

"That's not the Kamala Society's style," Kaleb said.

"He's right," Vira agreed. "It has to be magic based."

"It's odd, don't you think," Ronak muttered, "that a group that sought to destroy magic would use it to protect their secrets?"

Vira glanced back at him. He was leaning against the wall, his eyes half closed. He'd barely been able to make the leap across the last few tiles. Her stomach knotted and, irrationally, anger flooded her. How could he not be more careful?

"We need a better vantage." Riya frowned. "I think we need to go higher up—"

"What are you doing?" Vira asked, but before any of them could move, Riya was out on the ledge. "Riya!" Vira's heart leapt into her throat as she rushed forward just in time to see Riya grab a statue to pull herself up.

Vira's heart pounded as she watched her sister easily climb the tower, using the statues embedded in the gopuram as hand- and footholds. It was terror-inducing, but also beautiful somehow. Riya had always had an intense physicality about her. Even as children, while Vira had spent hours learning and perfecting every movement in their bharathanatyam and kathak lessons, Riya had strolled into class without having practiced and outperformed her. It was hard not to be jealous watching her climb with such ease and grace.

Riya stopped and swung her leg over a stone horse, sitting astride it as if she were about to charge into battle.

"What do you see?" Vira called up.

"Nothing." Riya turned to scan the rest of the temple compound. "Maybe I should go higher."

Riya disembarked, and as she did, the dagger at her waist knocked against the horse's head, slipping from her dupatta. It bounced once against the statue of a fish. Vira's fingers stretched out, lunging for it—but it slid past her hand.

And landed with a thud in midair.

Vira stared at it, uncomprehending.

Amrit edged forward. Vira grabbed his arm, but he turned to give her a reassuring smile as he gingerly put a foot out. Inch by inch, it lowered, until he had one foot on the invisible platform. He took a step forward and then bent to pick up the dagger.

"This is incredible." Vira's voice was full of awe as she took in Amrit standing on what looked to be air. "It's a bridge."

"A magical bridge," Kaleb said. "A magical invisible bridge."

Vira exhaled. The Kamala Society was certainly making it difficult for anyone to unearth its secrets.

Amrit turned back toward Vira. She pushed strands of hair out of her face and gingerly stepped out. Blood pounded in her ears as she inched forward, slowly, toward Amrit's outstretched hand.

Don't look down.

Her fingers touched Amrit's, and warmth flooded her, radiating from where his hand gripped hers.

"Let me go first," Vira said.

"Are you sure?"

Vira nodded. "It's just a bridge," she muttered to herself as she edged past Amrit, her body brushing against his. Just a bridge made of stone and magic that she couldn't see.

Amrit stood right behind her, holding her hand as she took a step forward. Then another. Then another.

And then she fell.

"VIRA!"

Vira tried to scream, but all the air rushed out of her lungs. Fear choked her, freezing her legs and arms and brain.

I'm sorry, Papa. I tried my best.

All she could do was fall to her certain death.

And then someone grabbed her forearm and she slammed into the side of the stone bridge. Her ribs were on fire. Her arm felt like it was being ripped out of its socket.

"Vira!" Amrit's face was twisted in utter terror as he held on to her desperately with both hands. "Hold on."

He pulled. Summoning all the energy she could muster, Vira reached up, her fingers fumbling to grab the invisible stone. Her heart slammed into her ribs, her stomach roiled, but bit by bit she inched herself up until her elbows were on stone. Amrit pulled her back from over the edge, and she tumbled into him, her face pressed into his chest as he pulled her close.

Vira was shaking. It wasn't an invisible bridge. It was an invisible maze. She willed her heart to stop racing as she finally pulled away from Amrit. Behind him, the rest of her family watched with slack-jawed horror.

She nodded. "I'm all right. I'm all right." But she wasn't sure if she was trying to convince them or herself.

"Do you want me to go in front?" Amrit asked. His grip on her arm was tight, as if he was afraid to let her go for even a second.

But Vira shook her head. Going first made her feel that she had some amount of control. Her leg trembled as she put her foot forward, slowly, until she felt stone beneath her. She exhaled and then took another step — and then jerked back, slamming into Amrit's chest as she felt air.

"Careful." Amrit's voice was a whisper against her ear. She nodded again.

She took a step to the left. Solid ground.

The five of them moved slowly, testing every step. The path twisted twice, once back toward the gopuram they'd left, then across the width of the gap — right above the crocodiles — before straightening again toward the second tower.

And finally they were across, the maze depositing them in front of another door. Vira pulled it open and stepped off the invisible ledge into the second gopuram.

CHAPTER FORTY

— KALEB —

KALEB'S HANDS SHOOK as he shut the door behind him, sealing them into the second gopuram. Once more, lamps flared to life around them, illuminating a second door on the far side of the room.

Ronak leaned heavily against a wall next to one of the two windows — as if he needed the support to keep him on his feet. Blood had soaked through the dupatta, and it was painfully obvious that the makshift bandage wouldn't last very long. Ronak needed a healer's attention.

For the first time, the true gravity of their situation was dawning on Kaleb. It wasn't about freedom or imprisonment. It wasn't about magic or war. It was about family. Life and loss. For the first time, it was occurring to him — and perhaps to all of them — that maybe not everyone would return to Dvar.

Next to Kaleb, Vira looked ashen. Her hands shook as she pointed toward the center of the room. "I think we found it," she said.

"Kaleb?" Riya waved him forward.

Kaleb approached the middle of the room, where the others were clustered around a shimmering, shallow pool. Around it, thin slabs of stone rose up in a spiral over the water, almost like a staircase of sorts. At the top of the stairs was a rectangular wooden box suspended in midair, spinning slowly. Everyone's eyes were trained on the box, but Kaleb's eyes stayed on the pool.

There was something about it that made him uneasy. There was a reason it was here — a reason the box was suspended above it. And Kaleb had a feeling it shouldn't be taken lightly. He reached into his pack and withdrew a coil of rope, cutting off a piece of the end and dropping it into the pool. It sank slowly — as if it weren't in water, but a more viscous substance.

"What are you thinking?" Riya asked.

"It's probably nothing," he said. "But don't touch the pool, just in case."

"Who's climbing the stairs?" Amrit asked.

Kaleb finally glanced up. This was it. This was why they'd come here. Why Ronak was injured. Why Vira had freed him.

"I will," Riya said.

She was the best suited to this task, but Kaleb put his hand out to stop her.

"I'm the mayaka. I should go first, just in case."

Kaleb gingerly stepped on the first stone slab. It sagged under his weight, wobbling like it would throw him off. He threw his hands out to steady himself, and Amrit immediately gripped his arm to steady him.

"I'm fine," Kaleb said. "Really." Amrit let go.

But he took the next step more slowly, testing his balance before pulling himself up. It wobbled again. Kaleb breathed deeply before climbing the next one. Riya followed him, balancing herself with surprising ease — and holding him steady. It was slow going, as he stopped every time to regain his balance, which was thrown off as soon as he reached for the next step. But then he was at the top, at eye level with the wooden box. Below them, the others stood still and silent — quieter than Kaleb had ever believed possible for his family.

The box was surrounded by the barest haze of yellow, but it looked like any other wooden box, with a metal hinge and a single clasp at the front. Far too simple for something that supposedly held secrets that members of the Kamala Society had died to protect. Kaleb put his palm out — and then retracted it.

"What's wrong?" Riya called up.

Kaleb stretched out his hand again, but he kept his distance, almost as if he were warming his hands on a flame. Magic prickled along his palm, the sheer power overwhelming, pushing against his skin with a kind of insistence he'd only ever felt in the quarries.

But it wasn't raw magic, that much he could tell. He exhaled, not knowing if the yellow haze would do anything if he touched it.

His fingers trembled as he reached for the box. His hands closed over it.

And then he pulled it out of the air.

CHAPTER FORTY-ONE

— RIYA —

THE FLAMES SUDDENLY turned green.

Riya's foot slipped. Kaleb grabbed her forearm, steadying her as they looked around in confusion. On the ground below them, Vira turned, her black braid whipping through the air as her hand snapped to her talwar.

"All the lamps are green," Ronak said, peering out the window.

"They're *all* lit?" Kaleb's brows rose. "How's that possible?"

"Magic," Riya said recalling the oil in the lamp she'd knocked over.

"We need to go," Amrit said, joining Ronak at the window. "I'm betting the troops in Ritsar will be able to see this."

Riya hopped down one of the steps, her arms thrown out on either side for balance as each stone rocked back and forth. Behind her, Kaleb followed, the box clutched tight in his hand.

Without warning, the ground shook. Riya screamed. Kaleb's leg buckled. The box tumbled out of his hands as his face slammed into the stone slab of the step above him.

"The box!" someone shouted.

Riya lunged after it, hurtling down the stairs. The unstable stairs propelled her down too fast. The box was going to fall into the pool any second, so Riya did the only thing she could. She leapt over the last three steps.

All thoughts flew out of her head except one: *save the box.*

"Don't touch the pool!" Kaleb bellowed.

She landed on the ground and lunged forward. Her fingers wrapped around the wood just as it smashed into the pool. Amrit grabbed her left arm, pulling her back from the edge. Riya held the box in her dripping wet hand.

Kaleb's lip had split open, and blood slid down the side of his mouth. He used the sleeve of his kurta to wipe it off. "Riya, are you all right?" He pulled the box out of her hand and reached for her palm, twisting it this way and that. "Does it hurt?"

As thick as the water had looked, it hadn't clung to her hand like oil. She wiped it on her kurta. "I feel fine."

Kaleb's gaze turned to one of horror as he looked down at the box in his hand.

"Vira," Riya said, her voice strangled. "Look."

The box was disintegrating in his very hands.

The world shuddered around them. Dust and dislodged rocks rained down on their heads, crashing at their feet. But they stood in stunned silence as the wooden box crumbled to dust.

"No," Vira gasped. "No!" She rushed toward them, but it was too late.

"I'm sorry," Riya whispered. "I'm sorry. I—"

The cylindrical hinge that held the box together was all that remained, slipping through Kaleb's fingers and tumbling to the ground. Riya watched it twist and turn and fall in a painfully slow arc—and some sudden reflex made her pluck it out of the air just before it hit the shaking floor. The moment her fingers touched it, magic surged through her.

Magic? She looked down at it, uncomprehending.

"We have to go. Now!" Amrit said, yanking open the second door, opposite the one they'd come through.

Riya didn't have time to think about it. She shoved the hinge into her pocket.

Amrit grabbed Vira's hand and tugged her toward the stairs. Kaleb snatched his pack off the floor and ushered a limping Ronak out. With one last look at the crumbling room, Riya followed.

CHAPTER FORTY-TWO

— RIYA —

THE STAIRWELL SHOOK, and Riya's shoulder slammed into the wall. She groaned as someone's hands — Ronak's — steadied her and shoved her down the stairs. Despite the windows, the green flames filled the stairwell with smoke and heat.

Somewhere below, Vira screamed. One of the lamps tumbled onto the stairway. Oil and fire spilled down the stairs. Riya coughed as smoke filled her lungs.

Behind her, Ronak was panting, slowing down.

"Come on, just a bit farther." Riya reached for Ronak in the dark, grabbing her brother's hand tightly as they hurtled down the stairs.

They burst out of the stairwell and into the temple. Vira and Amrit were well ahead of them, running through the hall until they reached the giant temple doors that opened onto the courtyard. Amrit shoved them open — and froze.

The temple was crumbling into ruins of ivory and stone, burning in a fiery green haze.

"Kausalya help us all," Riya muttered.

Above them, green flames covered the gopuram towers, which were collapsing into themselves. Cracks spidered through the floor, splitting the stone pillars with thundering snaps. Water rose up as the temple began to sink.

"There's no way we'll make it through that," Ronak said. He leaned heavily on his left leg. His right was still bleeding, the cloth entirely soaked through. Sweat beaded down the side of his face.

"We don't have a choice," Amrit said, his mouth set in a grim line. "Run."

They took off through the courtyard, jumping over the cracking stones, ducking as the temple walls crashed in a shower of stone and fire.

"Ronak! Move!"

Riya wrapped her hand around Ronak's forearm and pulled him out of the way as a huge pillar thudded down in the center of the courtyard. The force of the blow knocked them both off their feet. Riya threw up her hands to shield her eyes as rubble rained over them, dust mingling with black smoke.

"Ronak? Ronak?" Riya crawled toward where Ronak lay motionless on the ground. "Ronak!" She shook his shoulder, and he groaned. Riya exhaled.

His eyes fluttered open. "Where are the others?" His voice was hoarse from the smoke inhalation. He pressed two fingers to the side of Riya's head, and they came away bloody.

"Come on. We have to go." She could deal with her head later.

Ronak struggled to his feet. The dupatta had come undone around his thigh. He ripped it off, crumpled it, and tossed it aside. He swayed — and Riya caught him, wrapping her arms around him to keep him upright.

Ronak sagged against her heavily. "I'm fine," he mumbled.

But they both knew he wasn't. He'd lost too much blood.

"You have to go," Ronak said, pushing her away. "You have to get out of here."

"No. I'm not leaving you."

"Riya —"

"No. Come on." Riya tugged him forward.

But when Riya looked up, she realized that there was nowhere for them to go. The pillar had landed at an angle — sealing off their only exit. Sealing them away from the others.

No. No. *This can't be happening.*

The pillar was too tall for them to climb over. The stone too smooth for her fingers to find purchase.

The temple stopped shaking all at once. And then water spilled in at an alarming rate. Riya's eyes stung from the smoke. Her lungs burned as she pushed against the pillar, willing it with all her might to move. But it was too heavy. Ronak was breathing heavily, struggling to remain standing.

"Riya," he said quietly.

"We're going to make it," she said. "You're going to make it."

The water level was rising, nearly to their knees now. Ronak collapsed against the wall.

"No, come on, Ro," she insisted. "Come *on!* You can't give up."

She pulled Ronak to his feet, helping him stand. But it was only prolonging the inevitable. The broken temple was sinking into the water. And all Riya could do was wait for the water to swallow her.

"I'm sorry," she told Ronak. "I'm sorry I failed you."

Those words were meant for a hundred different people. For Kavita. For Vira. For Ashoka. She needed somebody to hear them.

The water was up to her chest.

She held Ronak, her arms around his waist, her face pressed into his shoulder. She didn't know when she'd begun crying, but a choked sob escaped her.

The water was up to her chin. Then the water pulled her under. Pried her away from Ronak.

Her lungs burned. She was running out of air.

No. She put her hand out. *Ronak.*

Something tugged at Riya's chest, pulled at the depths of her soul. Everything glowed blue. The pillar shattered into a million pieces.

I'm sorry.

And then there was only darkness.

CHAPTER FORTY-THREE

— VIRA —

VIRA GASPED FOR breath. The bridge had started to sink almost as soon as they'd begun running. Water covered her feet, the bottom of her kurta pants. But she couldn't stop. Not yet.

She ran and ran, fighting against the water even as it tried to stop her, to hold her back. *One more step,* she told herself. *Just another step.*

And then she felt grass beneath her feet. She tumbled to the ground, falling to her knees.

She'd failed. She'd come this far only to lose everything. Her only chance of protecting her country had crumbled right along with the box that held the Ivory Key.

"Vira?" Kaleb's hands were on her shoulders as he dropped before her, searching her face, scanning for injuries. "Are you all right?"

She shook her head. She could feel tears prickling at her eyes, and she knew that if she opened her mouth, said a single word, there would be nothing holding them back.

"Vira." Kaleb's gaze was soft. "I'm sorry."

She turned away, but Kaleb wrapped his arms around her. Helping her. Comforting her. After everything she'd done to him, she couldn't bear it. She pulled away and rose to her feet. Amrit stood a few feet away.

"Where's Ronak?" she demanded. "Riya?"

"They were right behind us," Amrit said.

But there was no one else on the bridge. With a strangled gasp Vira ran back toward the temple — but Amrit's arm caught her around her waist.

"I have to find them," Vira said as she struggled against his hold. "Let me go! I can't leave them behind."

Amrit didn't let go. "There's no use getting yourself killed, too."

"I don't care!" She'd lost *everything*. She couldn't lose her family, too. "Please. Let me go." He didn't.

They were gone. And there was nothing she could do but watch the temple crumble into ruins.

Then Vira knelt on the banks of the lake and wept.

✳

When the tears subsided, it was only Amrit beside her. He sat next to her, his knees pulled up to his chest. The smattering of items that had survived their trip lay on the grass beside him: a lantern, her bag that had Papa's journal, and her talwar.

"Kaleb went to look for Riya and Ronak," Amrit said quietly. He winced as he shifted, and Vira noticed the gash on his right shoulder.

"Amrit, you're bleeding." Guilt filled her. She hadn't even checked on him and Kaleb, to see if they were hurt.

But he shook his head in dismissal. "I'm fine. It's not that deep." He shifted closer, wrapping his good arm around her and pulling her to his side. Their clothes were still wet, but Vira didn't care as she pressed herself against him, resting her head in the crook of his neck.

"I was so sure we would do this," she whispered. "I was convinced we would find the key."

It almost didn't feel real. In every one of her dreams, her plans, they'd always walked out triumphant. Instead she felt the loss deep in her bones.

"We'll find another way," Amrit said. But they both knew those were just words. There was no other way.

"How long do you think we have? Before everything changes."

Before panic filled the streets. Before another country invaded. Before magic was gone, erased from time and memory until it was just a story for the children of whatever civilization rose from the ashes of Ashoka.

"I don't know." He rested his cheek on top of her head. "We'll face that together, too."

Out on the lake, the smoke was blowing over the water. The last remnants of her dream, snatched by the wind and dispersed as if it had never been.

"Maybe it wasn't worth it. Coming here. Failing." Vira laughed bitterly. "My mother wouldn't have failed."

"No, she wouldn't have," Amrit agreed. "Because she wouldn't have tried."

"All I ever wanted was to be the kind of maharani she was. Better, even. To prove to her somehow that I'm worthy. That I could protect Ashoka."

"You are worthy, Vira. How can you not see that?" Amrit pulled away, turning so they were face-to-face. "You came back to Ritsar — to the site of the battle that haunts your nightmares — all so you could protect your people. Don't you see how brave you are?"

Vira's eyes burned as she looked up at him, tears threatening to fall once more.

"Let her go, Vira," he said gently. "When you battle ghosts —"

"The living always lose. I remember."

"You have to be your own maharani." He gestured to where her talwar lay on the ground. "The one who pulled this talwar off the wall. That's who Ashoka needs." He looked up at her, the world in his eyes.

Wind blew hair into her eyes, and Amrit reached up to tuck it behind her ear. Vira shuddered at the light touch, suddenly all too aware of how close they were. Before she could think about it, she reached up and pressed her palm against the curve of his cheek.

He stilled, but his eyes were clear. "Vira." There was something about the way he whispered her name, a desperation, a reverence that made her breath catch.

And then she closed the gap between them.

She'd looked at his face so many times, studied it, traced it with her eyes. But it was a whole other experience doing it with her hands. The sharp edges of his cheekbones, the strong lines of his jaw, the imperceptibly crooked curve of his nose. And his lips. Softer than she'd ever imagined beneath the pads of her curious fingers.

And then beneath her lips.

Amrit, too, explored her, his fingers sliding around to the back of her neck as he tilted her head back to deepen the kiss. Vira gasped as his mouth left hers only to trail down the side of her face. Her neck. Vira flushed, her body heating from within as if every nerve had burst into flames all at once.

And then — too soon — he pulled away. Vira wrapped her fingers around his neck, pulling him back. She wasn't ready to let him go, not yet.

He pressed his forehead to hers. His breath, warm and fast, fluttered across her lips. His hand was still tangled in her hair, their breaths rising and falling in an erratic rhythm.

Amrit let out an incredulous breath of laughter. "What are we doing?"

Vira had absolutely no idea.

She exhaled. "Amrit —" The word died on her lips as she looked up.

They were surrounded by Lyrian troops.

CHAPTER FORTY-FOUR

— RONAK —

RONAK SWAM THROUGH the temple ruins — ducking between pillars, dodging floating statues. His chest burned. His leg stung. He felt like he was on the verge of passing out.

But he had to swim. He had to survive. For himself and for Riya.

Next to him, Riya floated along, barely conscious. His grip on her arm tightened as he pulled her up, fighting against the water. Then they broke the surface, gasping for breath.

"Riya?"

She didn't respond.

Smoke billowed all around them. The temple was still aflame, the green fire a beacon drawing too much attention.

Land.

He could make out the barest outline of the edge of the lake.

Summoning the last of his strength, Ronak swam.

❋

Ronak had no idea how much time had passed. They'd collapsed on the ground at the edge of the lake.

He blinked his eyes open and with a groan pushed himself up to his elbows and looked out at the temple, at the stone crumbling in the center of the lake, still aflame somehow. Another pillar collapsed, sending an enormous spray arcing through the air. But the water did little to douse the magical green flames that covered the ruins, and thick smoke billowed around him, working its way into his nose and mouth. His eyes stung, his head pounded, and with every breath his throat burned.

Riya was sprawled out next to him.

Riya.

He grabbed her shoulder, shaking her. "Riya? Riya." He shook her harder until she finally came to, gasping for breath.

Thank the goddesses. Ronak collapsed back on the ground. His energy was waning. The world around him swam, fading in and out. He reached for his leg. Everything was too wet — he had no idea if he was still bleeding. But he knew he'd already lost far too much blood.

"Ronak?" Riya's voice was hoarse. "Where's . . . everyone?"

"I don't know."

Riya looked out at the lake, pulling herself up to a sitting position. "How did we get out of there?"

Ronak didn't know that either. What little he'd seen made no sense. Riya's hand had glowed blue — and then the pillar had broken apart like it was made of glass. He looked down at her hand now. It looked normal.

"It's gone," Riya said, her voice hollow. "The key. Papa's dream. Ashoka's future. Everything."

It had never occurred to Ronak that they would emerge from the temple without the key. He didn't understand how it could just be . . . gone. He'd only wanted it to protect Kaleb, but the thought of Papa's — *Vira's* — lost dream hurt more than he expected.

"We have to find the others," Riya said, tearing her eyes away from the ruins. She was shivering. So was he. They were soaked from head to toe.

They struggled to their feet, wringing the excess water out of their kurtas. It didn't do much. The clothes still hung heavy on them. Ronak had let his bag sink to the bottom of the lake with his coat and what remained of their supplies. Riya's bag was gone too. He only hoped that Vira had managed to save Papa's journal.

"Can you walk?" Riya asked.

"I think so." The pain in his leg had subsided. Or perhaps his brain didn't have the energy to worry about it just then.

Huddling together for warmth, they followed the curve of the lake, desperately hoping that the others had survived.

CHAPTER FORTY-FIVE

— KALEB —

KALEB WALKED AROUND the edge of the lake, shoving his way through overgrown grass that reached nearly to his waist. He hadn't wanted to leave Vira, but Amrit, in his quiet, commanding voice, had told him to find Ronak and Riya.

Please let them be alive.

He gripped tight the talwar Amrit had pressed into his hands. Kaleb couldn't recall the last time he'd held a weapon, but he clung to it like it was his lifeline.

They made it out, he told himself. *They're alive.*

They had to be.

There was rustling in the grass ahead. Kaleb's heartbeat picked up as he squinted into the distance, barely able to make out a dark figure moving toward him. Logic told him to tread cautiously, that they were close to the Lyrian border, that the troops at Ritsar could easily see the destruction they'd wrought.

But panicked desperation won out. "Riya? Ronak?" A moment later they came into view, huddling together as they stumbled forward. Kaleb's relief was palpable as he ran to them. "Thank the goddesses. Are you all right?"

Kaleb scanned them in the fading moonlight. They were drenched, hair plastered to their scalps, wet clothes clinging to their skin, making them shiver. Riya had a cut across her temple. Neither had their pack of supplies on them. But they were here. They were alive.

"We're fine," Ronak said, though he looked anything but as he wavered on his feet. Kaleb's eyes drifted to the wound on Ronak's thigh. The dupatta he'd used to stanch the bleeding was gone.

"Vira?" Riya asked, coughing as she inhaled the smoke.

"They're back there," Kaleb said. "Here, let me help." He slid his arm under Ronak's shoulder, but Kaleb was unprepared to receive the full force of his brother's weight. His knees buckled. Alarm made him drop the talwar and use both hands to steady Ronak.

"I'm fine," Ronak repeated, even as he leaned heavily against Kaleb.

Kaleb glanced at Riya, seeing his worry mirrored in her eyes. Ronak had already lost a lot of blood, and they had a long way to walk back to Ashoka. Vira and Kaleb were the only ones who'd managed to make it out of the temple with any of their supplies intact.

"Let's find Vira." Riya picked up Amrit's talwar, and they set off in the direction Kaleb had come from.

"Look at Papa's dream," Ronak muttered, staring out at the temple. "Reduced to rubble and ash."

The thing Papa had searched for all his life, found and lost in the span of a single breath. Kaleb couldn't begin to fathom the depth of his father's despair at learning that the Ivory Key had been destroyed.

"Maybe it's a good thing Papa never got this far," Kaleb said. Papa had died with hope in his heart, faith that his children would someday succeed where he'd failed.

"I told you this was a bad idea," Ronak said. "We should have run when we had the chance." He looked at Kaleb out of the corner of his eye. "It's not too late now."

"You can barely walk," Kaleb said, knowing that wasn't what he was asking.

"Quiet," Riya hissed suddenly. The wind had shifted, and as the air cleared of smoke, Kaleb could see that they were no longer alone. There were at least a dozen soldiers pointing at the lake and shouting in Lyrian. "Troops. *Shit.* Get down."

"Vira." Horror washed over Kaleb. "She's right th —"

Ronak grabbed his shoulder to hold him back. "We can't help her if we get captured, too."

He was right. Kaleb reluctantly allowed his siblings to pull him down into the wild grass. The wind shifted again, carrying the Lyrians' voices toward them. Kaleb's spoken Lyrian was only passable, but even he could understand the directive one of the soldiers issued.

"They're taking them to the fort," Kaleb said helplessly, watching as they marched Vira and Amrit away from the lake at knifepoint.

✳

Ritsar was made up of a jumbled mess of intersecting roads, alternating between sloping streets and stairs that climbed up toward the highest point: the Simha Fort, built right into the cliffside. Kaleb had seen the sprawling expanse of Ritsar spread out over the two hills when they'd emerged from Visala, but it was different seeing it up close. Here, it was easier to see the way the Battle of Ritsar had changed the city.

The houses toward the base of the hill were largely Ashokan in style — rangoli on front stoops and garlands of marigolds or tulsi draped over door frames. But the higher up they walked, Kaleb could make out more Lyrian flags planted on rooftops or hung from verandas. Buildings were no longer colorful in the Ashokan style, but painted in dull whites and grays, their porches were full of strange potted plants Kaleb had never seen before.

He couldn't imagine what it would be like for these people — who'd spent their entire lives as citizens of one country, whose lives and rules had suddenly changed — having to answer to new laws and creeds.

"Stop." Riya tugged on Kaleb's arm when the fort came into view. "We need a plan."

Kaleb's gaze lingered on the troops walking ahead of them with Vira and Amrit, but he allowed Riya to drag him behind an abandoned building. "We need to free Vira," he said.

"I know," Riya said. "But we're not Lyrian. We can't just walk into the fort."

An odd silence fell between them as her words sank in. If anyone was infiltrating the fort, Riya would be the best option. She was a thief, and she'd always been gifted at physical feats. Even Ronak, who was excellent at thinking on his feet, could easily come up with convincing lies and misdirects.

But they wouldn't be able to avoid notice. Kaleb would.

"I'll go," Kaleb said after a beat. For the first time he could remember, the way he looked was an advantage. His paler features wouldn't draw attention here amid the chaos.

"It's too dangerous," Ronak said at once.

"I'll be fine," Kaleb said, though he didn't know whether he was reassuring Ronak or himself. He *looked* Lyrian, but that didn't mean he'd truly be able to blend in. He was fluent, but his accent was heavily Ashokan, and he'd stopped training with weapons nearly four years earlier.

"We need to know the layout of the fort," Riya said. "You need new clothes. And we need a plan for how to break them out of the dungeons."

"We can't get a layout without entering," Kaleb pointed out. "It's not like they would conveniently have a map lying around."

"And we don't even know how sophisticated or well protected the dungeons are. If there are magical barriers or rotating guard shifts — or even how many guards to expect," Ronak said. "Believe me, I've spent a lot of time thinking about breaking someone out of jail the last few months," he added dryly.

Kaleb decided to ignore that. "I'll figure something out." It wasn't ideal for him to go in without knowing anything, but they were wasting time. "You two should go back to Visala. I'll meet you there."

"You also need a way to get all three of you out of the fort," Riya said. "They might let you in, but they won't let you walk back out with two Ashokans."

"Wait—" Ronak said suddenly. "You don't have to. The entrance to Visala — there's one under this fort."

"That way was blocked," Riya said, frowning.

"It was locked from the outside," Kaleb said, understanding Ronak's plan. They'd left the door on the other side of the crystal wall unlocked. If this door, too, had an outer lock, they'd have access directly into Visala.

"Think about it," Ronak said. "It's safer for all of us."

"We don't know where the entrance is," Riya said. "We can't exactly —"

"The kitchen," Kaleb interrupted. "It was where we exited the other fort."

"I agree," Ronak said. "Knowing what we know about Visala, I don't think they'd leave it up to chance. It was a city, remember, not like the Kamala Society. Everyone would need to know how to get in and out using the tunnels. They would make sure the entrances were well hidden but consistently located."

"If you're wrong, we *all* get captured," Riya reminded them.

Kaleb looked at his brother. Ronak's breathing was already labored. It would be a struggle for him to go back down to the lake and then up a second hill to the Syena Fort and the tunnels. This would be the easier option for him, too.

"I think it's worth a shot," he said.

Riya gave the two of them a look. "Fine. Wait here," she said finally, and then disappeared into the night. She came back twenty minutes later, tossing Kaleb a clean Lyrian-style tunic. "I have a plan."

✹

Riya had briefly canvassed the outside of the fort and found that it had two entrances. The main door had four guards stationed outside, but there were Lyrian soldiers freely entering and exiting. The second way in was through the northern tower that had collapsed in the Battle of Ritsar. For whatever reason, the Lyrians hadn't bothered to board it up or rebuild it. This one was harder to access, as they'd have to climb over rock, but it had only one guard.

Kaleb's stomach twisted in knots as he squared his shoulders and walked toward the entrance, feigning confidence he didn't have. The clothes Riya had stolen for him off someone's clothesline were ill-fitting and uncomfortable, but he resisted the urge to tug at the collar. His breath caught as a whole squadron emerged from the fort, but they paid him no mind, a few soldiers skirting around him, talking excitedly about the temple ruins that no one could believe were still on fire. Kaleb forced his shoulders to relax. He nodded casually at the guards at the gate, and then he was inside. He expelled a breath.

Riya's plan was straightforward: he would walk in, and then he would make his way to the northern tower, where Riya and Ronak would be waiting. There, he would persuade the guard to leave his post and then would allow his siblings in.

But the *straightforward* part was entirely in its conception. Their chances of success hinged on Kaleb's ability to convincingly play the part of a Lyrian soldier, along with sheer chance.

The Simha Fort was constructed simply but efficiently with tall, unscalable outer walls serving as its primary defense mechanism. And despite the activity he'd seen outside, it was largely empty inside. Kaleb took a moment to look around the entrance hall. There was a courtyard directly in front of him where two soldiers in partial armor were sparring. A covered walkway wrapped around the open space, and Kaleb followed it toward an elaborately designed gate that had been left open and unguarded.

As Riya had instructed him, he looked around as he walked, trying to catalogue as many details as he could. There were soldiers walking around — enough that he could avoid close attention, but not so many that he could let his guard down. Lyrians didn't use magic in their lanterns, so flaming torches crackled around him, illuminating three distinct areas.

He was standing in the middle of a large, grassy training area, with obstacle courses, targets for archery and spear throwing, and a small dirt arena for combat practice. Beyond it were barracks and stables. To the left, a stone staircase curved up to the three-story manor that had once been the Viceroy of Maravat's home but now belonged to some high-ranking Lyrian officer. It was too far away for Kaleb to make out any details, but he could see lights flickering through open windows lined with gauzy curtains. The rest of the buildings — including the tower where he was supposed to meet Riya and Ronak — were to the right, so Kaleb followed the sloping ground toward a stone walkway.

The wind was shifting once more, and thick smoke from the temple obscured the stars above and irritated his nose and throat. He lifted his hand to scratch his forehead and subtly turn his face as another soldier passed him.

It was immediately apparent that this part of the fort was emptier than the training grounds. The torches were left mostly unlit, and he could hear his footsteps on the stone floors echo uncomfortably loud. The corridors were interconnected, so Kaleb wove through dining halls, servant quarters, and two kitchens before finally finding the northern tower. He took a deep breath and picked his way through the rubble toward what remained of the entryway.

Riya had coached him through a lie, making him practice until the Lyrian words rolled off his tongue easily. But the guard spoke before he could even open his mouth.

"You're late," she snapped. "My shift ended over twenty minutes ago. I'll see to it that Lieutenant Lukas hears about this."

"I — uh. Sorry?" Kaleb stammered, watching in bewilderment as the soldier stormed away.

He waited to make sure she was truly gone before he stepped outside. He couldn't see his siblings anywhere, and he hoped that Ronak's injured leg could handle the difficult climb up the rocky slope that led to this part of the fort.

"Riya?" he whispered.

A moment later, she and Ronak emerged from the shadows.

"That was easy," Ronak said.

"That was *lucky*," Kaleb corrected. "Come on. The kitchen's right through here." He pointed to the adjoining room, glancing over his shoulder as he heard someone approaching from the other direction.

"Where are the dungeons?" Ronak asked.

"Close by," Kaleb lied, hoping that was true. "I'll be fine. You have to go now."

"Be careful." Riya pressed their last remaining orb of smoke into his hand, and the two of them disappeared. Kaleb just had time to stuff it into his pocket before another soldier appeared.

He stopped abruptly when he saw Kaleb. "Who are you?"

"Finally," Kaleb said, throwing his hands up in irritation. "I was about to come look for you. You're half an hour late for your shift. You can be sure that Lieutenant Lukas will hear about this."

The soldier flushed and muttered an apology. Exhaling deeply, Kaleb watched as the guard took up his post. It was time for him to find Vira and Amrit.

CHAPTER FORTY-SIX

— RIYA —

RIYA PEERED AROUND the corner of the kitchen, watching Kaleb walk away into the darkness. Next to her, Ronak was leaning against a wall. A thin layer of sweat covered his forehead as his eyes flickered closed.

Panic had her reaching for him, gently slapping his cheek until his eyes cracked open a tiny sliver. "Ronak. Stay awake."

"I'm awake." But his voice was weak, his breath rapid and shallow. He was still shivering — they both were.

"Are you dizzy?" Riya pressed her fingers to his neck. His pulse was elevated.

Ronak pushed her hand away. "I'm fine." He tried to stand up straight, but a moment later he sank back heavily against the wall.

Anxiety knotted in Riya's stomach as she mentally cycled through the injuries she'd seen among the Ravens — scrapes that tore the flesh off their palms and knees, falls that left their bones fractured and in need of resetting, one terrible instance of diluted scorpion venom poisoning. But no one had ever been stabbed. Not like this. She had no idea how to help him.

Riya rummaged through the bag Kaleb had handed her, digging through the last of their supplies. "Drink this," she said, giving Ronak the last of the water they had left in the waterskin. "I'll be right back."

She cast her eyes around the room. There was a barrel of water in the corner. She filled a small pail and snatched a few clean rags that had been hung up to dry on a clothesline. They had to properly clean Ronak's wound if there was any chance of him surviving the night and making it out of Ritsar.

Riya was relieved to see that there was a bit more color in Ronak's face when she returned. She refilled the waterskin first, and once she and Ronak had had enough to drink, she used the cloth to clean Ronak's wound. She didn't dare take the lantern fully out of Kaleb's bag, but she widened the opening of the bag until it was just bright enough for her to realize that something was wrong.

The wound wasn't that deep. The arrow had grazed his outer thigh, but the cut was not nearly bad enough to warrant the amount of blood he'd lost.

"What is it?" Ronak asked, catching the look on her face.

"I think the arrow was magical," she said. "The wound isn't closing."

Ronak leaned his head back against the wall.

"We need more pressure," Riya said. "We'll tie it tighter this time." She tore one of the rags in half, knotted the two pieces together, and wrapped it around his leg several times, pulling it tight until she could tie the end.

"You learn this from the Ravens?" Ronak asked.

"I never did this with the Ravens." She turned to find him watching her, his brows furrowed, as if he wasn't entirely sure what he was looking at.

"What?" she asked. "Is it your leg?"

"Riya . . . do you remember what happened? When we were underwater, I mean?"

Riya blinked in surprise at the question. "No." They'd been trapped, and the next thing she remembered was Ronak shaking her awake. "Why?"

"You don't remember *doing* anything?"

"What do you mean, doing anything? What could I have done?"

"Right." Ronak turned away.

"No, Ronak. Tell me."

But he only shook his head. "It's nothing. Just . . . a trick of the light."

Riya watched him for a moment. "Why'd you really come on this trip, Ro?"

Ronak was looking at something off in the distance. She half expected him to make a snide comment, or just not answer, but he surprised her. "You were right. I made a deal with Ekta." He smiled wryly. "It seems you're not the only criminal in our family, sister."

"You promised her the key. Why?"

Riya didn't know if it was their circumstances — being stuck in Lyria, separated from their family — or just that he'd lost too much blood and was too weak to argue, but he told her the truth. "For Kaleb. She was going to get the two of us new identities. A way out of Ashoka." He paused. "Well, the three of us. But Jay's not coming." He exhaled deeply. "I didn't know what else to do. Who else to turn to. Kaleb was rotting in that cell. I was miserable. Ekta offered me a way out, and I took it." There was pain in his voice.

Riya wanted to be angry, but how could she fault him when she'd also run away? When she'd returned to her family only to steal for the Ravens? They were so similar, she and Ronak. She didn't know why she hadn't seen it before, but they'd wanted the same thing: a family. It had been different for Kaleb, but she and Ronak had grown up in Vira's shadow — in different ways, but they'd both been ignored and sidelined and forgotten.

But he'd stayed, and she'd left.

"Ronak, I —" She froze at the sound of voices echoing through the corridor. "We have to hide."

Riya silently grabbed the bag. *There,* she mouthed, pointing toward a gap in the wall that led to what looked to be a cellar. They quietly moved toward it.

Ronak took a step forward and then stumbled. Riya lunged forward to catch him, and she slammed into the side of the wall. She winced as something sharp pressed against her thigh, biting her lip to keep from making a sound.

The footsteps paused for a second.

"What's that?" someone asked.

Riya held her breath, her back pressed against the wall.

"Probably a rat," another voice said. The footsteps continued, and she heard the sounds of their voices getting fainter. She sighed in relief.

Riya dug her hand into her pocket, pulling out the small metal rod. It was the hinge of the box that had held the key. Miraculously, it hadn't fallen out in the lake. She looked at it in confusion. The metal had chipped where she'd hit the wall. Beneath it, something glowed white. And when Riya ran her hand over it, she could feel magic flutter over her fingers.

"I think this is the entrance to Visala," Ronak said, but Riya didn't look up. "What is that?" Ronak asked, peering over her shoulder.

"I don't know." She turned it over in her hand, and then used the edge of her nails to pick at the metal. It peeled off easily. And when it was all off, she could see that the hinge was made of something lighter — something easier to carve. Ivory.

Her heart was pounding as she realized that she knew what it was. The grooves in the ivory weren't arbitrary. They were just like the bangles the girls in the palace had shown her. At one end of the rod were seven notches. Seven turns.

What if the key had never been *in* the box? What if the box had always been meant to disintegrate?

The Ivory Key wasn't gone. It was right here in her hand.

CHAPTER FORTY-SEVEN

— VIRA —

THE LYRIAN SOLDIERS shoved Vira into a jail cell.

She crashed to the floor, throwing out her hands to keep her head from hitting the stone floor. Pain radiated from the force of the contact, traveling up to her already aching shoulder. A second later, Amrit landed on the ground beside her.

As the door slammed shut, Vira scrambled to her knees. "Amrit?"

"I'm fine." He twisted around to a sitting position and then looked her over. "Are you all right?"

They were in a small stone room. No windows. No way out other than the narrow hallway they'd come through. The doors didn't look like they were made of magic — but the moment Vira pushed her hand through the metal bars, she could feel that the lock had magic in it.

Panicked, she looked at Amrit. There had been many moments when Vira had felt the sharp despair of failure, but she'd always been able to do something — change something, decide something. But all she could do now was wait and hope. Hope that Riya and Ronak had somehow made it out of the temple. Hope that somehow Kaleb knew where she was and that he would come for her.

But as the minutes ticked by, it became increasingly clear that they were trapped in a Lyrian fort with no escape and no rescue. No one outside her family even knew where she was. She'd be the maharani who simply . . . vanished one day.

"You're thinking too much," Amrit said. His voice was low; she felt his breath flutter along the shell of her ear. "He'll come." His voice was sure and even, and Vira held on to his conviction even as she felt her own dwindle away.

Now that they were alone, it hit her all at once that things between them were . . . different. They sat shoulder to shoulder, her arm brushing his, their knees touching, and she was so aware of each of those points of contact.

She'd kissed him. *Vaishali's bones.* It wasn't like they had a future. Not without the key. Not stuck here. Her one hope was gone, and if she ever escaped, she would need to marry for money or troops or whatever the Council felt necessary. There were far worse things to worry about, but she felt an ache in her chest. One more thing she didn't get to want.

"There's not much else to do," she said sullenly.

"We could talk."

She glanced at him out of the corner of her eye. Amrit, who hardly spoke unless spoken to, wanted to *talk?* "All right," she said. "What should we talk about?"

"Tell me one of your wishes, and I'll tell you one of mine."

Vira turned to him in surprise. It felt like an age since she'd said those words to him on the balcony in Dvar. She'd felt brave then. Now she was terrified. "I thought wishes were too dangerous to share."

"We've courted plenty of danger already. What's a little more?"

"We shouldn't tempt fate," Vira said. But she faced him anyway, intrigued.

"Well, if you're scared, I'll go first," he said, and Vira was acutely aware that he was trying to put her at ease. "I wish I had a plan for how to get us out of here."

"That doesn't count. That's not really a secret wish."

He smiled a little at that. "You didn't say it had to be secret."

"I wish . . ." *I wish I was brave enough to tell the people I care about how much they mean to me.* But she wasn't even brave enough to speak that wish aloud. "I wish I knew where I stood with my family," she said instead.

"You could ask them."

If they were alive. If she ever saw them again. "Your turn," she prompted.

He looked serious. "All right," he said. "A secret wish. One that I haven't told anyone in my life." He thought about it, then said, "I wish I'd made a different choice at a juncture in my life."

He'd picked his words carefully, so Vira didn't pry. She trusted that he would tell her when he was ready. But she couldn't say nothing. "My mother used to say that once you've made a choice, you have to act as though it's been made forever. But I don't know if I believe that's true. Our lives aren't decided by one choice, but by a series of small decisions that build up to pivotal moments. You can always make a different choice at the next juncture."

"Maybe," he conceded, but Vira had the sense that he didn't fully agree. "Your turn," he said.

Vira exhaled. "I wish we'd found the Ivory Key." She held her hand up when he opened his mouth. "Not just because of the freedom it would have given Ashoka, but because of the freedom it would have given me." She looked away. "I know it's terribly selfish, but . . ."

"I wish you knew that I'll always protect you," Amrit said.

Vira's eyes snapped up to his, her heart beating painfully loud. He held her eyes in the dark. She was still searching for words when there was a soft cough outside their cell door. She and Amrit whipped their heads around in unison to see a figure in the cell across from theirs.

Vira scrambled to her feet. She hadn't seen anyone else, so she'd assumed they were alone.

"Hello?" she called.

"I recognize you," the shadowed figure said. "You're the maharani."

Vira froze, her mouth parted in shock. Next to her, she could feel Amrit tense up.

"What?" Vira asked, looking down the empty corridor, hoping no one had heard. "I'm not —"

"I saw you at the battle."

"You were there?" Vira asked, surprised.

"Yes." The figure stepped closer, and in the dim light of the single lantern hanging above, Vira could see a young girl — maybe not even fifteen. She had a haunted look about her, her skin gaunt, and her tunic hanging off her thin shoulders.

"What's your name?" Amrit asked.

"Esha."

"How did you end up here, Esha?" Amrit asked.

"My brother," she said. And then, "How much do you know about magic?"

Vira exchanged a confused glance with Amrit. "As much as anyone, I suppose. It's mined. Used in objects." *We're running out of it.*

"That's what we thought too. Until it happened."

Vira frowned. "What happened?"

"My brother, Shivesh, and I used to work in the kitchens here. It was usually quiet because the viceroy's family often stayed at the other palace, but the cook had gotten word that he would be returning soon. She hadn't ordered enough, so she sent me to the market. And that's when the Lyrians came."

"You saw them?" Vira asked.

Esha shook her head. "I didn't know what happened. It wasn't until I came back that I saw that the fort had collapsed right near the kitchens. But once they captured the fort, the Lyrians blockaded everything. There was no way for me to get inside to find my brother. So I hid. The next day, more Lyrians came, and Ashokans as well. There was fighting everywhere in the streets. The Lyrians were distracted, and I knew the back way into the fort. Shiv and I used it all the time to sneak out, so I made it into the collapsed tower."

Vira could hear the pain and fear in her voice as Esha spoke about that day. Guilt pierced Vira sharply between the ribs, and suddenly she felt that she couldn't breathe. She'd run from what happened at Ritsar — blocking out the memories, refusing to think about her failure as a warrior, as a maharani. But that was a luxury; those who'd been left behind couldn't simply forget.

"There were bodies everywhere," Esha continued, her voice trembling. "But none of them were Shiv's. I searched and searched until I heard it — a noise in the cellar. I was so scared, but when I went down there, I found Shiv and two others. We tried to get out, but there were too many Lyrians in the fort. We moved some shelves around to seal the entrance to the cellar, and then we saw it — a gap in the wall, like a door."

"A door?" Vira found herself pressing closer to the iron bars.

The girl nodded slowly. "We'd heard these rumors that there were tunnels beneath the fort, so we thought it would help us escape."

"Visala," Amrit muttered in Vira's ear.

"You went inside?" Vira asked.

Esha nodded again. "Shiv thought it would lead us toward the mountains, but he was wrong. We walked for no more than twenty minutes when we were in a large cavern. It was full of buildings — like a — like a forgotten city almost. But then we hit a wall. It was white and made of some kind of crystal. And it looked like something had gouged it out."

"Gouged it out?" Amrit asked, confused.

"You know, when a rat eats a mango and you see the bite marks?" Esha said. "The wall looked like that."

"Like it was receding?" Vira asked. Magic didn't work like that. If the crystal had been infused with magic, only the magic would wane. This sounded like the wall itself had been made of magic. But that was impossible.

"We tried everything we could to break it down, but nothing worked," Esha said. "We were there for over a day. We were starving and thirsty when Shiv found some barrels of water. Or what he thought was water. He reached for it, and something wasn't right. When he turned around, he'd . . . changed."

"Changed? How?"

"He suddenly had this incredible power. He could lift nearly anything. Smash through rocks. Bend metal with his bare hands."

Vira blinked at her. "Magic doesn't work like that." She glanced at Amrit, but his gaze was fixed on the girl.

"We didn't believe it either. Not at first. But that's what it had to be."

"It only worked on your brother?" Amrit asked, rubbing his brow. "Did you touch it too?"

"We did, but the goddesses chose him," Esha said.

The goddesses have nothing to do with magic, Vira wanted to say, but she bit her tongue. "So what happened next?" she asked instead.

"We made it out of the fort, but by then the fighting had ended."

Vira had retreated.

She took a deep breath and looked away from the girl. Amrit's fingers found hers, squeezing her hand tightly.

"We got caught," Esha said. "The general found Shiv trying to break through the wall. There were too many of them, and I think Shiv was tired, because the magic stopped working. They caught us all and made us tell them about the powers."

"You showed them the cellar?" Vira looked up, startled. The Lyrians knew about Visala.

"Yes. They took all the magic they could find in there. And they took Shiv. He made them promise they wouldn't harm me, so they keep me locked up here, but Shiv works with them now."

"Works with them how?" Amrit asked.

Esha shook her head. "I don't know. He's only allowed to see me for a few minutes every day. He said they were doing experiments, trying to get it to work again so more people can use magic like that."

Vira looked at Amrit again, her eyes wide. She'd thought that more magic would be the solution to Ashoka's problems. If she could just strengthen the borders and negotiate with Lyria, things would go back to the way they were.

But if all this was true — that Lyria was experimenting with magic, experimenting with *people* — everything had changed. They were no longer fighting the same war. And Vira felt powerless to stop it.

CHAPTER FORTY-EIGHT

— RONAK —

RONAK HAD DEFINITELY lost too much blood. With every step he took, he was feeling weaker. Even Riya's new bandage was starting to soak through. He touched his leg, and his fingers came away bloody. He exhaled. Riya was right. It wasn't uncommon for soldiers to put magic into their swords to ensure that the wounds they inflicted didn't heal well, but he hadn't expected an ancient stone statue to have that kind of magic.

He followed Riya down the tunnel until they reached the antechamber. Riya went ahead, and deciding it was safe, she pulled out the flameless lantern. Unlike its counterpart on the other side of the fort, this room hadn't been abandoned for centuries.

"Careful," Riya warned, kicking something out of Ronak's path. "Sword. Or it used to be anyway." It was broken, half the blade snapped off, as if the result of poor workmanship.

"And not the only one," Ronak noted. There were a handful of broken items — arrows and short swords and other useless weapons — scattered through the space.

"All Lyrian in style," Riya said, her mouth set in a tight line. "And they all look quite new."

Ronak winced as he crouched to tug out a few papers that were trapped under the weapons. They were Lyrian news sheets — some dated as recently as two weeks earlier.

On the other side of the courtyard, the lever had already been pulled, revealing the city of Visala. The Lyrians had set up lamps all throughout the area, so Ronak could see that the view abruptly ended where a crystallized wall bisected the fort at an odd angle.

And it seemed that the Lyrians had tried to break it down. Heavy axes and hammers littered the ground, but they had no effect on the crystal. Still, the Lyrians had managed to demolish nearly half the palace. Ronak's mouth fell open in horror as he realized that they'd broken down entire walls, allowing him and Riya to step into rooms as in a diorama.

"This way," Riya said.

"Just a second," Ronak said. It was his only chance to see the palace of Visala, and he couldn't resist looking inside. It was what Papa would have done, he thought.

"Ronak," Riya hissed, but he just walked away from her.

The palace wasn't as big as he expected — just a single story. The rooms were empty of furniture, of belongings, of tapestries and paintings, but Ronak could see how different they were in construction from the palace at Dvar. Everything was made of elaborately carved stone and wood, with only a few gold and silver embellishments. It looked simple and austere, but no less regal.

"Ronak, look at this," Riya called from somewhere ahead of him. She'd huffed and muttered under her breath, but she'd followed him into the palace.

"What is it?"

He stepped into the next room and discovered that, unlike the others, this one wasn't empty. But the furniture inside wasn't Ashokan. There were several chaises and Lyrian-style lanterns. To one side, flush against a wall, was a large desk with a few stacks of paper, an ink pot, and a candle. And across from it, a golden vault, its door cracked partially open.

"Bring the lantern over here," Riya said, looking up from where she was rummaging through the papers on the desk before pulling one from the very bottom.

"What are you doing?" Ronak asked.

She looked at him and then held up the thin white rod she'd been holding in the kitchen. "I think . . . I think this is the Ivory Key."

"*What?*"

"It sounds impossible, I know," she said, unscrewing the ink bottle. "But I have a hunch."

Ronak watched in confusion as she used her fingers to paint ink over the rod and then rolled it over the paper. She repeated this several times, and when she was done, Ronak could see slanted words that took up the entire page.

She stepped back, and Ronak took the rod from her. It certainly looked like ivory. And it was coated in magic. "How did you know to do that?"

"I've seen something like it before," she said. She looked down at the paper in despair. "More clues. Another treasure hunt." She shook her head. "I didn't want this. It was supposed to be the *end*."

More mysteries to unravel. More years to waste. Maybe this was their fate, to follow the same path Papa had walked, never to find what they sought, to live a life of perpetual dissatisfaction.

"We could get rid of it," he said softly. "We don't — The temple burned. No one has to know."

Riya's eyes were wide. "You're serious?" she asked incredulously.

"What if I am?" Ronak shrugged helplessly. "We don't know what lies at the end of this new quest, Riya. What if it's *another* puzzle? We can spend the rest of our lives chasing legends, like Papa, or we can let it go. Kaleb was right. We don't have to be them. We can make our own destinies."

"We need magic, Ronak. We can't just walk away from this."

But Ronak could. He could leave this all behind and start anew somewhere else. They *all* could. All he had to do was make sure that Ekta got the key, and it would be over. It would be her problem to solve.

"No. Ronak, you can't give it to her," Riya said, reading his mind. "She's a criminal."

"How is it different from what you're going to do when we walk out of here? You cannot tell me that you're not going to take this to the Ravens."

She looked away. "That's different. The Ravens protect people."

"How, Riya? Protesting? Stealing? You think that's making more of a difference than what the Council can do?"

"It's not perfect, but it's *something*," she snapped. "I don't expect you to understand."

"But I do," he said. "You think I didn't see the hypocrisy of Amma's words? Of Vira's lies? Why do you think I want to leave?"

"You can leave, Ronak, but not all of Ashoka has that luxury. Think of who you will condemn if you put the fate of our country in Ekta's hands."

That silenced Ronak. He'd never considered the fate of Ashoka with any seriousness. He'd never needed to. And he'd never considered the way that this one choice would alter the lives of innocent citizens — because their concerns were kept outside the walls of the fort, hidden from view.

But Riya was right.

They *were* running out of magic. And he couldn't trust that Ekta would help anyone but herself.

All at once, it hit Ronak that everything he'd wanted had slipped through his fingers. Kaleb was free. Jay didn't want to leave. He was already engaged.

He didn't know what he was fighting for anymore.

"All right," he said, his voice hoarse. "I won't give it to her." He'd find a way to keep Kaleb and Jay safe — to protect them from her — but he wouldn't give her the Ivory Key.

Riya nodded, stuffing the key and the copy she'd made into her pocket. "We should go."

"Wait," Ronak said, walking toward the vault door.

It opened into a spacious room made entirely of gold, and the moment they stepped inside with the light, the entire room seemed to glow brighter, as if the walls themselves were lit. All the walls had shelves built into them. And all the shelves were empty. In the center of the room were three wooden crates.

Riya tried to pry the top off of one of them. Ronak moved to help her, and together they yanked it open.

The nausea was sudden and immediate.

Ronak could see spots in front of his eyes. His breathing quickened until his breaths were so shallow he couldn't stand. He collapsed to the ground.

"Ronak!"

"The crates," he managed to say.

Riya dragged them away. His lungs filled with air. He gasped for breath.

"What was that?" Riya asked, shaken.

Ronak couldn't answer. He had felt something similar to this only once. When he and Jay transported the raw magic. "What's in there?"

"Nothing," Riya said.

"Check the others," Ronak said.

"Ronak —"

"Just do it," he said. His vision had cleared, but his stomach still roiled.

She pulled the tops off all three crates. "They're all empty." She swept her finger over the edge of the last crate and then lifted it up in front of the light. "Odd. This dust. It's . . . gold."

When she brought it closer, Ronak felt his body seize up again. He scuttled back, ignoring the shooting pain in his leg. "Get that away from me," he snarled.

Riya looked terrified. "What's going on?"

"Raw magic," Ronak said.

Riya looked stunned. "It can't be. I'm touching it."

"It's raw magic," he insisted.

She hesitated and then wiped her hand on her kurta. "Maybe you need more water."

Or maybe he was losing his mind. First he'd seen Riya blast apart a pillar with her hand. And now he was responding to dust like it was poison. All Ronak knew was that he had to put as much distance between those crates and himself as possible.

He put his hands on the ground to push himself up. His right hand slipped, and he looked down. He'd bled through the bandage once again. But now, blood was dripping out of his thigh and pooling on the gold floor beneath him. He was feeling light-headed again.

He fell back on the floor.

"Ronak!"

He saw Riya rush toward him just as his vision went black. The last thing he remembered was a flash of blue light.

CHAPTER FORTY-NINE

— KALEB —

KALEB HAD NEVER thought of himself as being particularly good at anything, other than working with magic, but as he walked through the fort, he couldn't help but be surprised at his own capacity. He'd traveled through a terrifying jungle full of traps, mercenaries, and poisonous plants. He'd survived harrowing magical obstacles and escaped a collapsing temple. And he was now sneaking around a Lyrian fort, plotting to break his sister out of jail. He could hardly recognize himself.

He'd intended to follow in Papa's footsteps, and having decided that at a young age, he'd never wavered. He would train to become the palace mayaka and, perhaps later in life, return to university as a teacher or a scholar. But that future had been abruptly taken from him. And now he was realizing that he had never allowed himself to explore other interests, to wonder what else he might have excelled at.

Kaleb tamped down his frustration as yet another corridor turned out to be a dead end. He closed the door to an unused storage room and continued down the hall toward the next building. He didn't know how much of the fort he had left to search — or how much time had passed since he'd left Riya and Ronak near the northern tower. He hadn't heard any alarms or seen any soldiers run past him, which he took to mean they hadn't been found. Yet that didn't comfort him. There was still a lot that could go wrong before the night was over.

He rolled his shoulders back and took a deep breath as he approached the next door. He eased it open, wincing as the hinges creaked. It turned out to be an empty office. He passed rows of desks piled with ledgers and littered with ink pots and walked to yet another door. Another hallway. More doors. As he tried them all, Kaleb mentally cursed whoever had constructed this labyrinthine fort. The first two were more storage rooms. The third was a private office with a single huge desk and a bookshelf stretching across the wall behind it. He was about to close the door when the placard on the desk caught his eye.

General Demitrios. He'd been the one who'd launched the attack on Ritsar.

He had to keep moving. He had to find the dungeons. But this was a chance for him to gain rare insight into Lyria's plans. He started to enter the room.

"What are you doing?"

Kaleb whirled around, his heart racing. A soldier stood in front of him. He was clearly important, with nearly half a dozen medals pinned on his chest. His thick dark brows were knitted together as he stared at Kaleb.

"I was, uh, looking for the general," Kaleb said, feeling his face heat as he tripped over the words. He could read and write Lyrian decently well, but his conversational skills were severely rusty.

"He went to the capital a week ago with the boy." The soldier eyed him suspiciously. "How did you get in?"

"The door was open," Kaleb said, but the soldier didn't appear to believe him. "I was just transferred here."

The soldier crossed his arms over his chest. "We haven't had new troops in days."

"I meant transferred from, uh, up there." Kaleb waved vaguely.

"From the tower?" the soldier prompted. "Do they not get news there?"

Kaleb felt his face heat more, but he was saved the trouble of responding by the arrival of another soldier. "Lieutenant Lukas? The carriages are ready for the journey to the capital, sir."

Lieutenant Lukas. Kaleb felt his stomach sink. He hadn't expected to run into any of the commanding officers. A bit young for a lieutenant, he thought. Lukas didn't look that much older than he was.

"Tell them not to leave. I'll be right there." Lukas turned back to Kaleb. "What's your name?"

"Kaleb," he said, and then realized immediately he ought to have given a false name.

"If you're reporting to me, Kaleb, you and I ought to get to know each other. Wait here for me."

"Yes, sir," Kaleb lied.

Lukas reached over and pointedly closed the door to the general's office before he walked away.

Kaleb waited until he could no longer see Lukas before he set off in the opposite direction. He quickened his stride as he rounded a corner, and he came abruptly upon a stone staircase that disappeared belowground. For a second, Kaleb could only stare at it, thinking how remarkably similar this dungeon entrance looked to the one in the Dvar Fort.

But he forced himself to keep moving, descending quietly until he came upon a single guard, who sat snoring behind a table that held Vira's weapon and bag. Behind him hung a brass ring with a dozen keys, and next to it, a bronze bell.

Kaleb swallowed. He could feel his heart thundering against his rib cage as he held his breath and inched forward, slipping the key ring from its spot. The guard didn't move. Kaleb clutched the keys tightly in his fist as he eased past the guard and toward the cell.

There weren't many prisoners, and Kaleb quickly found Vira and Amrit sitting on the floor of the same cell. Vira scrambled to her feet as she saw him.

"Riya and Ronak?" she asked at once.

"They're alive," Kaleb assured her, and she exhaled in relief.

For a moment the two of them just looked at each other, and all Kaleb could think was how odd it was being on the other side — being the one who held the keys.

"I wouldn't blame you if you left me in here," Vira said softly, as though she could read his thoughts. Kaleb looked at her. He could tell that something had changed in her. She wasn't the same Vira as the one who had locked him up — who had left him there month after month because it pleased the Council. This Vira understood the weight of what she'd done.

"Don't be ridiculous," he said, glancing over his shoulder before he crouched down in front of the lock. He fumbled with the keys, trying five different ones before the lock finally clicked open. The metal grate swung open noiselessly, and Vira and Amrit slipped out.

"The others," Vira said, tugging on Kaleb's arm. "We have to free them."

Kaleb turned to where she was pointing. There was a young Ashokan girl, her face pressed against the bars as she watched them unblinkingly. He hesitated. Freeing more people would take time they didn't have. But he knew what it was like to be on the other side.

"All right. I'll —"

"Hey! You can't be here!"

Kaleb whirled around to see the guard standing at the entrance, pointing at them, eyes wide with shock. He saw the keys in Kaleb's hand and lunged toward the bell.

"Wait—" Kaleb darted toward him, but it was too late. A clanging sound reverberated around the room, then up through the rest of the fort. Within moments, soldiers would be swarming the dungeons, searching for escapees.

"Kaleb, the keys!" Amrit ordered, holding his hand out.

Kaleb tossed them to him, watching as Amrit wrapped his knuckles around the key ring and used it to punch the guard. He went down after one hit to the temple, but Amrit hit him a second time, leaving him unconscious on the floor.

"We have to go," Amrit said, stepping over the body and snatching Vira's bag and talwar off the table. "Now."

"We don't have time," Kaleb said, looking apologetically at the girl.

"I'll come back for you," Vira promised the girl, and then the three of them fled.

CHAPTER FIFTY

— RIYA —

RIYA LOOKED AT her hand in confusion and shock and horror. She was sitting in the empty vault, her back against the shelf.

Blue light had shot out of her hand.

Out of *her* hand.

It was impossible.

Ronak stirred on the ground in front of her, and then he jerked up. "What happened?"

Riya couldn't answer him. He looked so much better. The sweat was gone. His breathing wasn't labored. He looked disoriented — and then he yanked the bandages off. Where moments ago he'd been bleeding to death, there was nothing but unmarred skin. As if he'd never been wounded at all.

She warily looked at her hand and then back at Ronak.

"You did it again," he said, eyes wide.

"Did *what* again?"

"The pillar," he said. "I didn't imagine it. It was you."

"It's not me." *It couldn't be.*

He looked around the room and then frowned as he pushed himself to his feet. "Did you do this too?" he asked, walking over to where the shelves on one side of the room had dislodged from the wall.

"I didn't do anything," Riya insisted, but it wasn't true; moments earlier, the shelves had not been in this position.

Ronak pulled the shelf forward, and it moved easily, revealing a second vault. It was constructed the same way, made entirely out of gold. But the shelves here were full.

"This must have been Savitri's private collection," Ronak said, awed. He looked at Riya, his eyes bright with shock and discovery. "Do you know how much this is worth?"

Riya was still staring at her hand — at Ronak's leg — uncomprehendingly. But she rose and followed her brother inside.

Ronak started to unroll one of several canvases that were tucked into a basket while Riya made her way to the desk in the center of the room. Unlike the Lyrian one outside, this wasn't constructed for efficiency. It was elaborately designed, the dark wooden legs carved with intricate patterns and the edges plated with gold. It was topped by more objects: illegible scrawls on yellowed papers, ink bottles that had long since dried up, a stack of clothbound journals, small knickknacks, and paperweights. It almost looked like it had been in use when it was carried inside this secret room and abandoned.

Riya thumbed through the journals. They seemed similar to the one they'd found in the monastery in Dvar, written in the same archaic form of Ashokan that would take her days to decipher. She left them alone and moved to one of the shelves. It reminded her of Papa's room — well, Ronak's now. There were compasses tucked between books, flowers made of colored crystal, and small silver boxes with strange-looking rings. The last small chest she opened gave her pause. Inside was a pendant — one that looked just like the mirror they'd found, just like the one on the girl in the mural in Visala.

Riya pulled it out, letting it dangle by the thin gold chain, letting the red stone sparkle in the light of the room.

"Riya." Ronak's voice was strange. "You need to see this."

She put the pendant back in the box, closed it, and turned to see that Ronak was looking at her with a mixture of alarm and confusion. "What's wrong?"

He pointed to four paintings he'd spread out on the floor, each corner weighted down by the objects in the room. Riya made her way toward him, and immediately she could tell that each painting had two things in common. The first was that every figure in them had a different-colored pendant around their neck.

The second was that each of them was accomplishing an impossible feat.

There was a long-haired girl with a yellow pendant, floating several feet above the ground, her legs emanating faint white light. There was a boy with a blue pendant, no more than ten, his mouth parted in a scream that was shattering a stone wall. There was an older, bearded man wearing a green jewel, his fingers glowing as he weaved a gold sphere out of nothing.

And finally, there was the girl from the mural—the maharani. It was the only painting that wasn't of a single figure, but of two. She was wearing the red pendant—the same one Riya had found just moments earlier—and she was crouched down beside a soldier in full armor, a grotesque cut down the young woman's arm. The maharani's hands were cupped around it as the soldier's skin had begun to stitch back together.

They looked like stories out of someone's imagination. *People* didn't have magical powers. This was a singular fact that everyone knew. Magic only worked on objects.

And Riya would have brushed it all aside if Ronak wasn't standing in front of her as if he'd never been hurt at all.

CHAPTER FIFTY-ONE

— KALEB —

THE HORRENDOUS ALARM was still echoing through the air as Kaleb emerged aboveground. The area was still empty, but it wouldn't stay that way for long. He had to get Vira and Amrit to the other side of the fort quickly.

"This way," Kaleb said, leading them back the way they'd come.

"Do you have a plan?" Vira asked as she hurried along behind him. "We can't fight them."

"Visala," Kaleb said.

"No," Vira hissed, alarmed. "The Lyrians know about it."

"What?" Kaleb glanced at her over his shoulder. "Well, we don't have a choice. Ronak and Riya are already there."

Amrit put a hand on Kaleb's arm to stop him. "Wait," he whispered. "Voices."

The three of them pressed themselves flat against the wall as Kaleb peered around the corner. He could see a group of soldiers gathering, confusion evident on their faces as they awaited orders.

"I have an idea," Kaleb said, pulling away. "Stay hidden."

He took a deep breath, then approached the soldiers at a run. "That way!" he shouted over the alarm. "Two prisoners escaped. They went—"

He pointed toward the training arena, panting. Even before he finished, most of the soldiers took off. But four lingered.

"Lieutenant Lukas said to wait for him here," one of them said.

Kaleb slid his hand into his pocket, fingers closing around the orb of smoke. He wasn't sure it would work on all of them, but he had no other choice. He smashed it on the ground, yanking up his tunic to cover his nose and mouth as the others coughed.

"What are you —" The soldier collapsed before she could finish the sentence.

Kaleb backed away from the four unconscious soldiers and ran to where Vira and Amrit were watching, wide-eyed. "Run," he ordered.

"The cellar is through here," Amrit said as they approached the kitchen. He lowered himself through the trapdoor first, then helped Vira and Kaleb.

Kaleb's lungs burned as they ran down the length of the tunnel. He kept hoping that Riya and Ronak were all right, that they'd found a way to open the door, and that he and Vira and Amrit would be able to simply walk through it. The Lyrians thought it was a dead end, but they would search here eventually. They had to escape before then.

But when they finally slowed to a halt in front of a large building that had been partially demolished, they found Ronak waiting for them.

"Ronak, your leg!" Kaleb said. He looked far better than when Kaleb had left him — the sweat was gone, the weakness, even the way he was standing.

Ronak's face was grim. "You need to come see this."

"We don't have time," Kaleb said. "There are soldiers —"

"You really have to see this," Riya said, appearing behind Ronak, her face equally somber.

"We have to be quick," Amrit said as the three of them followed Riya and Ronak back toward a vault.

"What is this place?" Vira asked.

"Best that we can tell, it used to belong to the first maharani of Ashoka," Riya said. "Look here."

She pointed to a set of paintings on the floor, of four people performing feats of magic. It was clearly a work of art, but when Kaleb looked up, he caught Vira and Amrit exchanging looks.

"What am I missing?" Kaleb asked slowly.

Riya held out a stack of papers, folded in half. Kaleb took it, confused. The first page was a letter addressed to Savitri.

"Read it out loud," Ronak prompted.

"'My dear Savitri,'" Kaleb read. "'It saddens me to know that this will be the last time I write to you. I hope this letter brings you some solace in the wake of your sorrows — the depth of which I cannot begin to comprehend. I trust that you will forgive me this moment of sentimentality as I send my deepest condolences and heartfelt regrets.

"'Everything you've asked of me is done. The quarries are hidden, just as you specified. The library has been destroyed, and with it, all knowledge concerning the true nature of magic. Enclosed are the pages we managed to retrieve, though I desperately pray to Kausalya that we never need to use them. As for the other matter — I dare not commit it to ink, even to you — rest assured that I personally ensured its completion.

"'It pains me that our children and grandchildren will never experience the true joy of magic as we have, but I take a great deal of comfort knowing that the world will be safer for it — that we have protected them from unnameable grief. The world must never know what once was, and to that end, I've done what I can to prepare the Kamala Society, for they must play their part in writing the history that is to come.

"'For my part, dear friend, I promise to spend my remaining days in

Dwar, ensuring that your vision is realized and that your sacrifice is not for nothing. Yours forever, L.'"

With trembling fingers, Kaleb flipped through the other papers in the stack. There were pages cut out from books, full of mathematical equations and calculations. It was the same type of calculations he'd watched his father do over and over in his lab as he forged magical objects—but these were different. Pages that spoke of extracting magic from the mines, of forging objects, of forging *people.* And beneath even those, there were notes that detailed plans: how to seal the quarries, how to manipulate people's minds to forget, how to ensure that the only future that survived was one the Kamala Society shaped.

Kaleb looked up at the others in shock. "What does this mean?"

"It means the Kamala Society isn't what we thought it was," Riya said. She hesitated. "There's something else." She held up her right hand. "I . . ." She trailed off, as if she didn't know what to say.

"Riya healed me," Ronak said flatly.

"What?" Vira's eyes were wide as she turned to Riya. "Really?"

"I don't know," Riya said, shrugging helplessly. "I—"

"This doesn't make any sense," Kaleb said. He'd spent his entire life studying magic, and what he held in his hands—what Riya was claiming—was impossible.

"When we were imprisoned," Vira said, "we learned that there was another boy who managed to get this kind of power when he touched a barrel of what he thought was water."

"The water," Ronak said. "In the temple. You touched it when you grabbed the box."

"You thought it was odd," Riya reminded Kaleb. "You warned me not to touch it."

"Because I thought it was some kind of trap," Kaleb said.

"What happened to the boy?" Ronak asked Vira.

"The Lyrian general took an interest in him," Amrit said. "Supposedly they're doing experiments with magic, trying to recreate what happened to him."

"The general went to the capital a week ago with the boy," Kaleb said, recalling the lieutenant's words.

"We can't just leave. We need to know what they're doing with magic," Riya said.

"How?" Vira asked. "They're not simply going to tell us, especially if the general's not even here."

"I'll stay," Kaleb said without thinking.

"What?" They all turned to face him.

But now that he'd said it, he knew it wasn't an impulsive choice. He wanted to be useful — to help Ashoka in some meaningful way.

"There are carriages leaving for the capital," Kaleb said. "I can go. Find the general. Find what he's doing with magic."

"That's absurd," Ronak said.

"It's not," Kaleb said. "If what Vira's saying is true, we need to know what we're up against. This is the best chance we have at getting those answers." He glanced at Riya — at her hand. He didn't understand it, but she needed those answers just as much as Ashoka did.

"You don't understand," Ronak said, panic evident in his voice. "If you leave, the Council will think you ran. They'll spin it, making it sound like you're working with Lyria."

"He's right," Vira said softly. "We'd have to tell them you ran away."

"I know." Kaleb exhaled. "But it doesn't matter what they think."

It was true, he realized. He didn't care what the Council believed. He'd been sure that once he left the dungeons, he could pick up right where he'd left off, go back to being a mayaka and following all the dreams he'd left behind. But he hadn't counted on the fact that he'd changed. That maybe he could want something different.

He'd never understood Riya's or Ronak's desire to run. He'd been content — or so he'd thought. But maybe that was just what he told himself because he had never been brave enough to dream, to wonder what else could be out there. Papa had been the same age when he'd traveled to Lyria alone. And Kaleb was already so close. He could get to know his family, to explore the place that had been his father's home for so long — all while learning what Lyria intended to do with magic.

"We can find someone else to do this," Ronak said. "Some other way just —"

"You don't have to protect me, Ronak. I'm not a broken boy."

"What?"

Kaleb ran a weary hand over his face. "I saw the painting. The one you did of me. I am not that boy in chains. You don't have to protect me."

"So you're doing this to prove something to me?"

"No. I'm doing it to prove something to myself. I *want* to do this."

"We have to go," Vira said. She held Kaleb's gaze. "Are you sure you want to stay?"

Kaleb nodded. "I am."

"Be careful," Riya said, drawing him into a tight hug.

They made their way toward the crystal wall. Amrit found the door and waved his hand over where the doorknob would be. Just as it had on the other side, one appeared. He pulled it open.

Kaleb lingered until his siblings and Amrit crossed to the other side.

Ronak's face was confused and hurt as he closed the door, severing the connection between the two halves of Visala.

This wasn't the way Kaleb thought his life would go, but as he passed his hand over the doorknob and watched it disappear, he felt a sense of surety about the future that he hadn't felt in a long time.

CHAPTER FIFTY-TWO

— VIRA —

THE EMPTY EXPANSE of Visala felt endless on the way back.

Vira's entire body ached. Her soul felt weary. Hunger gripped her stomach. So when Riya wanted to rest, she didn't protest. They'd lost most of their supplies and had very little food left, but they split what remained and then stretched out on the floor side by side — she and Riya and Amrit and Ronak, looking up at the dark ceiling as if they were counting stars.

She rolled her left shoulder uncomfortably. It stung from when Amrit had grabbed her arm to stop her from falling off the invisible maze. Her ribs hurt too, and she was certain she would have bruises along the left side of her body in a few hours.

Vira dozed off — for what seemed like seconds — when she felt Amrit shaking her shoulder. As she rubbed sleep out of her eyes, Riya crouched down in front of her.

"What is it?" Vira asked.

"I have something to show you." Riya pulled something out of her pocket. She held it out, and when Vira reached for it, Riya pulled back. "Don't make me regret telling you this."

"I don't even know what it is, Riya."

"It's the key."

"What?" Vira stared uncomprehendingly. "What are you talking about?"

"When the box disintegrated, the hinge was the only thing left undamaged," Riya said. "I don't know why I caught it, but I think the box was *meant* to disintegrate."

Vira desperately tried to quell the hope rising within her again. "How is this a key?" She turned to Amrit, her eyes wide.

"We can discuss this once we're home," Amrit said, his expression unreadable. "We still have a long way to go." He turned toward where Ronak had already gathered all their supplies.

"Later," Riya agreed and pocketed it.

But it was all Vira could think about as they trudged in silence through the never-ending dark. Was it possible? Had she actually been successful? Had they actually found the key?

"This way," Ronak said as they reached the far end of Visala, near the antechamber where they'd fallen in. He guided them to the right, toward a different lever that opened into a different antechamber and a different set of tunnels.

"We don't know where it leads," Riya reminded them. "We could end up walking for miles."

Vira looked at Ronak. "What do you think?"

"It's the easiest and fastest way to cross the border," he said.

"All right," Vira said. "We'll use the tunnels."

Vira lost all sense of time as they walked — stopping to rest when they grew too weary to continue, not paying any attention to how much time had passed — so she was surprised when they reached the end of it.

Riya went up first, unlatching the trapdoor and pushing it up to reveal the star-studded sky. They emerged in an abandoned compound in the center of a large stone courtyard. On one side were half-crumbled build-ings. On the other, a set of stairs, covered in moss and debris, that led down to a lower level.

"University of Amashi," Ronak read, dusting cobwebs off a broken sign. "I thought it was a monastery."

"It was," a voice said behind them. All at once, torches sprang to life. Vira whirled around, searching for the source. And when she turned back, her heart leapt into her throat. A dozen armed mercenaries stood before them.

On either side, her siblings moved closer to her. Riya's fingers were already curled around her dagger. Vira put her hand on Riya's. *Not yet.*

A tall, skinny man with long black hair that hung to his waist stood at the center, facing them. His skin was riddled with tattoos and scars, each blending together like a seamless tapestry. A scar stretched over his cheek and cut into the edge of his right eye, which twitched as he spoke.

"Welcome home, son."

Vira felt Amrit's steady hand on her arm. Reassuring her. Protecting her. She reached for him — then froze when she felt it.

A blade against her throat. "Give me the key, Riya." Amrit's voice was quiet.

Confusion muddled Vira's thoughts as she tried to move, but Amrit's grip on her tightened, holding her captive.

Vira didn't understand. "Amrit?"

"Give me the key," he repeated. His breath fluttered over her cheek, as it had so often in the days past. But now they were speaking words that made no sense. How could he be one of *them*? One of the people who had killed her mother?

Riya stood frozen in shock. "What are you doing?"

"I'd do it," one of the mercenaries said. The one who'd caught them in the net. The one Amrit had tied up. "See how he's holding that blade? It will take her less than a minute to bleed out."

"Don't," Vira breathed, her eyes pleading with Riya. "Don't give it to him." Ashoka would survive without her, but it wouldn't survive without magic, without the key.

Riya reached into her pocket and pulled out the long rod.

"Riya. *Don't.*"

But it was too late. Riya threw it. Amrit caught it. "I'm sorry," he breathed, so softly she might have imagined it. And the pressure around her neck vanished.

Vira lunged for him. She grabbed his arm and pulled him back.

"I trusted you."

Every moment had been a lie. Every word. Every smile. Every touch. Every kiss.

She didn't know she'd drawn her talwar until it was pressed against his chest. Amrit stepped closer to the blade, so the tip of it was right at his heart. His heart.

All she had to do was push.

She couldn't do it, and he knew that.

"One day you'll understand," he said.

He drew back, and Vira let the blade fall.

Then he was gone. All of them were gone. Only Vira and Riya and Ronak standing in the middle of an abandoned university.

CHAPTER FIFTY-THREE

— RONAK —

IT WAS DUSK when they returned to the palace.

Ronak had instructed the hired carriage to stop at the base of the fort, and he ushered his sisters in through one of the back entrances of the palace, hoping to avoid notice. But the palace staff had been trained to pay attention to the maharani, and within moments there were guards flanking them.

"We should talk tomorrow," Vira said as the three of them stood at the base of the stairs that led up to her room. They had stopped at another inn briefly to find new clothes and wash the dirt and blood off, but they all wore the stress of the last few days.

"Tomorrow," Riya promised, her eyes lingering on Ronak as she followed Vira.

Ronak continued toward his room, his heart heavy. This was to have been his last night in the palace, but he couldn't leave — not until Kaleb returned. He still couldn't believe that Kaleb had just . . . *left*. Frustration and fear warred within him. He wanted his brother to be safe, to be free of Ashoka and their family, but Kaleb had put himself in even more danger.

Ronak climbed up the tower and pushed open his door. He froze.

It wasn't empty.

Ekta stood in the middle, a slow smile curving over her face when she saw him. "Rajkumaara," she said. "I heard you'd returned." She was wearing a black kurta once again, and a silver clasp in the shape of a coiled snake pinned back her hair.

"How did you get in here?" he asked, all too aware that there were no guards nearby — no one who'd hear him if he called for help.

"I told you. I know how to find you." Her eyes gleamed in the light. "Do you have the key?"

Riya's words echoed through his head. *Think of who you will condemn if you put the fate of our country in Ekta's hands.*

"We didn't find it," Ronak lied.

Ekta moved faster than Ronak expected. He took a step back and realized that he was against a wall. She grabbed his jaw. Her sharp black nails dug into his cheeks. "I heard that your brother didn't return with you, but there are others you care about. Your sisters. Your friend Jay. Your betrothed."

Ronak felt panic clawing through him. "The temple collapsed," he said. "We couldn't get to it in time. We —"

"You know what happens to those who don't deliver what I want," she said. "I'll ask you one more time. Where is the key?"

"A seat on the Council," Ronak blurted out.

"What?" She drew back, loosening her hold, and Ronak wrenched himself from her grasp.

"You want power," he said, remembering the night of his engagement party — how she'd looked at the other nobles, how she'd spoken of the world she'd grown up in but had been kept apart from. "I never claimed my title formally, but I'm the Viceroy of Dvar. If I take my seat, I will be able to appoint a successor who takes over as soon as I step down."

"You can name anyone as your successor?" she asked.

"The seat will be yours," he promised. Traditionally, the position was passed through the maharani's family, but there were instances of outsiders occupying the role — a trusted war general or an expert in a specific field.

Ronak's heart thumped painfully loudly as she considered his words. It was the only thing he had left to offer — the only way he could ensure the safety of those he cared about.

Ekta stepped toward him, and Ronak tensed. "Our previous deal is void," she said. "You have two weeks to secure my seat. Or I kill Jay first."

"Two weeks," Ronak agreed, feeling sick to his stomach.

Ekta turned on her heel and swept out of the room, her cloying perfume lingering as a reminder of her threat.

Ronak collapsed against the wall. Two weeks to get Ekta into the palace. To find a way to keep Jay safe. It wasn't the same as giving her the Ivory Key, he told himself. She'd have power, but she would be one voice among fourteen. But somewhere in the back of his mind, Ronak had the horrible feeling that he'd made an irreversible error.

CHAPTER FIFTY-FOUR

— RIYA —

RIYA WRAPPED HER arms around herself as she stood on Vira's veranda and looked out at the ocean, the dawn air cold against her skin. She hadn't slept in two days. Her eyes burned and her head hurt where she'd hit it, but all she could do was stare at her hand. She flexed it, turning it this way and that. It looked fine, but she knew she couldn't do anything if the . . . *magic* wanted to come out.

This wasn't supposed to happen. If there was one thing she'd learned from Papa's lessons, it was that magic couldn't fuse with living things.

Yet there was no denying the energy simmering just beneath the surface of her hand. It didn't hurt exactly, but it felt insistent. As if it were yearning to escape.

"Riya?"

She started. She hadn't heard Vira awaken. "Out here."

"I thought you left." There was an accusatory edge to Vira's voice as she walked out onto the veranda.

"No. I just wanted some air," Riya said as Vira came to stand next to her, resting her elbows on the railing. "Are you all right?"

Vira had bathed, but Riya could still see the remnants of the last few days: dark circles under her eyes, scrapes across one cheek, the way she hissed whenever she had to use the muscles on her left side. Her hair hung loose around her shoulders, fluttering in the breeze as she looked out at the distant horizon. Riya had never seen her sister look so young — so lost — and she felt her heart clench.

Vira hadn't protested when Riya showed up at her room the night before and climbed into her bed. It was something Riya couldn't remember doing since she'd been eight and had woken up from a nightmare, but it had felt wrong to leave Vira alone.

Riya took a deep breath, her stomach tightening with nerves. "There's something I need to tell you."

"What is it?" Vira asked warily.

"We didn't lose the key."

"What?" Vira turned in shock.

"I made a copy. Before I gave it to — him."

"Made a copy?" Vira's eyes brightened for a second — and then the spark died out. "Well, it doesn't matter. It's too late."

"Stop it, Vira. You are not defined by one failure. Just because our trip didn't go as planned, it doesn't mean you give up."

Vira said nothing, looking down at her hands clasped on the railing.

Irritation burned through Riya. "Ronak didn't nearly die so you could stop protecting Ashoka. Kaleb isn't risking his life so you can stop being a maharani. I'm coming to you, Vira. Not the Ravens. You."

Vira's eyes shuttered closed. "Why? Why *are* you coming to me?"

"Because you were right. Ashoka needs magic."

She could take it to the Ravens — she could prove Varun wrong and repair things with Kavita and cement her place among them again. But . . . the world was different from what Riya had thought. Magic didn't work the way it was supposed to. The Kamala Society hadn't been created for the reasons she'd believed. And Vira was the only person who had the means to protect every single citizen.

"You say you want to help the people, Vira. So do it. Find the magic. Fortify our borders. Fix the economy." Riya reached into her pocket and pulled out the folded piece of paper. "I'm choosing to trust you."

Vira's hands trembled as she took it. "More clues." She traced her fingers over the dark ink lines Riya had copied from the Ivory Key. "And you'd come with me? To see what lies at the other end of this?"

"Yes."

The sky was a canvas of pinks and purples and oranges. Birds chirped in the distance, signaling the arrival of dawn. And the two of them stood side by side, watching the sun rise over the ocean.

Riya owed the Ravens answers. About magic. About the past — answers she didn't have or even fully understand. But not yet.

She looked down at her hand, full of magic and mystery. Full of power and destruction and questions. Maybe whatever the key led to would give her answers, too.

CHAPTER FIFTY-FIVE

— KALEB —

IT WAS NEARING dawn when the chaos of the temple fire began to die down. After his siblings had left, Kaleb had rummaged through the vault.

Riya had taken Savitri's letters with her, along with a ruby pendant. Ronak had wanted to take the paintings, but Vira talked him out of it. Kaleb longed to explore everything in the vault, but he didn't have much time. He selected a few journals that looked promising and a few valuables that he could sell to get Lyrian money, and then he made his way out of Visala and back into the Simha Fort.

The fort was quiet, and no one paid him any mind as he walked deliberately toward the row of carriages lined up at the back, getting ready to travel to Lyria's capital. There were several soldiers hovering around the carriages, shouting orders at each other and throwing their bags into an open wagon.

A Lyrian soldier stood with a ledger. She looked up at him as he approached. "Name?"

"Nikolas," he said, remembering to lie this time. It was a common name, and he hoped it was enough.

She frowned, flipping through pages before looking up at him. "I don't see you listed. Are you sure you were assigned on this transport?"

"I'm a new addition," he found himself saying. "Lieutenant Lukas gave me this assignment personally. I can find him if you'd like." There was no reason for her to doubt him, but he felt his pulse race anyway.

"Oh, that's fine, then," she said. "I'll make a note here."

She waved him on, and Kaleb made his way to one of the carriages. There were four others already seated when he climbed in. One of them gave Kaleb an odd look, as if he didn't quite recognize him, but Kaleb offered him a smile, and the soldier hesitantly smiled back.

As the carriage jerked to a start, Kaleb peered out the small window. It would be his last glimpse of Ashoka for a while. He exhaled as the winding mountain streets of Ritsar gave way to the gentle rolling hills of the Lyrian countryside, lush and green in the pale hues of dawn.

He would do what it took to find out what the Lyrians were planning—with Ritsar, with magic. To find answers not only for Ashoka and Riya, but for himself.

There was truth in what Surya said. Kaleb knew he didn't belong in the palace—not anymore.

I'm sorry, Ronak.

Going to Lyria to spy on the emperor wasn't the journey his brother had wanted for him, but this was something Kaleb had to do.

And he had to do it alone.

CHAPTER FIFTY-SIX

— VIRA —

SOMETIME AFTER VIRA's return, Neha had been promoted to act as the captain. Vira didn't know what Riya had told the Council about Amrit's disappearance, but no one had questioned her.

"Maharani," Neha said from the entrance. She stood with her spine straight, a serious look on her face. The swan-stamped silver bangle that denoted her status as captain was around her upper arm. "The Council is ready for you."

"I'll be right there," Vira said.

She sat in front of her vanity and looked at herself in the mirror. She looked the same as she always had: the same kaajal, the same jewelry, the same clothes. But somehow she felt like she was looking at a stranger.

Her eyes slid to where the copy of the Ivory Key was tucked beneath a gold plate that held her rings and necklaces. It was what she'd wanted — what she'd spent so many months hoping and searching for.

But looking at it now, Vira felt hollow.

She reached up to touch the necklace around her neck, stamped with the Kamala Society emblem she'd held close all these years. And for the first time in the seven years since her father had given it to her, she took it off and dropped it on the table among the rest of her jewelry.

She'd trusted the Kamala Society — trusted that everything Savitri had done was for the good of Ashok. But Savitri hadn't simply hidden the quarries, she'd hidden the very nature of what magic was. Secrets didn't stay buried forever, and Savitri's choice had doomed Ashoka. They were wholly unprepared to face the new challenges that were arising.

Vira exhaled, pressing her eyes closed. The quest was supposed to fix her problems, not create new ones. But Kaleb was all alone in Lyria. She'd felt the weight of Ronak's judgment that she'd let Kaleb go without any protection or support. Riya had powers that none of them understood.

And Amrit . . .

There was another knock at her door, and Vira forced herself to rise — to plaster a smile on her face and pretend that everything was normal as she opened her door. Neha looked apologetic.

"The meeting, Maharani," she said.

"I'm ready," Vira said, squaring her shoulders and stepping out of her room. She followed Neha down the corridors toward the Council meeting room. She would have to talk with Neha eventually and review the guard protocols, but for now all she cared about was the cold, impersonal presence of a stranger.

A stranger she hadn't touched. Hadn't kissed. Hadn't trusted.

Amrit had manipulated her and used her, and she'd fallen for it all. For his kind eyes. His silent strength. His heartbreaking words. And she hated that despite everything, she *missed* him. His reassurance, his belief in her, his sweet smiles. She was terrified that she didn't know how to be a maharani without him.

She reached back up to her bare neck. But Riya was right. She couldn't give up. Ashoka needed her. She wasn't her mother. She wasn't the Council. But she was going to fix Ashoka in her own way.

Vira had told herself so many times that she couldn't do it. But she had. She'd found the key. She'd survived. And now she wasn't going to let anyone stop her from finding more magic to protect her country.

Not her mother's ghost. Not the Council. Not Amrit.

And certainly not herself.

EPILOGUE

Once upon a time, there was a little boy who looked up at the stars and wished for a family. Every month on the amavasya, when the moon disappeared from the sky and the constellations glittered like shards of broken glass, the little boy squeezed his eyes shut and whispered his secret prayer.

The goddesses — who weren't always listening — heard the little boy.

Strong, said Devyani.

Lonely, sighed Kausalya.

Desperate, snarled Vaishali.

They waited and they watched as without fail, the little boy returned month after month, looking up to the heavens with pain in his eyes and hope in his heart. The goddesses — who didn't always engage — spoke to the little boy.

What is family to you, little boy? they whispered to him one night.

Home, the little boy said. *Belonging. Purpose.* He thought for a moment. *Love,* he added.

Hmm, said the goddesses, considering. *We can give you all you seek, little boy. But you might not like the weight of the legacy that rests upon your shoulders.*

I'm prepared for anything, the little boy avowed.

Dedicated, said Devyani.

Compassionate, sighed Kausalya.

Unprepared, snarled Vaishali.

But there was fire in his eyes and conviction in his heart. So the goddesses — who weren't always kind — granted the little boy his wish.

The path you walk won't always be virtuous, they told him the day they altered the threads of fate. *And the path you walk won't always be merciful. But this is the way of the path you chose.*

The little boy didn't understand it then, but his destiny had been re-made that day, a tapestry woven from carefully selected strands, twined with the life of a girl he wouldn't meet for many years to come.

✷

The little boy had found his family. He had a father, wise and bold. Brothers, brave and true. A kitten, tiny and rebellious. But as the moons passed, he found that he couldn't let go of the stars. Devotion — or perhaps fear — kept him glancing up at the skies, whispering new wishes. To be stronger. To be braver. To keep his family together.

"What are you doing, my child?" his father said one day when he caught the little boy standing at the edge of the battlement, his eyes pressed closed, elbows resting on a railing he couldn't reach without standing on the tips of his toes.

"Wishing."

"Wishes are for fools and dreamers," his father said, taking the little boy's chin in his callused hand and tilting it gently toward the earth. "You, my child, are a warrior. A warrior plans. And he executes."

"But how will I know I've made the right plans?" the little boy asked.

His father studied him for a long moment. "Come," he said, deciding. "It's time you learn the truth."

The little boy followed his father from the edge of the fort, through open courtyards, down to the small library on the lowest level. He watched as his father carefully selected five books from the single book-shelf and stacked them on a small table. A moment later, there was a quiet click, and the entire bookshelf swung outward, revealing a dark corridor.

"Our history," said his father, leading the little boy inside, "began with a rani who loved her sister very much." The little boy, who had al-ways loved stories, paid close attention. "The rani did everything she could to keep her sister safe, but her sister had made a choice that couldn't be undone."

The corridor ended, and the little boy followed his father into a stone room. It was empty except for a single column of yellow light.

"Heartbroken, she vowed that no one would ever suffer as she did."

The boy could make out three floating items in the middle of the col-umn.

"And so she created an organization to protect the world, composed of three branches. An organization trusted with the most important task."

A lotus in the center, crossed by a sword and a scroll.

"A lotus for the magic wielders. A sword for the protectors. A scroll for the secret keepers." The boy's father knelt in front of his son. "We are the sword."

"We're protectors?" the little boy asked, his wide eyes unmoving from the sword.

"You see, my child, the plan is already set. All you need to do is execute it."

✴

So the boy stopped looking up at the sky.

He planned. He executed.

And he grew up.

✳

Amrit stood on the battlement of his home, his elbows resting on the railing as he held the Ivory Key in his hands.

I trusted you.

Vira's voice rang in his ears, and he felt a sharp pang in his heart. He had done the right thing, but that didn't mean it had been easy. That it hadn't hurt.

That he didn't miss her.

You can always make a different choice, she'd said.

But some choices couldn't be undone.

This was what the Kamala Society had trained him for: to protect the key at all costs. Legend and time had twisted the truth of what it was, but no matter how much he wanted to, he couldn't give her the answers she so desperately sought.

There was a flutter in the air as his father came to stand beside him. "I contacted the Society."

"Good."

His father studied him. "Are you sure about this, my child?"

"I am," Amrit said. "It's time to end this."

And as he pushed away from the wall, he couldn't help but glance up at the glittering stars one last time. But this time he didn't make a wish. He made a promise.

I will always protect you.

ACKNOWLEDGMENTS

I wanted to say something profound here, but every time I sit down to write these acknowledgments, I get overwhelmed with a sharp sense of gratitude and wonder that I have so many incredible people in my life who've helped make this book happen.

My brilliant agent, Hillary Jacobson: you believed in this book and in me even when I didn't, and your unwavering faith gave me the courage to see this through. I could not ask for a better guide to help me navigate publishing. I'm also very grateful to have Felicity Blunt, Rosie Pierce, Roxane Edouard, Savanna Wicks, Liz Dennis, Will Watkins, Tamara Kawar, and the rest of the ICM team in my corner.

I'm so thankful to have not one but two incredible editors tirelessly champion this book. Nicole Sclama: from the first time we talked, I knew you got this book, and every conversation since convinced me that I couldn't be in better hands. Emilia Rhodes: I appreciate your wisdom and thoughtfulness so much, and I feel so fortunate to have the chance to work with you. A million thanks to the entire Clarion team for supporting this book from day one, especially Elizabeth Agyemang, Mary Magrisso, Kaitlin Yang, Samantha Bertschmann, Erika West, Maxine Bartow, Tracy Roe, Anna Ravenelle, Julie Yeater, Lauren Wengrovitz, Margaret Rosewitz, and everyone else who has worked on this book in any way. Huge thanks to

Emma Matthewson, Carla Hutchinson, and the entire Hot Key Books team for being the best champions I could ask for in the UK. I'm so lucky to have the most beautiful cover, and I cannot thank Doaly and Dana Li enough for the incredible illustration and design.

To the entire writer cult: thank you for inspiring me with your immense talent and for all the pep talks, brainstorming calls, and cultreats both virtual and IRL. Janella Angeles and Maddy Colis: thank you for being on every step of this journey with me from haunted hotels to bat signal wine nights. Axie Oh: I literally cannot imagine not talking to you every day. Thank you for being my voice of reason in your chaotically calming way! Ashley Burdin: you're the other half of my brain and this book literally wouldn't exist without your brilliance. Katy Rose Pool: my favorite travel, writing date, deadline, and tree buddy! Thank you for being my secret to productivity (and also that one phone call that helped). Mara Fitzgerald: I don't know what I'd do if I couldn't text you about the most important things in life . . . I'm obviously talking about Zumbo, Shrek, and D&D podcasts. Thanks to Amanda Foody for talking through my magic system every year, Tara Sim for the wine & whine nights, Ella Dyson for being the first one to read this book, Christine Lynn Herman, Kat Cho, Claribel Ortega, Alex Castellanos, Amanda Haas, Melody Simpson (my first CP!!), Meg Kohlmann, and Erin Bay. I'm so fortunate to know you all!!

Patrice Caldwell: every step of this journey was only possible because of your generosity, kindness, and wisdom. Thank you for the recycled pep talks, spontaneous macarons, "I told you so"s, and letting me be the more melodramatic friend. Susan Dennard: my publishing big sister and personality twin — I truly mean it when I say that meeting you changed my life. The rest of my writing community: Traci Chee, Julie Dao, Sara Raasch, Sara Holland, Roshani Chokshi, Swati Teerdhala, Hannah Reynolds, Cassie Malmo, Shveta Thakrar, Aneeqah Naeem, Adrienne Young, Kristin

Dwyer, June Tan, Sabina Khan, Sarena and Sasha Nanua, Karuna Riazi, Dhonielle Clayton, Sona Charaipotra, Samira Ahmed, Rebecca Mix, Tasha Suri, Lyndall Clipstone, and Alex Brown. Many of you took the time to give me thoughtful advice and encouragement long before I ever had a book deal, and your friendship has meant the world to me.

I wrote a book about a complicated family, but I'm so glad to have the most supportive one. I know I didn't go to med school, but I still hope I've made you proud!

I dedicated this book to my grandparents who told me my first stories and set me down this path. They taught me the importance of hard work, pursuing my passions, and trying new things. To my parents: thank you for instilling in me a love of the arts and the courage to pursue my dreams. None of this would be possible without your generosity, love, and the example you've set. And I obviously could not have written this book without my little demon cat who is my best brainstorming buddy and always the first to hear any publishing news.

Thank you to my aunts and uncles (Rajmohan, Baskar, Srividya, Vinod, Radhika, Krithikka, and Sridhar) for letting me steal your books every summer. Special shoutout to my little brother Arjhun for driving me to see temple ruins and the thevangu, and my baby cousins Atul, Ajith, and Riti who are all budding storytellers in their own right. Thank you Gayathri for always putting things into perspective, and Uthra Aunty and Sundar Uncle for your unwavering support. To the rest of my family and extended families — I'm so grateful for all of you.